MW01129247

The Archangel *Ariel*

A Sanction Mate Series - Book #5

© 2016 by EJ Brock

ISBN-13: 978-1540819208
ISBN-10: 1540819205

ACKNOWLEDGEMENTS

I want to thank author GMME for the cover picture. In fact, I thank you for the covers of all of my books.

Erica George, I could never pull a single book off without your continued support. I don't know what I'd do without you. (Probably go back to terribly edited books)

And to my twin sister, Emma Brock. Girl, you are my ride or die soul mate, and that special part of me. Thank you for always supporting and pushing me. Thank you for reading and questioning every scenario for continuity.

I thank Jehovah Elroi – The God who *sees*. Thank you for sending your angels to watch over me all day, and all night.

THE ARCHANGEL

Ariel

A SANCTIONED MATE SERIES
BOOK #5

A NOVEL BY

E J Brock

The Archangel ARIEL

PROLOGUE

ERIC GEORGE propped his elbow against the old Sycamore Tree. He palmed the side of his head, looked down, and sighed.

Loose bark had fallen by the wayside, and lay scattered at his feet. The rugged, and curled bark reminded him of the cycle of life. Here today…gone today.

No matter what your plans may be, predestination controlled every minute; of every day. And like the season, circumstances force plans to *change.*

The beautiful, and colorful leaves were a sign that the season was changing. Still yet, the dying leaves *stubbornly* hung on to the branches. After all, the branches were their lifeline. He understood that more than ever.

When he was a kid he loved the Sycamore tree. The patchwork colors of the trunk intrigued him. Plus, the way the trunk split allowed him to sit in the V, for hours on end.

The tree provided the needed shade from the California sun. The pointy lobes of the leaves allowed him to stay hidden from bullies, until the coast was clear.

He chuckled at the memory. He was a suspender wearing, book in hand, brainiac nerd. The kid everybody picked on, for no other reason than they could.

He could almost feel the snap of his suspenders, his classmates inflicted on him. Not to mention the feel of his underwear wedged between his cheeks. His classmates would stand around laughing, as he dug them out; only for them to repeat the process. The latter was painfully embarrassing, even now.

The last laugh was on them though. While they grew up to live mediocre lives, he kept his head in the books.

In the beginning he was a professional student. He earned Master's degrees in four disciplines. Law, Medicine, Accounting, and Banking.

He minored in Theology, because it fascinated him. When he was young he heard a young lady recite James Weldon Johnson's poem "The Creation". He became obsessed with it.

He developed a doggish thirst that couldn't be quenched by King James' version. He had to learn all he could about God. Not from a believer's stance, because he already knew that there was a benevolent God.

He delved into areas that the Bible left out. What happened between Genesis 1:1 and Genesis 1:2? In his heart he knew something had happened.

Scientists tried to explain it with their 'big bang theory', but they got it wrong. Others said some type of catastrophic even occurred, but they didn't know what.

He believed – no he knew for a fact – that God stomped His feet in anger, and the earth crumbled. How he knew he didn't know; but he knew he was right. He could see everything play out in his mind's eye. But how?

...

To his classmates' dismay he made a name for himself. He was no longer the butt of their jokes. His zeal for knowledge was no longer a laughing matter.

His careers of choice allowed him to rub shoulders with the elite, who's who in several arenas. He was both a renowned doctor, and a lawyer.

Prior to becoming White House counsel, and doctor; he was both to the stars. He treated everybody fairly, and was well loved by all. That was evidenced by the sea of people marching toward him.

His wife, four sons, and only daughter were leading the way. All he'd ever accomplished was for them.

Also in the processional were movie stars, politicians, Five-Star Generals, and lawyers. Limo drivers and busboys were all in line. The only one missing was his best friend. That was understandable though.

They'd all come from seventeen states, and three countries to attend this celebration. Even the POTUS, and FLOTUS, along with the Secret Service were in the crowd.

They were all dressed in their, all black, Sunday best. Everyone sported dark shades, to shield their eyes; but not from the sun. It was only 9:00am, and the sun wasn't that bright.

He sighed. Although a celebration, it was a solemn and somber one…

···

"Are you ready?"

He looked toward the voice. He'd only met his new friend five days ago. He shook his head. "Not yet. I'd like to wait until everyone makes it to the front. Is that okay?"

"Of course, but I do not understand why."

He shook his head again. He didn't have an answer. It wouldn't change the outcome. "I'm not sure."

"Very well."

They turned their attention back to the coming crowd.

···

CHAPTER 1

LIBBY GEORGE was grief-stricken, and mentally worn. She felt like somebody had cruelly, and mercilessly, ripped the right side of her body clean off.

The only reason she knew the left side was still there, was because her heart was exposed; and bleeding. She'd never felt this level of grief before. Even her baby sister's death hadn't produced this level of sorrow. Her parents' deaths either. Not even the valium they gave her dulled the pain.

That's because the pain transcended her flesh, and accosted her soul. There was nothing manmade powerful enough to heal the loss of a soul mate.

She believed in God, and the power of prayer too; but she hadn't prayed in over a week. She was angry with God, and didn't have anything to say to Him. And she wasn't trying to hear what He had to say to her.

What could He say? Every man has his appointed hour. She already knew that, but it should have been her that died.

The only voice she wanted to hear was Eric's, but God had muted that sweet voice…

···

She and Eric had been married twenty-three years. She fell in love with his brain, first. He was the smartest man she'd ever met. He had an addiction to knowledge, and always had his head in the books.

Then it was his heart that tightened the ties. It was made of gold. She'd never met a kinder person, in her entire life. Not before, and not since.

Finally, his face and his body, caught her attention. Most girls looked, and walked, right past him. That's because his eyeglasses were as thick as a coke bottle. They made his eyes look three times bigger than they were. They made him look almost challenged, but she saw *him*, and not the rims he wore. Or so she thought she did.

She was always hanging around him, and not to get the answers to homework. They weren't even taking the same college courses. She just found him intriguing, and fascinating.

When it became apparent that he was never going to ask her out, she asked him. He smiled the sexiest smile, and readily accepted her invitation.

He showed up at her house in a 1964, jet black, drop top Thunderbird. She asked him how he could afford that brand spanking new car. He was a student, and flat broke. He said he won it in the raffle that had been going on, on campus.

He also showed up without his glasses. He was wearing his contact lenses, instead of his coke bottles, and…damn! He was not only smart, but handsome too. Really…really…*really* handsome! That's when she noticed his body.

He was six-feet-five and, like his car, factory built. Kingdom factory! She wondered when he worked out. Not only that, but he had an authoritative swagger that seduced her core.

She, and everybody else, had gotten it wrong. He was *not* a nerd! Doctor, Esquire, CPA and Investment Banker extraordinaire; Eric George was a highly educated diamond in the rough. A Greek god!

He told her that he'd noticed her, long before she

noticed him. He said he'd always been attracted to her, but he didn't have time for games. He said the glasses, although he really was half blind without them, were a guise. He wanted to see if *she* would accept him as he was, and not just as a friend. She damn sure did, and from their first date he was *hers*.

...

She looked at the casket and grabbed her chest. Her throat was so thick; all she could do was moan. She struggled to breathe, as her tears flowed. She couldn't believe her husband was gone. She couldn't believe this nightmare had even happened.

Her Greek god had pushed her, and their only daughter Erica out of the path of a speeding car. He saved them, but not himself. The car dragged *him* for a block. The love of her life died saving her, and their daughter. She sobbed, and openly wept...

...

ERICA GEORGE stood at the front of the crowd. This had been the second saddest weeks of *her* life. The first one was nine years ago, when her birthmother died.

The beautifully polished Sycamore wood coffin sat just above ground. It had polished brass handles, and hinges. A brass placard was attached to the front of the casket. Embossed with brush lettering, topped and bottomed by three gold crosses, was her father's favorite scripture:

†††
"If a man die, shall he live again?"
~Job 14:14~
†††

A beautiful black and white rose spray was splayed across the top of the casket. There were dozens more flowers, from colleagues, friends, and loved ones stationed along the side of the grave. Even more were at the house.

Her stepmother and four half-brothers were standing beside her. All of them were too caught up in their own feelings, to notice how grief-stricken she was. Or how recklessly alone she felt.

Three of her brothers were feeling anything but grief. They were more interested in the reading of the will. How much they were getting, and how much *she* was getting. They blamed her for their father's death. If they had their way, she'd get the boot.

Her stepmother's brother, Pastor Perry Busby, was officiating the services. He was standing in front of them, with his back to the casket.

He was dressed in his long black robe, with a gold trimmed red sash draped around his neck. The sash had three gold crosses embroidered on each side.

She bowed her head, and tuned him out as he began to speak. Her uncle always embraced any opportunity to be longwinded, where the scripture was concerned.

Before long he was going to have these people all riled up. Waving and co-signing, like this was Sunday morning worship, instead of her father's funeral.

She knew what his words would be, and wasn't emotionally ready to embrace them. Not today. Possibly not ever again.

She'd never say it out loud, but she was so angry at God. He took her birthmother nine years ago, and now almost nine years to the day her father. How could He do this to her again? Didn't He know she needed them?

Her tears ran down her cheeks…

…

Pastor Perry Busby turned, and rubbed the question embossed on the casket. Then he looked out over the crowd. "Confronted with imminent death, Job posed this question, *'Will a man live again?'*. No one knows exactly when the question was asked, because no one can pinpoint when Job lived, or penned the book. We do know that he was having a monologue with God, because the Bible capitalized all the letters in LORD. Meaning Jehovah! God! Henceforth, we know it was before the *Lord* – capital 'L', small 'ord' – meaning Jesus – the Son arrived."

Erica heard that. She didn't know there was a difference. Nevertheless, she wasn't interested in the LORD, or the Lord. The Father, or the Son. Not today. She pressed harder to shut him out again.

...

Pastor Busby kept preaching. "Jesus answered his question, in the New Testament."

Then he opened his Bible and recited Jesus' answer, "In my Father's house are many mansions; if it were not so, I would have told you. I go to prepare a place for you."

He skipped a few verses, and said, "I am the way, the truth, and the life; no man cometh unto the Father, but by me. John 14 verses 2 and 6."

Then he closed his Bible, and laid his hand on the casket. "Eric was born and raised in the poorest ghetto, in California. His school mates made fun of him, because he didn't have much. Most days his lunch was a mustard, or ketchup sandwich."

Everyone nodded. They all knew that, because Eric boasted about it.

"But he had a brilliant mind, and was determined to pull himself up. With hard work, and resilience, he surpassed everyone's imagination. Not only did he become successful, he became a man of independent means. Over the years the very people who laughed at him, as a child; came to him with their hands out. He didn't hold it against them, or throw the past up in their faces. The mere fact that he was willing to help them, was a humbling reminder."

Some of those who'd taunted him were in the crowd. They bowed their heads.

"Eric didn't believe in, or carry, change. He said change reminded him of the years he spent scratching for every dime. I asked him for a quarter once," Perry said and chuckled. "He frowned, and replied, 'A quarter? Man, I ain't seen a quarter since 1969.' Then he graciously gave me a dollar."

The grieving crowd laughed, even Libby. That was Eric's idiosyncrasy, alright. The man did not do coins. He always rounded up to the next dollar, when paying for anything.

If someone asked him for a helping hand, he always doubled what they asked for. If they asked for five dollars, he gave them ten. If they asked for ten dollars, he gave them twenty. He said he didn't want anyone else scraping for change, either.

He believed that God sent blessings to those he could send blessings through. He was proven right every single time. The more he blessed others, the more God blessed him.

...

Perry continued. "He was blessed with a beautiful family, devoted friends, and unmeasurable wealth." Then he laughed, again. "I can shamelessly admit he was a handsome brotha."

The crowd laughed. Some of the women replied, "Amen, Preacha!"

"I offered the dude a mirror once, after I'd cut his hair. He said, 'No thanks, I trust you.' Then he said, 'My mirror image gets mad that it's not the real thing, man. It never reveals my handsome masculine face, but some strange looking dude.'"

The grievers roared. Perry did too.

"However, as fine as he was, his earthly body was flawed. That was evident by the thick glasses he wore. Now he has a glorified and perfect temple. He has perfect eyesight in his new body, and he will never grow old."

The crowd responded, "Amen, Preacha!"

"As elegant as his home here on earth is, it needs constant updating, and care. Eric had another home. A mansion waiting in Heaven. Prepared by the Lord, and it requires no repairs. It will keep him safe from the troubling evil, and wickedness that surrounded him," he added and looked out at his three nephews.

He patted the coffin and said, "Every man has his appointed hour. When that hour comes, Jesus promised He would come back for his own."

He paused. This crowd wasn't ready to hear what he almost said. He wasn't ready either. He turned and looked at the old Sycamore tree. As he suspected, Eric's spirit was looking on, and he was not alone. "No more weary days, brother-in-law. Your troubles are over."

...

Erica closed her eyes so she wouldn't see her uncle's next move. She heard, and saw, it though; in her heart.

...

Pastor Busby turned toward the coffin. Then he

raised his hand, and sprinkled a handful of dirt on top of it. "Ashes to ashes. Dust to dust."

•••

Erica wondered why ministers always did that! Why remind grieving family members that their loved ones would soon be nothing but dirt? It seemed careless, and coldhearted to her.

She cried out loud, "Don't leave me, Daddy!"

•••

CHAPTER 2

ERIC GEORGE, JUNIOR was just twenty-two years old. He was the man of the family now. His brother, Remington, was nineteen; even though he didn't act like it. The twins, Ian and Carson, were seventeen; but acted like they were five. Erica was eighteen. She'd graduated a week ago, the day their father died.

He pulled his sister into his embrace. She was the only girl, the *middle* child. But not his, and his brothers' *mother's* child.

She was the result of a one-night stand their father had over eighteen years ago. Their father didn't know about her, until her birthmother died nine years ago.

Their father didn't remember the one-night stand. Even when he saw a picture of her mother, he didn't remember her, or the night.

He wasn't a rolling stone, or one to cheat on his wife. He loved her too much, to risk losing her. He loved his sons too much, to disgrace them. He loved God even more. Nevertheless, Erica was here, and she was his.

The only thing he did remember was that he'd been on a business trip that coincided with the time of Erica's conception.

His lack of memory didn't matter to him, though. One look at Erica and *everybody* knew it was true. She looked like their father had spit her out of his own mouth. There wasn't a speck of her birthmother in her. Not her face! Not her stature! Not her smile! Not her hands! All of those were replicas of their father's. And just like their father, and *him*, Erica wore coke bottle glasses.

Their father was a family man. There was no way he was going to let Erica go into the system. He discussed Erica privately with their mother first.

Then he called a family meeting, and confessed his wrong. He informed them that Erica was only nine years old, and had no other family. He asked them all to forgive him, not just his mother. Then he asked them if they could find it in their hearts to accept his daughter.

Even though his mother was hurt over the betrayal, she knew it wasn't Erica's fault. She had the strangest look on her face, when she said, *"No child asked to be born, under any circumstance."*

She readily agreed to take Erica in. In fact, she insisted on it. To prove her sincerity, she went with him to bring *their* daughter home.

From day one she treated Erica like she came from her womb. It didn't hurt that Erica looked like Eric Senior, and not her natural mother. Although he doubted that would have mattered to his mother. The woman has a gigantic heart.

She took Erica on mad dash shopping sprees. She bought that girl so many clothes, they had to be delivered. Shoes too!

She took Erica to the eye doctor. When they came home, Erica no longer had her glasses. Like him, and their father, she had on contacts. He couldn't believe how different she looked.

They'd also gone to the hair salon. Both of them had their hair freshly styled. His mother was beautiful, and Erica was as cute as can be.

They went to the electronics store, and bought Erica her own television, VCR, and movies galore.

Seeing that Erica was Eric's daughter his mother knew what she might like next. The next day she took her to the bookstore. She damn near bought every children's book on the shelves. The girl was more excited about the books, than she was the clothes. Yeah, she was their father's daughter alright.

Her clothes arrived on the third day. They stayed up late, organizing her closet with all of her new clothes. Then they watched TV in Erica's room, until the wee hours. In under a week they bonded, and were mother and daughter.

Pretty soon it became obvious that their mother was making a difference in them; but the pendulum of affection swung in the wrong direction. It appeared that she loved Erica *way* more than she did her sons. She treated Erica like she was the crowned princess.

He loved *finally* having a sister, as much as his mother loved having a daughter. She was the sweetest little thing. Many nights he watched TV with them in her room. His father did too.

His other three spoiled assed brothers despised Erica. They were jealous of the bond between her, and *their* mother. They were jealous of the bond between her and *their* father. They were jealous that none of them looked like their father. They were even jealous that she had their father's name. They'd long hated that he was junior. They were too stupid to realize that they all had his name. They never let Erica forget that she was a *mistake.* *"You are a bastard, from a sleazy one-night stand,"* they declared. They constantly reminded her that their father didn't even remember screwing her *slut* of a mother.

In the beginning, she was always in tears. He and his parents couldn't figure out why. She wouldn't tell them what those jerks were saying to her. Or what they called her deceased mother.

The first time he heard his brothers verbally attacking her, he went physically off. *"If her mother was a tramp, what did that make our father?"* he'd shouted. Then, he beat their asses, like they deserved, and then some.

Their parents were livid when they found out. Their mother didn't practice corporal punishment, but she slapped the hell out of them. After that, his parents moved Erica's bedroom, so she would be close to them.

They actually gave her their bedroom, and they moved across the hall from her. That only fueled his brothers' hatred for Erica, because her new bedroom was huge, with its own bathroom.

He'd spent the next four years taking them to task every time they messed with her. In the end they couldn't stand him *or* Erica. They hated their father for bringing her home, in the first place. They hated their mother, because she loved Erica. In an effort to get back at their parents, they continuously acted out. Stupid childish things, like urinating in the swimming pool whenever Erica was in it. Destroying her bedroom. Tearing pages out of her favorite books. It was one thing, after another. To this day, his brothers were filled with venom, and hatred for their sister. And it was about to get worse.

...

Erica laid her head on Eric's shoulder, and sobbed. "What am I going to do without Daddy, Eric?"

He squeezed her tight. He knew she was feeling like she was all alone. First to lose her birthmother, and then her father. Now she was stuck with three brothers who hated her, and blamed her, for their father's death.

"You still have me and Momma, Erica," he assured her, and kissed the side of her head.

"We still have each other, Erica," he promised. "I'm not leaving." He was grateful that he'd just graduated college. He decided to move back home, for Erica's and their mother's sake.

•••

When Erica cried out, Libby snapped back to her right mind. Her daughter was hysterical. Her oldest son's face was drenched, but he was silent. She wrapped her arms around both of them, and cried right along with them.

Eric's voice trembled, when he promised, "We're going to be just fine."

He'd made arrangements with the funeral home not to lower the casket until the family left. He didn't think his mother, or sister, could bear to hear the crank; or see the casket lowered. He wasn't sure he'd be able to handle it either.

•••

Pastor Perry Busby said a closing prayer, then added, "This is the end of the services. Please join us at the country club, for the repast."

He walked over to his grieving sister, and wrapped his arm around her. "Let's go, Lib."

He wasn't surprised when she and Erica let out screeching screams. They knew that this was it. The grand finale! Their husband, and father, was gone; and he wasn't coming back.

They both fell across the top of the casket and cried, uncontrollably. They were both begging Eric not to leave them.

His sister screamed, "What am I supposed to do without you, Eric?"

He lifted his shades, and wiped his own eyes. This was a hard one for him too. His brother-in-law was a good man. He'd made a mistake when he had the one-night stand. However, he didn't compound that mistake, by pretending it never happened. He stepped up to the plate, and owned it. He first asked God to forgive him, and then his family. That was in order, because the sin had been against God. That made him respect his brother-in-law even more. He was going to miss the man.

He reached for his sister. He didn't have the heart to remind her, or Erica, that Eric wasn't inside that casket. It was just the empty vessel, lying beyond the lid. He and Eric Jr had to practically carry Libby and Erica to the waiting limo.

...

"It is time for you to leave, Eric."

Eric wanted to cry. He couldn't though, because he was a spirit. He sure hated to leave his family. They still needed him. He saw the way his three sons were looking at Erica. They'd never accepted their sister.

He was concerned, and he needed to be. On this side of the glass darkly he saw beyond the veil. He saw the answer to the mystery of his daughter's conception. It was no wonder he didn't remember.

It didn't matter though, because he loved her as much as he loved his sons. "Will my daughter be safe, Michael?"

"I can assure you she will. Her mate has arrived."

Eric nodded. He almost laughed, because on this side of the veil there were no mysteries. No secrets! "Will they ever learn the truth?"

"Her mate will make sure that everyone knows," Michael replied.

"Will I still be able to see them, once we leave, Michael?"

"Perhaps. From time to time."

Eric looked up at the Sycamore tree, one last time. Surprisingly all the leaves were falling at his feet. "The cycle of life." Then he looked at his family one last time. "To everything there is a season."

"Indeed."

They vanished…

…

CHAPTER 3

ARIEL leaned against an old Sycamore tree, high on a hilltop. It overlooked one of California's ritziest subdivisions. He gazed across the landscape at all of the beautiful homes below. Most of them could only be seen from an aerial view.

No two were alike, but they all were indicative of humanity's *idea* of living large. In their minds the bigger the more impressive. Some of them were two-story, and mostly glass. All of them had private pools.

The homes were spread far and wide. There were acres of sprawling meadows, and forestry between them. Each home had groves of seven-foot boxwood hedges on the backs and sides, along their peripherals. Those hedges allotted the homeowners privacy, and in some cases, anonymity.

Some of the homes had shorter bushes up close to the dwellings that were shaped like different beasts. He smiled when he noticed one of the homes had two bushes shaped like lions.

The only uniformity was the large white wrought iron fences at the front of each yard. Each fence had a single gold letter welded to the spikes. No doubt the first letter of the family's surname.

All of the circular driveways were filled with expensive cars. Bentleys, Mercedes-Benzes, Maseratis, Ferraris, classic Corvettes, Rolls-Royces, on and on. All of the homes had five and six car garages.

...

He was mesmerized not only by the luxurious scene, but the Pacific Ocean backdrop as well. The marina was lined with large covered boats. His heart clinched when he noticed one was named "Eric's Liberty".

...

Spanish speaking yard service employees were busy catering to the expansive yards. Some were pruning the trees. Some were weeding the flower beds. Others were blowing fallen leaves; while some edged along the sidewalks, and driveways. He watched as they worked clearing out the debris, before mowing the lawns. The way they were working together brought order to the process. Get rid of the tares, before they shaped the lawns. Brilliant! Their organizational skills reminded him of what God had done, during the re-creation. Prior to creating His 'so' loved, He set the universe in *order.*

...

On *day one*, He called forth the *Light*, to overpower the darkness that was on the face of the deep. The waters!

On *day two*, He created a *divide* in the middle of those waters. He called that divide the *firmament.* The Sky! The heavens!

The waters above the firmament became the river of the water of life, in Heaven. It is as clear as crystal, and flows from the throne of God and of the Lamb, down the middle of the great street in the Holy City.

The waters under the sky, He commanded to gather itself in place, and allow the dry terrain to appear. The waters rolled back, and formed the *seas*. The now exposed terrain instantly *dried.*

On *day three*, He called forth plant life. Grass, fruit trees, and other vegetation. He commanded the greenery to regenerate themselves, by producing seeds, after their kind. Those seeds would allow for continuous new births. Most of which would be sustenance for His 'so' loved. Others for their shade, and eventual clothing.

On *day four*, He called forth the planets. The sun, moon and stars. He set them high in the firmament. He commanded the sun to bear witness by *day*, and the moon by *night*. He declared that they would be signs that separated the seasons, and one day from another. After which, the *Light* subsided.

On *day five*, He called forth the sea creatures, great and small. And the birds of the air.

One *day six*, He called forth land creatures, and four footed beasts.

Then, and *only* then, did He lean down and create His 'so' loved. *After* everything they needed, was in *order*.

That's was what he was here to do. Bring order to the chaos, in his mate's universe.

•••

He could have made himself invisible, but he chose not to. He could have also pretended, like Jeremiel, to be human. He wasn't going to do that, either. Too much was at stake.

It was imperative that everyone knew who he was, from the onslaught. Especially, those who had intentions of hurting his mate. That was their plan, but he had another one. One they would not comprehend, or see coming.

After all, he is the LION OF GOD.

But, speaking of order…

•••

He slowly shook his head. *"I declare by Heaven, I don't understand you, Michael!"*

"Why is that, Ariel?"

"Why does the situation always have to be dire?"

"I do not understand your question."

"You understand me!"

"I assure you if I did, I would have said so. Now explain yourself."

"Why couldn't you tell me where my mate was last month, or even last week?"

"She was not yet eighteen."

"You are splitting hairs, man. One week wouldn't have made a bit of difference, as far as our mating. It did make a difference, as far as what happened."

"You know as well as I do, that her father would have departed, anyway. Your presence would not have changed the outcome."

"It would have allowed Eric to leave his family in peace, man. It would have allowed him to leave, in peace."

"How do you figure? Eric did not know himself, until he moved beyond the veil."

"That may be true, but I live beyond the veil, Michael. The minute I arrived, I...KNEW! You should have allowed me to come sooner. I would have provided him with the knowledge he lacked, prior to his exodus."

"You were not allowed to rescue Daniel, before he was imprisoned."

Ariel actually smiled, at the memory.

...

Back in the day, the Jews was taken captive by the Babylonians. Daniel had been just a young man, when captured. The first thing the king did was change his name, from Daniel to Belteshazzar.

Nevertheless, Daniel knew who he was, and who he

came from. He was proud that he was from *Judah* lineage. He didn't let his circumstances define him, or resonate in his heart. He still believed what his forefathers had told him. He still believed what he knew, in his heart. God was the only God! In his darkest hour, he never lost his faith; or hope. He still believed in Him. He still trusted Him for deliverance. He still prayed to Him, three times a day; while looking eastward.

Even though in captivity, he rose in the political arena of the pagan king, Darius. The other governing officials became jealous of his relationship, and political sway with Darius. They devised a plan. They told Darius to decree that within a thirty-day period no one could pray to another God, or bow to another man; but *him*. Darius' ego got in the way, and he fell for it. Of course, it never crossed his mind that he was being played. He gladly issued the decree.

Daniel, like everyone else, heard the decree. Even so, he held steadfast to his tradition; and his faith. He went home, and bowed down to his God, in prayer. The governing administrators spotted Daniel on his knees praying, as they knew they would. They immediately brought him before Darius, and the court. Darius' countenance fell, because he *loved* ole man Daniel.

Being the king, he couldn't make an exception. Not even for Daniel. The punishment was already set in stone. Anyone caught would be thrown in the lion's den, even ole man Daniel.

God had sent *him* to be the mane that, His greatly beloved, Daniel laid his head on when he was thrown in the lion's den. No other lion would come near Daniel. They recognized that *he* was the very first lion. The original alpha king of the jungle. In fact, the lions were surprised to see him appear in their den.

The first thing he did was lock their jaws. They couldn't roar or meow, and they knew better than to even growl. They nervously pranced back and forth, but did not come near Daniel; for fear of *him.*

The king could not eat or sleep. He tossed and turned all night long. Worried, and remorseful over what he'd done. The next morning, he went running to the lion's den. He was actually *joyous* when he saw that Daniel was still alive.

He asked Daniel if his God had saved him. Daniel replied, *"My God sent His angel, and he shut the mouths of the lions. They have not hurt me, because I was found innocent in His sight. Nor have I ever done any wrong before you, O king."*

In the end, that situation was God proving His sovereignty to King Darius. Darius immediately had Daniel's accusers, and their families, thrown in the lion's den. Then he issued another decree. He ordered the people to fear, and reverence the God of Daniel.

However, that situation had nothing to do with this one. Erica and her family knew and worshiped God, and His Son. Eric had taken Joshua's stance, *as for me and my house*, when they were little. He did not send them to Sunday School. He showed them the way, by taking them.

...

"I'm not talking about Daniel, Michael. I'm talking about my mate. You cut it too close, man. You can hear her crying, like I can. It's breaking my heart! I should have been at her side, offering her comfort; that only I can give her."

"Perhaps you are right."

"I know I'm right! Now I'm going to have to go in

and nut up! You know how I am when challenged, man. You know the beast within! Personally!"

All of his brothers cracked up. Ariel could be ruthless, but quite entertaining. In truth, they all could. After all they were warring angels. But, when Ariel locked his metaphoric teeth down on you, you knew you'd been bit! Him being the lion, and all...

...

Michael did not laugh. *"No matter what, these people are Yahweh's 'so' loved, Ariel. Not all of them are evil."*

"Yet you allowed Chamuel to kill a few!"

"I did no such thing, Ariel," Chamuel replied. *I did not lay a finger on any of God's 'so' loved."* He'd never harm a single one of them. At least not physically.

"Why do I remember seeing a few salt pillars, in that cemetery?"

"They did that to themselves, boy."

"How about Winston and his cousins. You're telling me I didn't see you hit them with that bat?"

"I did not hit them. I just commanded Pain to attack them."

"You hit them, man!"

Chamuel frowned. *"What are you talking about?"*

"Your mate hit Mammon, and then Winston, but your hands were on the bat! Your might was the force behind it!"

"Oh," Chamuel replied. Ariel was technically correct. He had indeed directed that bat. *"I guess I did."*

"I know you did," Ariel arrogantly replied. *"And what about Jeremiel? He knocked that Leslie around, didn't he?"*

"Do not put me in the middle of this, Ariel,"

Jeremiel replied.

"You did, didn't you?" He chuckled at the memory. *"It is a wonder that boy could walk, let alone dispel his bodily fluids."*

"He came at me, first. I just defended myself," Jeremiel defended.

"Um Hmm!" Ariel murmured. All he knew was he didn't have the time, or the inclination, to pretend to be something that he was not. He planned to go all in, and through the *front door.*

"You liked it," he replied to Jeremiel.

Jeremiel laughed. *"Yeah, I did."*

They all laughed at Ariel's murmur, and his thought.

Michael still did not laugh. He appeared next to Ariel. "What you have to do is get rid of those pesky spirits, *A.r.i.e.l!*"

Ariel didn't appreciate neither the inflection in Michael's tone, nor the way he modulated his name. For Michael to have no emotions, he sure could invoke it in others. Especially him!

"I have no intentions of doing that, *M.i.ch.a.e.l.,"* he replied. "You waited until the last minute to let me know where Erica was. Now I'm going to do it my way. Those spirits will help me to get my point across."

"Ain't that the truth," Chamuel agreed. *"You did the same thing with Kay, big brother."*

"Because she was too young, Chamuel!" Michael roared.

"Yeah well, she was eighteen, and that was old enough."

"What difference does it make how old our mates are? We can't make a move until you get off the pot. So to speak," Ariel added.

"Wait a minute! Our mates are eighteen too. I'm ready to be reintroduced to Charlotte, Michael. Now!" Zadkiel said.

"That's right! Wanda has turned eighteen too. Where is she?" Jophiel asked.

"Where is Brandi? Reintroduce us, before they get in dire straits, Michael."

Michael sighed. They did not understand why he held off reintroducing them. It had more to do with his and Verenda's relationship than it did theirs. They were not fashioned like him. It was evidenced by Ariel's desire to embrace those spirits. Specifically, Rage, Anger, and Revenge. Nevertheless, they were probably right. Their mates were all legally grown now. Plus, they knew the rules. Until he did, they could not.

"I will need you boys to stand by Ariel, first. Then I will tell all of you where your mates are."

"I do not need their help. Trust me," Ariel replied, and started to walk away.

"STOP!" Michael shouted. Ariel thought he had the upper hand, because the others agreed with him. He was grossly mistaken.

Ariel stopped and turned to face Michael. He smirked. "What?"

Michael's eyes twirled. "You will need their help, and you will take it. Am I clear, Ariel?"

Ariel knew he'd rubbed Michael wrong, and he meant to do that. He was more than a little upset with his big brother. He'd felt and heard Erica's cries at the graveside. He should have been allowed to be there.

He could hear her crying, this very moment, in the limo. The feel of her emotions, and the sound of her cries, was searing to his own. In all of his existence, his eyes had never released a tear, not even when they crucified the Son. However, they were on the verge of a straight up flood.

The caravan of limos was moving toward the country club. He really needed to go to his mate. The only way Michael was going to let that happen was if he complied.

"Perfectly," he replied, and vanished.

...

CHAPTER 4

The repast was a catered affair. The white gloved butlers, and maids of Eric's neighbors pitched in to help his own.

His neighbors, and friends, were all posthumously roasting him. They stood at their seats, and one by one shared their experiences with him. Each one proclaiming 'they' were his closest friend.

Movie stars declared he was more than just their friend, or doctor. He was family. They all spoke of his big heart, and giving spirit. Some spoke of his helping them overcome their addictions with love, and patience.

"The man never met a stranger," one proclaimed. "And as smart as he was, he never made anyone feel stupid."

"He never made any of us feel our acting careers were less noble than his. Even though they were," one actress said.

"He never looked down on anyone," another stated. "He'd just as soon bring a homeless man home for dinner, as he would the President."

"Eric's knowledge of medicine was unmatched. Even in fields he did not practice, he was the 'go to' man," one said.

Erica looked up, and actually smiled. That was her and her mother's doctor, Dr. Grayson. Her father recommended him for both of them.

Their closest neighbor, Nanette Kelley, was sitting at the table next to them. She stood up and looked at all the people pretending to be Eric's favorite. She almost laughed. Then she looked at Libby, and said, "You and I know that my husband, Kal was Eric's closest friend; and vice versa. They were closer than any two brothers. When they were in town, they spent every evening together."

Libby nodded. Kal and Eric were inseparable. So were she and Nanette. Their children were a little older, but they were family to her children, too.

"As hard as he tried, Kal couldn't make it back in the country in time," she explained. "He and I, and our children, love you guys too, Libby. When everyone else is gone, we'll still be here for you."

Libby nodded, and smiled. Kal traveled more than Eric had. On many occasions they ended up in the same cities. Sometimes the same country.

She stood up and hugged her friend. "Thank you, Nanette."

...

"He will be sorely missed," Lucinda Hopewell said. She was a well-known rising star. Her manager introduced her to Eric, years ago. The man was a shrewd investment genius. They'd hit it off, because they both came from nothing. She owed her wealth to him. She raised her glass. "Here's to Eric George."

Everyone stood and raised their glasses. "To Eric!"

...

Erica hadn't been listening to any of them. She'd cried so hard, she now had a throbbing headache. She did not want to be at the repast. Everyone was fellowshipping, and having a splendid time. They called it the celebration of her father's life.

She never understood how people could bury their loved one; and then eat, drink and be merry. Her emotions didn't flip like a switch. Her mother and Eric didn't want to be here, either. They were just as mournfully solemn as she was.

Remington, Ian and Carson were having the time of their lives. They were laughing and talking with their girlfriends and schoolmates. They shamelessly spoke of their desire to hear the reading of the will. All of them were making plans as to how they were going to spend their portion.

"I wonder how much Dad left us?" Ian asked.

"Show some respect for once!" Erica snapped.

Remington smirked. "You're acting all sad, but you want to know too." In truth, he was devastated too. He was handling it the only way he knew how.

"Can't you guys at least let the dirt settle on Dad's grave?" Eric asked.

"What difference does it make?" Ian replied. Then he smirked. His heart was just as broken and Eric's, Erica's and their mothers. He just didn't know how to deal with it any other way. "Listen, I am going to miss Dad. I hate that he died, but he ain't coming back."

"Close your mouth, Ian," Pastor Perry demanded. This conversation was upsetting his sister, and niece. His nephew Eric had turned beet red. "Before I close it for you, boy."

Ian went to respond, but wisely thought better. His mother may not believe in the rod, but his uncle sure as hell did. Over the years he'd slept with more than a few icepacks, thanks to his uncle.

Remington glared at his uncle. He was so angry that his father had died saving that *bastard*. She's the one that should be dead, not his father. "Just because Dad is dead doesn't mean you are in control."

"Actually it does," Perry replied. "Your father-"

Libby grabbed her brother's hand. "Not now, Perry." She knew what he was getting ready to say. She also knew her three youngest sons were not going to be happy about it. She didn't want it to play out amongst all of these people. Family laundry should be aired in the privacy of their home. "Let's just get through this repast."

Perry gingerly patted his sister's casted hand. Her wrist was broken when Eric pushed her, and Erica, out the way of that car. "Okay, Lib."

"Don't stop. My father what?" Carson asked.

"Didn't you hear your mother say not now?" Perry replied. "Now if the three of you can't control yourselves, leave."

"Who the hell-" Ian started.

Perry rolled up out of his chair, with his hand already in motion.

Ian jumped out of his seat, and stumbled a few steps backward into one of his classmates. Remington and Carson knocked over their chairs, trying to get out of the way. Or out of Perry's reach!

Their uncle was a big man. Freakishly big! With long…long arms!! Big hands, too! Hands that made your peripheral the interior view. Hands that made your tongue flap, and put on the airbrakes!

Thank God they moved in time. Otherwise he would've gone down the line; and with one swift swipe tagged all of them.

Perry's voice was blistering, when he warned, "Now you boys listen up. I will not tolerate your unruliness, today of all days. I don't care if this is Eric's repast. I will fine tune your disrespectful butts. You understand me?" He took a few steps toward their side of the table. "Now I said take your disrespectful butts *home!*"

Remington, Ian and Carson angrily pushed past their friends. They had no intentions of leaving, but they did move to the other side of the room. Remington turned around and shouted, "My father is dead! I don't need another one. Especially you! I'm a grown ass man!"

Perry took a couple of angry steps towards them, but Libby grabbed his arm. "Let them be, Perry."

She didn't want him making a scene. There were too many dignitaries at her husband's repast. It would diminish her husband's legacy, if the real Perry rose up. She was grateful that the POTUS, and the Secret Service Agents, did not come to the repast. Nevertheless, a lot of her husband's associates were curiously watching.

She and her brother were closer than most siblings. They'd gotten even closer after their sister, Annette, overdosed on heroin seventeen years ago. That day had been as sad as this one.

Perry pulled Libby's hand off of his arm. He wasn't about to let these boys get out of hand. Not today, and not tomorrow. He wasn't their father, but he was their uncle.

He and his wife never could have any children. He'd married her, twenty-seven years ago, knowing she was terminal. The doctors gave her three years to live – tops. But he believed God, and her cancer went into remission.

They celebrated their twenty-fifth anniversary, two years ago. She went to sleep that night, a happy woman, but didn't wake up the next morning.

He couldn't entertain the thought of another woman in his life. He imagined his sister would never remarry, either. No one could follow in the footsteps of the greatest love.

He sat back down. "I'm sorry, but your sons are out of control, Lib."

...

Erica actually chuckled. Her three brothers were doofuses, and clumsy, on a good day. There had always been a rivalry between them, at least on their part. They resented how much she, and Eric, looked like their father. The three of them certainly didn't. Plus, they were short like their mother. Nerd Smurfs.

They despised her most of all, and treated her like crap. They always called her 'the bastard', when no one was around. When she first arrived they stole from her, and vandalized her bedroom. Her parents finally put a deadbolt lock on her door.

When they were young, they used to triple team her. Her stepmother told her to stop letting them bully her. She confessed that she was afraid to fight back, because she thought *she* would take their side. Mainly she was afraid her stepmother would kick her out. After all they were her real children, and she was the *bastard*. Her stepmother told her that she was as much her daughter as they were her sons. Then she kissed her forehead and said, "Kick their booties."

After that she started fighting back. In fact, she'd hit them, before they could hit her; just because she felt like it. The last physical altercation was two years ago. It ended all physical altercations. That's when she pushed Remington down the stairs, and broke that fool's arm.

She'd had enough of them, and went after Carson and Ian. Those two midgets ran down the other stairs to get away from her. They tripped over the flippers they called feet; and fell down those stairs too.

Her father had been furious with her. He'd shouted,

"He could have broken his neck, Erica!" After he set and casted Remington's arm, he tore her butt up! He said he wasn't whipping her because she finally fought back. He was whipping her, because she deliberately pushed her brother down the stairs. She guessed he was probably right.

As terrible as her brothers treated her, they didn't *mess* with their Uncle Perry. That man did *not* play with children. His motto was, *"Children should be seen, and not heard."*

When he found out about her, he made her feel like she was part of his family, too. It didn't matter to him that she was her father's - his *brother-in-law's* - outside child.

He told her that although her father's action was sinful, she wasn't the *sin*. He told her that she wasn't a mistake, because she came from the breath of God. He said God's breath was not, nor had it ever been, foul. He actually had a church service dedicated to the newest member of *his* family. He introduced her to the congregation as his beautiful little niece.

His voice rang out, *"Take heed that ye despise not one of these little ones; for I say unto you, that in heaven their angels do always behold the face of my Father which is in heaven."*

Even at nine years old, those words were not hollow to her ears. They'd resonated in her *soul*. She didn't know how she knew, but she *did* have an angel. She just wished he'd been there a week ago, to save her father. She wished he'd come and save her from her three brothers.

"Can we just go home, Momma?" she asked.

Libby nodded. They'd stayed long enough, anyway. Too long, as far as she was concerned. She didn't want to be here, either. She didn't want to celebrate her husband's life. She wanted to mourn his death, in the privacy of her home. With her children, and brother.

She stood up. "Let's go, baby."

Perry reached for Libby's hand. Eric did the same to Erica. Before they could take a step, a stranger walked in the door…

...

CHAPTER 5

Ariel walked through the door of the country club, and paused. He spotted Erica right off. She looked the same, but different. Their eyes locked, and his heart clinched. She was exhaustingly, and numbingly, beautiful. So much so that his legs weakened.

There was something about her smooth sable flesh that was enticing, especially in that dress. She was exotically, and sexually alluring. She was beautiful, and glowing, even in her present state of mourning. She was turning the king of the jungle into a household pussycat.

He moaned. *"You were right to keep Erica hidden from me, Michael."*

Michael chuckled. *"I am always right, Lion."*

"You need to get busy with your woman, man. I'm not sure I have the fortitude to keep my hands off my luscious mate."

He heard all of his brothers co-sign his demand.

"You had better control yourself, Ariel," Michael replied. *"I told you that you would need help, did I not?"*

He knew Ariel would need help in this arena. His brother was a wild beast. A ferocious lion, in all things.

"You had better handle your business, Michael. I am not playing! My mate already has me weak in the knees. I have a desire to crouch down at her feet. Wag my tail, and tongue; and meow until she pets me, man. Seriously!"

His brothers let out a full throated belly roar. None of them had seen Erica. They all took a peek, and immediately stopped laughing. Every one of them had the same thought. Sheba!

"Oh man. I feel for you, Ariel," Zadkiel said.

"We all do," Jeremiel added. *"You are where I am this very moment."*

"Where we both are. Maybe you should go home for a fresh anointing," Chamuel suggested.

"I just got here, man. I'm not trying to leave. Besides, I couldn't if I wanted to."

"I can help you leave," Michael replied.

"Why are you still in the conversation, Michael? If you want to help somebody, help Verenda come to grips with her destiny, man. That's all the help I need from you...big brother."

Michael grunted.

His brothers roared. Ariel and Michael were going to be fun to watch. Those two were the definition of complete opposites. Because of the way Michael was fashioned, he was overly disciplined. Because of the way Ariel was fashioned, he had no discipline...at all!

...

Ariel smiled, and closed the distance between him and Erica. He stopped in front of her, and caressed her cheek. In all of his existence, he'd never touched the human flesh; with his hands. Teeth yeah, but never hands!

Her flesh felt better than it looked, and that was saying something. He stroked his thumb back and forth, and declared, "I have missed *you*, Ms. Erica George."

Erica was caught off guard. Strange men were always coming on to her. Normally she would have told him to step off. She didn't this time, because he felt familiar. Instead, she asked, "Do I know you?"

He nodded, but couldn't respond verbally. If he did,

he'd sound like a croaking bullfrog. He just kept nodding.

...

Even through swollen, and red eyes, she could tell he was exceptionally handsome; and big. He was at least six eight, and dark chocolate. He was, without a doubt, the finest brotha she'd ever seen.

His eyes were strange, but intriguing. They were dark, with more than a hint of purple. Probably contact lenses, but they looked good on him. Natural! He had a purple amethyst stud in his beautiful Afrocentric shaped right nostril. His lips were full, and plush. He was clean shaven, with the exception of a thin square patch below his bottom lip. That was too grown, and sexy.

A row of that same stone, in various sizes, graced the whole of his right earlobe. They mirrored the stones in her own. His hair was pulled back in five thick cornrows. Soft baby hair lay smoothly along the edges.

He was appropriately dressed in a black linen suit, with a lilac shirt. However, the first three buttons of his shirt were open, allowing his smooth chest to be exposed.

His touch felt familiar, and not just to her flesh. To her soul! "How do I know you?"

"You have always known me, and I you." Then he stroked his thumb across her cheek. "I've missed you so much. Not a day has gone by without my wondering if you were safe," he added.

She was wondering if maybe they knew each other, before she moved here. She'd left a lot of school friends behind. Before she could ask, he planted the scene of their past in her mind. And not just hers!

...

Every person in her family was seeing them together...in Heaven. He let them see his purple, and white tipped wings. He let them see her, before she had her sensuous flesh.

He let them witness how much they had *loved* each other…in Heaven! He allowed them to see every single moment they'd ever spent together. He allowed them to witness him, as the lion of God; during and after the Great War. He allowed them to see her, leaning on the balcony of Heaven, watching him do battle.

He allowed them to see the day she left, and the promise he made to her. He let them see that he couldn't see her, because Michael had blocked his view.

He let them see that once Michael got out of his way, he'd seen *everything* she'd been through. And had come straightaway, to her.

He allowed them to read his thoughts about her mistreatment, by her three brothers. He advised them that he knew about the trouble and hurt they felt over Eric's infidelity.

He whispered to their hearts, *"The truth will make you free."* Then he let them *witness* her conception.

···

Libby almost lost her footing. Her eyes welled. "Eric," she sobbed. "My husband died, never knowing the truth! He never knew the truth!"

···

Perry's eyes watered. Eric was a good man. He'd always known that. He wished he could tell him one more time, how much he admired him.

Not only that, but he'd been looking beyond Ariel and Erica. His gaze had been on Heaven. The Throne! God! He always believed in God. Never once did he doubt His existence. But to see Him! He whispered, "Sweet LORD!"

...

Eric was in total shock. Over everything! He mumbled, "What?"

...

Remington, Ian, and Carson were frozen in place. Erica – *the bastard* - used to live in Heaven? They saw God kiss her cheek. They saw the angels celebrating her coronation. They saw God breathe. They saw her soul land in her mother's womb, and take form. They resented her, all the more. They jumped when Ariel roared, like a lion...

...

"You are moving too fast, Ariel!" Michael warned. *"Humans cannot take everything at once."*

"You need to get out of my business, and handle your own. Stop stalling, Michael; and get with your woman, man," Ariel replied. *"You have all of us hanging in the balance. I think you are afraid, big brother."*

His brothers cracked up.

"Do not reveal anything else! You understand me!" Michael demanded.

"Perfectly! The other is of no concern to me. At least not at the moment."

He closed down the vision.

...

When the vision slipped from Erica's view, she blinked, and stared up at him. She remembered him now. She remembered them. He was her *angel.* She didn't know it, but she'd missed him all of her life. That's why she'd begged the lawn service to shape the shrubs, off her patio, like a lion. Her soul knew the lion was...

"Ariel," she whispered. She palmed his hand, closed her eyes, and whispered again, "My fierce lion."

He was her hero. He'd saved her from the wrath of God, in Heaven. He was ferociously powerful, but wondrously gentle. She was experiencing dueling emotions. Excitement and regret.

'What if' was doing a number on her. She opened her eyes, and stared up at him. "If you'd been here last week, my father would not have died."

His heart sank. Her words, and the tone of her voice, reminded him of Mary and Martha. Martha said the same to Jesus, when Lazarus died. Faith didn't get any stronger than that. Accusation either, for that matter.

It was true, as a son of God he was as powerful as the *begotten* Son. They all were. However, what they lacked was the *authority*, the begotten Son had.

As powerful as Michael and his son were, they still needed *permission* from God to put a spirit back in its body. Just as Sammael needed permission to take a soul.

That's why Sammael wasn't at the crucifixion. He had neither the permission nor the authority to touch the Son. Jesus himself said, *"No man takes my life. I have the authority to lay it down. I have the authority to pick it up again."*

That is why Michael didn't invite Sammael, or his apprentices to take Eric last week. Michael was commanded, by God, to do it himself. Eric was a special man. His heart soared…and sank. Michael should have let him come earlier.

He pulled Erica into his embrace, and eased her spirit. Then he whispered, "Your father-"

Michael muted him…

"I am about sick of you, Michael!"

"Not now, Ariel," Michael demanded. *"Control your tongue. Control those spirits!"*

Ariel sighed. Michael was right. This was neither the time, nor the venue. Not with all these guests present. "Were you on your way home?" he asked.

Erica nodded.

He looked over her shoulder, at her family. They, and every person in the banquet hall, were staring at him. "Let me escort you guys."

Perry was more than ready. He had a million questions for this angel. He addressed the crowd. "Thank you all for coming, and expressing your love for Eric. Please utter our names, when you pray." Then he reached for Libby's trembling hand.

Ariel knew everybody in that room wasn't *friend*. In fact, some were more than *enemy*. They were *foes*. But, just like King David's foes, they *will* stumble and fall!

He hoisted his wings, and wrapped them around Libby, Eric Jr, and Perry. Before everybody's eyes...they all vanished.

The crowd gasped!

...

Everybody's nerves, in the hall, were on edge. They couldn't believe what they'd just witnessed. Or even *if* they'd truly witnessed it. Some wondered if it had been an apparition. After all he had on a suit, didn't he? No way wings could just burst through the fabric. Could they?

Those who had evil machinations trembled, including Remington, Ian and Carson. If that really happened, they were in serious trouble.

They looked at each other with fear in their eyes. Did that angel know that they planned to run Erica off? She didn't belong in their family anymore, because her one connection was dead!

After seeing what they just saw, they were afraid. Should they stay, or should they go? They were too afraid to do either.

Before they could decide, for themselves, they vanished…

•••

Michael wiped the crowd's memory of Ariel, and the entire incident. Lucinda Hopewell was in that crowd. She could not know about *'sanctioned'* mates. If she remembered, she'd tell Seraphiel. His son definitely could not know. Plus, their neighbors, Nanette and her children were present.

Ariel was like a wild beast. He acted without thought. It was not his fault, though. He was the untamed lion that Yahweh used time and time again.

When he was called to action it was usually without restraints. His job was to stay, until the job was done. His instructions were by *every* means necessary. But this was a different situation.

He sighed. He imagined they would all have to play cleanup man, for Ariel. Well not him! Ariel was right. He needed to tell Verenda. *"You guys keep your eyes on Ariel."*

His brothers silently nodded, even Jeremiel. They'd all been there for him, four years ago. Chamuel didn't see what the problem was. He'd shown Kay who he was on the first day too.

"Not in front of an audience, you didn't," Michael replied to his mind. *"Unaware is the key, Chamuel."*

"True."

•••

CHAPTER 6

Ariel didn't appear in the house. Instead, he appeared at their front door. He retracted his wings, and released everyone but Erica. He couldn't bear the separation, and neither could she. She was holding on to his waist, for dear life.

"Why didn't you take us inside?" Libby asked.

"You haven't invited me in," he replied.

"You are most definitely welcome," Perry replied, and put his key in the lock.

"Hold up," Remington said from behind them.

They all turned around.

"How do we know he's really an angel, and not a vampire? He evidently can't enter unless invited."

"One thing we do know for sure, Remy," Eric replied.

"What?"

"You stupid as hell, boy."

"No, he's not. Vampires can make us see what they want us to see. Even if it's a lie," Carson argued.

"Yeah, but vampires can't come out during the day, right?" Ian asked.

"Stop this nonsense, right now!" Libby shouted. She was so embarrassed, she could die! "Just stop it!"

Ariel smiled, but Erica felt his stomach muscles rapidly flexing. She knew that he was inwardly laughing. She squeezed him, and laughed. "Ariel!"

He kissed the top of her head, and chuckled in her mind. He missed their days together. *"Vampire! Your brothers are quite hilarious."*

"More like retarded."

He squeezed her and laughed out loud. Then he said, "Is it not a human custom to be invited into someone's home? Do you not stand at the door, and knock?"

"If you are with the homeowner, you don't!" Remington replied.

"In that instance does not the homeowner say, 'Come on in? Make yourself at home.'"

Remington smacked his lips.

Ariel chuckled.

Erica laughed.

"Forgive my nephews," Perry said, and opened the door. "C'mon in, man. Make yourself at home." Then he stood to the side and held the door open.

"If you don't mind, I'd like a few moments alone with Erica," Ariel said. "We'll be back shortly."

"Alright," Libby replied. "That'll give me a chance to change clothes, and make some coffee."

He noticed Libby's wrist was casted. He reached for it. "Allow me." He vanquished the cast, and healed the bone. Then he stroked her wrist, and the bruises disappeared. "That's better, yeah?"

She rubbed her wrist, and nodded. "Thank you."

Ariel nodded. Then he and Erica vanished…

•••

They appeared on the mountain that he'd been on earlier. This was the only private space he could think of. He begrudgingly released her, and immediately felt the void. He was into his mate, more than he should be. More than he could afford to be, at the moment.

His wings had been around her family, but his arms

were around her. His hands had rested on her backside.
Man, he *loved* the way her soft cheeks curved out. He was
feeling a wealth of need for her. He had to temper his
desire; otherwise there would be no turning back.

Nevertheless, he pulled her back in his arms, and
kissed her. It felt completely different from kissing her in
Heaven. Her flesh was pliable, and extremely soft. He
could get used to this. He pulled back, and stared into her
eyes. "I have missed you, girl."

"Do we have God's permission to do this, Ariel?"

He stroked her cheek, and nodded. "We do."

"What happened after I left?" she asked.

"Michael told me that when the time was right he'd
let me know where you were."

"That doesn't mean we have permission." She knew
about the fallen and she didn't want that for her Ariel. She
loved, needed, and wanted to be with him. But she'd
rather live the remainder of her days alone, with the
memories intact. That way when she did die, he'd be in
Heaven waiting for her.

He heard her thoughts, and again his heart melted.
She was concerned about him, and his relationship with
God. She was willing to sacrifice them, to preserve him.
He loved her more.

"We are 'sanctioned' mates, Erica."

"What does that mean?"

"God has sanctioned our union, like he has Michael
and Verenda's."

"He did?"

"Chamuel and Jeremiel have already been reunited
with their mates."

She squinted, because she didn't know who they
were. Then she remembered. "Kay and Anita! Oh my

God, I forgot them too. I forgot everybody, Ariel. How does that happen?"

"Everyone forgets, Erica. I allowed your family to see you, in Heaven. None of them realize that they started out there too."

"They did?"

"Every soul does."

...

She realized that they were just chit chatting. It was for her benefit. This had not been a good day for her. A good week for that matter. She'd been surviving on pure adrenaline. Now she was mentally drained, and physically exhausted.

Her emotions were still dueling. Happy and sad! She was so glad to have Ariel back in her life. She was so sad her father died, before meeting him. She was so angry that her father died, *in the first place!* She wanted to thank God for her mate, but she wasn't speaking to Him these days.

She hadn't slept more than a couple of hours at length, since the accident. Every time she closed her eyes, sleep or awake, she relived the accident. She was tired, and weary.

What she really wanted to do was stretch out, on this mountain, and sleep. She wrapped her arms around him, and sighed. "I'm so glad you're here, but I wish you'd come sooner."

...

Ariel could restore her physical strength, and ease her troubled mind, but he wouldn't. Grief was a natural human condition. Like a baby, it needed to be birthed. Likewise, physical exhaustion was best relieved, when done naturally.

As far as her being angry with God, that was okay with his Father. Being angry was different from losing faith in Him. Besides God created that spirit too.

He materialized a goose down comforter, under the old Sycamore tree. He lifted her, walked over to the tree, and physically laid her down. He removed her four inch heeled shoes, and started to massage the soles of her feet. "Weeping endures, but for a night," he told her.

Then he stretched out beside her, and pulled her into his arms. He kissed her temple and whispered to her mind, *"But joy comes in the morning."*

Erica laid her hand on his chest, and sighed. As physically ripped as he was, she didn't feel his muscles. Wrapped in his arms, all she felt was his mane. His soft *lion's* mane.

She stroked her hand back and forth across his chest. "I'm so tired."

"I know, baby," he replied, and kissed her temple. He pulled her closer. "Sleep."

She dozed off...

...

Erica knew she was dreaming. She had to be. She was sitting under the Sycamore tree, talking with someone. She didn't recognize the face, but she knew him.

She'd spent years in this spot sharing secret moments with him. This was their hiding place. Just hers and her...

"Daddy!"

"It's me, Erica."

"I miss you so much!" she said, and hugged him.

"I'm here now, aren't I?"

"How do I go on without you?"

"I'll always be here, when you need me. I am so

proud that you are my daughter. No matter what, don't ever let anyone convince you otherwise."

"I feel like you let go of my hand, Daddy."

"Never!" he replied, and reached for it. He placed her hand, and his, over her heart. *"I'll always be right there."*

She sobbed, and hugged him. He felt so good, but different. Like a spirit. *"I can't think straight, Daddy. All I see is that car hitting you. Over and over again! I don't want to do anything, but turn back time."*

"Don't let my death keep you from reaching your dreams. Live your destiny, baby. Make me proud," Eric replied. Then he leaned over and kissed her. *"Let this moment be your memory, not the accident."*

"I will," she sobbed.

"I'll see you soon," he said…and vanished.

...

Her eyes popped open. "Daddy!"

Ariel squeezed her. She'd been asleep for over an hour. He stood in the background, in the peripheral and watched. He felt it when Peace eased in her spirit, and Calm her body. He felt the exodus, when Trouble left her mind.

He smiled, and asked, "Pleasant dreams?"

"Did you do that?" she asked.

"What?"

She smiled. "I saw my father. He looked different, but it was him. He didn't have a scar on him."

She wondered if that was what happened to everyone who died. It certainly had happened to Jesus. No one recognized him, either; not until he spoke.

Ariel smiled. "Everyone gets a glorified body, when they take off mortality. Your father is now immortal,

Erica."

"Will I see him again?"

He squeezed her. "I'm sure you will."

She sat up. "I need to check on Momma. I need to tell her about my dream."

He stood up, and pulled her to her feet. "Don't. She'll probably have her own."

Erica slipped her feet in her shoes. Then she hugged him. He didn't feel soft anymore. All she felt was rock solid muscles. She wondered if the softness was an illusion. It didn't matter.

"I'm so glad Michael finally let you come." She leaned back and looked into his eyes. They were dreamy. "I love you, Ariel; and I missed you."

"I love you too, Ms. Erica George," he replied.

He leaned down and kissed her. They both moaned. Yeah this was going to be hard. He pulled way. "Let's go."

They vanished...

• • •

"Thank you for allowing me that visitation, Michael."

"You are welcomed, Eric."

• • •

CHAPTER 7

They appeared at the foot of the porch. Her family was sitting outside. They'd all changed clothes, and were anxiously waiting. He sensed Perry really wanted to talk with him, but not about Erica. He wanted to talk to the *angel.* Libby had a million questions, about both Erica, and Eric.

Her brothers were staring at them. Three stares were filled with anger. They resented her…and him.

Eric Jr couldn't believe how rejuvenated Erica looked. She looked at peace for the first time in a week. Whatever Ariel had done for her he wished the man would do for him, and his mother. They both were quietly tormented.

Everyone stood up. Perry opened the door again. "Let's go in?"

Ariel kissed Erica's cheek, and said, "Shall we?"

Erica smiled and held his hand behind her back as they walked through the door.

He looked down, and groaned. His hand was resting against her rear. Man! This was going to be challenging.

Chamuel laughed, and spoke to his mind, *"I feel ya, Ariel. Just imagine how I feel. I live with my mate. Have been for years!"*

"Michael needs to get his act together," Ariel griped.

•••

When Remington went to enter the house, Perry put his palm on his nephew's chest. "Give me a reason to beat your butt!" he warned. "Any reason at all."

"Lest you forget, I'm too old for whippings!"

"Did I say whip you? I said beat your butt. Trust me there is a difference."

Remington pushed his way past his uncle, and stormed in the house. He didn't need this crap. He'd already made up his mind that he was not staying here. As soon as he found out how much money he was getting, he was out. Forever!

Ian and Carson walked past their uncle with their heads down. They knew life had just gotten hard for them. Their father was always traveling, and they paid their mother no attention.

Their uncle was a different story. He lived by Leviticus, as it related to children. He'd moved in with them, last week, after their father died. Things were about to change.

They both wished they were old enough to leave. Not only that, but just how much did this angel know?

...

Ariel looked around the large foyer, and then down the hall. There were double doors on each side of a wide staircase. One led to a large family room, the other Erica's bedroom.

He reached further to see her bedroom. He really should not have done that. It did not look like a young girl's bedroom. Not! At! All!

The walls were deep purple, with gold crown molding, and chair rails. Her bed looked so inviting, like it was designed just for him. And her of course!

The bed was a king size brush brass. At the foot of the bed was a brass seat, with purple, gold and white cloth padding.

The bed was covered with a silk purple coverlet that had gold eyelets along the edges. Mounds of pillows with the same design were at the head. Even her dresser and chest were purple, with gold knobs and handles.

On the wall over the bed were three heart shaped mirrors, trimmed in gold. The ceiling was an amazing mural of the galaxy. It had deep purples, black, and golds running through it. The white stars were as vivid as the real ones. If you looked close you could see an outline of *his* wings, hidden in the background. It even had one singular black hole.

It was the most amazing thing he'd ever seen. It was obvious her soul remembered him. It was obvious she was waiting on him.

There were double doors that led outside to a patio. At the base of the patio, two lion shaped shrubs stood on each side of the walkway. Yeah, she was waiting on him.

Metallic wrought iron stairs led to a loft, in her bedroom. The loft was a sitting room, and study area. A white and purple flowered sofa, and love seat was on one end. A roll top desk on the other.

It did his heart good to know that his mate had lived a life of luxury. At least in the last nine years.

···

"You have a lovely home," he voiced, and squeezed her hand.

"Thank you," Erica and Libby replied.

They both were thinking that it's just a building. That structure is not what made it lovely. It was the love, and warm affection of Eric that did that. Now this was just a building haunted by memories.

Everywhere they looked, they saw his ghost. Him hugged up with Libby, eating popcorn, watching a movie.

Him helping Erica with her homework. Him telling her boyfriend, just last week, that she didn't want to see him anymore.

Him wrestling with his sons, and sliding down the banister, like a kid. His setting Remington's arm, after Erica pushed him down the stairs.

Him teaching all five of them how to drive. Him playing football with his sons on the lawn. Him cooking BBQ on the family patio. Him sitting at the head of the dinner table, blessing the food.

Nothing would ever be the same again, because the heart of the family was gone.

···

Ariel was listening to their thoughts. It warmed his heart that wealth hadn't made her forget where she came from.

···

Perry moved to the front, and said, "Let's have a seat, shall we."

Everyone followed him toward the den. Ian decided he wasn't going to be led by his uncle. He rushed in front of him, opened the double doors and marched in.

Remington and Carson pushed past everyone. As rude as it were, it was their way of rebelling.

Libby shook her head. "You boys are acting like you have no manners!" she shouted at them.

"Whatever!" Carson replied.

Libby had reached the end of her patience with her sons. They were acting like caged animals testing the fences. Her being the fence! She reared back, and smacked Carson in the mouth. The sound bounced off the walls.

"I have had enough of your, and your brothers'

mouth," she said. Then she looked at her other two sons. "Don't you think for a minute I am going to accept this behavior, any longer. I will beat every one of your asses! You all understand me? Now get somewhere and sit y'all asses down!"

All five of her children were stunned. Perry was too. Libby did not believe in hitting, or using foul language. Eric cussed, a lot, when he was really angry; Libby never did! She didn't even say 'lie, or butt'; let alone *ass*. Her terms were fib, and booty.

"Momma!" Erica shouted.

Libby turned around and looked right in Ariel's eyes. She blushed. "Please forgive me. This has been a trying day."

Ariel chuckled. "That's quite alright."

"Please have a seat," she offered. Then she noticed Remington was sitting in Eric's chair, behind his desk. "If you don't get your-"

Remington jumped up, and frowned. When did his mother get so mean, and so damned controlling? "Listen, just tell me how much money I've got coming, and I'll be out!"

Libby could not believe her son was challenging her, especially in front of this angel. She imagined it was her fault. She wasn't much of a disciplinarian. She'd always left the punishment up to Eric, and Perry. But Eric was gone, and he wasn't coming back.

It angered her that that was all her sons were concerned about. Money! How much they'd inherited was more important to them than how much they'd lost.

She frowned back at her son. Then she sat in her chair, looked under eyed at him, and said, "You don't have a damn *dime* coming, boy!"

The room went quiet…

…

CHAPTER 8

Remington knocked all the papers off of his father's desk. "I know you're lying! My father would not have left me out of his will!"

He glared at Erica, then back at his mother. "You're trying to steal my inheritance for that *bastard!*"

"Why do you insist on calling my mate *bastard?*" Ariel snapped.

They all jumped from the rage in his voice.

"Let me explain something to *all* of you. I will *not* put up with your mistreatment of Erica. In case you haven't figured it out, I am not here on a visit. I'm here to stay. To protect my mate. Understand? Now just in case you are confused, let me be break it down."

"Easy, Ariel," Chamuel demanded. He could feel his brother's rage, all the way in New Orleans.

Ariel ignored him. "I am an angel, but I'm not a Seraphim, or Cherubim. I have never sung in *anybody's* choir. In fact, I can't hold a monotone note. I was not fashioned to do so."

Remington, Ian and Carson jumped, when they saw his shadow appear on the wall. They were the only ones to see, with their mind's eye, the worlds that had been destroyed.

Cavemen, and Neanderthal, were mercilessly wiped off the face of the earth. Prehistoric beasts were being obliterated! Not by God, but by Ariel, and other warring angels.

They trembled when they saw the hunter become the

hunted. They trembled when they saw Ariel take down one T-Rex, after another, with his bare hands.

"I am bound by neither chain, nor rein," Ariel declared. "I was fashioned to be untamed. Called to be methodically monolithic, and profoundly prolific in battle. I am commanded, by God Himself, to be His ferociously animalistic annihilator!"

He released Erica, and stalked toward her three brothers.

Erica remembered the Great War in Heaven. She knew what Ariel could do. As mean as her brothers were to her, she didn't want him to hurt them.

She grabbed his hand. His hand had turned furry, like a paw. No one could see it, but she felt it. "Don't, Ariel. Stop!"

"In case you boys missed it, I am the Lion of God! The king of the jungle. In every realm! Every dimension! I am JEHOVAH-GMOLAH'S *untamed* rage! His attaché of recompense! Now go ahead, and disparage my mate one more time. I will feed you your own tongu-"

...

Michael felt his brother's rage, and the boys' trepidation. He heard Erica's plea. Ariel hadn't exactly told the truth, or maybe he really didn't know.

He, himself, held the rein on Ariel's rage. He shouted, *"Back off those boys, ARIEL!"* and literally yanked the lion's chain.

Ariel's entire body snapped back, and it pissed him off. Michael was working his nerves, again. He did not appreciate his impudence, in the least bit. *"Do not ever do that again, Michael! You understand me!"* he snapped. *"You need to get out of my business, and handle your own! Now back off!"*

None of his brothers laughed. They knew that Michael was listening to Ariel's heart. They all were. They knew he wasn't going to touch those boys. To do so would hurt his mate. Michael knew that. They wondered why he asserted his authority, in that manner.

"That was uncalled for, Michael," Gabriel reprimanded from the balcony. *"You were way out of line, brother."*

"That was a foul move, man," Raphael added. *"Ariel knows what Father expects of him."*

Michael grunted. His brothers were only paying attention to Ariel, and his antics. He was charged with protecting all of humanity, especially 'sanctioned' mates.

"I am sorry, Ariel. Your mate, and her family, did not know you would not hurt them. You are doing harm to their peace of mind," Michael advised. *"Right now they are all fearful of you, Lion. Even your mate."*

Ariel looked around the room and then backwards at Erica. Everyone looked frightened of him, especially her. That had not been his intentions. *"Fair enough. However, there is nothing wrong with my hearing, dude. Next time just tell a brotha,"* he added. *"Do not ever choke me again. Understand?"*

His brothers exhaled.

Michael laughed, at them all.

...

Ariel hugged Erica, and said, "Forgive me." Then he looked over her head, at Libby. "Tell your children the *truth*, Liberty," he demanded. "Or, by the throne of God, I will!"

Libby had kept quiet all of these years. She told Erica to stand up for herself, against her brothers. She didn't want to pick and choose between her children, because she loved all of them.

It hadn't worked. They continuously agitated her, and called her that awful name. Even seeing what Ariel had showed them didn't soften their hearts.

She saw the look on Erica's face, but that wasn't the worst. She saw the look on Ariel's face, and felt his rage. She was sure she saw fire in his eyes.

She nodded. It was time. Eric never wanted the truth to be known. He was such a good family man, but he wasn't here. She almost resented him for leaving her with the fallout.

She looked at Perry. He'd known all along, and helped keep the secret.

Perry knew what his sister was thinking. What they'd done wasn't a sin. It was for the children's sake. Maybe they should've been truthful in the beginning. If they had these boys might've seen Erica differently. He balled his mouth, and nodded. "It's time to tell them the truth, Lib."

...

Libby looked at her daughter, and sadly smiled. Her baby was not a bastard; no more so than Jesus was. She felt an unfamiliar anger toward her three sons, for labeling Erica as such.

She glared at Remington. Her tone was acerbic, when she declared, "If Erica is a bastard, Remington; then so are you, Ian and Carson."

Everyone in the room was shocked, and it showed. That is except Perry and Ariel.

"What?" Erica asked.

"What are you talking about, Momma," Eric asked. "How can that be? I'm the oldest. You and Dad were married, before you had *me*."

Libby looked at Eric, and Erica. They looked just like their father, but Eric had her smile. She nodded and said, "You are the only child, on God's green earth, that was nurtured in *my* womb, Eric."

"WHAT?" Eric asked.

Libby continued, "You and Erica are the only children - in this room - that came from Eric's *seed*. God only knows how many more of Eric's children are out there."

She leaned her head back, and closed her eyes. "My husband took the blame for something he hadn't done." She slowly shook her head and sighed. "He died never knowing that he had not been unfaithful to me."

Erica, Eric and Perry nodded. Ariel had let them all see Erica's conception. She was Eric's daughter alright, but he was *not* in the bedroom when she was conceived. He wasn't even in the house. The state either, for that matter.

Eric Senior had been a sperm donor, before he ever met Libby. He'd needed the money because he was a professional student.

Although he was able to secure full scholarships, that didn't include spending money. His parents were extremely poor. They not only lived on the margin, they *were* the margin.

His contributions were supposed to be anonymous, and identified by an assigned number. He was a regular at the sperm bank, and the entire staff knew him. By face, name and number.

Eric had a brilliant mind, and was godly handsome. A technician charged with collecting the specimens wanted *his* baby. She stole a vial of his donated sperm. Then used a turkey baster, and impregnated *herself*.

She never told a soul what she'd done, because her actions were unethical; and criminal. She would have lost her job if anyone had found out. Possibly gone to jail, too.

She never told Eric, or asked him for a dime. That was because he'd only been a donor. Plus, he might have sued her, and on top of everything else took her baby.

He didn't know her, but she kept tabs on him. When she found out she was dying, she told her nurse to mail a letter, and picture of Erica, to him. Even then she didn't reveal in the letter how Erica came to be. She'd feared Eric, and his wife, would be repulsed by a turkey baster daughter.

She'd already died, and was buried, by the time Eric got the letter. There was never a question that Erica was his daughter, because she looked just like *him.*

...

Even after her dream, Erica was concerned over that revelation. She wasn't really her father's daughter. He'd only been a sperm donor. He'd evidently forgotten that he'd been one. Otherwise, he would've realized what happened, as opposed to taking the blame for being unfaithful.

"I'm sorry, Momma," she whispered. She realized that she didn't even have the right to be here. That broke her heart, because she loved her stepmother. "I should leave. I wasn't an accident, or a mistake. I wasn't his daughter, either."

"You damn right you weren't!" Remington replied. "You were just one of many donations he made jacking off, at a sperm bank."

Perry backhanded Remington before he knew it. "I've had enough of your disrespectful mouth, boy! Now shut up!"

Remington grabbed his mouth, but didn't say anything. He couldn't! He felt the growl coming from Ariel's throat, vibrating in his own. He moved to the far side of the room.

Libby saw the hurt on her daughter's face. Her own face softened. She stood up, and walked over to her. Then she palmed her cheek.

"I have loved you from the day I knew you existed. One look at your picture, and I was a goner. There was no doubt that you were *Eric's* daughter, so that made you my daughter, too. I don't care how you came to be. I never did! I'm just so grateful you are here, baby. I am so grateful that you are *my* daughter, Erica. Don't ever doubt that. Eric was your father, and he loved you, too. His very last act proved how much."

Erica hugged her mother back, and started crying. That car had come out of nowhere. Her father died, saving her. "I love you, too, Momma."

"Don't leave me, baby," she desperately begged. "Your birthmother gave me a wonderful gift. A beautiful daughter. I'm your momma. You and Eric are all I have left of your father's flesh and blood. This is your home. Please stay."

...

Remington, Ian and Carson were freaking out. How could their mother lie like this? There was no way in hell they weren't her sons. There was no way they weren't their father's sons.

"We may not look like Dad, but we damn sure look like you, Momma!" Remington shouted. "Why are you lying?"

"Remington is right!" Ian shouted, and kicked the chair. "You're trying to steal our inheritance for that bas-"

He felt what seemed like hairy claws stroke his bottom lip. He looked across the room at Ariel. The man's eyes were glaring.

He jumped, and respectfully said, "Erica, and Eric."

•••

Libby released Erica, and walked over to Remington. She slapped him again. "Make that the last time you call me a liar, son. It does not benefit me, one bit, to reveal the truth to you boys. I may not have birthed your unruly butts, but I am *still* your mother. You all are going to respect me."

"What truth?" Carson asked. "If we are not your sons, whose sons are we?"

She looked at Perry again. This was going to be hard. It was going to reveal an awful truth that they never wanted these boys to know. She was having a hard time saying it out loud.

Perry was feeling his sister's angst. It was both of their silent shame. He decided he'd take it from here.

•••

"Libby and I had a younger sister. Her name was Annette. She and Libby looked alike. They could've been twins, were it not for the five years between their births."

"What?" Eric asked. His mother had never talked about another sibling. He'd never even seen a picture of the woman. None of them had.

"She was an unruly, and wild child; from day one. Much like you boys," he said, and looked at his three nephews.

"Even as a toddler she'd just haul off and kick whoever was closest to her. Biting and spitting at everybody. Spanking her only made her behavior worse. She was always getting into trouble. Always fighting against the grain. First one thing, and then another. She drove our parents to the brink, and an early grave. She'd just as soon curse them out, as she would a stranger on the streets. Ditching school, and sneaking out at night; all before she turned fifteen. Hanging out with the scum of the earth. The more our parents punished her, the more she rebelled," he told them.

He took a seat, and rubbed his forehead. To this day he believed she had a demon in her. She had to have had. No one is born inherently evil. Sinful yes, but not evil.

"When she was fifteen she got hooked on drugs. She started stealing things from us. Momma's jewelry. Dad's tools. Libby's first set of wedding rings. My car. She stole any, and everything, not anchored down."

He rubbed his face again and mumbled, "Lord, have mercy Jesus."

This next part was going to be hard. He leaned his head back, and in the middle of his story, had a conversation with God.

"Help me, Father," he prayed. "If I tell *any* of the story, I have to tell *all* of the story. Ease my mind. Guide my tongue. Remove the resentment that still lingers in my heart."

...

Everyone in the room felt his distress. They'd all deduced that this sister, that none of them ever heard about; was their real mother. That revelation was bad enough, but it was more to it than that. They all sensed this was going to be bad.

They all moved to take a seat, except Ariel. He stood behind Erica, with his hands on her shoulders. He eased her spirit.

Libby leaned her head back, and closed her eyes.

This next part was going to make, or break, her family.

They nervously waited for Perry to start talking again…

...

CHAPTER 9

"A few months later she found out she was pregnant," Perry informed them. Then he opened his eyes, and gazed at Remington. "With *you*. She was in no condition to take care of a baby. Hell, she couldn't even take care of herself."

He closed his eyes again, because he couldn't bear to look in his nephew's eyes. "You were born, on her sixteenth birthday; addicted to *heroin*."

At first, Remington could not say a word. He knew his uncle wasn't lying. Good or bad, the man never let a lie slip from his lips. He'd never heard his uncle utter a single curse word. He'd just done that, and for good reason. "I was born addicted to *drugs!*"

Perry nodded, but did not open his eyes. "The state took you from Annette, because she was unfit. That girl didn't care. She didn't want you anyway, because you would've cramped her style. She said they could throw you in the trash, for all she cared. In fact, she threatened to do it herself, if they didn't."

"The trash? Like garbage?" Remington asked.

"Her exact words were, 'Either y'all throw the *bastard* in the trash, or I will!'" Perry replied.

He never understood that. He looked at Ariel, and frowned. "What happened to her maternal instinct, man? How do you carry a baby for nine months and have no attachment to him, whatsoever?"

Ariel shook his head. He felt Perry's heart racing, and breaking. This was still a sore spot for him. In his heart he wondered why some of those who had children took parenting for granted. Yet, he and his wife wanted them, badly; but couldn't have any.

He wondered how Perry and Libby would feel, when they found out that Erica couldn't have children either.

He eased Perry's spirit…

...

Perry finally opened his eyes, and looked at Remington. "My wife and I wanted to take you, because we didn't have any children. Couldn't have any. But, my wife wasn't well enough to deal with the stress of raising a child. Especially one addicted to drugs. They were going to place you in a foster home, Remington. Libby wouldn't have it. She asked Eric if she could bring you home. Eric didn't hesitate. He said, 'Let's go and get our baby.' You were only two weeks old. The only reason the state agreed to Libby and Eric taking you, was because of *Eric's* credentials."

Perry looked at Ian and Carson. "Even after what she did to Remington, Annette kept doing drugs," he said, and wiped his face. "That girl just couldn't break the curse. There was something wicked in her. I prayed and I prayed. Night and day I prayed for my baby sister. My prayers fell on deaf ears."

"That's only because she did not want to stop doing drugs, Perry," Ariel informed him. "God will not answer your prayers for someone else, if they don't *want* His help. Your sister had the same free will you do. The curtain was torn for her too, Perry. Jesus knocked on the door of her heart, like He did yours. All she had to do was let Him in. She didn't, because she didn't want to be healed."

Perry's tears gathered at the edge of his lids. He

actually groaned. He knew his sister was in Hell, and that broke his heart. He whispered, "Annette."

...

Libby knew Perry was at a breaking point. They never discussed their sister, because it was too painful. There were only two options for the dead. Heaven or Hell. Annette wanted no part of God. She just didn't buy into the whole creation notion. She didn't believe there was a God. She believed when it was over...it was done.

They gathered up all of her pictures, and burned them. They didn't need them anyway, because Annette's image was still there. All she had to do was look in the mirror, to see her. All Perry had to do was look at *her.*

They decided never to speak her name, in front of the children; for fear they'd ask questions. They never wanted these boys to know how reckless she was. How uncaring she had been.

She took up the story. "Annette had sort of a dry rot in the fabric of her *heart.* She loved no one, not even herself. Two years later she got pregnant *again.* A set of twin boys. Both babies hooked, like the first. Only this time her dry rotted heart was weak, because of the drugs. It couldn't handle the trauma of giving birth. She was only eighteen years old. Mother of three beautiful babies, yet her heart was too weak. She died two days later. I couldn't bear any of you boys being placed in the system. I already *loved* all of you," she said and wiped her eyes. "I asked Eric if I could bring two more babies into our home."

To this day she didn't understand why her sister couldn't stop using drugs. Why she couldn't love her children, more than the heroin.

"Your father had such a big heart. He said he

already planned to, but there was a stipulation this time. He said we needed to make it *legal*. We hadn't adopted Remington, because we hoped Annette would get her life together. If she had, we would've given her, her baby. Once she died, Eric didn't want anyone to come along and claim his sons as theirs. Or even possibly splitting you boys up. If he was going to raise you boys, you needed to carry *his* name."

Eric didn't understand. As sad as this story was, something didn't ring true. He was in agreement with his brothers. His mother, and uncle, were lying. But why?

"Our initials spell out Dad's name, Momma. That can't be just a coincidence."

"What?" Ian asked.

"What are you talking about?" Carson asked.

"**E**ric! **R**emington! **I**an and **C**arson!" Erica shouted. "You can't be that stupid that you never realized that." She wanted to say *'you bastards'*.

"Shh!" Ariel whispered, and chuckled. *"Let them finish."*

Libby nodded. "Eric was afraid that one day the truth would come out. He wanted to make sure that all of *his* sons were connected to him. He wanted you boys to know you were just as much his sons, as Eric was. Ian and Carson hadn't been named yet, but you were already two years old, Remington. When he drew up the adoption papers, we changed your name from Quincy to Remington."

"Who is my father?" Remington asked.

"Eric was your father," Libby replied.

"Who was my sperm donor, then!" he snapped.

He couldn't believe these people had kept this secret all of these years. No wonder they made a difference in them. He and his brothers were not Eric's sons.

"I don't know who any of your birthfathers were. I imagine no one does, other than God; and perhaps this angel," she replied. "It doesn't make a difference though. You are all Eric's and my children."

"Eric didn't give a damn about us. That's why he didn't leave us any money!" Carson shouted.

"That's not true," Perry replied.

Remington smirked. "You said yourself that where your money be, there also is your heart!"

"Since he didn't leave us anything he couldn't have loved us. Ain't that right, Unc?" Ian challenged.

"That is a loose interpretation of that scripture. A manipulative, and vulgar one, I might add," Ariel injected. "If you'd stop resenting my mate long enough, you'd remember how much your father loved you."

Then he planted a scene in their heads…

•••

CHAPTER 10

Eric was sitting in a rocking chair, in a dark room. He was holding a little baby boy. The baby was screaming, and tremoring. Eric reached for a medicine dropper filled with some type of liquid, and placed it in the baby's mouth. Being raised by a doctor, they all knew that it was methadone.

The baby's screams immediately quieted, as he suckled the drug. His fix! He was making loud suckling sounds, as he desperately consumed every last drop. They saw the baby's body immediately relax, and heard him sigh.

Then they saw Eric place the baby over his heart, and soothingly rub his back. He kissed his head, and started gently rocking back and forth. They heard him whisper, *"I love you, son. I'm so sorry this happened to you. We're going to get through this together, okay. You and me. One day at a time."* They both fell to sleep, right there in that rocking chair.

They saw Eric go through this same ritual day after day, night after night. Until he finally weaned the baby off the Meth. The baby was Remington.

•••

The next scene showed Eric holding, and rocking, two babies. He performed the same ritual that he'd performed with the first baby. He made the same promise to both babies. He slept in the same rocker, rocking them all night long. Night after night!

•••

The next scene showed Eric squatting down in front of Eric Jr. He was five years old, and feeling neglected. *"Rock me, Daddy!"* he demanded.

Eric stood up with little Eric in his arm. Then he went to the rocker, and sat down. Little Eric didn't need to be rocked gently, so Eric made a game of it. First he rocked real fast. Then he lifted little Eric up in the air with one hand, and twirled him over his head. Little Eric was giggling and having a ball.

When Eric finally brought him back down he hugged him against his chest. *"I'm sorry I've neglected you, son. I love you, but your little brothers needed me more,"* he whispered, and kissed his cheek.

...

Then they saw a tent, pitched in their backyard. Eric and his four sons were inside the tent. It was his idea of boys' night out. Just him, and his sons, and they were all healthy.

He was telling them ghost stories. Ian and Carson were scared. They were hiding their faces in Eric and Remington's laps. Eric and Remington were scared too, but they were the big brothers.

Then they flipped over on their backs, with their heads outside the tent. Two on each side of Eric. They were gazing up at the stars. He was pointing toward the sky, showing them the big dipper and other star formations.

They heard him say, *"There's a whole other world up there, in the galaxy. Angels walk on the air up there."*

"Nobody can walk on air, Daddy," Remington replied.

"Angels can," Eric replied.

They saw the wanderlust look in his eyes.

The memory was faint, but the brothers remembered it. Ian was closest to Eric, and Carson to Remington. They'd all loved those weekend getaways, because their father made them all feel loved.

...

Ariel smiled. Maybe he wouldn't have to tighten these knuckleheads up, after all.

...

"I remember that," Eric said. He missed those days. "We camped out every weekend, whenever Dad was in town. I loved his ghost stories."

His brothers nodded; they remembered too. "He was a good father, until Erica came along," Remington voiced. He looked at Erica and frowned. "The minute you got here, he stopped spending time with us."

"That's not true, Remington. Eric always catered to the one that needed him most, at the time," Libby replied. "Your sister had just lost her birthmother. She was shipped across country, to live with a bunch of strangers."

"It didn't help that you three jerks treated her like crap, from day one. Your behavior perpetuated her need for Dad's attention," Eric added.

"That's because we knew he cared more for her, than he did us," Carson replied. From the vision, he knew better than that. He just wasn't ready to admit he'd been wrong all of these years. "Now it makes sense. We weren't his natural children. And that's why he didn't leave us any money."

"That is not true, Carson," Perry replied. "He loved all of you guys, but he knew you. He knew you'd behave the way you are behaving now. Even though he and Libby raised you boys, we all saw Annette's rebellious spirit in you."

He looked over at Libby and chuckled. "Your mother didn't have it in her to whip you guys, but your father and I did. We wanted to keep that spirit tamped down. I wasn't about to lose you boys, like I did my baby sister. You boys are all we have left of her. Understand?"

"Your father had to make sure that you guys didn't go wild, and spend everything he'd worked so hard for…in an instant," Libby added.

Perry sat up and crossed his legs, knee to knee. "He knew you three would try and run over your mother. He knew she'd let you. So he made me the executor of his estate."

"What?"

Perry nodded. "The house is your mother's, flat out. All of the furniture, too; including your bedroom furniture. He left everything he owned to your mother. The cars, the boat, stocks, bonds, you name it."

"He really didn't leave us anything?" Remington asked.

Libby shook her head. "Not one penny. Not to you! Not to Ian! Not to Carson! Not to Eric Jr! Not to Erica!"

Perry nodded. "He didn't think it would be healthy to leave that much money to you guys. He left it all to Liberty, the love of his life. He knew that she'd be fair, and share with you guys."

"But she's not sharing," Carson reminded him.

"Per her instructions, as executor I setup a trust account for all of you. Ten million dollars each."

Remington, Ian and Carson smiled. Remington looked at his mother. "I thought you-"

Perry kept talking. "However, the account cannot be touched until you reach thirty. Longer if you haven't matured."

Their smiles faded.

"What?"

"Your mother, and I, will decide if you guys have reached a level of maturity to handle your inheritance."

"That is not fair!" Ian replied.

"I have setup an account in each of your names," Perry continued. Then he reached in his pocket, and pulled out five cards. He handed them to his niece, and nephews. "Each of you will get a monthly allowance. I will put it in your accounts the first of every month. If you run out before the month is over, too bad. Neither your mother nor I will spot you guys an advance."

"That means you're going to make us live below our means!" Ian shouted.

Perry laughed. "Everything you have, your father provided. The cars you drive are in his name. Even this roof over your heads. You haven't worked one day to help pay the mortgage, have you? You haven't offered to buy groceries, or put anything in this house? So exactly what means are you referring to, Ian?"

"So we have to live here until you decide we are mature enough?" Remington asked. He was in college, and only here for the funeral. He planned on dropping out of college, and hitting the road.

"By no *means*," Perry replied. "You can leave tonight, if you want to. I'll help you pack. You'll just have to get a job to pay your bills."

A giggle slipped from Erica's lips.

"What about college?" Carson asked.

"Of course we will pay for college, Carson," Libby replied. "Education was very important to your father. However, you *all* will have to maintain at least a B average."

"Eric has already graduated college. Does he get his money now?" Ian asked.

"Is he thirty?" Libby asked.

Ian didn't respond.

"Another thing," Perry said. Then he looked from his nephews to Erica, and back. "Your father died with the knowledge that you guys never accepted Erica. I'm here to tell you that broke his heart, because he loved you all. You know the truth now. I hope this knowledge will help you guys overcome your disdain for your sister. I am sure Ariel does too."

Ariel's eyes twirled.

Remington, Ian and Carson looked down, but didn't respond.

"If that's all, I'd like a private moment with Ariel," Perry said, and stood up.

"Why?" Erica asked. Her uncle was taking his role seriously, but she didn't like this. She did *not* want her uncle grilling Ariel. Although she imagined her father would've, if he were still alive.

"I just need to talk with him, in private. Is that a problem, Erica?"

She shook her head. "No, sir."

Ariel kissed her cheek. *"Don't worry, I'm a big boy."*

Everyone left the room, but Perry and Ariel...

CHAPTER 11

Ariel took a seat in the oversized wingback chair. He was surprised how soft and plush the cushions were. He looked at Perry and smiled. "Nothing but the best, right?"

Perry laughed, and walked over to the mini-bar. He retrieved a bottle of wine from the built in wine cooler and examined the label.

"Domaine de la Romanee-Conti Grand Cru, Cote de Nuits," he recited. "One of the finest wines known to man. This single bottle is worth over three grand. There are dozens more laying on the rack. Chillin'. All of them gifts to Eric by rich and famous people who loved, and admired him. People were always giving him things as their way of saying thank you."

He reached up and grabbed two crystal tumblers from the shelf. "Eric graciously accepted any gift someone gave him. He believed it was rude to turn down anything that was given from the heart," he said, and laughed.

"Man, you should have seen some of the clothes. He graciously accepted them, and then donated them to charitable organizations."

Ariel sensed that Perry needed to talk. His voice was nostalgic, as he walked backwards down memory lane. "Sounds like he was a good man."

Perry nodded. "I've never met a finer one." Then he popped the cork. "Eric didn't drink wine, or any other spirits. However, I do imbibe on occasion. 1st Timothy says, *'Do not drink just water. Drink a little wine, for thy stomach's sake.'*"

"Indeed," Ariel replied. "After the week you've had, I'm sure it is a necessity."

He had no doubt about that. Perry was holding his own, for his family; but his heart was broken. Eric was more than his sister's husband. He was Perry's brother. The only one he'd ever had.

"Umm," Perry replied. He tilted the bottle toward Ariel. "Care to join me?"

Ariel nodded twice.

He poured a good measure of wine in both tumblers. Then he walked across the room with the bottle, and tumblers, in hand. He handed Ariel his, and sat the bottle on the cocktail table.

He then sat down across from him. He took a sip, reared back and crossed his legs, knee to knee. Then he quizzically stared at Ariel...

...

"You know, I've always wondered why we couldn't see angels, like the saints of old," he said, and chuckled. "Was I ever wrong! Maaan, you being here just gave Hebrews 13:2 a pulse."

Ariel laughed, and said, "Do not neglect to show hospitality to strangers, for by so doing some people have entertained angels without knowing it."

"Exactly!" Perry replied, and laughed. He took another sip of his wine. "I just pegged you for another brotha trying to get next to my niece. I was thinking this was not the time, nor place. That is, until I saw your wings." He would have never imagined seeing an angel, let alone a black one. With cornrows to boot! "Are all angels black, man?"

Ariel shook his head. "We have no ethnicity. However, with our home being close to the sun, it is a given that we all have a dark tint. Nevertheless, we come in whatever form people can embrace us. For instance, I would never appear to a separatist in this form."

Perry bellowed. That was priceless. "Can you imagine a Klan's man's response if he knew the truth?" he asked. Then he frowned. "Is this not your true form?"

"It is, when I am not in battle. However, if it is more comfortable for you to see me as less human, I can accommodate," he replied and took a sip of wine.

Perry went to respond, but saw the metamorphosis of Ariel's shadow, crouched on the wall. He jumped. "Nah man! That's okay! We cool!"

Ariel chuckled.

"I'm curious. Where were you guys during Slavery, and the Civil Rights Era?" Perry asked. "And not just those times. America has a dark history, man. We got our start from taking the land from its original owners. Then we, as a nation, massacred thousands of the Natives. The trail of Tears is still a sore spot to the Indians. Let's not forget the Salem witch trials. Women burned to death, because of nothing more than rumors. When the Irish got here, they were treated just as badly. And what about those citizens who ventured to California during the dust bowl. They were just seeking their God given right to survive. America seems to always need an underdog to trample. Yet, we proudly proclaim that we are the land of the free. That certainly didn't include the Slaves. Home of the brave. How much bravery does it take to oppress the minority?"

"We have been on hand, in all of those instances. One angel even decided to be enslaved."

Perry's eyes bucked. That was absolutely absurd. "Why, in God's name, would he do that?"

"To experience the woes of life, from a human standpoint."

Perry nodded. "I imagine there is nobility in that. I, as a man of God, have never learned to turn the other cheek."

"Me either," Ariel agreed.

They both laughed.

Perry downed his drink, and refilled his glass. It was time to get down to the business of Erica...

...

He took a sip of his wine, and placed the glass on the table next to him. He leaned back, and closed his eyes. "This has been an amazing week. Sorrowful, wondrous and disturbing."

Ariel nodded, but didn't respond.

"The entire family had gone out to celebrate Erica's graduation from high school; and Eric's from college. Eric, and even Remington, had come home for the celebration. Everybody was getting along, for once. Ian and Carson were excited because Erica would be leaving for college. Eric would be going back for his Masters. Remington was already in college. That meant that they'd have their parents to themselves."

Ariel nodded again. He'd seen the celebration, the minute he arrived. He remained silent. It was important to let Perry retell the story.

"Like her father, Erica is a bookworm. Retaining what she reads, and is taught, has always come easy for her. Her comprehensive skills, and her ability to apply them, are without a doubt unmatched. She graduated with honors. A slew of ivy league colleges has already offered her full scholarships."

"Has she decided which one?"

"Not as of yet. I'm sure she'll want to stay close, after what happened to her father," he replied.

He scowled, and shook his head. Erica and Libby had walked out ahead of him and Eric. His nephews were behind him and Eric.

He and Eric were talking about the vacation the family was to leave on, the very next day. They were going to be gone for two months.

One month was Erica's graduation gift. The other was Eric's, for graduating college. Eric had planned to go back to college, after their vacation, and further his education. He wasn't so sure now. He understood that. Both of them were the men of the house now. It would take both of them, to fill Eric Senior's shoes.

No matter how detailed your plans were, all it took was a split second to ruin them. One split second that seemed to last an eternity…

…

When he walked out of the restaurant, he'd looked to the left. Their cars were parked across the street. He'd seen the car sitting a block away, with its lights off. He'd heard it rev its engine the minute Erica and Libby hit the edge of the parking lot. He saw it pull out of its space, and speed up; with the lights still off.

He'd shouted, *"Watch out!"* That was the wrong thing to do. His shout caused Erica and Libby to pause, and look back at him.

Eric had already taken off running. He got to them just in time. He pushed both of them with all the force he had. They hit the ground, but were out of harm's way. Eric wasn't so lucky. That car dragged him for more than a block. Then it stopped backed up, turned left; and sped off.

The shocking thing was; he'd seen Eric's spirit when it left the body. And he wasn't alone…

•••

"I imagine you know that it was not an accident," he stated. "That car was *aiming* for Libby, and Erica."

"Not Libby," Ariel replied.

"Erica?"

Ariel nodded. "That's why I am here this early."

"Early?"

"Michael dictates when we can meet our mates. He wants them to be grown, first."

Perry nodded. He had a lot more questions about angels, and human women. When did God decide it was okay? What about the ones that had fallen? But now was not the time.

"I assume you will take her away from here. Somewhere safe."

"Absolutely not," Ariel replied. He took a sip of his wine. Even though it was made by the hands of man, it was quite good. His eyes twirled. "Tell me, Pastor, where have you read that God commands his servants to run from evil?"

Perry shook his head. "Nowhere."

"In fact He told His beloved to do what?"

"Put on His full armor, so that when the day of evil comes, we will be able to stand our ground, and after we've done everything, to *stand.*"

"That's what you have to do, Perry."

"Is that what you plan to do? Just stand!"

"Nah man. Those instructions were for His 'so' loved, not me. My previous assertion was not hyperbolic.

I *am* the king of the jungle, and I'm going in. That's the nature of my beast *within*. Erica's stalkers have just become the stalked."

His brothers cracked up laughing. Perry actually heard them, and jumped. It sounded like thunder, rolling back and forth. "What is that!"

"My brothers. They will assist me, if the need arises. Are they welcome in your home?"

"YES! YES!" he shouted. He was a big man, and actually jiggled with excitement.

He thought about the scripture, *'He will give his angels charge over you.'* Angels...plural! Somebody was after his niece. They'd already killed her father trying to get to her. Who would be next? Libby? His nephews? Him? Or would they succeed in getting to Erica? This house had too many windows!

"C'mon in the building, y'all! Stay as long as you like!"

The Archangels appeared, including Michael.

Perry stood up. He would have tagged every single one of them as human. That is with the exception of Michael!

"Merciful Savior!" he voiced. That biggest angel was with Eric when he died!

...

CHAPTER 12

Erica changed clothes, but she didn't hang her dress up. She knew she'd never wear it again. If she did it would remind her of why she'd bought it in the first place.

She placed it in the chair, on top of the dress she'd worn the day of the accident. She would never wear that one again, either.

She was sure her mother was going to donate all of her father's clothes to a charity. Her parents were fanatics when it came to the less fortunate. They never donated old tattered clothes that couldn't be used. They said it defeated the purpose of giving.

They donated their favorite clothes, and shoes; as a sacrifice. Once a year they even shopped for clothes, just for the underprivileged. Her father always said, *'to whom much is given.'*

Her mother could donate these items too…

…

It was only 4:30, but she was physically and emotionally tired. She stretched out on the bed and closed her eyes.

This had been her parents' bedroom, before she arrived. The loft had been her father's private study. They moved across the hall, on the second floor after she arrived.

Her mother was an interior decorator, and had put everything she had into their home. Including redesigning the upstairs floor plan.

She had carpenters come out and install a door in the

loft. That door led to an upstairs hallway. Across the hall was a bedroom that had originally been a guest bedroom. Like her room, it had its own bathroom; and was extremely large.

Her mother had the contractors close off the original door, and place another on the side facing her room. She, and her father, wanted to be close in case they were needed.

Both rooms had large picture windows that faced the west and looked over the Pacific. That allowed them to experience the sun going down, across the ocean. Her bedroom also had sliding glass doors that led to her private patio.

...

The sun was still up, but it had been a long day. One that left a sweet, salty, and sour taste on her palate. It baffled her that in the midst of her grief, she found joy.

Joy that Ariel had come for her, when she needed him the most. Joy in knowing that, unlike the humans she loved, he would never leave her. Joy in knowing, without a doubt, that she'd never walk away from him. Joy in knowing that he'd never give her reason to leave, like her boyfriend had done weeks ago. At the same time, in the midst of her grief, and joy, she was confused.

Why had her birthmother felt the need to steal her father's sperm? Why didn't she get married, and have a baby the natural way? With a man that she loved, and that loved her?

She frowned at that though, and then mumbled, "Oh man!"

She hadn't thought about it, but come to think of it; she *never* saw her mother with a man. Not once in the nine years she'd lived with her. She had close female friends, and they would go out. But never once did she go out with a man. It all made sense, now…

It didn't matter. Her mother was good to her, and she still missed her. In the end, she made sure that her father knew about her. She made sure that her daughter wouldn't be left alone in the world.

It didn't matter to her father that he didn't know about her. He immediately embraced and loved her. He never let her feel like she was not wanted, or was a mistake. She was daddy's little girl, from day one. She wiped her eyes, and whispered, "I miss you *so* much, Daddy."

She could swear she felt him kiss her cheek…

•••

She heard a loud crashing sound across the hall and jumped. She ran up the stairs, and out the door. Right into Eric! "What was that?"

"I don't know," he answered.

Remington, Ian and Carson came running. "What was that?" they asked.

"We don't know," Erica responded.

They all rushed in the room…

•••

They didn't see their mother in the room. "Mom…ma!" Ian shouted. "Mom…maaa!"

"I'm in here!" Libby replied. "I'm trapped!"

Her muffled voice was coming from their father's walk-in closet. Their parents had two separate closets, because their father *insisted* on it. He'd said he loved the smell of Liberty's perfume, but not so much on his clothes.

They rushed to the closet and opened the door. The racks had toppled, causing the shoe shelving to collapse, as well. Mounds of their father's clothes, and shoes shelves, were on top of her.

The pile was rocking back and forth. It looked like their mother was trying to get out, but couldn't. The pile was too deep. Their mother was making noise under the stack. If they didn't know better they'd swear she was laughing.

They all went to work trying to get her out. "Are you alright, Mom!" Eric shouted.

Libby was holding some of Eric's clothes up to her nose. They smelled just like her husband. She was rocking his suit jacket back and forth, and taking deep healing breaths.

She didn't know if it was real, or imagined; but she felt Eric kiss her cheek. Then she felt him whisper up against her heart, *"Remember the last time this happened? I was there then. I'm here now. I'll always be with you, Mrs. Liberty Belle George."*

"Your father is here!" she shouted. "He's here!"

Her children looked at each other. Had their mother lost it? "What?" Remington asked.

"Get me out, son!" Libby shouted. "Hurry up!"

•••

It was taking more than a minute for them to uncover their mother. The strangest thing was happening. As they wildly moved their father's clothes, another rack fell. And then another! Their mother was laughing the entire time. So much so, that they started laughing too.

This reminded them of the time Ian and Carson were playing hide-and-seek. Ian decided to hide in their father's closet. He thought he'd hide on top of the rack, because Carson wouldn't expect him to be that high.

Unfortunately, their father had personally installed the racks, and shelving. And he didn't know a *thing* about carpentry.

He'd used nails, instead of toggle bolts, to secure the racks to the wall. Nails were okay, so long as they didn't pull on the rods.

As small as Ian was, he had to *pull* himself up. The entire rack collapsed on top of him. Their mother was furious over the mess he'd made. She started scolding him for playing in their room.

Their father quieted her rant by jumping on the pile of clothes, and taking her down with him. Then he started tickling her, until she got over her mad; and started laughing. Just like she was doing now.

Then he pulled a scared Ian on his lap and said, *"Nothing man made can't be fixed, or replaced. These rags are not as important to me as you are. The only thing that is important to me is that you are not hurt."*

After he said that, a jealous Carson plopped down on him too. *"Am I important?"*

Their father replied, *"You, your brothers and sister, and your mother; are my treasures, son."*

Before long, they were all in the closet, on the floor, rolling around in their father's clothes. Erica too!

It was one of the best days of their lives. In the twins' innocent minds that proved that he still loved them; in spite of Erica being there.

They'd all forgotten that simple confirming incident…

...

When they finally uncovered Libby, Eric asked, "What happened?"

"I was going through your father's clothes, getting ready to pack them for charity. I had a moment. I started snatching them down, and yelling at Eric for leaving me.

Then the rack just crashed on me. I think your father did it, to let me know he's still with us. All of a sudden the room filled with the smell of his cologne. He didn't leave us, he's here."

She sniffed Eric's jacket, again. Then she reached up and said, "Smell."

Eric reached for it. He closed his eyes and took a big whiff. No one could have told him that it would have an effect on him. "It smells just like Dad. It's like I can feel his essence," he said. Then he passed it to Erica.

She smelled the cologne before she reached for the jacket. She also smelled her father's natural scent. Her eyes watered, and she squeezed the garment tightly. "Daddy," she said, and sat down on all of his fine suits, and shirts. His presence was as real as it was in her dream. "Daddy."

Her brothers all followed suit. One by one they smelled their father's clothes. They actually sensed his spirit, and literally felt his presence. They were amazed that one whiff, and one touch, of his garment eased their spirits.

"He *is* here," Carson voiced. "I can feel him, can't y'all?"

"Yes," Remington replied.

They started talking, and laughing, about special moments they'd had with him. Ones they'd long forgotten.

...

Libby smiled while her children sat on their father's clothes and remembered when. She realized in that moment that you could grieve, and still laugh about the memories; at the same time.

She closed her eyes, and sighed. She felt Eric's

arms around her, just as sure as she was alive. She heard him, in her heart again. *"Weeping may endure for a night, but joy comes in the morning."* Except he was pronouncing it...*mourning!*

She opened her eyes, and looked at her children.

...

Remington wrapped his arm around Erica's neck. "Will you forgive us?" he asked.

He, Ian, and Carson had been talking in his room. After the revelation of their births, they had a different attitude.

Seeing their father's determination to heal them, was a sobering sight. It put things in perspective. He'd hung in there with them through their darkest days. He'd healed them with paternal love.

Now they understood why he catered to Erica. She'd needed healing too. When they admitted that, they also had another revelation. He never stopped being a good father to them.

He never stopped spending quality time with them. He just didn't give them the quantity of time, like he'd done prior to Erica's arrival.

"Are you going to stop calling me the bastard?"

"Nope! We're all bastards, sis," he teasingly said.

Erica elbowed him. "Shut up!"

Ian laughed. "Yeah, Mr. Eric Jr is the only legit in this bunch."

"I knew I didn't like him for a reason," Carson said, and threw one of Eric's shoes at him. "We should start calling him Legit!"

Eric caught the shoe, and threw it back at him. It hit Carson in his chest. Eric cracked up. Then he stopped laughing. "It doesn't matter to me, or Mom, that you were not Dad's blood sons," he told them. "It didn't matter to Dad, either."

Then he looked at Erica. "It has *never* mattered to me, or Mom, that you were not hers biologically. I was so happy to finally have a sister. Mom was thrilled to finally have a daughter."

He scanned all of their faces and said, "None of you are bastards. We are *all* Eric's and Liberty's children. You all are my little sister, and brothers. Not adopted, not step, and not half, understand?"

They all wrapped their arms around each other, smiled, and nodded.

"Can we all finally start getting along? For Mom's sake."

Erica shook her head. "Not just for Momma. For all of our sakes. We are the only ones in the world who knows how *each other* feels, in this moment. Momma's loss is a different loss than ours," she said, and her eyes clouded. "In time, she can get another husband, if she chooses. We'll never have another father."

...

Libby watched her sons hug their sister, and each other. That was the first time that had *ever* happened. For the first time, since Erica arrived, her children identified with each other. Losing their father was the tie that was binding their hearts together.

That scene gave her peace, and she felt joy sweep through her soul. Eric was right, joy comes in the *mourning*. Ariel was also right. The truth did make them free. Erica was wrong on one point, though. She would never love again.

She felt Eric's arms around her. She felt him kiss her cheek. Someone else might think it was the memory of his touch, and his kiss. They would call it nostalgia, but she knew better. Eric was definitely in this closet...

•••

"I surely am, Liberty..."

•••

CHAPTER 13

Perry and Ariel both stood up. Ariel made the introductions. "This is Chamuel, Jeremiel, Zadkiel, Raguel, Jophiel, and Michael. This is my mate's uncle, Pastor Perry Busby."

They extended a firm handshake to Perry.

Perry's heart, and the blood in his veins, literally froze. Ice Age frozen. Cryogenics frozen! He could not believe angels were encamped all around him. War angels! Ready to do battle, for Eric's family. His family too.

They all had on street clothes. However, if he'd seen these men on the street, he would have definitely noticed them. Not because they were angels, but because they were inhumanly tall. Not even steroids could produce their physique, especially Michael's.

"Please, everybody, have a seat," he instructed. He was ecstatic, as he watched them ease down on the sofa, and wingback chairs. He wished he could share this moment with Eric, but he couldn't.

He looked across the room, and said, "I've seen you before."

"Who?" Ariel asked.

"Michael. He was at the crash site. I saw him standing beside Eric's spirit."

Michael nodded. "Indeed."

"I was concerned, because even though I saw you with Eric; I didn't see the light. I was afraid my brother was on his way to Hell. Why-"

Ariel changed the subject, before Perry could finish the question. Mostly to deny Michael's answer. Michael was built without the embodiment of spirits, including Discretion. If he was asked a direct question, he would answer it head on. Without cautious consideration, mindful deliberation or embellishment.

Michael had stopped him from speaking at the repast. He was right to do so. Now it was his turn to stop Michael.

"I don't mean to harp, but why are you here, Michael? I hope it is to tell me that you have handled your business, with your mate."

His brothers roared. Michael did not.

"Well, have you?" Ariel asked again.

Michael grunted. Of course he had not worked things out. "No, I have not, Ariel. I have been busy keeping my eye on you. I had to clean up your debris, at the repast. The fact that I had to do so leads me to believe that I have to keep monitoring you."

"What debris?"

"I said unaware was the key, did I not? Yet, you left everyone at the repast's memories, of your antics, intact."

Ariel nonchalantly hunched his shoulders. "You didn't tell *me* unaware." He'd meant to leave their memories intact. A couple of wolves, in sheep's clothing, were in the room.

Michael, and all of the Archangels, heard his thoughts. He wanted to forewarn the deceitful wolves that the king of the jungle had arrived.

That was true. He'd actually told Chamuel, but Ariel heard him. "Humanity does not always respond in a good way, when fear is in play, Ariel. More often than not, they act out their fears in an aggressive manner. If I had not removed their memories, they would have come for you; in a mob style. Just to prove to themselves that they weren't afraid."

"I wish they would," Ariel warned.

"You may very well get your wish."

"My greatest wish, and desire, is for you to have a talk with your mate. Do I get that wish, too?"

Michael did not respond, but his eyes twirled.

Ariel smiled and, antagonistically, twirled his eyes back at Michael.

His brother roared, but abruptly stopped. Michael was not amused with Ariel's insolence. The room got seriously quiet...

...

"Wait a minute," Perry said, and broke the tension. His mind had just processed this discussion. "Michael has a mate *too?*" Then he looked at the other angels. "All y'all have human mates?"

They all nodded.

"God flooded the *earth,* because of the Fallen mating with human women. When did He change His mind?"

"Yahweh did not change His mind, Perry," Michael replied. "He sanctioned the unions between Archangels and human women, before He fashioned Adam."

"Then why-?"

"Our brothers that fell are no longer Archangels," Jeremiel answered.

"Or the sons of God," Zadkiel added.

"They are men of vile, and evil, repute," Chamuel added.

"Therefore, they forfeited their reward of having a 'sanctioned' mate," Ariel added.

"Once they fell, they became enemies of Yahweh. Demons," Michael explained. "Yahweh would never bind His 'so' loved's hearts to His enemies," he added.

"I see," Perry replied.

This was a fascinating revelation. He'd always known that the Bible did not cover it all. It couldn't, otherwise the book would be too big. Not only that, but the fact that angels had mates was extraneous to humanity's salvation.

In fact, it might hinder some. There wasn't a mother, or father, alive who wouldn't attempt to become a matchmaker. They'd run their daughters' true mates off, in hopes of snagging an angel for her.

They would be like Zebedee's wife, Salome; wanting something special for their daughters. And being mated with an angel was indeed special.

Michael responded to his thoughts, "You are correct, Perry."

Perry nodded, but didn't respond. His mind was in overdrive. His wished Eric was still alive to witness this astonishing turn of events.

They'd had many conversations about artificial insemination. He'd always been *against* it. Eric had always been *for* it. As a doctor Eric said it helped parents who couldn't conceive the natural way.

His personal opinion was that it was God's will. He'd even pointed out that there were many women in the Bible that were barren. Eric had pointed out that God opened Hannah's, and several other women's wombs.

He'd come right back and said doctors were trying to act like God. Eric didn't hesitate when he said, *"Not at all, Perry. Until we figure out how to replicate sperm, God still gets the glory. Until we can capture His breath,*

He still gets the praise."

Eric had been adamant about science and divine will not being mutually exclusive. In all of their debates Eric never once told him that, in the past, he'd regularly donated his sperm.

Now he realized Eric was right. When he examined the situation, God had to have had a controlling hand in it. The vision Ariel allowed them to see told the entire tale.

Eric stopped donating his sperm, after he met and married Libby. Eric Jr was twenty-two. Erica was only *eighteen*. Seeing that each specimen is unique in its own right, her mother had to steal the *right* vial. And look what God did with that stolen specimen. He breathed! And Erica became a *living soul*. That right there made him want to shout.

He looked at Ariel, and said, "The daughter, who by law, Eric should've never known…was made known. The sister, who her brothers call 'bastard', is *favored* by God. The daughter Libby readily accepted as her *own* had to be born, because she had a predestined future, with *you*."

He stomped his foot, and hit the arm rest. "Man, I feel a sermon coming on!"

Ariel, and his brothers, heard the awe in Perry's voice. They'd heard his thoughts, as well. The man was experiencing a spiritual awakening. Although a minister, he'd put limitations on the sovereign power of God.

It went further than that, though. Perry had equated what Eric had done, to masturbation. In his mind, because of what Onan had done; he thought of it as 'wasted seed'.

"You have misunderstood Onan's story, and God's displeasure with his actions," Ariel replied.

His brothers nodded.

"God was displeased with Onan's behavior because

of the condition of his *heart*. Onan refused to impregnate his brother's widow, because by custom the child wouldn't be recognized as his. But his dead brother's!" Ariel added.

"By spilling his seed on the ground, Onan usurped God's divine will to breathe life into it. That angered God," Chamuel added.

"Since Onan refused to let God breathe on his seed, God refused to continue to lend *Onan* His breath, too," Zadkiel added. "He died not a moment later."

"What Eric did in no way resembles Onan's actions, Perry. In fact, his actions were quite the opposite. Eric wasn't one to spread his seed around; haphazardly. In doing what he did he allowed the seed that would become Erica, to be preserved. Frozen until the time was right," Michael assured him.

"When that time came, her mother stole the vial, God breathed," Ariel said, and smiled. "And my mate became a living soul."

Perry grunted. Eric had told him the exact same thing. He hated that Eric would never know that he was right.

"He knows," Michael replied to his mind.

Perry nodded. He imagined he did. He also imagined that these angels had the answers to a few other things.

He looked at Ariel and asked, "So tell me who is after my niece? And why?"

Ariel didn't answer his question. Instead he stood up, and said, "It is getting late. I need to make a run, and then check on my mate."

"That's another thing," Perry replied and stood up. "Do you guys sleep? And if you do, exactly where do *you* plan on sleeping?"

Ariel's brothers laughed, said their good byes and vanished. This conversation was not their business.

"No worries, Perry," Ariel replied. "Above all else, including my love for Erica, I am an *Archangel*. I am governed by a higher authority. Therefore, you can be sure that I will not disrespect Eric's home, *or* his daughter's honor," he added, and vanished.

"You still didn't answer my question," Perry said to the empty space.

Ariel laughed in his mind, and replied, *"Here!"*

•••

CHAPTER 14

Jacques Bouvier couldn't shake the festering rage he felt, and he didn't want to. He walked around with a smile on his face, but he'd been stewing for weeks. He knew his thoughts were morbid, but he couldn't help himself. He knew that he would die soon.

He looked forward to the nothingness of the great beyond. He thought for sure he'd be dead by now, but not yet. He couldn't die, until he witnessed *her* death. She had to go first.

He, his father, Beaux, and his friend, Tristen, were huddled together in the greenhouse. This two-thousand-foot glass building was his mother, Dorothy's, pride and joy.

She spent hours on end out here. Not that she was a botanist, or anything; but she did have a green thumb. She liked working in the soil. She said it kept her mind off things she'd witnessed, and experienced, in her youth.

She bought little seedlings and transplanted them to larger pots, with richer soil, and compost. She always added coffee grinds. She said they provided a nitrogen boost.

She named every single one of her plants. She even talked to them, like they understood her. Maybe they did. In no time they'd spring up.

Rows of large potted palms lined the walls. In most cases they were taller than his six feet frame. On the bottom row, in front of the palms, were large pots of begonias, four o'clock, orchids, and impatiens. Their blooms spilled into the aisles, making the passage narrow. Ferns, ivy, chrysanthemums, petunias and coleus hung in baskets above. The ivy leaves dropped down, shielding the inside from any outsiders' view.

His father had installed an irrigation system along the top of the greenhouse. It was set on a timer, so that the flowers were watered at the same time every evening.

His mother wouldn't come near the greenhouse after the sprinklers came on. She had a fear of falling on the slick concrete floor.

That worked out perfectly for him, his father, and his friend. They could talk openly. *Plus,* they didn't have to worry about being busted for getting high. Not to mention the smell of the manure blocked the smell of the blunt.

...

"I don't understand why you didn't just talk to the girl," Beaux said. "I told you that in her state of mind she would've appreciated the support. You missed your opportunity to win her back."

His son had been moping around for two weeks. He and Erica had been going steady, since they were in the ninth grade. Then out of nowhere she dropped him.

His son suffered from ADHD. When he was younger they tried to keep him drugged. He didn't like what they did to his son.

He and his wife decided that wasn't right for their son. Dorothy started all kinds of home remedies. She was proud of herself, because she believed it was working. He knew better. He started giving Jacques marijuana, and that's what calmed his son.

"She was surrounded by her family. They know she doesn't want anything else to do with me," Jacques replied. "What I don't understand is how they got past us, without us seeing them leave." He'd planned to offer her a ride home, and then kill her.

"I don't know, man. We were sitting close to the door," Tristen replied. He'd gone to the funeral, and repast with Jacques.

The country club had been crowded, but that wasn't an excuse. They were still able to see her, seated at the table. In fact, they never took their eyes off of her.

She had been sitting with her family, in the banquet hall. Her uncle was giving her brothers hell. They stood up to leave, and then all of a sudden they were *gone!*

...

Beaux took a drag from the blunt, and let it marinate in his mouth. His son had told him what had happened. Unfortunately, it brought back unnerving, and unwelcomed memories.

He was born, and raised, in New Orleans, Louisiana. Sin City! The Big Easy! The capital of hoodoo, voodoo, and every other '...*doo*' you do. He knew all about weird, unexplainable things. He'd seen it all with his 20/10 vision. That's why he lived in California, *today.*

Over eighteen years ago he'd witnessed an angel battling demons in St. Louis Cemetery. It scared him enough to make him crap himself. He would have too, except his bowels locked down. His bladder had no such restraints.

When that angel shouted, "RUN!" he took off running, and pissing, down I-10. He was so scared, his mind tried to outrun his own feet. He ran so long, his pants dried! But, he never *once* looked back!

A truck driver stopped, and tried to pick him up, but he kept running. Another truck driver drove past him, and pulled his big rig over on the shoulder. The driver jumped out of the cab, and grabbed him, just before he hit the back of the truck. Even while the driver was holding on to him, his feet kept stomping. In his mind, he was still running!

The driver instinctively knew something terrible had happened. The man started praying, right there on the side of the road. He was asking God to give his angels charge over the situation. That scared him even more, because he was running from an *angel!*

He knew the only way to stop the dude from praying was to calm down. He did! But he was so scared, his feet kept tapping the asphalt, like a sprinter. On your mark! Get Ready! Go, at a moment's notice!

The driver was en route to California. That seemed as good a place as any. And as far away from New Orleans, as he could possibly get. He hitched a ride.

When he found a place to stay he called his girlfriend, Dorothy; and apologized for leaving her in the cemetery. She was furious with him, and blessed him out. Then she told him she was pregnant.

He may have been a coward, but he loved her. He told her that he'd marry her, but he was never…ever coming back to that Hoodoo town. She came to California the next week. They got married on a California beach. They'd been in California ever since. He didn't even go to his own parents' funerals. What the hell for? They were dead, and gon' be buried in that same cemetery!

...

His hands were trembling when he said, "There is no way they could've gotten past you guys, unless something supernatural happened."

"Squash that shit, man," Tristen replied. Even though Beaux was Jacques' father, he liked him. He was the coolest old dude he'd ever met.

Not only did he get high with them, he supplied the dope. He said he'd rather Jacques get high at home, instead of in the streets. That way Jacques would never be arrested for using, or buying. The man had issues, though.

"How do you explain it then?" Beaux asked. "As crowded as that parking lot was, you should've at least seen them driving away. I'm telling you guys there was something paranormal at work."

"C'mon, Dad. Don't start with the angel versus demon crap again," Jacques replied.

He liked hanging with his ole man, except when he started talking like he was a mental case. There was only room for one such case, in the family. That was him!

He'd always known he had issues. Dark thoughts! Erica was so sweet, that her presence eased his spirit. Since she broke it off with him, all he could think about was death. His and hers!

He wanted to experience murder/suicide with her, and had told her so. She told her father, and the man put his foot down. *"Stay away from my daughter!"* he'd shouted.

He hoped he'd get a chance, now that her father was dead. He was going to miss his father, the most. "Stop trippin'."

Beaux took another drag. He didn't care what these boys thought. He knew what he'd experienced. He knew there was a spiritual war going on.

"I'm telling y'all that angel spanked those demons' asses. Turned their butts into solid concrete!" he insisted.

Jacques shook his head, and took the blunt from his father. "You've had enough."

Tristen laughed. Then he stopped. The sprinklers

had long gone off, but he heard something up front. "Y'all hear that?"

"What?" Jacques asked. "Don't tell me you are trippin' too."

"Nah man. Be quiet, and listen."

Jacques and Beaux tilted their heads sideways. Then they heard it too. Assuming it was Jacques' mother, they rushed and put the blunt out. Beaux and Tristen led the way, as they walked through the plastic sheet makeshift door.

"What was in that blunt?" Tristen asked, and laughed. He couldn't be seeing what he was seeing. He was too high.

Sometimes Beaux came home with Bohemian marijuana, laced with formaldehyde. That shit will have you jumping out of a moving car. "This cannot be real. I'm hallucinating, right?"

"The hell you say," Beaux whispered. He was nowhere near high. Feeling no pain, sure; but not high. "I told y'all supernatural, didn't I?"

...

They watched the dark shadow of extremely large bat wings move towards them. Stalking almost.

"What *is* that?" Jacques whispered.

"That's a Popobawa!" Beaux replied.

"What's a Popobawa?" Tristen asked.

"A degenerate demon spirit," Beaux replied. "It sexually attacks its victim."

"What?" Jacques replied.

"Men, women, and children," Beaux replied. The thought of that made his shiver. "It is also a shapeshifter. It can change its form."

Before they could ask what he meant, the shadow

dropped down and crouched. It was now a *lion,* and stalking toward them. The thing looked prehistoric. It was almost as tall as they were. Its slow, but sleek movement was hypnotic; and predatory. They were too intrigued, or fearful, to run.

When the shadow got within striking distance, its paws materialized, and it struck out. Neither Beaux nor Tristen were affected. Jacques, who was standing behind them, got the full brunt of the blow.

He rubbed his lips. "Wow! That shit felt real," he declared. Then he looked at his hand. It was covered in blood. "It is real!" he screamed. "RUN!!"

•••

Beaux had a flashback. He'd be damned if Jacques' clarion call…RUN…didn't sound like that angel's in New Orleans. He took off running to the right, with no thought for his son.

Tristen was right behind Beaux, but the floor was wet and slippery. Beaux fell, and he fell on top of him. While down they both rolled under the table holding the flowers. They hoped the blooms would shield them.

They were wrong! That lion's face materialized, right in front of their faces. Its canines were elongated. Its eyes were blood red! They screamed and turned the table over. Then they jumped up, and took off running. More like slipping and sliding…

•••

CHAPTER 15

Jacques told his father and Tristen to run, but he did not. He watched as the ghost lion antagonized them. He knew it was just toying with them. If it had wanted to, it could've gone through the wood table; instead of under it.

He watched them virtually destroy his mother's greenhouse. They'd toppled over all the palms trees. The blooms were knocked off their branches, on the smaller plants. The seedlings on the floor were smashed by their slipping and sliding feet. His mother was going to be pissed.

He was mesmerized by the creature. Every which way they ran, the beast was there waiting for them. Only now it was back to being the silhouette of a bat-like creature, with purple wings.

His thoughts went one step beyond darker. He was stimulated! What would it feel like for him and Erica to die together, this way? He envisioned their deaths at the paws, and teeth, of this creature. They'd scream in painful ecstatic harmony. Awesome!

He wondered why it wasn't attacking him. Maybe it knew he wanted to die.

...

Beaux's heart was about to beat out of his chest. He thought for sure he'd put enough distance between him, and weirdness.

These past eighteen years had been quiet, and uneventful. He knew he should be trying to protect his only son, but what the hell! That creature seemed to be after him! Why? What had he done to invoke its wrath?

He kept running…

···

Tristen knew why the demon was behind him. Behind being the operative word. Nevertheless, he wasn't about to let that creature rape him.

He squealed when the thing nipped his butt again, and sped up. He jumped on one of the tables holding plants. He knocked them all off as he rolled to the other aisle. The creature was right behind him. He shouted, "I don't want to have sex with you! Leave me alone!"

···

Ariel's brothers were watching him terrorize these humans. They knew that he was just taunting them, for now. Chamuel remembered Beaux. He'd challenged the validity of his story. He'd asked, *"What was the name of that city?"* As if he was lying!

"He was the first one out the gate, in the cemetery. He plowed his way through the humans in front of him," he said and cracked up. *"A lot of them fell, and crawled the rest of the way out. The man left his woman behind, like he just left his son."*

His brothers cracked up laughing. Beaux's actions proved that he was friendly with the first law of nature. Every man for himself!

Chamuel and Jeremiel were allowing Kay and Anita to see too. "That's Beaux," Kay voiced.

"You know him?" Chamuel asked.

"We went to school together. I never knew what happened to him."

Chamuel laughed. He was seeing, for the first time, what happened. "He ran out that cemetery and never stopped running. He ran almost to the state line."

They all roared.

...

Beaux was trying to get to the only door, but couldn't. Ariel was blocking his path. Beaux would come to a slippery halt, and skid around another corner.

Tristen felt Ariel's teeth nip his butt. He was running, screaming, and holding his butt at the same time! He remembered that Beaux said the creature raped men, too! He was screaming, "Get off my ass, you evil demon ghost!"

Ariel's brothers, and their mates, were all screaming with laughter. They were making so much noise they drew Michael's attention.

...

Michael realized that Ariel was right. He needed to at least inform Verenda of their connection. She needed to know that they were more than just friends. Much more!

He knew her feelings for him were slowly changing, but she had reservations. She was fearful of them, though. She was remembering what Yahweh did to his fallen brothers. She did not want God to banish *him.*

In addition, she thought something was wrong with her. She was torturing herself, over her feelings for him. He decided to give her some mental relief, by explaining why she felt the way she felt.

They were sitting at the table, in her suite at Georgia House. She had taken to not looking him in the eye. He lifted her chin. "Verenda."

Verenda looked at him. His voice swept clean through her heart. Her eyes were tormented. "What is it, hon?"

"We need to talk."

Her hand trembled. Michael was an angel. Hers!

She wondered if he knew her most intimate, ungodly thoughts about him. She was sure he did.

They'd been together for twenty years. Even when Cappy was alive, Michael was there. At no point had he ever shown her anything, but friendship. Platonic companionship.

They worked together day and night taking care of, and protecting the little children, and their mothers. She knew about his son, Seraphiel. She knew about Seraphiel's spirit mate, Jodi. This house had been set up sixteen years ago, in case she needed shelter from the demonic forces looking for her.

As the years went by, she began to depend on Michael more and more. It was more than dependency. She needed him. Nope! She *wanted* him! She *loved* him!

How in the world did she get here? How could she have let herself fall for the most powerful Archangel? Was she that desperate to be loved? She was in real trouble here.

"About what?" she asked.

Michael heard her thoughts. He perused her form, and his eyes twirled. He was about to let all of those pesky spirits in.

Love, Desire, and Passion, were all waiting on the sideline. They were excited, and anxious. They couldn't wait to embody the 'like god' Archangel.

Before he could respond, he heard his brothers, and their mates, laughing. He sighed. He had no doubt it had to do with Ariel, and his antics. Otherwise, they would not all be laughing at the same time. He took a look...

He shouted...out loud, "ARIEL!"

"What?" Verenda asked. "Who is Ariel?"

"We will finish this conversation later, Verenda," he

replied and vanished.

...

He appeared inside the greenhouse, invisible. Ariel was on a rampage. He was not at the point that *he* wanted to kill them. He was going to make them kill themselves.

The healthiest of human hearts still had frailty. Even the purest of hearts was fashioned with one singular flaw. It was purposely *designed* to give up, and out.

YHWY knew His 'so loved' humans would fall, in the Garden. He created them, with that knowledge in mind. It was the condition of their hearts that caused the death of their relationship *with* Him. Their separation *from* Him!

From that day forward, the human heart has dictated when the soul and spirit separates from the clay vessel. It is the heart that causes the death of the trifold being. Not cancer, or any other disease. Not a knife, bullet, or any other tool. Not even the car that rolled over Eric decided his fate! Lots of people have been knifed, shot and ran over, yet they lived. That is because their hearts kept beating. In fact, doctors record the time of death, based on when the heart stops.

Death only shows up, when Reaper snatches the rhythm and the beat, from the heart. Reaper answers to Time's eviction notice. Time answers to YHWY'S request for His breath back!

Their phrase 'scared to death' was not a metaphor; at least not in this instance. He sensed all three of their hearts beating beyond the healthy eighty beats a minute.

The spirit Fear was bearing down hard, on these humans' hearts. Like an elephant's foot on a flea, they were struggling to even breathe; especially the innocent ones. They all thought Ariel was the demon Popobawa.

That made perfect sense, because Ariel was behaving like him.

In truth Popobawa was not his name. It was the name given to him on the island of Pemba, a few decades ago. Other islands knew him by different names.

In Chile they called him either El Trauco, or La Fiura; depending on if he was attacking male or female. They saw him, in either form, as a dwarf. In the Brazilian rainforest they called him 'Encantado' – the beautiful enchanted one.

In Hungary, they call him 'Liderc' the demon that attacks the family members of the dead. He made them think that their loved ones have come back, and raped them.

In truth, his name was Samjaza. The Fallen who had raped a human woman, and fathered *his* adopted son; Seraphiel. That demon was consumed with lust.

Humans all over the world believed that he could manifest, and sexually assault them. He could do no such thing. What he *could do* was make them *think* he had a physical form; and was violating them.

The human mind was fragile and swung like a pendulum between fact and fiction. That was how folktales started. One person, of good report, convinced another. Then that one spread the word, and so on and so forth. In no time, everyone was afraid of a *tale.*

Sometimes Samjaza appeared as a succubus, or an incubus; depending on whose mind he was tormenting. However, it was just an illusion. That was why he only attacked when humans were in a twilight state.

Like all other original Fallen, Samjaza's physical body was trapped in Hell. He should know, because he trapped Samjaza there.

This course of action was offensive to *him*. Ariel knew better than to behave like this. He could hear their thoughts, too. He knew they thought he wanted to rape them. That's why he kept nipping at Tristen's hind side. He was stoking the boy's greatest fear.

Stalking humanity in a sexual fashion was unbecoming for an Archangel. Since when did angels take their lead from demon behavior?

He shouted, *"STOP, ARIEL!"*

•••

Ariel stopped, and glared at Michael. He wasn't in the mood to get in a verbal tussle with Michael. At the end of the day he answered to his big brother. He nodded once and looked back at Tristen, and then Jacques. He allowed his lion head to be seen. Then he roared, and vanished.

Jacques ran past his father, and Tristen, out the door. He jumped in his car, and sped off.

•••

CHAPTER 16

Erica was back in her room, stretched out on her bed. This day had been emotionally draining. Highs and lows in a matter of minutes, was not good. She felt like there was a battle going on, in her mind.

She wanted to be elated, because Ariel was here. But, the loss of her father was overshadowing that elation. She wanted to be happy that she and her brothers were getting along. But the fact that her father would never know saddened her.

In addition, she was wondering why her ex-boyfriend Jacques was at the services. Their breakup had been *ugly*. Her father had had to step in, and get him to leave her alone.

She didn't love him, but she liked him. That is until out of nowhere he got weird. Talking about them dying together. Saying that it would be the epitome of their love. What love? She didn't love him. She certainly wasn't willing to commit suicide with him, and no one else for that matter.

She sighed, again. It was only early evening, but it had been a long day. She was looking forward to spending time with Ariel tomorrow. They had so much catching up to do. She couldn't wait to hear what her uncle said to him. She wished he was with her now.

She turned over on her side, right into his arms. "Ariel!"

"I'm here, Erica," he said. He kissed her temple.

She wrapped her arm around his waist, and snuggled

up closer to him. In his arms felt like soft fluffy down. "Does Uncle Perry know you're in here?"

He chuckled. "No."

She laughed. "I didn't think so."

He squeezed her. "Tell me about Jacques."

She looked up at him. "How do you know about Jacques?"

He smiled down at her. "I know everything that has ever happened to you, Erica."

"Everything?"

He laughed. Humans had secrets that they never shared with a soul. They had things they did as little inquisitive children, that they themselves forgot. Erica was no different.

He smiled mischievously, and said, "I know that you liked being the wife, when you played house."

She gasped. Then hid her face in his chest and cracked up. She hadn't thought about that in years. She couldn't have been any more than six or seven.

She and the little boy next door were always playing house. He and his parents had a screen enclosed back porch. It had a bed on it. His parents used it for the nights it was too hot to sleep in the house.

The porch was their playhouse during the day. He was the husband, and she was the wife. Her dolls were their children. They did everything they imagined grown folks did.

Of course she'd never seen her mother with a man, but the boy had a mother and father. He told her that he knew what to do, because he'd seen his parents.

His mother finally caught them, and she was livid. She spanked his butt good, and hers too. Then she told her mother what she caught them doing.

Her mother spanked her, too. Then she told her that she could get pregnant, just by *kissing* a boy. That ended her days as being his wife. As a matter of fact, she couldn't even play with him anymore.

"Oh my God, Ariel," she said through her laughter. "I can't believe you!"

He was still laughing, too. "What? You did, didn't you?"

She didn't answer. She just kept laughing.

Her warm breath, against his chest, was allowing him to experience chills; for the first time in his existence. He never knew that warmth could produce chills. He liked the way it felt. He liked the way she felt.

He tickled her side. "Why do humans call it 'doing the nasty'?"

She screamed. This was the weirdest conversation to be having with him. She had never told anybody about that. She couldn't even remember the little boy's name. She wondered if he remembered. She hoped not.

Ariel was laughing at her thoughts. She was so embarrassed. She didn't need to be, though. It was natural for little humans to be inquisitive about their bodies. They innocently explored sexuality, even though they didn't understand it.

He leaned down and said, "That was the first time you saw the male anatomy."

"Stop!" she screamed. She couldn't believe she was laughing, today of all days, but she was. And it felt wonderful. "Stop!"

"It was, wasn't it?"

"I am so embarrassed, Ariel!" she replied, but didn't look at him.

"You thought something was wrong with him. You

asked him, *'What's those?'"*

She squealed, and beat his chest. That was exactly what she'd said. She'd been shocked to learn that boys and girls have different bodies. At first she'd thought he was deformed. He told her his father had them too, but his mother didn't. He said his father's weeny was as big as his arm.

Ariel was still listening to her mind, and still laughing up a storm. Innocent embarrassment was a beautiful thing. Laughter during, and after, a storm was healing for a troubled mind.

It didn't escape him that her spirit had eased. That was what he was trying to do. She'd had such a strained life. First losing her birthmother. Then being shipped across country, to live with virtual strangers. Half of whom could not stand her.

Then she felt guilty because she loved her stepmother. Deep in her soul, she felt like she was betraying her birthmother. That's why she always said, 'my stepmother'. She didn't want to ever forget her birthmother, or hurt her feelings.

That was too much of a load for her to have borne, most of her life. He was going to spend the rest of his existence making sure her spirit was at ease.

...

They were laughing, and making so much noise, Libby heard them. She knocked on the door. "Are you alright, Erica?"

Erica jumped up. "Uh-oh." Her mother was not going to appreciate Ariel being in her bedroom, let alone in her bed. "You gotta go," she whispered.

He chuckled, and shook his head. "Nope!"

"You're going to get me in trouble, Ariel," she

whispered.

"Erica, baby! Open the door," Libby said, a little louder.

"Here I come," Erica responded. Then she looked back at Ariel, and fanned her arms. "Hurry up and hide!"

He put his face in the pillow, and roared. His reply was muffled, "Nope!"

She rolled her eyes, and ran up the stairs. When she got to the top, Ariel was sitting on the couch. *"Is this better?"* he asked.

She huffed, and shook her finger at him. Then she whispered, *"If I'm in trouble, so are you! Momma is going to invite you out of her house. She won't let you ever come back, either!"*

He chuckled, and winked at her. *"Nothing and no one will be able to keep me from you, ever again. We still need to discuss Jacques, Ms. Erica George."*

The last person she wanted to talk about was that psycho. She sighed. *"You are exasperating me, Ariel!"*

"But you still love me."

She gave him the finger.

He meowed, and laughed.

...

She opened the door, just as her mother was getting ready to knock again. "Sorry I disturbed you, Momma," she innocently said.

"What were-" Libby said, and paused. For a minute she thought for sure Eric was in here with Erica.

She looked past Erica and saw Ariel, sitting on the sofa. She frowned, and walked past Erica. This was not acceptable. She didn't care if he was an angel. "We do have several guest bedrooms, Ariel."

Ariel smiled. "I am aware of that, and I appreciate

the offer."

"Would you care for me to show one to you?"

Ariel chuckled to himself. Then he said, "Sit with me, please."

Libby took a seat on the loveseat. Erica rolled her eyes at Ariel. Then she plopped down on the couch next to him. She was in trouble, and so was he.

"I am-" he started and stopped. Perry was standing in the doorway. "Come on in," he said.

"I planned on it," Perry replied. Libby was right. Ariel was not staying in this room, even if he is an Angel.

Michael spoke to his mind, *"Remember you are a guest in their home, Ariel."*

"Have you told Verenda yet?" Ariel replied.

Michael actually laughed. Ariel was strong willed, like him. However, Ariel had no middle ground. He was hot or cold. Laughing or roaring. Fighting a battle or playing around. Even in Heaven!

Because he was the lion, he hardly ever left Heaven. That is unless Yahweh sent him on an assignment, or when he was assisting his brothers.

This was the first time that he'd left Heaven to tend to his own business. *"I tried to earlier. Your antics interrupted me, like they have now."*

"I'll behave, if you do what you need to do."

"Alright. Just remember you are a guest in Libby's home."

...

"I am-" he started, and stopped again. All of Erica's brothers were standing in the doorway. That was actually okay. Might as well get his business taken care of in one conversation.

"Come on in," he invited.

Her brothers filed in the room, and took a seat on the railings. They were all wondering what was going on. Why had their mother allowed Ariel to be in Erica's room?

Their father never would have let that happen. No boyfriend, or girlfriend, was ever allowed upstairs. And certainly not in their bedrooms.

There was a game room on the first floor. That was the only place they could entertain guests. Their father was adamant about that. They couldn't believe their mother was willing to discard his rules.

"What's going on in here?" Eric asked. "What are you doing in Erica's room?"

"I was about to explain," Ariel replied. Then he reached for Erica's hand. He squeezed it, and smiled at her.

Then he looked at Libby. "In addition to being Erica's mate; I am an Archangel. As such, I know what is required of me. I not only answer to God, but to Michael as well."

"The Archangel, Michael?" Libby asked.

Ariel nodded. "In saying that, there are rules that I must abide by. They, like our mating, were decreed long before Erica received her earthly vessel."

"What rules?" Perry asked.

Ariel told them about the covenant that Verenda made with God regarding her and Michael. Then he told them about the boundaries that had been set by God. That Michael and Verenda were the test subjects.

He told them that Michael had been with Verenda for years, but she didn't remember him. Or them! He told them about his other brothers, and that two of them were already with their mates. In fact, one had been with his mate for over eighteen years.

Then he smiled, and said, "Until Michael and Verenda do, Erica and I can't. Those are the rules that I am bound to live by. I agreed to those rules because, unlike my fallen brothers, I love my Father. Nevertheless, I have no intentions of leaving my mate's side. Now, we have two options. I could make you *think* I'm sleeping in another bedroom. Or you can take me at my word, and know that I will not disrespect your home, or my mate."

Perry went to speak, but Libby cut him off. "So let me get this straight. You can't do *anything* with my daughter, until Michael and his mate...mate?"

Ariel chuckled. "I wouldn't say *anything*."

His brothers roared.

Libby nodded, and said, "That's what I figured." She knew better than that, too. She just wanted to see if he'd be honest. She and Eric hadn't made love until they got married, but they did a *whole lot* of other things before the actual I do's.

If Erica and Ariel were mates, mated by God, they had the same desires. She'd seen it in their eyes, at the repast. She saw in their eyes now. If angels could make love, they could do the '*whole lot of other things*', too.

She read between the lines. Lines that this angel had not considered. "So here's my thought," she said. Then she looked from a blushing Erica to a smiling Ariel. "You are correct. I would have no way of knowing if you were in Erica's room. I believe you when you said that you can't, until Michael does."

Ariel nodded.

"Nevertheless, if the daughter of God, Eve, could be tempted, so can the daughter of Eric. So, if you plan to stay in *here,* in Eric's garden; you are going to have to marry his daughter. Tonight!"

"What?" Erica asked. This was so embarrassing.

Libby frowned at Erica. "I said what I mean, Erica. Whether he marries you tonight, or after Michael and his mate get together doesn't matter. He can't go all the way until Michael does, but he *can* improvise. I will not have you playing house…in my house."

"MOMMA!" Erica shouted. Her parents had always been strict, but this was ridiculous.

Her brothers cracked up laughing. Ariel did too.

"I'm not about to let you shack up, in my house. It's disrespectful to me. It's disrespectful to your father's memory. It sets a tone where your brothers may think they can bring girls up in here. Archangel or not. Covenant or not. I will not have that, young lady. You understand?"

Erica bowed her head. "Yes, ma'am."

•••

"I like that lady," Zadkiel said, to Ariel's mind.

Ariel chuckled. *"Me too. Now why are you here?"*

"Michael told me to keep an eye on you, brother."

"I'll just bet he did. What you need to do is look and see if he's doing what he should be doing. All you guys need to be riding him, not me."

"You're full of it! Are you trying to get Michael to put our eyes out!"

Ariel cracked up. That was a good point. Michael would not be pleased with them snooping on him. In truth he wondered if they could. The window probably had a one-way view. He could look out, but no one could look in.

"Whatever," he retorted. *"Now if you don't mind, I have some business to handle here."*

"I'm out!"

•••

"I have no problem marrying Erica today, or any other day, Libby. However, are you sure you want her wedding day to coincide with the day you buried your husband? Her father?"

"No!" Erica and her brothers shouted.

Libby frowned. That was a good point. A damn good point. She didn't want that, either.

...

Eric senior was standing in the corner, listening to his family. He loved that his wife wanted to preserve his dignity. He didn't mind his transition, he just wished it had happened a week later. He wished he could walk his daughter down the aisle. Even so, he didn't like the way this was going.

He spoke to Ariel, *"Can you allow them to see me?"*

Ariel shook his head. *"You have not yet been transformed, Eric. As long as you keep hanging around here you never will be. You are as bad as Michael, man,"* he said and laughed. *"Now take your ghost butt on away from here!"*

Eric laughed. It was amazing what revelations were revealed in the darkly. He'd met Ariel shortly after his transition, or at least he believed that to be true. He couldn't really say when that was. Time was different without a body.

He missed talking to his children, especially his three youngest sons. He needed them to know that it didn't matter who their birthfather was. He'd loved them the moment he first held them. He should have told them the truth, years ago.

He'd talked to Erica, but only in her dreams. She wasn't ready to hear him now, either. It's something about humans that makes them afraid of ghosts. He wasn't open to speaking with them either, before he became one.

He was grateful that his wife was open to feeling, and hearing, him. He wished she could see beyond the darkly. See him.

Perry had seen him, but he didn't tell the family. He was afraid that they'd think he was crazy. He didn't know that Liberty could feel him.

On this side of the darkly, he realized humanity left a lot unsaid, and undone. That was a shame…

•••

"Would you go, man?" Ariel said. *"Even without a body your energy resonates."*

He nodded. Then he kissed Libby's cheek, and spoke to her mind, *"Joy comes in the mourning, Liberty."*

Libby caressed her cheek, and smiled…

•••

CHAPTER 17

Libby knew Eric had just sanctioned their having the wedding so close to his death. He was saying embrace the joy, in the midst of mourning. The joy will help you *get through* the mourning.

It was amazing to her that he was gone, but not really. She'd felt him in the closet, and she felt him now. Not only that, she'd felt him in the cemetery. She was just too grief-stricken to know it was him. But it was! For obvious reasons he could not leave them.

Her children would think she was crazy if she mentioned his approval, but she sure wanted to. She wanted to shout that he hadn't left them, after all. She wanted to shout that he loved them too much to walk into that glorifying light.

Nevertheless, having the wedding today wouldn't seem right. Even if it would mean for the rest of their lives this day would represent joy...and mourning.

She shook her head. "Not tonight, but how about tomorrow?"

"Very well," Ariel replied. Then he thought about it. "No, wait. This is all wrong," he added.

This felt like he and Libby were bartering. My daughter's hand, for your room and board. It reminded him of ancient days, when women had no voice. When they were nothing more than property.

In those days, there was no room for feelings. The young girl had no voice in the decision. They were obedient for the good of the family. Most of them learned to love the man their families chose for them. But then again that *learned love* had no feelings either. He liked being the recipient, and the giver, of feelings! Emotions!

There was no dollar amount in this agreement, and no promise of anything tangible. Nevertheless, it reminded him of what Mammon and Pandora had done to Kay.

He'd never do that to Erica. He'd never swap anything, to marry her. He loved, and respected her too much. Plus, she'd shouted *'NO!'*

He stroked her cheek. God it was soft. Even without make-up, it was velvety. He'd declared that he'd spend the rest of his existence making her life easy. He hadn't voiced it out loud, but his Father heard them.

She didn't feel easy in this moment. She felt embarrassed, and humiliated. Trapped! The fact that her entire family was witnessing this didn't help.

He wished he'd done as she'd asked, and hid. If he had none of this would be happening. Her dignity, and pride, would still be intact.

...

"Michael!"

"I know you are not calling for my help, Lion," Michael replied.

"I hear ya, man. Nevertheless, I am."

"Ask your mate for her opinion. Let her voice be the deciding factor. If she does not want to, explain to her family why you are insistent on staying in her room. Also, keep in mind you do not have to stay in her room. You can protect her from the balcony, Ariel. You know this."

"I agree with everything you said. However, that last statement is not true. Yes, I can protect her from the balcony, but I can't bear to leave her side, man."

Michael actually laughed. *"Believe me, I definitely understand. However, how do you think I feel every time I have to leave my mate, because of your antics?"*

He ignored Michael's last statement, even though it was true. Now was not the time. *"I'm not very good at explaining, Michael. You know that."*

Michael agreed. Ariel was the lion. He had never once given an explanation for his actions. Plus, the only time he ever confronted humans was to destroy them.

"Before you do anything, talk with your mate. Get her feel of the situation. Then go from there."

...

Erica was embarrassed over this entire situation. She loved her mother, but she didn't appreciate how this was going down.

Her uncle and brothers were staring at her. Of course her uncle was for the marriage. Her brothers were wondering what happened to her spunk. Even they knew this was degrading.

It felt like she was an item at a swap meet. Marry my daughter, in exchange for room and board. Her mother was concerned about her own respect, but what about *hers?* She certainly wasn't feeling respected; by her mother or Ariel.

Not to mention Ariel had said no. He said this was wrong, too. Yet, he remained silent. He did not stand up for her. Her eyes teared.

She snatched her hand from Ariel's grip, and jumped up. She needed to get away from all of them. She ran down the stairs.

"Erica!" Eric shouted, and took off after her. He could feel his sister's discomfort. He'd always been her protector. In the past it had been from their brothers. Now it appeared it was from their mother. "I can't believe you are doing this, Momma!"

Remington frowned at his mother. "That was jacked up, Mom! Did you even consider Erica's feelings? Nobody, in their right mind, wants a shotgun wedding!"

Then he, Ian, and Carson ran down the stairs. They were feeling Erica. After all, none of them were Libby's birth children, but Eric.

Ariel's heart broke, because Erica's was. He vanished.

•••

He reappeared in front of her, just as she reached the glass sliding doors. Her eyes were drenched, and it tore him to pieces. He pulled her into his embrace, and palmed the back of her head. She was sobbing, and trembling; more from anger than hurt. He just held her, and let her cry; but his eyes were wet too.

Her brothers stood at the base of the stairs. Her tears had never affected Remington, Ian, and Carson before. But they did now. Once again their sister was being pushed around, and they didn't like it. Not this time!

Theirs and Eric's eyes glazed, with the same anger. Angel or not, Ariel had no right! They all wanted to comfort her, but realized they were not who she needed. Ariel was!

•••

Ariel eased her spirit, and then whispered to her mind, *"Forgive me, Erica. I did not mean to hurt you, or make you cry. I love you. I've waited eons to hold you in my arms. Day and night, my thoughts were consumed with you. Us, and our future together; was all I thought about. Please forgive me. I have no intentions of taking over your life, or ordering you around. I am not that type of man. I only mean to love you. I just want to share this world with you."*

He decided to speak out loud. It was important for her family to know their destiny lay in her hands, alone. He pulled back and gazed in her eyes.

"We have been sanctioned by Father, but the choice is yours. It would break my heart, but you have the option to reject our union."

"What?" she asked.

"You have the option to walk away, and never look back. I have to honor whatever your decision is about us," he said and scowled. The thought of her rejecting him, after all of this time, didn't sit well.

Humans had a habit of making rash decisions, when angry. And she was angry at him, and her mother. If she rejected him, based on her current state of mind; that decision would stand. There would be no do overs. No second chance. No reconsidering. No saying I didn't mean it.

He stroked her cheek. "I will do anything to keep you, *except* defy my Father's rules. But, it is you who have the power over the life and death of our relationship...in your *tongue.* Please listen to your heart, and not your emotions, before you answer." Then he released her face, just in case, and asked, "Do you still want me, Ms. Erica George?"

Erica gazed in his eyes. He looked as afraid as she had, when she messed up in Heaven. She'd been afraid of God banishing her. Ariel was afraid of her banishing him. How foolish! That thought never even crossed her mind.

She looked around her room, at all the purple. She looked up at her ceiling, the constellation. Everything in her room was a precursor to his arrival. Even if she hadn't known it.

"You know I do, but not like this," she replied. "This doesn't feel right. I don't want you to marry me because you are forced to, Ariel. I don't want to be forced to marry you, either. I love you. I always have. And even though I didn't remember you, I *missed* my lion. I just can't marry you, like this."

He breathed a sigh of relief. "Then we will wait and marry on your timeframe," he said, and kissed the top of her head.

"But-"

Shots rang out, and the glass sliding doors shattered. She felt his body forcefully jerk toward her, and knew he'd been hit. She screamed, "Ariel!"

• • •

Two bullets caught Ariel in the center of his back. The shots paused, and then started up again. More rapidly! He grabbed Erica's arms by the elbow, and snatched them from around his waist.

He folded his upper body around her. Then he snapped his wings, and swaddled her. Shielding her!

She heard him grunt, and then growl. He was being hurt, possibly killed! She screamed again, "ARIEL!"

"Shhh," Ariel responded to her panicked scream. He couldn't move until the firing stopped. If he did, others in the room might be hurt. He squeezed her tighter. "Shhh."

The bullets kept coming...

• • •

CHAPTER 18

Libby's heart stopped when she heard the shots, and saw the door explode. She jumped up, and shouted, "Nooooo!" She ran down the stairs screaming, "Nooooo! Noooo!"

She just knew her daughter had been shot. She couldn't handle losing anyone else. Her eyes were blurred, from her fresh tears. She tripped, and grabbed hold of the banister. "Erica! Erica!" she shouted, as she tumbled the rest of the way down.

Perry shouted, "God, nooo!" He'd forgotten that Ariel had warned him somebody was after his niece. That was why Ariel refused to leave her alone in her bedroom.

That sliding glass door was a major security risk. Erica's bed was directly across from it. If she'd been in the bed, she'd be dead.

If Ariel hadn't vanished, and appeared in front of her, those bullets would have riddled her *head*. Whoever was out to get her, meant to hit his mark this time. Thank God Ariel was in her bedroom!

He promised Eric years ago, that if anything ever happened to him he'd protect his children. He would've done it anyway, even if he hadn't promised.

He jumped over the railing, and ran toward his niece and nephews. They were all in the line of fire. "Get down!!" he shouted. "Lord have mercy, Jesus! Y'all get down!"

Her brothers were at the base of the stairs, helping their mother to her feet. They all shouted, "Erica!"

Eric ran toward his sister, and Ariel. He resented that this bedroom was this large. He resented that that glass door was there. He resented that the house had sliding glass doors, leading to patios and balconies, in most of the bedrooms.

They thought they were safe from crime in this upscale neighborhood. They had been, until now! But why?

He and Perry were in the lead to get to Erica. His brothers, and mother were right behind them. They were all shouting Erica's name.

They saw Ariel's body jerking. The bullets kept pelting him in his back. How much more could he take? Had any gone through him, and hit Erica?

"Is she hit!" Remington yelled.

He, Ian, and Carson didn't realize until now that they had always loved her. They just didn't like her. To be truthful they were jealous of her, but they never wanted *this*. They never wanted her dead!

After finding out that none of them were Libby's biological children, they saw things differently. After their meeting in the closet, they liked her too. They each prayed that it wasn't too late for them to finally start acting like siblings.

...

Ariel saw everyone running toward the shots, even the brothers who'd had aught against Erica. Most humans run in the other direction, when bullets rang out; but not his mate's loved ones.

He was listening to their heartbeats. They were about to explode, with fear and remorse. Her brothers were consumed with regret over the way they'd treated her. They wanted another chance to get it right. That did something to his heart.

He snapped his wings backwards, and blocked the opening. They were no longer purple, but silhouettes.

He growled, when another round of bullets hit his back. This was getting old, fast. Trite! Blasé! Certainly the shooter knew his better option was to run.

He squeezed Erica tighter to him. He didn't want to release her, but he had to. He kissed her cheek. She looked to be in shock. He calmed her, palmed her cheek, and asked, "Are you okay?"

She nervously nodded. She noticed that his whole demeanor had changed. This was the face of the warrior she loved, in the ages. "Are you?"

He nodded, but did not smile. "I'm going to handle this right now." Then he gently pushed her toward her family, and very calmly said, "Everybody move under the loft, and get down."

He turned around, retracted his wings, and glared across the vast backyard terrain. He was off his game. No way should those bullets have travelled that distance.

...

Everybody's back was to Ariel, as they encircled, and hugged, Erica. That is all except Perry's. He gasped when he noticed Ariel's back. It was riddled with bullet holes. Dozens of them. He watched as one bullet after another ejected from the angel's silhouetted body, and vanished. Midair!

"C'mon," he demanded, and led them to the large bathroom, under the loft.

Thank God the bathroom had no windows. Thank God Ariel was here. If his being in Erica's room was what would keep her safe, he was all for it. Married or not! Libby would have to just get over it.

Besides, no preacher ever stood before Adam and Eve, and spouted man's version of the wedding vows. He had no intentions of bucking against the goad.

God had joined them together, in the Heavens. Neither he nor Libby had a right to put that union to sunder. They had no right to put any stipulation, or restrictions, on it, either. God had already done that. This was God's business, and His alone.

He started humming, in his spirit. *"All night…"*

•••

Another bullet caught Ariel in the chest. He roared, in anger, and the bullet popped out. It flew across the yard, toward the shooter.

"Michael was right. I will need you guys' help. Protect my mate's family, please. Michael, would you please see after Ms. Erica George?"

He didn't wait on a response. His eyes were ablaze, when he stepped through the broken door in silhouette. He spoke to the fool's mind. *"I'm coming for you…"*

•••

None of Ariel's brothers were watching, but their ears were tuned. They heard the round of shots, first. Then they heard Ariel's grunt, growl, and request. They all cast their eyes toward him, and then vanished from their positions.

They appeared in the yard, and formed a line across the yard with their wings spread. Nothing would get past them.

They heard the balcony creek…

•••

Gabriel was keeping an ear bent toward Ariel. He knew his brother was untamed. He was fashioned that way. Michael was their Father's wrath. Ariel was imbued with their Father's *vengeance.* There *was* a difference!!

Michael administered their Father's wrath, without emotion. Ariel, on the other hand, was consumed with the spirit of revenge. Payback, reap what you sow, turnabout, and every other negative connotation associated with remuneration.

He'd spent his entire existence as a God sanctioned destroyer of man, and beasts. Worlds even! And he reveled in it!

He was the lion, and he had a primal nature. He did not care if you were someone's mother, father, brother, or sister! You knew what you were to others, before you did what you did!

The Heavenly host could almost smell the scent, and taste the blood. *"They have messed with the wrong angel, Raphael."*

Raphael was sure Ariel would need help calming down. Right now that boy was embracing every retributive spirit one would imagine. *"It has been a while since he has been in action. He's going to take his time."*

...

Michael and Verenda were sitting at the dining room table. He was finally going to tell her the truth. Not necessarily for him, but for her. He hoped the knowledge would give her a sense of peace.

It would also be beneficial to his brothers, especially Ariel. That boy had no filter! No middle ground! If he did not get this handled, Ariel would continue to be agitated. And agitate him!

Just as he started to speak, he heard the shots. Then he heard Ariel's request. He took a look, and sighed. Although this time it wasn't Ariel's doing, it was still a distraction.

This situation had been handled wrong. Ariel should have handled his business pre-emptively, like he always did.

He felt Erica's fears. He imagined that was partly *his* fault. He should have acted sooner. He should have let Ariel come, last week. He'd kept them away from their mates for too long, and now none of them were at their best.

He appeared in the doorjamb with his back to the entrance. Shielding the family from an approaching unwanted guest.

He saw his brothers had already arrived, as backup. Their wings were stretched across the yard, like a rainbow. There was one missing.

···

"Sammael!"

"Yeah, Michael."

"Are you not back on the job?"

"You know I am."

"Why are you not here?"

"Gale and I are hanging out. My apprentice can handle that situation."

"Do you not understand what back on the job means?"

"On my way."

Sammael sighed. Michael was right. He wouldn't be able to hang out every night like he'd been doing. He'd have to find a way to squeeze time in, for Gale.

"I gotta go to California, Gale," he told her. "I'll be back, when I can."

"Okay," she replied. They were in the Bahamas, dancing on the beach. She didn't want to stay here by herself. "Do you have time to take me home?"

"Of course," he answered, and wrapped his arm around her waist.

He took her back to the house they shared in Houston. At least Jeremiel would be there for her. Plus, she knew all of Anita's family. They treated her like she was family. "I'm not sure when I'll be back."

"I understand," Gale replied. "I'll be here."

He hugged her and vanished.

•••

He appeared, invisible, next to Michael. He hadn't been paying any attention. When he saw the door was shattered, he said, "Man!"

Michael nodded. "Stay at the entry," he ordered. "Another unwanted intruder will be here, momentarily."

Then he turned and walked in the house.

•••

CHAPTER 19

Ariel heard Perry's melody. Humans sing the song, 'All night, all day. The angels keep watch over me,' but most of them don't really embrace the words. They take the song to mean the angels were protecting them.

That was, in point of fact, *true;* and not just angels! Jehovah-Elroi, the God who sees, has never turned a blind eye.

However, they don't consider that in order for angels to watch over them, they had to *see* them. All night...all day! If they did some would certainly *act* accordingly. All night...all day!

...

The shooter could not believe his eyes. "OH MY GOD," he shouted.

That shadowy creature just appeared out of nowhere. One minute it was a shadow of a man, the next a lion! A lion walking upright, like a man! A man on all fours, like a wild beast. A shadowy winged thing, like a gigantic moth! A prehistoric lion with wings! Was there even any such thing? Evidently so, because it was stalking him. Where in the world did it come from? How did it know he was here?

He kept shooting, but it wasn't working. This shadowy thing seemed to be bullet retardant. What in the world was it? Where did it come from? Why was it here?

He'd come for Erica. She had to die! She possessed something that he needed to destroy. Why was this thing protecting her? Was it her father's ghost? Did that thing know what he was after?

He started to back up, while continuing to shoot. "What are you!" he shouted. "What do you want?"

"YOOOOU!" Ariel roared.

...

The bullets kept flying. This time all of them were aimed at *Ariel.* Although vexed, he was amused. He heard Gabriel, and Raphael. They were right. This foolish human had messed with the wrong Archangel. Although, to be to frank, to contend with any Archangel was foolish. However, he was different, because he was the *lion.*

He sniffed the air, and smiled. He savored the smell of fear. He loved the pounding sound of his prey's accelerated heartbeat. He physically felt the veins of his prey, constricting in distress.

He didn't hurriedly charge his soon to be victim, and he didn't roar. Predators don't make a *sound* when they have prey in sight. They *quietly* hunt, as they stalk their dinner. The beast in him liked that. He *liked* playing with his food. He unconsciously licked his lips.

He felt the overload of his prey's brain, wondering if he had a way out. He spoke to that quiet inquiry. *"None!"*

"What are you? What do you want?" the shooter shouted.

Ariel replied to his mind, *"A few pounds of your wretched flesh!"*

The shooter was freaking out. How was he hearing this thing, in his mind? He shouted, "WHY?"

"R.E.C.O.M.P.E.N.S.E.!"

...

Even in the bathroom they could hear the bullets still being fired. Erica panicked. How much could Ariel take? She jerked away from her family, and ran out of the bathroom. She ran towards the shattered door, shouting, "ARIEL! ARIEL!"

Her family was behind her, shouting for her to get down.

She ignored them. She'd seen him fighting in the Great War. He was a force, but she wasn't sure he'd survive so many bullets! "ARIEL!" she screamed.

Ariel didn't hear Erica. He'd blocked her voice out, the minute he stepped out the opening. Like any other predator, his mind was solely on his prey. In this moment, nothing else mattered.

$\cdots$

"Hello, Erica," Michael greeted. Then he smiled.

All of the 'sanctioned' mates were poreless beauties, and Erica was no exception. However, unlike Verenda, Kay and Anita, Erica came from mega wealth. She didn't wear discount clothing, or anything off the rack. Designer wares caressed her body from top to bottom, and she wore them well.

She had gone to one of the finest private schools in California. The country club, tennis court, and the marina, were her playgrounds. Yet, she was level headed. That was due to who her father was.

Eric was level headed, and knew that it could all be gone; in a split second. He set the example, by not worshipping the things money could buy.

He had taught his family to be grateful for their blessings, but not to make them their God.

"Ariel will be fine. Stay inside," he added.

$\cdots$

Erica immediately remembered Michael. The general in God's army had arrived. She relaxed, because she knew everything was going to be alright.

She jumped in his arms. "MICHAEL!"

Michael hugged her. He heard her thoughts, and laughed. "Everything would be alright, even if I had not come, Erica. Ariel is most capable, at least in battle. In affairs of the heart, not so much."

Then he kissed her cheek. "It has been a long time, Little One."

...

He noticed her family was staring at them. Perry had already met him, but not the others. They looked like they wanted to run back in the lavatory. And not just to hide!

There was so much about humanity that *fascinated* him, especially their bodies. All of their bladders leaked, when they were fearful. No doubt, his size was unnerving.

He reduced his size to a less frightening, and intimidating measure. Then he snapped his wings, to cover the gaping hole. They were not reduced.

No introductions were necessary, on either end. Michael was an Archangel, so he knew them all by name; and deed. They'd all heard Erica call out his name. Plus, they'd seen him in the vision Ariel showed them.

"Who's after my sister?" Eric asked. "And why are they after her?"

For once Remington was using his brain. There was nothing coincidental about the incident that killed their father, and this one. "That car accident wasn't an accident, was it?"

Everyone looked at him, then at Erica, and then at Michael. "What?" Libby asked.

Erica whipped around and looked at Remington. That couldn't be the truth, could it? Were both occurrences connected? If it was true, her brothers were right to blame her.

She looked back at Michael. "They're connected? Is this all about me?"

"Yes," Perry replied.

Everyone turned their attention to Perry. He had a look of anguish, anger, and concern, on his face.

"You knew!" Libby shouted.

Before Perry could respond, Erica asked, "Is it Jacques, Uncle Perry?"

This family was going to give themselves whiplash. That snapped their heads back toward her, and they questioned, "Jacques?"

Carson never cared for that dude, and it had nothing to do with Erica. He didn't like the pretentious French spelling, or the fake pronunciation. He frowned, and pronounced it correctly, "Jock killed Dad, trying to kill Erica?"

None of them would ever forget that Eric had pushed Erica, and Libby, out of the way. Erica had been closest to the car. Libby on the other side of her. Even so, he would have killed their mother too.

"Why would that boy want to kill you, baby?" Libby asked.

"I broke up with him, because he wanted us to commit suicide together."

Perry's chin dropped. He knew Eric had intervened on Erica's behalf, but he didn't know the details. "Suicide?"

"Is he *crazy!*" Eric asked.

Erica nodded. "Even after I broke up with him, he wouldn't leave me alone. He said if I was afraid to kill myself, he'd kill me; and then himself."

"Why didn't you tell us?" Ian asked.

She looked at him and frowned. Was he serious? "Up until a few hours ago you, Remington, and Carson would have welcomed my death."

They all slowly shook their heads. That was unequivocally not true. They didn't like her, true enough; but neither wanted her dead. They'd never wished the dirt nap on anybody, until now.

"That's not true. We never wanted you dead, Erica. Just gone," Remington replied.

"But not anymore," Ian added.

Carson was shaking his head. It was strange how they identified with her now. None of them were Libby's children, yet they all were. Just like they all were their father's children. "Not anymore, sis."

"Why didn't you tell me?" Eric asked.

"You were away at school, Eric," she replied. Plus, Eric was going through his own issues, with his girlfriend. She'd vanished without a trace.

She looked at her mother, and said, "I didn't want to worry you, Momma. I told Daddy to make him leave me alone."

Perry looked at Michael. The angel was too quiet. Something wasn't right. They could still hear gunfire, but it was further away. "What's wrong?"

Michael's eyes twirled…

•••

CHAPTER 20

Jacques pulled into Erica's driveway, with his stereo on full blast. He loved the rapper, Ice-T. That dude was gansta, for sho. His song 'Cop Killer' was thought provoking. The video was even better. It was a shootout between police and LA gangs. It evoked an over-the-top need in him to act out.

He envisioned him and Erica as a murderous couple, on the lamb. The black version of Bonnie and Clyde. Taking out their anger on rogue cops, was even better than dying together. Although he was sure they'd die in the end. But at least they'd die together. At least they would go out with a bang.

Seeing that shadowy thing heightened his desire to experience death. He'd always known that there was another world, somewhere. That thing had just confirmed it. It had to come from somewhere, right? Maybe there was a portal, or something that it came through. Maybe in that world he wouldn't be so messed up in the head.

...

When the song ended, he turned the engine off. He immediately heard gunfire. Automatic weapon type gunfire! It was coming from Erica's backyard. What in the world was going on? No one did things like that, in this upscale part of town. He got out of the car, and ran around the side of the house. He froze in his tracks.

That ghost was in Erica's backyard, and it was huge. What was it? How did it know to come here? Who was that, in the brush of trees, shooting at it? It didn't matter, because he didn't want no part of that creature.

He'd fantasized about dying at its hand, not a minute ago; but he just changed his mind. Plus, that creature wasn't alone.

There were others in the yard, too. Their wings were multicolored. Unlike that creature, they looked like really big humans. If not for the wings, and more than one being there; he'd mistake them for Erica's father. Her father was a big, inhumanly ripped dude, too.

Her father had come at him, like a hitman. Somehow he'd gotten in their locked house, while they were asleep. He'd blasted their stereo, and woke them up. When they all came running downstairs, he was relaxing in the armchair. His best friend, and sidekick, Kal was standing beside him, like a damn henchman. Not only had Mr. George threatened him, he threatened his parents too.

The so called good man glared at his parents, and said, *"You both better keep your psycho boy away from my daughter."*

His voice was eerily calm when he added, *"As you can see, locked doors cannot keep me out. If I have to come back, there will be no courtesy warning. I will kill all of you; while you sleep."* Then he stood up and walked out the door.

They believed him, because there were no signs that he'd broken into their home. The lock hadn't been tampered with. The alarm hadn't even gone off.

His mother had been unnerved by the entire incident. He promised her that he'd leave Erica alone. Although he had no problem dying, he didn't want his parents killed because of his obsession.

He'd been elated when Mr. George died. That left an opportunity for him to get with Erica again. Now he wondered if this thing was Mr. George's ghost. That thought scared him even more.

He tiptoed backward, until he was even with the house. Just as he turned to run, curiosity got the best of him. He flattened himself against the house, and peeked around the corner.

...

Sammael saw Jacques, and started to intervene. Ariel could be single minded when he was on the hunt.

Ariel replied to his thoughts, *"I see him. Leave him be. I'm real hungry."*

Sammael laughed, and turned his attention back to what Ariel was doing...

...

The shooter was hiding in the trees. He was sure he couldn't be seen, because of the leaves on low hanging branches. He was not thinking. If bullets weren't stopping this *thing*, what made him think branches would?

He was going for all of the vital points on Ariel's body. Everywhere he attempted to strike, Ariel's hands were preemptively poised.

He started flicking the bullets with his fingers, like they were pesky bugs. They boomeranged back, at a much faster speed from whence they came. He was deliberately making sure they did *not* hit the shooter. Unlike human hunters, Lions didn't need their prey wounded prior to the attack.

...

"Why don't you just take him out, Ariel," Chamuel asked.

Ariel did not respond.

"He always did like toying with his prey," Zadkiel injected.

Chamuel nodded. Ariel could do this all day. However, he really needed to change his ways. He wasn't a one man show anymore. There was a young lady in the house that needed him. All of them felt her dismay. That is all except her mate. Ariel had a one track mind, when stalking his prey.

...

Erica was worried. Ariel had been out there a long time. The gunfire had not stopped. She wondered why the police had not showed up.

More importantly, she wondered if Ariel was alright, or hurt. She'd seen him fighting in The Great War, and he was magnanimous. She couldn't see him now, and her imagination was running amuck.

Jacques was a star skeet shooter, and an avid hunter. He didn't even eat meat. He just loved the sport. He just loved killing defenseless animals.

Ariel wasn't defenseless, but still…

"Why is it taking Ariel so *long?*" she asked, but she was looking at Michael. They all were.

Michael responded to Erica's unspoken worries. "Even though arrogantly voiced, Ariel did not lie. He is a destroyer, of worlds; as are all Archangels."

"He named off other types of angels," Ian stated. "What is the difference between those and Archangels?"

"Archangels are the manifested fingers of Yahweh."

"What does that *mean*," he asked.

Michael pointed his finger at Ian, and then he arched it; to give him a visual.

"Explain that," Carson replied. Everyone thought he was stupid, but he wasn't. He asked because, for once, he wanted his sister to be comforted.

"Humanity could not withstand the actual touch of

Yahweh's hand. His touch is too powerful. His hands are too holy."

"That does not make sense. He touched them to create them," Carson replied.

"Indeed," Michael replied, and nodded. "Then His handmade 'so' loved fell, in the garden. They lost their innocence. They lost their purity. They lost His image, and likeness. They became sinful beings. Yahweh cannot touch sin, without destroying it. As Arches, we are the strong arm of Yahweh. He uses us, as His warriors, to reach out on His behalf. We stand in the gap fighting in Yahweh's stead, for His 'so' loved; against His and their adversaries."

"So you guys only battle?" Eric asked.

"We are His messengers as well," Michael replied. He knew that they already knew this. Perry was a student of Theology. Eric had been obsessed with knowing God, and His angels. Especially, the angels. "Humanity's ears cannot withstand the full magnitude of Yahweh's voice. That is why when He does speak, He whispers."

Perry remembered and said, "Gentle is His whisper."

Michael nodded. "That is correct. When He does speak, for Himself, He always whispers to humanity's heart."

Michael looked at Erica's brothers. These boys were trying to calm their sister's nerves. He appreciated that. "If you understand the phrase 'arch' then our role becomes clear."

"Ariel said he was the lion," Eric added. "Are the Archangels all animal in nature?"

Michael shook his head. "Lion is only Ariel's persona. Each of us are unique in our charge."

"How many different personas are there? I mean Archangels?" Remington asked. He wasn't trying to comfort Erica, although it wouldn't hurt. No, he was extremely curious.

"There are millions of us. One of my brothers is the purity of Yahweh's abiding love. Another is the comfort of His hope. One is the deliverer of Yahweh's blessings. One of my brothers is the calm of His peace. This list goes on, and on. Every good spirit you feel, is essentially an Archangel reaching out; on Yahweh's behalf. They offset whatever negative spirits that weasel sends your way."

"Who is that weasel?" Carson asked.

Michael smiled. "Lucifer."

"You call him weasel?"

"Among other things."

They laughed.

Carson looked from Michael to his brothers, and back. "So envy, jealousy, and those types of emotions are all spirits?"

Michael nodded. "They are spirits, but they are not from Yahweh. Those, along with rage, vengefulness, hatred, fear, spite, and resentment are all demonic spirits."

"Demonic?"

Michael nodded.

"What is your persona?" Libby asked.

Michael's eyes twirled. His glyphs lit up, on their own accord. Then he, without arrogance or apology, said, "I am the personification of YHWY's wrath."

"Whoa!" Ian replied. "Look at his arms."

"But isn't wrath rage?" Eric asked.

"Yes," Michael replied. He knew what Eric was alluding to. He'd just told them that rage was a spirit from Lucifer. "However, Yahweh's wrath is just. He uses me, and my brothers, to administer His wrath on our fallen brothers, and their sons."

"I thought Jesus did that," Eric replied.

Michael shook his head. "The Son is not a part of Yahweh's phalanx of warriors. That is not why He came to earth."

"Jesus came to save a dying world from her sin, not to fight humanity; or demons," Perry replied. "That's what the Archangels do. Fight spiritual wickedness."

Michael nodded. "That is correct."

Erica's voice trembled, as she slowly nodded. "If what Uncle Perry said about his dead sister is true, then it also applied to Jacques. Ariel is fighting a demon possessed Jacques, isn't he?"

"What?"

"Ariel is a hunter, Erica. That is who he has been since being called into existence. It is his natural instinct to hunt."

"But why is it taking him so long?"

"The chase is integral to who he is. He enjoys the sport of the chase, more than the capture," Michael assured her.

•••

"Erica is concerned about you. She, and her family, can still hear the gunfire. They are speculating as to who the shooter is. Erica does not think you are winning this battle," Michael informed Ariel, and chuckled. *"Do not leave her spirit troubled."*

Erica wasn't his only concern. He wanted to get back to Verenda. Every time he started to explain to her, Ariel needed help. He decided he would wait until things settled down, because this shooter was not Erica's only adversary. *"This is not the jungle, Ariel. The shooter is not a prehistorical beast. End this thing now, Lion."*

...

Ariel scowled, and slightly slowed. He'd literally forgotten about Erica. He hadn't lied when he said he was monolithic. He had a one track mind, when he was on the hunt. Nothing else, and no one else, was on his mind; except his prey.

The minute Michael mentioned Erica's name, the animal in him checked itself. WOW! Just the mention of her name momentarily turned the lion into a helpless kitty cat. This was a poignant first for him. No doubt, she would be the one to hold the reins on the beast within.

He took a look see. She was staggering. She would make him forget his mission. No wonder Michael said he'd need help. He did...and would. He shook his head. It was time to get down to business.

He crouched, and leaped...

...

The shooter jumped, when he saw the silhouette go airborne. Like a shadow, the higher it rose - the larger it got. Except this wasn't a harmless shadow. It never lost its shape, as it descended through the branches.

In fact, it solidified into a lion, on fire. But, like the burning bush, the foliage was not burning! He had no way out! No way to escape!

He dropped his gun, leaned back, and shielded his face with his upper arms. It didn't help! He felt the thing when it pounced. It went straight through his body, and encompassed him; at the same time. It was over, under, and all around him.

It knocked him to the ground. He felt claws swiping every part of his body, except his face. He felt the thing biting his *brain,* one minute. The next he felt his wounds being burned closed. Cauterized!

This creature was not going to let him bleed out, and die. No, it was going to continuously torture him. Bite! Burn! Cauterize! Every part of his body! Bite! Burn! Cauterize! Over, and over, again!

He let out a high pitched, painfully agonizing scream...

•••

Everyone in the house jumped, and stared at the opening. That is all except Michael. He remained stoic.

That screaming was piercing, unbearable, and unnerving too. It didn't sound like Jacques, but the pitch was so high they couldn't be sure. They could hear Ariel's angry growls. He sounded like a wild beast.

Erica put her hands up to her ears. She quietly wondered if Ariel would be able to turn his emotions on a dime. She couldn't! What if he couldn't either? What if he was out of control?

•••

"Shame on you, Ms. Erica George. Don't start doubting me now. You remember me fighting in The Great War, don't you? I came back to you calm, did I not?"

Erica moved her hands from her ears and smiled. *"Yes, you did."*

"I'll always come back to you calm. You hold the reins, to everything that I am."

She smiled and nodded. Ariel saw it, and smiled...

•••

Jacques had seen enough. Really too much! His heart was beating too fast. He recognized that scream! Why was *he* at Erica's house? Why was he shooting at that thing?

He'd thought he wanted to die, by that creature's

hands; but to hell with that. He was not *that* crazy, *or* suicidal! Shoot, not even Ice T was man enough to go up against that thing.

There had to be an easier, less painful, way to die. Shoot himself! Jump off a bridge! Take a bunch of pills! Slit his wrists! Hell, even setting himself on fire would be less painful. Well, no it wouldn't!

Painful death no longer seemed appealing to him, after seeing it up close and personal. Death in general didn't. No matter the method, it looked like it still might hurt.

Maybe he should just start back taking his meds. Not what his father gave him. Not even what his mother concocted. "What I need is some good ole doctor prescribed shit. Something to calm my *crazy* ass down!" he whispered.

He could still hear screaming, and growling. That creature must be taking his time, devouring that dude. He needed to get the hell out of here. He sensed that if he didn't leave now, he wouldn't be able to.

For years he'd thought his parents lied about what they saw in New Orleans. He didn't anymore. He now believed everything they'd said. He also understood why his father ran off and left his mother. He would have too.

In fact, he wondered if that thing was in Erica's yard to kill her, next. Or if it had already killed everybody in the house. NOT HIS PROBLEM! He took off running down the driveway. Straight past his parked car!

"He's his father's son," Chamuel said, and chuckled. The Archangels roared.

•••

CHAPTER 21

Ariel walked through the opening, and immediately replaced the shattered glass. He looked like he'd just taken a fresh shower. He showed no sign that he'd been in a battle. He showed no sign that he'd just killed someone. In fact, he hadn't killed anybody, *yet*.

He shoved the culprit at Erica's family's feet, then wrapped his arm around Erica. His lion rubbed up against her and purred, like a kitten.

He knew the answer, but he asked, "Do you all know him?"

The man was a tattered, bloody mess. Claw wounds covered every stitch of his body, but they all knew him. "Dr. Grayson?" they all asked, more so than stated.

All of them had a confused look on their faces. He lived a few houses down from them. Erica had just started going to him, a few months ago; before she broke up with Jacques.

Her father was a doctor, but not a gynecologist. Even if he had been, he would not have been hers. That would've been unethical, and *too* weird.

Her parents knew she was not sexually active, but they knew she would be one day. Since she'd dated Jacques since the ninth grade, they assumed it would be with him.

Her parents were in no way hypocritical. They talked to her and her brothers at the same time. They'd both talked to them about the importance of being sexually responsible.

Her father said jumping in and out of bed didn't look any better on boys than it did girls. It fact, he said it looked worse on boys, because males were mannish users.

He told them that there was more to be afraid of, than unplanned pregnancies. He told them about that actor Rock Hudson.

He said, *"This actor has come down with a venereal disease that don't give a damn how much money he has. Fame and fortune are no match. Race, creed, or color; are not a consideration. Not to this disease! It's true that he is gay, but don't let that trip you up. Some are bisexual. Some straight people have sex the same way gay people do! Anyone who has been promiscuous is susceptible."*

Then he frowned and said, *"If your partner isn't a virgin, you will be having sex with everyone they have ever had sex with. No amount of bathing cleans them up, or this disease off."*

Their father wasn't trying to scare them, but he was. He handed them snapshots of the disease. They were shocked. It almost looked like smallpox blisters. It not only looked nasty, but painful.

One picture showed the inside of a mouth. It had white blisters all over the roof, and throat. Even the jaws, and gums were blistered. While they gazed at the picture, he kept talking.

"The disease has been named, Acquired Immune Deficiency Syndrome...AIDS. Penicillin, and every other antibiotic, runs from it! There is no cure, and you can't hide the effects. That actor has lesions, just like those pictures, all over his body. Even on his private parts. They bleed, and secrete contagious infectious pus. It has spread throughout his entire bloodstream. He left the country, and went to England, in hopes of finding a cure.

There is none! This disease is a pac-man killer. The infected die in a matter of months. Even in death the body is still contagious."

Then he said, *"Your mother and I love all of you. We've fought too hard, to keep our children healthy, and safe. We're not trying to bury any of you, for any reason; let alone this disease. Keep your pants zipped, and your panties up!"*

Nevertheless, he didn't take for granted that they would listen to him. Even though she was put on birth control; she and her brothers were given a box of condoms.

"If that boy won't use them, don't have sex with him, Erica. Keep your drawers on!! You understand me?" her father insisted.

She'd been so embarrassed, she couldn't respond. Her parents didn't believe her when she said she didn't like Jacques like that. But she didn't.

He was a catch, as far as his looks. Her school friends were always tripping over themselves, for his attention. Even before he went crazy, he hadn't been able to unlock her hormonal treasure chest. Now she knew why. Ariel was the only one who had the combination.

But why was her doctor trying to kill her?

...

Perry reached down and grabbed him by the throat. His fingers wrapped almost completely around Grayson's neck. He and Libby had gone to high school with this bastard. "You tried to kill my niece? You killed Eric?"

"I didn't kill Eric," Grayson gurgled. "He was my friend, and colleague."

"Your friend!" Libby shouted. "He may have been your friend, but you damn sure weren't his! Why are you after my daughter?"

Grayson tried to speak, but choked. Perry loosened his grip. "Answer her!"

Grayson looked at Erica, and then Libby. "When she came to visit me I took her blood, like I do with all of my new patients. Like all doctors do."

The lab techs had called him freaking out! They had never seen anything like it. He hadn't either. He started experimenting with it. And WOW! The results were catastrophic.

"She has the purest blood I have ever seen. The purest anyone has ever seen. The pathogens in *her* blood are *inhuman*."

"What?"

"I tested it against cancer patients' blood. Her blood cells overtook their diseased cells, right before my unmagnified eyes. It healed every single one of them. I tried it on blood from an AIDS patient. Cured! Diabetes blood…cured! Sickle cell…cured! Just one drop of her blood healed every disease known in the modern world. Every single one. Common cold…cured! Flu…cured!!"

"What?" Erica asked.

"What?" everyone else asked.

Perry was so shocked, he released him. "What!"

He nodded. "It is not on any type chart, known to the medical field. Not A, B, AB, or O. It is neither negative nor positive, of either type. Yet, it is compatible to every single one of them."

Erica looked at Ariel. She knew it had to be true. She assumed it had something to do with him. She'd never been sick a day in her life. Not a cold, not a fever. Not one childhood disease.

She hadn't lost a single adult tooth. She didn't even know what an aspirin tasted like. She'd never had a headache until her father was killed. It was excruciatingly painful.

With trembling fingers, she rubbed her head. She felt another headache coming on. She looked back at Dr. Grayson. "So that was worth killing me?"

"YES!" he shouted.

Ariel squeezed Erica, and growled. "The only reason you're still in one piece is because Erica needed to see who tried to kill her. Raise your voice one...more...time. Please! I declare by my mere existence; I will rip you to shreds!"

Grayson jumped. Then frowned. He hadn't noticed that Erica was hugged up with that creature. He looked human now, but he wasn't. Were they all like that thing? He knew Libby wasn't, because he was her doctor too. Her blood type was one hundred percent human. AB!

"You took an oath to first do no harm, man," Eric said. "Why would you want to kill my sister?"

"The good of the many," he replied.

"I don't understand," Remington stated.

"Neither do I," Ian added. "You want to kill her, instead of utilizing her blood?"

"Don't you get it," Carson replied.

Everyone looked questioningly at him.

He scowled at Grayson, then back at his family. "Imagine if Erica's blood were bottled. It could cure the entire world."

Their eyes bulged.

"She would put the entire medical profession out of business," he added. He looked at Grayson. "Ain't that right?"

"That's right!" Grayson shouted. "Researchers, and doctors! Her blood would destroy the pharmaceutical industry. Colleges would lose money, because no one would need to study medicine. Lawyers would have no more medical injury claims. The insurance companies would go broke, because no one would need health insurance, or life insurance. Funeral homes! Casket makers! Grave diggers! Headstone masons! All of them out of work, because people would not die! There would be no end to wars! Her blood would allow friend, and foe, to live. To fight another day!"

"What's so bad about that?" Eric asked.

"God did not plan for man to live forever," he replied.

"Don't even try it. Your track record leaves much to be desired, as it relates to what God wants. Especially, seeing that you are in this house, because you tried to *kill* my niece," Perry replied. "God also said, 'Thou shalt not commit adultery'. Yet, you are on wife number three. Why is that? Oh yeah, you committed adultery against the other two."

"You don't understand," Grayson replied. "I was trying to save the world! Because of Erica, it will be over crowded. We'll run out of food. Her blood will literally destroy the *world's* economy. Even super powers, like America, will become third world nations."

"But, I bet you tucked the vials you have, safely away. For your own loved ones. Didn't you?" Carson asked.

Grayson didn't respond at first. He had four vials of Erica's blood tucked away in a freezer, at his house. And yes, it was for him, and his family. Diseases had no respect of person. They don't care what your station is in life.

Doctors die from cancer, just like anyone else. They

died from heart disease, and diabetes. They are dying from AIDS. They are not immune because of their profession, and neither are their families.

"Who wouldn't?" he arrogantly asked.

"That's what I thought," Carson replied.

•••

Libby looked from one of her children to the next. While Remington, Ian and Carson were sickly children, Erica and Eric never were. Her gaze paused on Erica and Eric.

Children carry their father's blood. Those two carried Eric's. Her husband had never been sick a day in his life, either. He had more energy than humanly possible.

This doctor didn't know that Remington, Ian and Carson weren't Eric's biological sons. Prior to today, no one did, outside of Perry, Eric, and her.

Eric's parents died before she met him. Her parents knew, but they died not long after Annette. Mainly from broken hearts.

The obvious slapped her in the face, and she gasped. She looked at Grayson, and scowled. Her mouth tightened. "You would *not* have stopped with killing my daughter. Would you have? You would have come after all of my sons, next."

"What?" Perry asked.

Grayson nodded. "They don't belong in this world. They are a freak of nature."

"You being a doctor, you had to know they have Eric's genes. His blood. You killed my husband, didn't you?" She reached down and picked up a broken piece of glass. Then she moved within a breath of him. She stabbed the broken edge against his throat. "You ran my husband down, like a dog in the streets."

He carefully shook his head. "No, but whoever did, did the world a favor. That man may have been wrapped in human tissue, but he was an alien living amongst us."

"WHAT! ARE YOU CRAZY!"

He looked at Erica, with disdain. Then back at Libby. "Look at your daughter. She's all hugged up with that creature, who attacked me. She knows that he is not human. All of you know. Eric must have been like him, too. You were bedding an alien. You spawned its children! I would have killed you too, Libby."

"You son of a bitch!" Eric shouted, and punched him in the face. "I'm going to kill you."

That move saved Grayson's throat from Libby slitting it, with the shard of broken glass. He fell back into Remington.

Remington grabbed him in a chokehold. Then he twisted his arms behind his back. "Get him!"

His three brothers beat the offended crap out of the bastard. And the angels let them...

...

Perry finally snatched the bloodied doctor, by the throat, away from his nephews. He never once carried a weapon. With his hands, he didn't need to; because they were lethal.

He'd chosen a form of self-defense that didn't require a physical altercation, or exertion. Dravidian martial arts, or as it is commonly known, "Varma Adi."

You just had to know the right pressure point to attack, to achieve your desired outcome. Which nerve to manipulate.

His hands could cause momentary unconsciousness, in a charging assailant. Paralysis! Or death! At this moment, he was in the mood for the latter.

He bore down hard on Grayson's windpipe with one hand, but his other hand was poised. He looked at Michael. "You are the wrath!"

Then he gazed at Ariel. "You are the lion! I know you both know that there is a *time* to kill. Either you kill him, or turn your heads and allow me! I'll square up with the LORD, in my dying hour."

"I believe I will take it from here."

•••

They all looked in the direction the voice came from. The owner of the voice was standing in the doorjamb. He was dressed in black leather pants and vest, with cross bone buttons. He had curly hair, and it was white as snow.

Erica squeezed Ariel. "That's Sammael."

"Who?" Perry asked.

Ariel wrapped both his arms around Erica, and kissed her temple. He was grateful his brother was here, because he couldn't bear to leave her side so soon. He answered, "Humans call my brother *Death*."

"Death is an Archangel?" Remington asked. He was looking at Michael.

"Indeed," Michael replied.

"You mean death, as in death?" Ian asked.

Ariel and Erica nodded.

"Man! Hollywood got that wrong," Carson added.

"Hello, Erica," Sammael greeted, and smiled. "It is good to see you again. I regret that it is under this vile circumstance."

She relaxed, and smiled. "Hi, Sammael."

Then he swaggered toward Perry. "You will have to release him first. Otherwise, the current will travel through him to you. It is not yet your appointed hour."

"Step back everybody," Perry instructed. He didn't want the bastard trying to hide behind his family. When they were far enough away, he squeezed his throat, one more time, and released him.

Grayson bear hugged Perry. At this point Perry was his lifeline. He had too much to live for. Too many things he still wanted to do. To many places he wanted to travel. What would happen to his wife, and children?

"No! No! I didn't know!" he shouted. He assumed everybody in the room was angels, except Libby, and Perry. "I can't die yet! I'm too young! I don't want to die!"

"My mate didn't want to die either," Ariel voiced. Then he vanquished Perry and made him reappear next to his family.

Grayson was standing in the center of the room hugging the air. He screamed when Sammael snatched him. He didn't die right away. At least not on the outside.

This doctor wanted Erica's blood running cold. Sammael decided to let him feel his own, doing the same. It was slowly, and tortuously, running cold in his veins. Brain freeze had a whole new meaning. So did frostbite. His eyes froze, wide open, but he was still alive.

Being a doctor, he knew that the human body was sixty-five percent water. His was now sixty-five percent ice, yet he was still alive.

His veins were pumping slushy ice-blood in, and around, his heart. Thus, giving a new meaning to 'cold hearted'.

He wanted to scream, but the saliva in his mouth was ice. Not even his tears were liquid. They rolled from his ducts, like shaved ice.

He was from California. He'd gone skiing, every winter. Yet, he did not know that cold could be so cold…it burned!

•••

"That is enough, Sammael," Michael commanded. "You may take your cargo, and go."

Sammael nodded and went to vanish.

"Wait!" Erica shouted. This had been disturbing to witness, for obvious reasons.

Sammael paused.

"Is this what you did to my father?"

Sammael smiled. "I am Sammael. The Archangel of Death, remember," he replied. "I only transport the *dead.*" he added and vanished.

Michael shouted, *"S.A.M.M.A.E.L.!"*

"Man, were you on vacation too long, or what?" Chamuel asked. He and his brothers were still standing guard, in the yard.

"Sorry!" Sammael replied. *"I just assumed Ariel had told this family everything."*

"I would have assumed the same thing," Jeremiel agreed.

"Did you tell Anita?" Zadkiel asked.

"No, because it has no bearing on her family."

"You guys can go home," Ariel added. *"I don't need you at the moment."*

"What about Jacques?"

"He won't be back tonight. I'll deal with him later."

"And the other one?"

"Same!" Ariel replied.

They all vanished…

•••

"WHAT!" the family shouted, but Sammael was gone.

They all looked at Ariel and Michael. Michael's eyes were twirling. Ariel was smiling lopsided.

"What did he mean?" Ian asked. They'd witnessed their father's horrible death.

They'd seen his body smartly dressed, laying in the casket. They'd kissed, and touched, his cold stilled hands and cheek.

Perry looked at Michael. He knew that he'd seen Eric's spirit standing with Michael. His body was on the ground, but his spirit was upright. Still he didn't understand. He frowned, and asked, "Did he mean that Eric's *not* dead?"

Libby's heart was racing. Eric had never left her! She'd felt him with every turn she took. She felt him kiss her cheek, and wrap his arm around her. She felt him tickling her in the closet. He was still here!

That is until the bullets started flying. "Where is my husband?" she asked.

•••

Ariel was cracking up, in Michael's head. Big brother looked like he wanted to kill Sammael. *"And you thought you would only have to clean up after me,"* he said, and chuckled.

"You are both out of control. Do not let me hear you complaining about my not talking with Verenda, again," Michael warned.

•••

"If a man dies, will he live again? All the days of my struggle I will wait until my *change* comes."

~Job 14:14~

CHAPTER 22

Eric had been fighting for what felt like days. He couldn't really be sure, because Time was different in this place. Even so, he wasn't tired. Maybe that was because he no longer had a physical body. At least not one made of clay.

His favorite scripture was in the book of Job. 'Can a man live again?' He'd first come across that verse in his youth. It peaked his interest, and he found himself asking the same question.

Of course he knew about the afterlife. He believed that those who believed in God, and more importantly Jesus; went to Heaven. Those who didn't, went to Hell. But, his mind kept telling him there was more to it.

If the human body is made of matter, and the spirit and soul are a consciousness, what happens next? Matter certainly doesn't disappear. Similar to the cocoon and the butterfly, it moves from one form to another. He believed that it never lost awareness, during the transformation.

He'd spent his quiet time searching one scripture after another, looking for the answer. He found it interesting that when Cleopas, and his friend, were on the road to Emmaus they encountered Jesus; after He'd been crucified.

They didn't recognize him, because His face was different. Is that what happens? Or was Jesus' situation different? He had to know! He'd taken to studying other religions' doctrine, on the subject.

...

He discovered that *Buddhism* isn't a religion, so much as an ideology. They believed in the philosophical concept of rebirth, through reincarnation. They believe that your current life, and behavior, determines what you will come back as. You could be human, in one life... a dog in the next. Many Indian religions, Eastern, and American, believe in that same tenet.

He didn't quite buy that one, because of the pecking order set in the Garden of Eden. If you went from human to dog, because you misbehaved; what happens after you were the dog? Animals have no concept of right and wrong, or good and bad. So behavior as the determiner was moot.

Druids don't have a spiritual document, like the Bible. They believe in oneness with nature. They also believe in reincarnation, and that you could come back as a tree. In his mind that meant trees had consciousness. What happened to the tree's mind when you were cutting, or burning it? That just didn't sound pleasant, at all.

Although Druids and Buddhists were similar, there is a difference in the two. Druids believe in 'other worlds', or realms. Much like this place.

He'd studied Islam, and Judaism, as well. They were closest to Christians, as far as Heaven and Hell. All three religions believed in Angels, or Messengers. But, Islam and Judaism weren't enough, at least not for him.

The one thing that Christians had that no other religion had was Jesus Christ. The Son of the Living God! He believed in Him! He taught his children to believe in Him!

He knew for a fact that Jesus took the sting out of death. That car had dragged his body a good city block, yet he felt...nothing! Not even the initial impact.

One of his favorite writings did not make it to the King James version of the Bible. It was the Book of Enoch, and it *fascinated* him. It took his mind away from can a man live again, and it opened another inquisitive thought pattern. What's up there, beyond the sky?

Not Heaven, because he knew about that place. But what else? According to Enoch there was another dimension. One that religious leaders didn't talk about. He'd been obsessed with Enoch's claim, ever since.

Enoch told about the offspring of the fallen angels, the Nephilim. Born to human women! That was no different than King James' version. He'd always felt a kindship to those giants! There was, however, one *big* difference.

King James declared that God wiped the Nephilim off the face of the earth, during the flood. Enoch repudiated that notion.

Enoch claimed that he was a mediator between the Nephilim, and God. He claimed they reached an agreement. A covenant of sort. The Book of Enoch claimed God granted those Nephilim a stay of execution, by ushering them off to another plane.

It was neither Heaven, Paradise, nor Hell. But a safe place, whereat they could hide from the flood. Much like the other realm that Druids believed in. That concept *fascinated* him to the point of sleeplessness.

His mind's eye saw the place hidden beyond one of the black holes. The names of the Nephilim, and the scene of that hidden place, had seemed so familiar to him. They stirred a longing in him. He spent many nights looking up at the stars. Trying to get a glimpses of a black hole.

When Erica first came to live with them, Libby redesigned her bedroom. Erica wanted the constellation drawn on her ceiling. His heart lurched at that. They told her they would see, but weren't sure; because her ceiling was vaulted.

Libby commissioned a Spanish artist, from Indiana, named Leevearne Walker to draw the mural. She turned out to be one of his clients, Lucinda Walker's, sister-in law. The woman was gifted.

They decided to surprise Erica. He and Libby took the family on a week's vacation. They asked the maids to stay at their house, to let the artist in. He told Libby to instruct Leevearne to put a black hole in the mural. Just one! Then he told her what star formation to put in front of it.

He didn't know how he knew it had to be put in a certain place, but he knew what was in the hole. He didn't know how he knew, or even why. That is until now!

...

He stopped fighting, and looked around. "This place is as dry and drab, as I remember. It is *exactly* what I had in mind, when I imagined it, Raphael. It's a wonder I can even breathe."

Raphael was personally training Eric. He personally trained all of his warriors. He stopped, and laughed. "You aren't breathing, Eric. You no longer need to."

"That's true, but still. I want to."

Raphael kept laughing. The newbies always had a hard time adjusting. They felt like they were suffocating, even though they weren't. They didn't have clay bodies, how could they. "Just relax, Eric."

"I always knew I was different. My mind was driven to reach beyond human's ability to imagine. I gazed at the stars for nights on end, trying to see this place."

"That's why your vision was what it was," Raphael replied.

Eric stopped. His eyesight was terrible. Without his glasses, or contacts, he was virtually blind. His glasses had looked like recycled coke bottles.

Now his vision was beyond anything he could've imagined. With just a glance he could see past, present, and future. With his bare eyes, he could see Heaven, Paradise…and Hell. And everything that was going on in all three places. But, for some strange reason he couldn't see earth!

It wasn't that he could see beyond the glass darkly. This place *was* the darkly. It was safely hidden from man's view.

"Why?" he asked.

"You would have been able to see more than you were supposed to."

"Like what?"

"Even from earth, you would have been able to see beyond the darkly. Beyond the black hole. You would have known all of the mysteries of Heaven. Seen your loved ones in Heaven and Hell. It would have been too much for you to handle your *origin.*"

"I may be able to see it all now, but I still don't understand."

Raphael laughed. "It'll take some time."

"Will I be able to see my host Watcher?"

"You can see him now, if you like."

"Let's go."

Raphael laughed again. Eric was in a hurry to get off this plane. Not just to see his Watcher. He wanted to check on his family.

He couldn't let him do that, because he'd interfere

with what was going on. That's why once he got him here, he blocked his view. It wasn't Eric's place to protect his children. That was Ariel's responsibility.

He'd also had to hide his memory of Ariel. "You will remember Ariel, but your host Watcher can't know about the 'sanctioned' mates. At least for the moment."

"Okay. Let's go."

"He will come here, Eric."

"I miss so much about being human, and not just my family. I miss my face, man."

It wasn't like his new face was ugly, because it wasn't. At first he looked more like her...than him. He needed to man up, and fix that with the quickness. He gave himself a mustache, and goatee!

He dispensed with the long hair, too. And that leather had to go! He'd never worn leather, a day in his human life. He looked foolish! Like a pretty motorcycle rider, with big muscles. Like a she-man!

Then he realized he was basically a eunuch. That didn't work either. He was very close, and personal, with his male identifier. He fixed that too! Although he didn't know why. Other than he liked his three buddies, hanging around.

Raphael howled. He'd taken Eric on a tour of Paradise, before coming to this place of invisibility. The man got a glimpse of his new face, when he leaned over the river. He thought he was looking at somebody in the water. When he realized it was him, he almost cursed.

He told him that he could add dressing to his new face, and physique. The man jumped at the opportunity.

He hadn't told him that he could change his face back, also. He wouldn't tell him that until he got used to his new state of being. Otherwise, he'd go back to looking like Eric, and return home to his family. He couldn't do that. Everyone who knew him thought he was dead, including his family.

"You'll get used to it," Raphael advised and kept laughing.

"I hope so," Eric said. "So, are you going to call my host Watcher?"

"Yep!"

...

CHAPTER 23

Kalaziel is the Ultimate Watcher over the California region. He, and his team, had been monitoring the coast, for close to one hundred years. It was one of the hottest spots in the states, and not because of the temperature.

The demon Quake did his worst damage on this coast, especially along the San Andreas. That demon was forever testing the earth, trying to break out of Hell.

He was persistent in his efforts. So much so, that he had humanity thinking California would one day break away from the main land, and become an island. If that happened, it would leave a crevice deep and wide enough to open up Hell. It was Kalaziel's, and his team's job to make sure that did not happen.

He had to admit it was a unique strategy. It would be catastrophic, if Quake could pull it off. A fault line, called San Andreas, stretched from Eureka to Brawley. If Quake's plan worked, it would separate the North America and Pacific tectonic plates. Quake did a lot of damage to the surface of the foundation, but the core and mantel were still intact. And they would remain that way. Kalaziel made sure of that!

...

He was in a good mood tonight, excited in fact. He'd waited almost fifty years to get a shout out. He knew a week ago it would be coming, but he didn't know the day; or the hour.

He leaned down and kissed his wife, Nanette. How ironic that today was their fifty-year anniversary. "This is the best anniversary present *ever*."

Nanette stroked his chiseled jawline. Her black Egyptian king was the love of her life. On most days he dressed the part, but not today. Today he was dressed for battle.

Watchers didn't need to sleep, as often as humans did. That was a good thing, because her husband hadn't slept in a week. "You are acting like the children did on Christmas morning, Kal."

"I feel like that too, Net," he replied, and laughed. "You think the kids will want to come home, for this?"

Nanette laughed. She always loved his jovial, and playful nature. He took fatherhood to the next level. He took care of all three children, all day long, with very little help from her. He dressed up as Santa Claus, the Easter Bunny, and any other character the children liked. Even Big Bird. When the children were small, he turned their den into one big playroom.

She took care of them in the evenings, and at night, while he was at work. She got the best part of parenting, because they were asleep most of her shift. She still spoiled them rotten, though. And they all slept in the bed with her.

"I think they will be upset if you don't tell them, Kal. They were extremely upset over what happened. They need to see him for themselves. They've waited as long as we have."

He kissed her again. "Not quite."

They were married almost twenty years, before they had children. Not only was Net not ready, in the beginning; he wasn't either. Both of them had enjoyed the pleasure of no responsibility.

They understood life would be different once the

children came. More dangerous too. He'd have to work out how to protect them during the day.

Nanette was scared of Quake. She didn't want her children in any more danger, than they'd already be in. Plus, there was a selfish element to their decision. They'd have to settle down, and act like grownups.

When they decided it was time, they had two beautiful daughters, back to back. Amber was their oldest, and Aniesha came nine-and-a-half months later. Two screaming babies in under a year was taxing. Especially at night, when he was working. Nanette shut her own womb down, after that!

He wanted a son, but Nanette said it was not going to happen. It took him five years to convince her, but she finally agreed.

He hadn't been watching when his daughters were conceived. He was all eyes on deck, when their son was. He knew this was his last shot. Literally!

Amber and Aniesha looked just like their mother. All three were beautiful, both inside and out. All of them had a small gap between their two front teeth. That was the cutest thing he'd ever seen.

Their son looked just like him. He was dark, and had the strong features of *his* chosen ethnicity. The ancient African Egyptians. The kingly, and royal Moors.

His features were so striking, Nanette insisted on naming him Prince Kaiden. He was more than fine with that. In his heart, all of his children were royalty.

Like their mother, his daughters were 'spirit' mates to Watchers. His son was married to the daughter of a Watcher.

His daughters' husbands were jealous, because their Alter-Egos were demonic. They'd never heard of one not being. They all knew Eric, while he was alive. Now, they couldn't wait to meet him, after the change.

...

"I'll reach out to them, as soon as I get back," he promised, and vanished.

"Love you!" she shouted. Yeah, he was excited. He never left her without telling her that he loved her. She understood though. She just wished she could go with him.

She wondered if Leizalak would remember either of them. It had been a lot of years. He certainly hadn't remembered them when he was human. Then again, he didn't remember himself.

"Sorry, baby!" he replied. *"I love you, too!"*

She laughed. *"I understand, but let me see through your eyes."*

"Okay."

...

He was anxious when he appeared in the place of invisibility. He hadn't been back here since the flood. Under normal circumstances he wouldn't have wanted to ever come back here. This time was different.

He'd waited almost fifty years for this day. Although, he wasn't happy that it happened this soon, or the way it happened.

He, and his inner circle, was in a battle in Oakland when it happened. None of his field team knew what Eric was to him, so it wasn't urgent to them. As a rule, they didn't interfere with humanity, and their struggles.

They were commissioned to get involved, only if demons were the culprit. A demon hadn't done this deed. By the time he got the report, the next morning, it was over.

The only reason they even told him about the incident, was because Michael was on the scene. He'd searched the report for the name of the victim, and almost lost it. He should have been there. He'd been waiting ever since to reintroduce himself.

•••

His heart lurched when he saw him standing with Raphael.

"Eric!" he gleefully greeted, and smiled. "Or can I *finally* call you Leizalak."

•••

CHAPTER 24

Erica saw the confused look on her family's faces. It mirrored her own. She slightly pulled back from Ariel. "What was Sammael talking about?"

Ariel looked down at her. When he opened her mind, he let her see all the mysteries. She knew the answer. She just wasn't embracing the memory, because their past was in the forefront. Or maybe she wasn't sure what she'd truly seen.

"Hold on," he replied, and pulled her back in his arms. He looked at Michael, and said, *"Are you going to erase their memories?"*

Michael's eyes twirled. He'd told Ariel not to tell too much, because Eric was still hanging around. If Eric knew his family knew, he would have never left.

"I would have liked for the family to be use to Eric being departed. However, Sammael's slip of the tongue put a different spin on that notion."

Ariel chuckled. It had not been a slip of the tongue. Sammael believed in revealing everything upfront. That's why he told his friend, Gale Amos, who he was.

"Humans never get use to loss. Any loss! There's always a void in their hearts, Michael. You of all people know that. Verenda has never gotten over her loss of Smith Walker. Cappy either. Has she? They cling to the past."

Michael did not respond, but it was the truth. They cannot see what they have because their eyes, and heart, are fogged with the past. They get on with their lives, but the past is a constant ghost.

"This truth will give them peace of mind. Especially my mate. Her guilt is eating her up, man. She blames herself. Can you not feel it?"

Michael did feel it. Erica was blaming herself, for her mother losing her husband. For her brothers losing their father. *"Not to mention her blood, Ariel. She is trying to understand it all, but her mind will not let her embrace it."*

"I know," Ariel replied. She was thinking that he had something to do with it. That was nowhere near the truth. *"I know that I have given you a hard time about Verenda. That's because I believe in being candid, Michael."*

"What you believe in is getting everything out in the open. Bluntly laying it on the line, regardless of the consequences."

"Consequences can be managed, if they are birthed out of truth. It's the consequence of lies that create discontent. If you were to tell Verenda the truth, I am sure the consequences would work in your favor. Just as my being truthful to Erica will work in mine."

"Perhaps. However, an easy approach would be best."

"I am not capable of being lukewarm, Michael. It is the way Father fashioned me. We were all fashioned to be what He deemed necessary; to bridge the gap between Him, and mankind."

Michael nodded, but didn't respond.

"He fashioned Jeremiel to be Hope, for His down trodden 'so' loved. He fashioned Varachiel to administer blessings."

Varachiel was in Galveston, blessing Foster House.

He paused when he heard his name. He knew that his mate had not even been born yet. *"How did I get in the middle of this conversation?"*

Ariel knew Varachiel was with Jeremiel, that's why he mentioned him. He kept talking to Michael. *"He fashioned Zadkiel to extend freedom of guilt, mercy, and forgiveness, to troubled souls. He fashioned Raquel to bring justice for the innocent. He fashioned Jophiel to overpower ashes with beauty. He fashioned Chamuel to be the world's biggest sap."*

"Hey!" Chamuel shouted. *"I heard that!"*

His brothers laughed. As the Archangel of abiding love, Chamuel could be a sappy romantic. Still, he was also a consummate warrior, and Ariel knew that firsthand. The two of them had reduced Sodom to rubble.

God had sent Chamuel to soften the blow, and be the messenger. He knew that Ariel had no middle ground. Ariel would have destroyed the 'lot' of them, without uttering a single word.

"In His infinite wisdom, Father fashioned all of us with what our mates need. Long before He breathed life into the first Adam, He called us. For them! Me for Erica. You for Verenda. He knew how cruel this new world would be. He knew they would need us."

"He surely did," Jeremiel responded. *"Anita had definitely needed hope. Kay had needed love. Sappy or not, she needed Chamuel. Anita needed me."*

"Stop calling me sappy!" Chamuel protested.

"Does cupid sound better?" Ariel asked.

"Worse," Chamuel replied.

His brothers laughed. Michael and Ariel did too. Chamuel hated that name. It was synonymous to a big baby in a diaper. Bow and arrow in tow.

Zadkiel, Jophiel, and Raquel stopped laughing. If what Ariel said was true, their mates must need them badly. Michael's, Jeremiel's and Ariel's mates were in dire straits, when they were reintroduced. If their lives were an indicator, what ugly, unjust and merciless predicaments were their mates in?

···

Ariel ignored his brothers, and kept staring at Michael. He kept pleading his case. *"YWHY fashioned you with no emotions, because your mate would make you wait. He fashioned me just as I am, also. You make no apologies for who you are, and neither do I. I am the Lion, Michael.* JEHOVAH-GMOLAH'S *ambassador of recompense. So loved, or not; He wants me to handle my mate's foes. My mate is still under attack, and she needs me. More importantly she needs me to be open, and honest, with her."*

Michael chuckled. Everything Ariel voiced was accurate. YWHY knew which 'sanctioned' mate would need which Archangel. He knew that Erica had many unwarranted enemies.

Two had been taken care of tonight. Dr. Grayson, and Jacques. Jacques was being driven by mental illness. That was the only reason YWHY allowed him to continue to breathe. Dr. Grayson, on the other hand, was driven by self-righteous indignation. He was more offensive to YHWY, because he claimed to know the heart of YHWY. Dr. Grayson appointed himself to be a messenger of God. An Arch!

There was one more person after Erica. That one is extremely dangerous, and determined. That one will not give up, or fall apart; like Jacques. He would strike again. Soon!

Humanity *fascinated* him. Affairs of the heart got them in trouble more often than not. They allowed themselves to be pulled into demonic webs of deceit. Then they justified it by saying their victims asked for it.

Erica had not done anything to anybody, to deserve her foes' disdain. Even if she had, it was not up to humanity to exact punishment on her. Vengeance belonged to YHWY. He often used Ariel to exact it.

YWHY had tied *his* hands, because Erica was Ariel's mate. He could not handle her foes. Only Ariel could.

He also heard his unmated brothers' concerns about their mates. They were right to be concerned. He nodded, but remained silent.

...

"No matter what, I know I am still under your command," Ariel admitted. *"I need to tell Erica the truth. I need you to allow me to do that, Michael."*

Michael nodded. *"Very well, Ariel. However, I caution you to go slow, in your explanation. They will be doubtful, at first. They will ask many questions. In addition, I will only allow you to reveal what has happened to Eric. Do not mention the other."*

Ariel actually agreed with Michael on the last part of the statement. He had never seen this happen to an entire family. He hadn't known, himself, until her brothers had a change of heart.

They were *all* under attack, and not from humans. If they knew the whole story, as to *why*, they'd be fearful. Especially with Eric no longer being around.

Just like the beasts of the wild, children and wives, put their trust in the Alpha male. Even though he was here, they still felt the loss of a sense of security. Because

Eric was their safety net. Little did they know, he still was.

He'd wanted Michael to get out of his business, and talk with Verenda. He was grateful that Michael ignored him. He would need his help bridling his own tongue. *"Thank you, Michael."*

"Zadkiel, Jophiel, and Raquel, you may go to your mates now," Michael said. Then he showed them where their mates were.

Jophiel and Raquel jumped. *"What!"* they both shouted.

"How could you allow this to happen to Wanda and Brandi, Michael?" Jophiel asked. *"Haven't you kept an eye on our mates?"*

Raquel's rage jumped. *"Why didn't you stop this before it got this far, Michael!"*

"I move at YHWY's will, even where 'sanctioned' mates are concerned. This is as far as YHWY wanted it to go. Arguing with me is not helpful. It is up to you, and Raquel to make sure this is as far as it goes."

"And we shall!" Raquel replied, and vanished from the balcony.

Jophiel and Zadkiel vanished also.

Michael went to vanish too.

"Stay," Ariel voiced, out loud. "I may need your assistance explaining."

Michael's eyes twirled. The lion had never once, in his entire existence, asked *him* for help. This was twice in one night. He nodded. "Very well, but you may not like my input."

"I'm sure I won't."

Michael laughed. *"Before we get started, lay off Jacques. You have done your job, where he is concerned,*

Lion. He is no longer a threat."

Ariel laughed. That sucker was still running. He did one more thing.

"L.i.o.n!"

Ariel laughed, out loud. *"I'm done."*

...

CHAPTER 25

Jacques didn't live anywhere near Erica. It was a thirty to forty-minute drive between their homes. Nevertheless, his feet were doing an impressive job as his mode of transportation.

He was running down the middle of major intersections, where it was brightly lit. He was weaving in, and around traffic. Cars were blowing their horns, and swerving, to keep from hitting him; and each other.

He kept going!

He knew without a doubt that his father had not lied to him, about running from New Orleans. Put enough fear in a brotha, stopping was not an option.

He decided to slow down, and catch his breath. Then he heard, *"Go ahead, run as fast, and as far, as you can. My bandwidth has no bounds. I can reach you anywhere, anytime. When you least expect it, I'll be there. Stay away from Erica, Sucker!"*

He sped back up!!

...

He'd almost reached his yard, when he saw his car was sitting in the driveway. His heart almost ran off, and left his body; right along with his bodily fluids. He knew damn well he left his car at Erica's house. That's why he was running, in the first place. How in the hell was that possible?

The engine revved. The stereo started blasting. Then he heard the voice, coming through the stereo, *"I figured you'd need it! Do not let me catch it, or you, in*

Erica's yard again."

He ran past the driveway, and across the lawn. He was shouting, "HELP! OPEN THE DOOR! LET ME IN, MOMMA! DAAAAD!!"

...

Beaux and Tristen were still in the greenhouse. They were trying to put the greenhouse back together, before Dorothy saw it. Beaux did not want his wife to know what happened.

They both kept nervously looking around. Their ears were on dog whistle alert. That creature had not come back, since it left. Thank God. Nevertheless, they were watchful.

Beaux was worried about his son. He'd been gone for a good while. He was sure that Jacques had gone to Erica's house. "I hope Jacques and Erica can work things out," he repeated for the hundredth time. "My son really loves that girl. He always has."

Tristen grunted. "Jacques is pathetic. He can't see what's right under his nose. Erica doesn't want him. No amount of groveling is going to change her mind. He needs to accept that, and move on."

Jacques was handsome, in every way imaginable. He could have anybody he wanted, just for the asking. Yet, he was trying to make Erica want him. He shook his head. "No woman is worth making a fool out of yourself," he added.

"You've never been in love, Tristen."

"Sure I have, but begging someone to love you back is crazy."

"That may be true, but my son doesn't underst-"

They both stopped when they heard Jacques' high pitched frantic cries. Something was definitely up. They ran out of the greenhouse.

Jacques' mother, Dorothy, had come downstairs to get some ice water. She knew her husband, and son, were still in the greenhouse. They thought she didn't know what they did out there, but she wasn't stupid. Plus, there wasn't a thing wrong with her sense of smell.

She'd just opened the freezer door, when she heard her son's terrified voice. The glass slipped from her hand, as she rushed to the front door. She snatched it open, and shouted, "What's wrong!"

Jacques was no longer there. He was still on the move. He was running along the side of the house, banging on the windows, shouting, "Momma!"

Dorothy beat him to the side door. She yanked it open. "Jacques!"

Jacques ran inside, and right past her. He ran up the stairs, two at a time. "Where's the Ritalin!" he shouted. "I need some dope! I need some dope now! Where's the Ritalin, Momma?"

"What's wrong with you, Jacques?" she asked. "What's happening out there?"

She had not seen this side of her son since she started treating him with organic herbs. She'd tried many things over the years. For a long time, nothing worked. Then she lucked up on Synaptol, and it did the trick.

She put it in everything he ate and drank. She did the same to her husband. He didn't realize it, but he was a basket case too! She loved them though.

•••

She ran up the stairs behind him. "Talk to me, Jacques," she shouted behind him. By the time she got to the bathroom, Jacques was pulling all the meds out the cabinet.

He didn't see what he needed in the cabinet. "Where's the Ritalin!" he shouted. Then he started yanking the drawers out. Everything was spilling on the floor.

"Jacques!" she shouted.

Jacques was paying her no nevermind. He was on his knees rummaging through everything from the drawers. "I need some real dope!" he shouted.

She ran out the bathroom. "Beaux! Beaux!"

Beaux and Tristen were running up the stairs. "What happened?"

"Something is wrong with Jacques! What happened out there? Did you give him some bad weed?"

Beaux almost stopped. He didn't know Dorothy knew what they were doing. That was an argument waiting to happen, but first things first. "No!" he replied, and ran past her.

He was going toward Jacques' bedroom, but stopped. He realized Jacques was in the bathroom. And he was unhinged.

···

One look at his son and Beaux knew what had happened. That creature had followed Jacques. He was not only frantically screaming for dope, he was quaking.

Beaux experienced a pregnant pause. He did not want to be trapped in this little bathroom, with only one way out. His entire being was on the mark. One sign that that creature was in the bathroom, and his feet were ready to go.

He needed to help his son, God knows he did. He couldn't handle seeing Jacques trembling, and out of control. That desire overrode his personal fears.

He walked in the bathroom, and dropped down on

his knees next to Jacques. Then he grabbed his cheeks, and said, "Look at me, son."

Jacques looked toward Beaux, but his eyes weren't focused. "Where is the dope, Momma? I *really* need it."

Beaux was afraid of supernatural beings. Anyone in their right mind was, or would be. He was afraid *for* his son, but not *of* him. He'd always had the ability to calm his son's storm, with just the right touch.

When he was a little boy, and out of control; Dorothy easily got exasperated. Jacques would be bouncing off one wall, Dorothy off of another. Not him. He knew what to do then. He knew what to do now.

He hugged his son, and stroked the back of his head. Then he gently whispered in his ear, "It's me, son. Tell Dad what happened."

As crazed as Jacques was, he realized it wasn't his mother, on the floor with him. He'd know that swaddled embrace anywhere, even if he were blind. He wrapped his arms around his father's waist, and whispered, "That creature killed Dr. Grayson, Dad."

"Grayson?"

That unnerved Beaux to his core, but it also gave him a semblance of peace. Ever since the thing left the greenhouse, he'd been wondering why his family had been targeted.

On the peace of mind side, maybe it wasn't about them after all. On the unnerving side, maybe there was a broader insinuation. It plagued his mind with even more questions.

Was that thing just going wild, stalking all of California? Where did it come from? Why was it here? If Jacques saw it kill Grayson, why did it let him escape?

He remembered that thing had charged him, and

Tristen. It hadn't gone anywhere near *Jacques*. He looked over Jacques' shoulder, at Tristen, and frowned. Why was that thing after them? The thing kept snipping at Tristen's backside.

Tristen was like a son to him, too. For the last four years, he hung out with them, day and night. Ever since he'd moved to California, with his father. The boy didn't have a happy home life.

His father was a wife beater, and child abuser, even when he wasn't drunk. His mother had walked away, two years ago. She'd moved back to North Carolina, but left her son with the abuser. That didn't make a damn bit of sense. Didn't she know about Francine Hughes?

That chick had set her abusive husband on fire; while he was asleep in a drunken stupor. They'd even made a movie out of it called 'The Burning Bed'. That movie had abusive husbands, all over California, sleeping with one eye open. Cheating husbands too.

...

He knew about all kinds of demons, and demonic spirits. After experiencing New Orleans, he studied up on them. Why was a Popobawa after him, and Tristen? Why had it attacked a local doctor?

He squeezed his son tighter, and asked, "That creature killed Grayson?"

Jacques nodded, and trembled. "It tore him to pieces, Dad."

"Dr. Grayson is *dead?*" Tristen asked.

"What?" Dorothy asked. She was a Nurse Practitioner, and Dr. Grayson was her boss. "What creature, Beaux?"

"It's coming for me next, Dad," Jacques whimpered. "It said it was going to get me, too."

"WHAT CREATURE!" Dorothy screamed. She saw the same fear in her husband's eyes, that she'd seen in New Orleans.

She knew he wanted to book now too. He wouldn't though, because he loved his son. As long as Jacques was in this state of mind, Beaux wasn't going to abandon him.

"I'll explain later, Dorothy. Let me take care of Jacques first," Beaux replied. "Would you get him one of your Valium, please?" He hadn't realized it until this moment, but they all had emotional issues.

His and Dorothy's started in New Orleans. Dorothy's was amplified when he ran off and left her. The first years of their marriage they'd both been plagued with nightmares.

She'd wake up screaming. He'd wake up in a cold sweat, exhausted from running down I-10; in his dreams. Undoubtedly Jacques inherited his mental instability from both of them.

"Okay," she replied, and left the bathroom. She never left her meds in the guest bathroom. She'd always feared her son would purposely overdose.

She resented his ex-girlfriend, Erica. Her son had been doing well the last four years. The minute Erica broke up with him, his personality reverted back to the dark side. Not even her homemade remedy was working anymore. She was tempted to call the heifer, and demand she come and see what she'd done to Jacques.

•••

Beaux stood up and tried to help Jacques stand. "C'mon, son, let's get off the floor."

Jacques tried to get up, but he couldn't. "I can't." He had neither the strength, nor the will. He'd run all the way from Erica's house, and now his legs were on strike.

This floor seemed as good a picket line, as any.

"Give me a hand, Tristen," Beaux said. When Tristen didn't respond, he looked over his shoulder. He hadn't realized that Tristen was gone.

He lifted Jacques off the floor, like he was a baby. "I got you, son."

Dorothy was waiting in Jacques' bedroom with the pills, and a glass of water. It took a few minutes for the pills to kick in. When it did, she looked at her husband. This scene was a rerun, of an old real life movie.

Many nights he slept in their son's room, when he'd had a bad emotional day. Only this time, Beaux was rattled too.

"You're not going to run off and leave us, are you?" she asked.

Beaux's guilt could be seen in his eyes. She had every right to ask that question. His past behavior dictated it. He shook his head. "I'm sorry I did that to you, Dorothy. I was young, and afraid."

"You're afraid now."

He nodded. "Petrified. That creature attacked us earlier in the greenhouse. I ran in the opposite direction of Jacques, and drew him away from our son." That sounded really good to him, but he knew better. It just worked out that way. He'd had his own skin in mind. "But I won't ever do that again. I promise."

"You need to tell me about this creature, Beaux," she whispered. "Was it like the one in the cemetery?" She never knew that angels could be destructive, until that day. Now she feared angels, and demons.

...

Chamuel was listening, but he wasn't laughing. He hadn't thought about what he'd done, in the cemetery in years. He hadn't even realized what he'd done.

He'd left a lasting impression on this couple. A negative one. Neither of them ever prayed, or went near a church. They were as afraid of angels, as they were demons. More so, even; because those demons were as powerless as humans, next to him. He sighed. *"I need to fix that, Michael."*

"Indeed," Michael replied. *"Take Uriel and Varachiel with you."*

…

Beaux nodded his head. Dorothy had a right to know, just in case it came back. He leaned forward, reached for her hands, and started talking.

…

CHAPTER 26

Ariel turned his gaze back to Erica, and smiled. Then he panned the room. All eyes were on him. Questioning eyes. Eyes impatiently waiting for an explanation. Eyes that were begging for what Sammael said to be true. Even though they knew it was not possible.

"Let's take a seat in the loft, shall we," he suggested. The loft was half the size of this bedroom. It was cozy, and intimate.

They all nodded, and moved towards the stairs.

...

Once everyone was seated, Michael was the first to speak. When he was present, he always took the lead. He knew more about the subject at hand, than Ariel did. Plus, he needed to set some guidelines.

"Before we get started, let me assure you that Ariel will behave himself, Libby. He will not disrespect your house, in any manner. I will make sure of that."

"How?" she asked. She'd forgotten why they all were in Erica's room, in the first place. "He has already admitted that he can be in here without my knowledge. Although, seeing what happened I'm not completely opposed to it now."

"Indeed. Nevertheless, your current mindset is seeded in fear for your daughter."

Libby nodded. She was afraid for Erica to stay in here tonight or any other night.

"Fear not, Libby. Ariel has fortified the windows

and doors, throughout your home. No foreign object, or unwelcomed guest, can penetrate your dwelling."

"You did?" Erica asked.

Ariel swooned over her voice, alone. "I did. Your windows are as secure as the windows of Heaven, your glass doors too. No one with evil intent will be able to even step on the driveway."

She leaned over, and kissed him. "Thank you." That gave her more peace than she imagined, but it still wasn't enough. "What happens when I leave the house? What happens when my family leaves the house? Eric and Remington are going back to college. What happens to them?"

"I'm not going back, Erica. I'm going to transfer to a local college."

"I am too. What about you, Erica," Remington added. "Mom needs all of us."

"I'm going to go locally, too," Erica replied.

Libby smiled. She loved that her children were getting along. She loved that they wanted to stay with her. She wasn't looking forward to the empty nest, now. Especially since Eric was gone.

"Still we will have to leave the premises," Carson added. "Ian and I are still in high school. Uncle Perry is pastor of the church. Is his congregation going to be in danger?"

"That's a good, and considerate point, Carson," Perry replied.

He'd never forget that the KKK blew up a church, back in the 60s. They didn't care that innocent little children were in the building. They killed four of those little children. To this date, no one has ever been charged in those murders.

He didn't want his congregation to become a target, because they were after his family.

"Yeah! They killed Dad, trying to kill Erica. They almost killed Mom, too. Who else will get caught in the crossfires?" Ian asked.

Erica bowed her head. "They're right. Everyone is in danger, because of me."

"It's not because of you, Erica. None of this is your doing," Libby assured her. "It's whoever is doing this fault."

"She's right. It's about them, not you," Ariel agreed.

Libby reached for Erica's hand and patted it. She wanted to get off the subject of the danger her family was in. "How will I know if Ariel sneaks in here?"

"You will not know, but I will. Be sure I will not let that happen," Michael replied. "He has no need to even cross the threshold. I am hereby forbidding him from doing so, after today."

"Will he listen to you?"

Michael looked from Libby to Ariel. His eyes twirled, and he looked back at Libby. "I can assure you he will."

Erica and everyone else looked at Ariel.

He smacked his lips, and huffed. He should have let Michael leave. *"That's wrong, Michael. You live with Verenda."*

"He's right, Michael," Chamuel interjected. *"And I live with Kay."*

"Cupid has been living with Kay, from day one! She was only eighteen, also," Ariel added. *"He has slept in the same bed with her all along. Why is it okay for him, and not me?"*

"Now see, I was on your side; until you opened your mouth, and insulted me," Chamuel replied. *"You're on your own now, A.r.i.e.l.!*

"The difference is Kay was all alone. She had never felt loved, Ariel. She needed Chamuel. She had no family. She had no parents to object," Michael replied. *"You have watched Melvin run Jeremiel back to the balcony for the last four years."*

Jeremiel roared. *"My mate's father definitely kept a watchful eye on me. Even when I lived down the street. However, we are all under one roof now, and Melvin still keeps his ears pointed toward Anita's room."*

Chamuel laughed. *"I should be grateful I don't have in-law issues, but my struggle is harder. Trust me, Ariel; you don't want to lay next to your mate every night."*

Ariel grunted. *"No one is making you lay by her. If it's too much for you, sleep somewhere else, Sap!"*

Ariel was getting on Chamuel's last nerve. That boy was too combative, when he didn't get his way. *"I hope Michael takes thirty years to tell Verenda! And I hope that he makes you stay out of Erica's bedroom all of that time."*

"Hey!" Jeremiel shouted. *"That move will affect all of us, Sap!"*

"Oh that's right," Chamuel replied. He was about to cut off his own nose, to spite Ariel. He needed to get out of this conversation. *"I'm out!"*

"Me too," Jeremiel added.

Michael roared. His brothers were as comical as Erica's brothers. Except they were older than Time Archangels.

It has always amazed him that humanity wanted to worship *them*. It amazed him that some had erected monuments, in Archangels' honor; including *him.*

If only humanity could hear their back and forth now, they would draw a different conclusion. They would see that angels are not deities. They are merely more powerful servants of YHWY.

...

Erica, and her family could tell by the way Ariel was staring at Michael that they were talking. She had no doubt Ariel was arguing with Michael about his decision.

She hunched him. "Ariel?"

Ariel kept staring at Michael, but replied, "Give us a minute, Ms. Erica George."

...

"Libby and Perry believe this will set a bad example for her brothers."

"You heard Libby say she didn't care if I stay. You heard Perry's thoughts, like I did. Neither of them cares anymore. They know that God sanctioned our mating. My mate's enemies are after her, man!"

Michael spoke out loud. "I am aware that Erica has more enemies. You are here to protect her, and her entire family, Ariel."

"What?" Erica asked. She looked from Michael to Ariel. "Why? What have I *done* to anybody?"

"Nothing," Ariel assured her, and squeezed her hand. "You don't always have to do anything to make someone hate you."

"It is the evil that resides within the hearts of men," Michael added.

"Sometimes it is the way you look, or carry yourself. Sometimes it is the fact that you have more wealth. Sometimes it is because of a convincing lie that someone has crafted about you. Sometimes all it takes is for you to be in someone's way," Ariel added.

Michael's eyes twirled. "Even if you are not aware that you are."

They nodded again. All of them were guilty of one or more of those reasons. Carson didn't like the way Jacques spelled, and pronounced, his name. He couldn't stand the guy, for simple stupid reasons. Although, he had sufficient reason to dislike him now.

"In this instance, you are in someone's way, Erica," Michael stated.

"Whose way am I in?" Erica asked. "And how am I in their way?"

Ariel looked at Michael. He wanted to tell her this part himself. She should hear it from her mate, the Lion. Her one true love. After all, it was the reason her father was dead.

Michael nodded. Ariel should break the news. "Be easy," he cautioned.

"You broke up with Jacques, but he can't let go. He still loves you, to the point of wanting to die with you. As a matter of fact, your rejection of him has heightened his need to carry out his murder/suicide plan."

"Did Jacques kill my father?" Eric asked.

Ariel shook his head. "No."

"There's someone else that wants my sister dead?" Remington asked.

Ariel nodded. "Yes."

"This list is getting too damn long!" Libby added. "Who killed my husband? And why do they want to kill my daughter?"

"Allow me to tell the entire story, Libby. As crazy as it is, it will make sense if you know all of it," Ariel replied.

"Okay."

"Oft times, what humanity calls love is in fact an obsession. They eat, sleep and breathe, that obsession. Like a drug, they want more, and more. No amount of intervention can help them," Ariel informed them.

Then he reached for Erica's hand. "Jacques is obsessed with you, Ms. Erica George. No amount of time is going to change that. In his mind, if the two of you die together, he will have you forever. With no interference from anyone."

"I can make him have a change of heart," Remington replied. "Where is Jacques now?"

"Let me finish," Ariel said. "He sees your deaths, as a way of saving you from your brothers."

"What?" Ian asked.

"You're kidding," Carson added.

Michael and Ariel both nodded. Ariel kept talking.

"However, there is someone else who is obsessed with *him*."

"They can *have* him, Ariel!" Erica replied.

"As long as you are still alive, Jacques' heart will always belong to you."

"Where is Jacques?" Remington asked. He knew the remedy to this problem. Kill that bastard.

All of Erica's brothers wanted a piece of Jacques. Sure, they were mean to her, but that was sibling rivalry. Even when they didn't like her, they didn't let outsiders mess with her.

Many of the fights they got in, in school, were because their classmates called her names like 'four eyes'. Although, truthfully that was what they themselves called her. Their classmates were just repeating their words.

It was like, I can call my baby ugly, but you can't. I

can call my brother the "N" word, but you can't. I can call my momma fat, and play the dozens with my siblings about her, but no outsider could. It was the nature of the beast.

···

"Where is Jacques, Ariel?" Eric asked.

Ariel cracked up laughing at their thoughts. That was the truth. It even applied to Archangels. He could call Chamuel a sap, or even Cupid, but no demon could. He could give Michael a hard time, but it made him mad when Lucifer challenged him. It was the ties that bind.

"Jacques is no longer a threat," he guaranteed, and chuckled again. That dude's mind was *gone.*

···

CHAPTER 27

Beaux was telling Dorothy everything that had happened in the greenhouse. He held nothing back, including the fact that they were getting high.

She thought smoking marijuana was wrong, because the government said it was. He, on the other hand, believed everything God made was good. You just needed to know its purpose. Marijuana had a calming effect on him, and Jacques. Both of them were basket cases. As quiet as it was kept, she could use a puff, or two.

Not only did their past haunt her, she was still troubled over how Eric George had gotten in their house. She'd had all the locks changed, and a new alarm system installed. Yet, she was still afraid.

...

"It was worse than what happened in New Orleans, Dorothy," he told her. "Jacques and Tristen thought it was a hallucination, but I knew better. I knew it was that demon."

Dorothy turned beet red, and her hand trembled. She didn't want to relive that night, eighteen years ago. Beaux studied demonology, but her mind couldn't handle the subject. She couldn't even watch a movie, or read a book, about demons. Angels either.

It hadn't surprised her that Kay Young was involved with creatures from other worlds. Her mother, Pandora, dabbled in all kinds of weirdness. She just never thought she'd see any of them with her own eyes. She certainly never thought she'd witness a battle between the two. She slowly shook her head. "I can't handle this, Beaux," she whispered. "Not again."

He squeezed her hand, when he felt it tremble. As afraid as he was, he didn't have the desire to abandon her; or Jacques. Not this time. "We'll be alright," he promised.

He really hoped that was true. He believed in God, but he hadn't prayed in years. Not since that dreadful night. He'd been afraid, ever since, that God would answer his prayer; by sending His representative. An angel! From what he'd seen that night, angels were much more *vicious* than demons. He did not want to see either one of them. Angel or demon!

He knew he would, though. The demon had already showed up. It stood to reason that the angel would follow, shortly. His own hand trembled.

...

Chamuel, Varachiel, and Uriel, were standing in the room listening. Chamuel's countenance fell. This was not the fear that YHWY had in mind, when He commanded, *'Fear the LORD, your God with all your heart, mind, body and soul.'* This fear was brought on by trauma.

"Good Lord, Chamuel. What did you do to this family?" Uriel asked.

"You and Ariel," Varachiel added. *"They are afraid of us, man."*

Chamuel didn't respond. His mind was reeling. How in the world was he going to fix this?

...

"Where did that thing come from?" Dorothy asked.

"I don't have any idea. It just appeared out of nowhere, Dorothy. It kept chasing us. It was really after Tristen."

Dorothy snatched her hands back. That gave her a sense of ease. She didn't care for Tristen. She couldn't put her finger on it, other than he was always around.

She'd watched that boy hanging around Jacques and Erica for years. He went on dates with them, but never brought his own. He'd even gone to the prom with them. She'd long been suspicious of him, and his motives.

She looked at Beaux and asked, "Tristen?"

Beaux nodded.

"It never went at Jacques?"

Beaux shook his head. "Not until the end. Then it looked at Jacques, and back at Tristen; and roared."

"Maybe it was trying to tell Jacques that Tristen was not his friend."

"What?"

"Erica is a beautiful young lady, Beaux. Well mannered, and respectful. She comes from a good family, with a hands on father. I've long thought that Tristen was in love with her. He needs a family unit."

"What?"

"I think that that's the reason Erica broke up with Jacques. They must have gotten together behind Jacques' back. Maybe that creature was trying to warn our son."

"Then why was it after me?"

"I don't think it was. I think Tristen was behind you, and the creature behind him."

That almost gave Beaux some peace of mind, but he remembered where he was. "If that were the case, why is Jacques traumatized, Dorothy? Why does he think the demon is coming after him next?"

She paused and looked down. She couldn't bear to say the words out loud. She couldn't bear to face the truth, but she had to. They'd already stolen her peace of mind.

They would crush her husband.

...

"Ease her spirit, Uriel," Chamuel instructed. *"She knows why, but she's too terrified to embrace the truth. She's too terrified to say it out loud. She knows she has the power of life, and death, in her tongue. She's just applying it incorrectly."*

Uriel surrounded Dorothy with the spirit of Peace. They all felt it when she relaxed, both physically and emotionally. Nevertheless, she was still in denial. She was not willing to cast her voice across the ether. In her heart she believed if she verbalized it, it would be set in stone.

She didn't want to say it out loud, because then it would be the truth. It would come to pass. She wasn't thinking clearly, though. If she were, she'd realize that Jacques had already said it out loud.

"Cover them both with Truth, Gabriel," Michael injected. *"Ariel is correct. The consequences of Truth are manageable."*

Gabriel had not been watching. The minute Michael called out to him, he took notice. This family was in trouble, and had been for a very long time.

He appeared in the room, invisible. *"In this case, the consequences will not only be healing, but lifesaving."*

His brothers nodded.

He covered them with the truth about what really happened in the cemetery. He covered them with the truth about what they were dealing with now.

Truth took hold of both their minds, and dispelled that spirit of Confusion. Once Confusion was gone, Peace was able to be effectual.

The Archangels nodded, and waited…

...

Dorothy looked at her husband, and took a deep breath. "I found some notes that Jacques left on his bed, a week ago. He's *been* spiraling out of control, Beaux."

"What did the notes say?"

"That he was going to kill Erica-"

"WHAT?"

"And himself."

"What? He wants to kill her, because she broke up with him?"

"That's *why* she broke up with him, Beaux. He wanted them to commit suicide together. When she refused, he decided to kill her, and then himself. That's why Erica's father broke into our house. He was concerned for his daughter. Our son needs help, Beaux. I'm afraid that he killed Erica's father. Everybody says the car was aiming for her."

Beaux looked across the bed, at his only child. He wondered if Jacques' desire to die was the reason that creature didn't attack him. Maybe it chased *him* because he wasn't giving his son what he needed. Maybe that creature was warning him that marijuana wasn't the cure.

His mind tripped back to the New Orleans cemetery. The scene began to unfold in his mind. He remembered something that he hadn't taken into consideration. He abruptly sat up in his chair, when the truth became clear.

That angel hadn't attacked *a single* human, in that cemetery. He'd only attacked the demons that were after Kay Young.

He told them to run, and not look back, true enough. Now logic told him that was so the humans wouldn't feel the backlash of his assault.

When he was a kid, he spent most weekends with

his cousins. One weekend they got in trouble, and their mother whipped their butts. He had been standing too close. When she swung backwards, he got hit.

He learned that day to get out of the way, when his cousins were getting a beat-down. That was the same scenario. Get out of the way before you get hit by God's wrath.

He grew up in the church. He was a member of one of the few Baptist churches in New Orleans. He knew the scripture *'He will give his angels charge over you, to keep you.'*

He knew that angels were messengers of God. He also knew they were watchers. The only way that angel knew Kay was in trouble was he was watching over *her!*

He remembered something else. Kay had come to the cemetery *with* that angel. They both evidently knew that demon would be there, waiting to attack her.

Every time that demon tried to grab her, that angel prohibited him from doing so. More importantly, Kay Young was not afraid of him. Neither were Winston, Sherman or Spencer. In fact, he remembered that that angel had his wings wrapped around Kay, and Ms. Viola.

That eighteen-year heavy load released his heart, and evaporated. He never realized until now, that he'd witnessed a miracle in that cemetery.

He breathed so deeply, he blew his own shirt collar. He reached for Dorothy's hands, and did something he hadn't done since that fateful night.

"Gracious Father, LORD of the universe. Forgive me for my doubts, and fears. Forgive me for forgetting what my mother, and grandmother, taught me. Forgive me for abandoning my faith in You. Forgive me for not introducing my son to your Son. Thank you for restoring my right mind. Thank you for giving me time to get it right. I know that you are a God that has no respect of person. You sent Kay Young an angel, in her time of need. Send one to help my son, this very hour."

Those words made his hand tremble. He knew the truth now, but he wasn't sure he was strong enough to see one. He kept praying though.

"Help me, and my wife, have the courage to do what is right for our son, Father. Help us to embrace another miracle. We humbly seek your guidance, in every area of our lives. If my son killed Eric George, please forgive him. Please let the court system have mercy on him. Let them see that he is sick. He needs help, Father. We all do. It has taken me a minute to put my trust in you again, but I trust you, Father. You are no shorter than your word. Thank you for your unseen mercies. In Jesus name. Amen."

He opened his eyes, and his heart thumped.

•••

CHAPTER 28

"You boys asked me earlier about the different types of angels."

They nodded.

"Ariel told you about the Seraphim, and Cherubim. I explained the Arcs, and our role in YWHY's plan."

They nodded again.

"There are many more types of angels. Many that you can find in different religious doctrines," Michael stated. Then he looked at Libby. "However, there is one that directly affects Eric."

"I knew it," Libby whispered. "I knew he wasn't gone. I've felt him all week."

"Wait! Are you saying Eric is an angel?" Perry asked. He never believed that when people died they become angels. Angels and humans are two different species. Or so he thought. "Eric is an angel now?"

"What kind of angel is Dad, if not Seraphim, Cherubim or Arc?" Remington asked.

"Does he have a body like you guys?" Carson asked.

"Can Dad just appear, too?" Ian asked

"Does he have wings?" Eric asked.

Erica squeezed Ariel's hand, and shook her head. "I wasn't dreaming, was I? My father was really on that hillside, wasn't he?"

He smiled, and nodded. "He was really there, but he is not an angel."

"He's a ghost?"

"No," Ariel replied, and chuckled.

Michael chuckled, too. The disciples thought that Jesus was a ghost too, when they saw Him walking on the water. "Eric is the Alter-Ego of an angel."

"What?" Erica asked.

"A *Nephilim* angel," Ariel added.

Perry sat up. He knew all about the Nephilim. This can't be true. "Nephilim weren't angels. They were demons. And they were all killed, during the flood."

"What?"

"Not all of them were demons, Perry. And none of them died during the flood," Ariel informed him.

"How is that possible? Our Bible tells us that Noah and his family were the only humans to survive."

"But remember, Nephilim weren't human, Uncle Perry," Carson reminded him.

"They were *half* human," Perry replied. "Giants at that!"

"They *are* half human, and half Fallen Archangel," Ariel corrected. Then he said, "Eric's best friend Kal, is a Nephilim. Eric is his Alter-Ego."

"WHAT!" they all shouted.

"*Kal?*" Libby mumbled.

"You are moving much too fast, Ariel. I told you to ease into it. You should have explained the history, before dropping that on this family."

Ariel nodded. The looks on Erica's and her family's faces said as much. He just didn't have it in him to ease into anything.

He was either all or nothing! Hot or cold! Fire or ice! Fighting or laughing! This whole meeting of his mate was going to be a learning curve for him.

He knew about his nephews, the Nephilim, but he had no dealings with them. He'd never met a single one of them. Whatever information he shared would be rushed, and uncensored.

However, like all angels, they were under Michael's command. It would be advantageous to let Michael take it from here.

He looked toward Michael. *"Would you like to explain?"*

Michael nodded. "My Fallen brothers wanted to go to war with us again. They knew that they were outnumbered, two to one. They decided that they needed to build an army, so that they would have a fighting chance. The decision was made to use human women, specifically their wombs, to achieve that goal. So they deceived the women into thinking they were in love."

"The women had no way of knowing they would die, giving birth to the seed of an Archangel. Even a Fallen Archangel," Ariel injected.

"They died?" Perry asked.

Ariel nodded, and hated he said anything. They all knew that he and Erica were mates. He'd boldly said that as soon as they met. Now, every one of them was wondering if Erica would die. "Oh man!"

"Don't worry, y'all, I still have a whole box of condoms," Erica said and laughed. She remembered that she could never be a birthmother. She didn't tell her family, because they weren't ready to hear that.

Michael chuckled. "Allow me to continue my story, Ariel. Can you do that?"

Ariel smacked his lips. "Yeah."

"You didn't blame Erica for her birth, did you, Libby? Not even when you thought that Eric had been unfaithful to you."

"No. It wasn't my daughter's fault."

"You were very wise in your rationalization. YWHY is infinitely wiser," Michael responded. "He knew that the Nephilim had not asked to be born, any more than Erica had. No more than any of you had."

"So He let them live?" Perry asked. "How?"

"There are more mysteries to this world, than humanity can imagine. More than humanity can embrace. You know of Paradise, Heaven, and Hell."

They all nodded.

"There are other dimensions that are not known to mankind."

"There are?" Perry asked. Although truthfully that didn't surprise him. There was an entire universe beyond the sky that hadn't been explored.

"One such place is on the other side of a black hole. It is a place called 'the place of invisibility'. The Nephilim were all ushered there, until the waters receded."

"Noah's flood?" Eric asked. He knew from Perry's teaching that more than one flood had occurred.

Michael and Ariel nodded.

"That was almost five thousand years ago! Kal is five thousand years old?" Libby asked. "He doesn't look a day over forty-five."

"Ariel is older than that, Momma," Erica reminded her.

They all looked at Ariel. The man didn't look a day over twenty-two.

Ariel smiled at the expression on their faces. "Eric is also close to five-thousand years old," Ariel replied.

"What?" Libby asked.

"Would you please let me tell this story, Lion!" Michael demanded. It was no wonder Ariel asked him to stay. His brother was messing this up royally. "Please!"

Ariel laughed, and not just at Michael. The family was looking at him like he'd lost his mind. "My bad."

Michael continued…

...

"Because the Nephilim were seeded by the Fallen, they all possessed an Alter-Ego, or inner demon."

"Demon?" Carson asked.

Michael kept talking. "The only way for them to get the demon out, was through their 'spirit' mates. The one and only woman they could love. She was given to them by YHWY, in the ages. She is their only means to redemption."

"How is she able to do that?" Ian asked.

Ariel leaned back in his seat, rubbed his closed eyes, and cracked up laughing. This was going to be hilariously funny. He sent a shout out to his brothers, *"Y'all need to hear this!"*

They all leaned their ears toward Erica's bedroom.

Ariel sat back up, and wiped his face. Then he looked at Michael, and said, "Go ahead, and tell them. In fact, be my guest."

Michael laughed, too. "As you are all well aware, there has never been redemption without the shedding of blood."

They all nodded.

His eyes twirled and he added, "They have to ingest their 'spirit' mate's blood."

"VAMPIRES!" Ian shouted.

"KAL IS A VAMPIRE!" Carson added. "THAT'S WHY WE'VE NEVER SEEN HIM DURING THE DAY!"

Remington felt vindicated. "I KNEW IT!"

Eric didn't whisper a peep. At this point, he agreed

wholeheartedly with his brothers. That unnerved him, to his core.

Ariel let out a high pitch screech. He knew they'd go there, especially since Kal couldn't come out during the day. He was laughing so hard, Michael had to laugh too.

Humanity fascinated Michael. They were often lost, because of their imagination. They jumped to a conclusion; instead of waiting to see what the end was going to be. "There is no such thing as Vampires," he assured them.

"Yeah well, why they gotta take the woman's blood? And how do they take it? They bite them, right?" Remington asked.

Michael nodded.

"See! I knew it," Remington added. "Vampires!"

Ariel rolled over sideways, and howled. His head was on Erica's shoulder, and he was cracking up. His brothers were laughing in his and Michael's heads.

Erica had remained silent. She didn't know what to make of it. The Nephilim really did sound like vampires, but she knew there was no such thing. She pushed Ariel off of her shoulder. "Get off me!" He wasn't helping at all.

He kissed her cheek, and squealed.

"Y'all stop this foolishness and let Michael finish!" she demanded. Then she looked at Michael and frowned. "How does this relate to my father?"

"As I stated, Nephilim have one of two things in them: inner demon or Alter-Ego. Eric was, and is, Kal's Alter-Ego. When Kal ingested Nanette's blood, she released Eric from Kal's body."

Erica's head jerked, and her eyes popped. She started flapping her hands in confusion. "Okay! Okay!

Hold up! Wait a minute! Say *what?*"

Ariel stomped his foot, and cracked up, again. His mate looked totally confused. She was wondering exactly how her father exited Kal's body. Where in the world did he come out?

Erica looked at him, and frowned. In her mind, men only had two orifices. Their mouths, and their rectums. Oh and maybe their nostrils. Neither one sounded good to her. Then there were the ears, but nope; not big enough.

Ariel screamed. She was too funny! He tried to wrap his arm around her stomach, but she pushed him away. He laughed harder. He went to say something, but Michael muted him.

...

"Eric didn't have a physical body, Erica. Just like none of you did before your births. Nanette released his spirit, from Kal's body," Michael informed her.

"Then how did he get a body?" Perry asked.

Michael explained to them how it happened. They all seemed to be satisfied with his explanation, especially Erica.

"So are you saying that Daddy was half blind, because of what he wasn't allowed to see?" Erica asked.

Michael nodded.

"What about my eyes? Why are Eric's and my eyes so bad?"

"For that same reason. However, since you know now, your eyes have been corrected."

"What?"

Ariel smiled. "You both can take your contacts out now. Your eyes are fine. However, Michael has blocked you from seeing what you do not need to see."

"What's that?" Eric asked.

"Beyond Time and Space," Michael replied.

They both popped their contacts out, and *wow*. They could see better without them. It was late and the sun had gone down, but it didn't affect the brightness.

Erica looked over at Ariel. "You can take yours out too then, right?"

"My what?"

"Contacts."

"I do not wear contacts. I have no need for them, Ms. Erica George."

"Your eyes are naturally purplish?"

He nodded.

"So Erica's blood is a natural healer because of who her father was?" Libby asked.

"In a manner of speaking," Michael said. "The baby was sick, so Kal gave him some of his blood. That blood was passed on to Erica and Eric."

"So that means my blood can heal too?" Eric asked.

Michael nodded. "Yes. However, Dr. Grayson was correct. If society ever found out, you both would be in danger. Scientists would treat both of you like lab rats."

Eric and Erica nodded.

"So where is my husband now?" Libby asked. "And why wasn't he here when we were under attack? He had to know."

"He is with my brother, Raphael; beyond the black hole. He is not aware that you were attacked, because Raphael blocked his view."

"Why would he do that?"

"Eric is not just a spirit. He is a warrior. There is a job he needs to do. He needs to vigorously train, for that job. He cannot be distracted."

"Is he happy?" Libby asked.

Michael nodded.

"Will we see him again?"

"In due season," Michael advised. Then he stood up and gazed at Ariel. "Shall we?"

Ariel didn't bother to argue. He felt how tired Erica was. They all were exhausted. Plus, he had something else up his sleeves. He learned over and kissed her cheek. "See you soon."

He and Michael vanished.

...

CHAPTER 29

Eric smiled, then frowned. That's right. He forgot that his name was Leizalak; the reverse spelling of Kalaziel. He remembered the day Kalaziel placed him in that baby's body.

They'd discussed, in advance, that he wanted to be a male human. He hadn't cared the station of the family, just so long as it was a boy baby.

When they arrived at the hospital Mrs. George had just been brought in. She was hemorrhaging so badly; the doctors weren't sure she'd survive the birth.

She kept moaning, *"Please save my baby! Don't let my baby die!"*

Kalaziel was touched by her lack of concern for her own survival. It reminded him of how his own mother died, bringing him in the world. He healed her, by giving her some of his blood.

The baby was still attached to the umbilical cord. He was able to get some of the blood, but not enough to save his life.

The baby had a heart murmur, caused by a hole in his heart. Kalaziel put him in the baby's body, but the hole was still there. The body would survive, but it would be sickly, because of the hole. Kalaziel gave him some of his blood, and the hole closed.

There were several babies in critical condition, that day. All boys. One Spanish, one Jewish and one other Black. He chose the Georges' son's body, because all they had was their love for their baby.

The other couples already had older children, but this was the Georges only one. Not only that, but Mrs. George had just barely pushed him out. The doctors had to perform a hysterectomy on her, as soon as they delivered the baby. The Georges couldn't have any more children.

His childhood had many shortcomings, but none of which was a lack of love. They'd made the right decision. But now…

…

"I could kick your sorry ass, Kalaziel! What the *hell!*" he replied. Then he hugged the best friend he'd ever had.

He hadn't known how much of a friend, until his change came. Then everything became plain. What he knew in part was fully revealed.

He'd always known he had a kindship to the angels. He'd always known that at his physical death, he'd live again. He'd always known that he was different, but not to this degree.

Now he knew that everything he was, and everything he'd ever accomplished; was due in no small part to Kalaziel. His health. His strength. His face! "Got me round here looking like Nanette," he added.

Kalaziel roared, and hugged his Alter-Ego. He'd kept an eye on him, from the moment he placed him in the baby's body.

He never interfered with Eric's impoverished life; not because he hadn't wanted to. He tried, but his father wouldn't accept handouts. Neither would his mother. They both said they gave their son what was important. Love and devotion.

Unbeknown to them and Eric, he paid for his college degrees. In the form of scholarships. He also faked a raffle, so that he could provide Eric with a car. A brand new Thunderbird.

He never let Eric see him, though. It would've been hard to explain why he wasn't aging. He didn't allow Eric to meet him face to face, until after he graduated college.

His own wife, Nanette was a real estate agent. She sold Eric and Libby their house. It was just to the right of *theirs*.

Then Nanette hired Libby to decorate the vacant home that she was going to put on the market. Afterward they all became best friends.

He was displeased with what happened, but was grateful the façade was over. He pulled away and patted Eric's jaw. Man, he looked just like Nanette.

"Thanks for adding the stache, and tee. Tighten up them brows, too. That shit is arched just like my woman's. Makes you look like a carnival she-man," Kal retorted and frowned. "That…is…so…*not*…cool!"

"Yeah well, you should've seen me in that leather crap. I looked straight up butch, man. Especially since, for some reason, I was castrated. What was up with that?"

Raphael and Kalaziel burst out laughing at his comment and expression.

...

Leibada appeared on the scene. "Hello everyone."

Eric looked Leibada up and down, and frowned. "Who are you?"

Raphael made the introductions. "This is the Ultimate Watcher, in Iowa, Adabiel's Alter-Ego. Adabiel was the first to have an Alter-Ego."

Kalaziel had never met Leibada, either. He couldn't believe how much Leibada looked like Gabriella. There was more of a feminine aura to this Alter-Ego, than Eric.

Maybe that was because Eric had dressed himself with a male persona. He was glad he had.

He and Eric both shook Leibada's hand. "Good to meet you," they both greeted.

"Same here," Leibada replied.

"Are we the only two?" Eric asked.

"Not by a longshot. We have been fighting demons for what seems like forever. The war keeps getting more and more intense. Lucifer is getting frantic."

"Why?"

"A child will be born that will make him obsolete. He's on the lookout for him."

"What?"

Leibada and Raphael laughed. "The thing is he has the gender wrong. He has the timeframe wrong. He has the lineage wrong."

"What do you mean?" Kalaziel asked.

"Suffice it to say that the baby has already been born. And she is a beauty," Raphael replied.

He wouldn't and couldn't say anything else. No one could know who this child was, who her mate was; or even where she was. The Alter-Egos knew, because they could travel through time, and space. But no Watcher did, or could. Not yet! He changed the subject.

"From this point on your training will be vigorous, Eric. The two of you, against Kalaziel and me." Then he materialized four spears that looked like steel batons.

Eric looked at Kalaziel and laughed. The man had a war room in his house. Kal had trained him how to use, and master, the Kenyan 'Samburu' spear. Kal had been adamant that he become a master with that tool. When nightfall fell, they always took it outside. Many nights they battled in the open fields, along with a few of Kal's coworkers.

He frowned. He just remembered something else. "Oh wow! You can't go outside while the sun is up, Kal."

Kalaziel shook his head. "Nope."

"That's why you weren't at my funeral!"

"Believe me that was the *only* reason," Kalaziel replied. "I'm sorry I wasn't there the night it happened."

"It's about Time, isn't it?" Raphael asked. "Nothing happens outside the will of God."

Then he looked at Eric. "Let's do this!" he shouted and jabbed his spear at him.

...

Eric jumped back. He was more grateful than ever that Kal had been training him for years. He was holding the actual spear he'd been trained with. The weight and balance was a little off for his human body. It was perfect, for this one.

His spear was vertical, and spot on, when he counteracted Raphael's horizontal attack. He swiped with uninhibited strength, and knocked Raphael's spear out of his hand.

The steel rod was as long as Eric was tall. Raphael had assumed it would take a minute for Eric to get comfortable with it. He hadn't realized that Eric was already trained, and proficient, in this discipline.

"Alright then," he said, and materialized another one. Then he, and Kalaziel, charged Eric.

Eric twirled his spear over his head, and threw it in the air. When it came back down, it pierced the brittle ground behind Kalaziel and Raphael. He vanished, appeared behind them, and gripped the spear with both hands. Then he rode it like a stripper; on steroids.

He was *much* more agile, powerful, and lethal,

without the clay. His new body felt almost weightless. He walked on the air…sideways; as he goose-stepped across Kal's and Raphael's backs.

They both staggered forward, from the impact. By the time they turned around, Eric had done a complete circle. He walked across their chests. They staggered backward.

Before they could get a grip, he was standing in between them. He placed his arms on both of their shoulders. "That was fun!"

Leibada was impressed. "I don't believe I am needed, after all."

"I trained him too damn well!" Kalaziel complained.

"He's good, but not *that* good," Raphael replied. He was an Archangel! Eric's boss, in fact. No way was he going to allow Eric to think he was more powerful.

"I was trying to go easy on you, but not now!" he added. Then he reared back, and elbowed Eric. The impact sent Eric flying six feet across the brittle ground. By the time Eric landed on his butt, Raphael was standing over him. He swiftly jabbed his spear towards Eric's navel.

Leibada forcefully, and angrily, hit Raphael's spear. The point hit Eric's thigh, instead. "That's foul, Raphael! You know he doesn't know to protect his navel!"

Kalaziel helped Eric up. He was offended by Raphael's move. He'd been protective of Eric all of his life. Nothing had changed. He glared at Raphael, and shouted, "What the hell is wrong with you? That was literally below the belt, man! Don't think for a minute I'm going to let you, or anyone else, hurt Leizalak, Raphael!"

Raphael laughed. "I am an Archangel. Lest you forget. I am always in control. I was *not* going to pierce him. If you remember, I trained you in this same manner, Leibada."

"And damn near killed me!"

Raphael laughed again. He'd had to bring Leibada down a notch too. He'd broken Leibada's skin, but that was on purpose. He'd wanted the first Alter-Ego to know who was in charge. Plus, the importance of the cord. "You know that is not true!"

"What's up with my navel?" Eric asked.

"That is where your silver cord is," Kal informed him. "It connects your lifeline, and span, to mine. If your navel is pierced, the cord will be severed. You'll die, and I won't be able to save you."

Eric looked down at his navel. Being that he'd been a doctor, he understood. Silver cord – umbilical cord! He remembered teasing Libby about cutting the cord, as it related to letting the children grow up. Even though she'd only given birth to one of their children, she rebuked him.

She said, *"They are my children, Eric. I'm not about to do that. The cord will never, ever be severed."*

He looked back at Kal. For all intents, and purposes, Kal had *birthed* him. He'd made sure that he was taken care of, all of his life.

He remembered a conversation they'd had once about his name. He'd asked him if Kal was short for anything. Kal lied, and said no.

He'd never heard the name before, so he looked it up. He found out that Kal means 'origin'. He wondered if Kal knew the meaning. Of course he did! That was why he introduced himself with the abbreviated version of his name. In a roundabout way, he was saying, *'you got your origin...from me.'*

He felt the discomfort of his first headache *ever*.

This was too mind boggling for him. He always knew there was something more. He always knew that there was something else, beyond the sky. He'd always known he had a connection to angels. But he never expected this!

He rubbed his throbbing temple. "Damn!"

"Let's take a break," Kalaziel suggested.

Raphael nodded. He could see what Eric needed, more than training, was to reflect with his host. He and Leibada vanished.

Kal felt how overwhelmed Eric was. "Let's get out of here, for a little while."

Eric nodded. "I want to go home, and check on my wife, and children. Is Erica safe, Kal?"

"She's safe, but you can't go home. Not yet."

"Is Jacques still after her?"

"I'm not sure, but I won't let anything happen to her, or anyone else in your family. Neither will Michael."

Eric nodded. "Alright."

They vanished.

...

CHAPTER 30

Beaux's feet were nervously tapping the wood floor. He was so used to being afraid, he didn't realize he wasn't. Not anymore. He reassuringly squeezed Dorothy's hands. "Don't be afraid."

"Of what?"

He looked over her head, and back at her. "That angel that was in New Orleans, is standing behind you. And he is not alone."

Dorothy went to jump, but he had a firm grip on her hands. "I prayed that God would send help for our son. He did, Dorothy. Those angels came to help. They are not going to hurt us."

Chamuel smiled. Then he walked from behind Dorothy. He gently placed his hands on Beaux's, and her foreheads, and eased their minds. "I am sorry that I frightened you, eighteen years ago. I am sorry that you have carried that fear, all of this time. Angels are not omnipotent. You never asked God for help, so I was not aware of your plight; until recently." He did not tell them that he'd seen Ariel chasing them. This wasn't the time.

Beaux's feet immediately settled, along with his heart. They both felt unbridled love flowing through their minds. It was encapsulating their bodies, like a second skin. It felt like a new beginning. Hope without all the white noise of doubt.

"Did our fears do this to our son?" Beaux asked.

"No," Varachiel answered from behind Dorothy. He walked around and stood on the other side of the bed.

Jacques was still sound asleep, but he was tormented. He placed his hand on Jacques' head, and smiled.

He looked across the room at Chamuel and said, "He's wrestling."

Chamuel slightly nodded once.

Varachiel permeated the room with rose scent, and blessed Jacques. Then he reached out and touched the wall above the bed. He frowned, and shook his head. "This house did this to your son. It has affected both of you, as well."

"This house? How?" Beaux asked. Lord help him if the angel said it was haunted. His anxiety level jumped. His feet started tapping again.

Varachiel almost laughed, except it wasn't a laughing matter. "You ran from the cemetery, because of what you saw Chamuel do. However, that is not what has kept you in fear."

"It's not?" Chamuel asked.

Varachiel shook his head. Then he began to pound the wall with his open palm. The paint began to buckle, and flake, under the angelic attack. "These walls are painted with lead based paint."

"They don't even make that type of paint anymore," Dorothy replied.

"You bought this house in 1970, but it was built in 1965, right."

Beaux nodded. He'd gotten a good deal on it, and couldn't turn it down. "Before we moved in, I painted every room. I've repainted at least twice over the last eighteen years."

"You painted over the original paint, with lead paint, didn't you?" Gabriel asked.

Dorothy jumped, and turned around. She hadn't

realized there were two more angels in the house. Four angels were in her house!

Chamuel realized that he'd forgotten to introduce himself, and his brothers. "I'm Chamuel. These are my brothers Uriel, Varachiel and Gabriel. We are messengers of God."

"Hi," Beaux and Dorothy greeted. They were dumbstruck.

Varachiel continued, "You painted over the paint that was already on the walls. That new paint was also lead based. Then you repainted twice. The last time with lead paint, also. As lead paint ages, it easily peels, and produces lead dust. Every time you bump up against the walls, you stir dust in the air. It has affected your entire family's mental stability. More damage was done to your son, because children are more vulnerable. However, it has affected both of you. It has affected your emotional, and spiritual logic. It had also affected your fertility. That is why you couldn't have more children."

Dorothy and Beaux looked at each other. Now it all made sense. Never once did she take any form of birth control. Not in eighteen years. In the beginning they'd tried, and tried. She just could not get pregnant, again.

They had Jacques, and he was more than enough. A handful in fact, but they loved him. "Can you help our son?" Dorothy asked.

"My brother Raphael can. He is the Archangel of Healing. He can help you too," Chamuel answered.

Dorothy looked around. She didn't see another angel in the room. "Where is he?"

"I will call him shortly," Varachiel replied. "We need to heal this house, first."

"How?" Beaux asked. "All of the sheetrock needs

to be replaced, upstairs and down. I can't get that much from the hardware store tonight. Even if I could, I can't replace it in one night."

Guilt was eating him alive. He looked at Dorothy, and then at Jacques. They were all he had. All he'd ever wanted or needed. He worked hard, as a longshoreman, to provide for them. He never ran the streets, and never messed around. He went to work, and came home; to his family.

He frowned, because something just occurred to him. As long as he was at work, in that hammerhead crane, he was relaxed. It wasn't until he came home that his emotions became unstable.

"I tried to provide a home for my family. Instead I provided a death trap. Look what I did to my son."

Chamuel patted his shoulder. "But you finally called on the LORD. We're His answer."

"You can fix these walls?" Dorothy asked.

All the angels nodded.

"Tonight?" Beaux asked.

"You will soon understand that God is a right now God," Gabriel replied. "There is nothing too hard for Him, or us."

His brothers all nodded.

•••

They could've replaced the walls with just a thought, but didn't. Beaux and Dorothy had seen Chamuel at his worst, and lost faith. They needed to see him, at his best; to restore it.

Not only that, but Beaux and Dorothy needed the assurance that the walls had been replaced. Like doubting Thomas, they needed to see it. They started in the room they were in.

...

Beaux and Dorothy watched as the sheetrock vanished from the walls and ceiling. They watched the insulation vanish, exposing the studs and the outer wall. Then they watched as the reverse happened.

New insulation rolled itself out. It was covered by sheets of thick black plastic. New unpainted sheetrock appeared, out of nowhere, and replaced the old. Headless nails pierced the sheetrock, straight through to the studs.

Joint compound spread itself along the lines, and connected the separate sheets of drywall. It smoothed itself over the headless nails. Sheetrock tape covered the still wet compound. Then everything instantly dried.

Chamuel smiled, and asked, "Do you want this room to remain the same color?"

"Yes," Beaux replied.

"No!" Dorothy replied.

The angels laughed.

Beaux was looking at Dorothy. It amazed him that out of nowhere his love for her had just grown. He was sure it had something to do with these angels being there.

She deserved so much better than she'd gotten, these past eighteen years. Of course he now knew it wasn't all his fault, but still she stayed. He felt blessed that she'd hung in there with him, even though he wasn't up to par. Not emotionally.

He chuckled and said, "It's my wife's house. Whatever she wants."

Chamuel patted his shoulder. "Good decision, man. Kay has the last word in my house too."

"Kay?" Beaux asked. "Kay Young?"

Chamuel nodded.

"You live with Kay?"

"She's my mate. The love of my life."

Beaux didn't know that angels even had mates. He always assumed something was going on. It all made sense now. The viciousness of this angel, that night, was a stark difference from the man standing in front of him. This man exuded kindness, and compassion. Love even.

He leaned back in his chair. "That's why you were so angry in that cemetery!"

Chamuel nodded. "I was protecting my mate from those demons."

"We gotta talk!" Beaux replied.

The other angels laughed.

"And we shall," Chamuel replied. He needed to talk with them about Jacques and Erica, also. "However, allow Dorothy to instruct us on each room first. We'd like to get this house in order, first, before we call Raphael."

"Of course," Beaux agreed. He stood up and shook all of their hands. "I can't thank you guys enough."

Dorothy stood up. She leaned over the bed and kissed her son's cheek. It amazed her that what she'd tried to do, and failed at, for eighteen years, God was going to do in a matter of minutes.

She started talking, more so to herself, "I haven't prayed in years. Somewhere along the line, I lost faith. It didn't have anything to do with what happened in the cemetery. It didn't have anything to do with Beaux running off and leaving me."

She looked up at Chamuel. "It had everything to do with the fact that my son had an illness, that wasn't curable. People kept saying that it was a lack of discipline. I knew they were wrong. I knew something was seriously wrong with my son." She stroked Jacques' head.

"I hadn't realized it until now, but I have been in a

constant state of dismay. I shutdown on God, and placed my faith in my nerve pills. I placed my hope for peace in the greenhouse Beaux built for me. In the beauty of Mother Nature. But, Mother Nature answers to God, doesn't she?" she stated, more so than asked.

The angels nodded.

"Year after year He kept showing me that He was *still* there. Still in control. I planted the flowers, in my greenhouse. Beaux watered them. But God provided the increase, didn't He?"

Beaux nodded. This was the Dorothy he'd married. Even though they were teenagers, she was active in Sunday School. She was a Sunday School teacher, and the junior superintendent.

"Did not the deep move at His will?" she asked. "This entire universe was nothing but dark, and murky water. The earth void, from a previous calamity. Yet, at His command, all things became new again. If God could set the universe back in order, certainly He could've healed my son. If I'd asked. But I didn't ask. My mother used to always say, *'Take your burdens to the LORD, and leave them there.'* I forgot that."

She was filled with so much joy, her eyes watered. "For the first time in his eighteen years, our son is going to be normal, Beaux."

Beaux hugged her. "And so will we, Dorothy."

Chamuel's eyes watered. He guessed Ariel was right about him. He was a sap! But his brothers were feeling the same emotion. Angels always rejoiced when the lost sheep, came home.

The angels heard Michael. *"Well done, gentlemen."*

•••

CHAPTER 31

Nanette jumped up, when Kal and Eric appeared in front of her. She hadn't seen Eric when he exited Kal's body. Kal had told her that Eric looked like her, but she hadn't realized how much.

"Oh my goodness," she exclaimed, and hugged him. He was built like Kal, but had her face. Or the male version of it. "We could be twins."

Eric blushed. He remembered something that he didn't want to remember. Something he had no business remembering. Something he shouldn't even be allowed to remember.

He was right there, the first time Kal made love to Nanette. He couldn't shut his eyes, because Kal wouldn't close his. He burst out laughing, and said, "Man, Nanette!" Then he kissed her cheek. "I saw you naked, girl! I need to wash my eyeballs."

Nanette pulled back, and punched him. "Shut up, fool!" She wasn't embarrassed though. Eric was like a brother to her, when he was human. He always had been.

Kal roared. He'd forgotten about that. It had taken him more than a minute to take Nanette's blood. He'd been so glad to finally find her. He wasn't about to rush the process.

The fact that Eric wasn't a demon made that decision easy. He wasn't that anxious for his oldest friend to leave him, either. So he took his time.

Her body became his playground, and he played for more than an hour. Eric had kept shouting in his head, *"Close your eyes, man! Close your damn eyes!"*

Eric laughed, and hugged her again. "You are still stacked, woman. With your fast tail."

He didn't need to remember that, because he never forgot. When he had his human body he'd noticed her figure. It wasn't his preferred body type, though. Libby's body was what he'd craved. What he still craved.

"Would you please shut up!" Nanette demanded. She was laughing too.

He stopped laughing. "How are my wife, and children?"

His question surprised Nanette. He lived beyond the veil now. He should be able to see anything, and everything. If it were her, the first thing she would have done was check on her family. Unless his eyes were still bad. She didn't see how that was possible. "You don't know?"

He shook his head. "Raphael won't allow me to see them. I've been forbidden from going home."

She nodded. That made sense. Plus, it would probably scare them to see their dead husband, and father. "They're dealing with it as well as expected. I called Libby earlier, but she didn't want any company. She said she and the children needed time alone. I told her I'd come over tomorrow."

"Thank you," Eric said.

"Let's have a seat," Kal suggested.

...

Eric was still concerned about the threat against his daughter. He could not believe who was behind the wheel of that car. Or why? None of them saw that coming. "You can't protect my family during the day, Kal. My daughter's adversaries are still after her."

"You know better than that, Eric. I may be trapped inside, but I can venture out with my mind. Trust me, man. I am never going to let them get to her."

"Michael won't either," Nanette added.

"Michael let that car run me down, didn't he?" Eric questioned. "For him to be on the scene, he had to know it was going to happen. Yet, he didn't stop it."

He had no problem with his new state of consciousness. With the exception of losing his family, he delighted in it. But, his fate was not his wife's or children's fate.

Not only that, but he was forbidden from protecting them. That was something he was not comfortable with. "What's the use of having this body, if I can't protect the ones I love?"

Kal smiled one sided. "First of all, are you sure your fate is not your family's fate?"

"What?" Nanette asked.

"Secondly, how do you know that Michael wasn't there to protect them? Is it possible that you got in the way, man?"

Eric sat up straight. Forget the second question. The first one gave him pause. Could it be? "Are you saying what I think you are saying? Don't jive with me, Kal!"

Kal smiled wide. "I know that Libby and your sons, with the exception of Eric, are just like you."

"What?" Nanette asked again. Kal had never told her that. "What?"

Eric's eyes bulged. "My wife, and sons, are Alter-Egos!"

Kal slowly nodded. "You didn't think that their mother could consume such large amounts of drugs, and they'd survive, did you?"

He had never told Kal, or anyone else, that he didn't father his three youngest sons. It surprised him that Kal knew. "You're saying they didn't survive?"

Kal nodded. "Just as Mrs. George's son didn't. Your three sons were all *stillborn*, Eric. The doctors were shocked when they drew their first breath."

"Why were they so sickly? Why didn't their host do for them, what you did for me?"

"Each Watcher has a different gift, Eric. One of mine just happens to be my blood can heal."

"Why didn't you do that for my sons?"

"We don't advertise when we find our mates. There is no big party, or billboard," Kal informed him. Then he looked at Nanette and smiled.

He looked back at Eric. "If you remember, once I found my woman, I never left her side."

That was true. He didn't tell his team, or any other Ultimate Watcher. He spent days, weeks even, just getting to know her. In truth, he was building up the nerves to tell her what they were to each other.

He nodded. "But how did my twins live? Two Watchers must have told each other."

"They showed up at the hospital at the same time. They didn't know about you, or our connection."

"You know who my sons' Watchers are, don't you?"

Kal nodded. "Of course. You know them too."

"Who?"

"My right hand man, my strategist, and my analyst."

Prior to having experienced his change, those descriptions wouldn't mean a thing to Eric. They did now. They were Kal's friends who sometimes fenced with them. "Oh my damn! Jed, Dale, and Sid?"

Kal laughed. Like him, his men had all shortened their names. It was necessary, because they mingled with humans. Some humans understood, and knew, angel names. The 'el' meant 'of God'. "Jeduhiel, Dalquiel, and Sidriel."

"What about Libby's host?"

"Hers is one of my field fighters, Zachriel."

"I met him once, didn't I? He introduced himself as Zach."

"That's him."

"Man!"

Kal laughed again. "They've all kept a close eye on your family."

"Not close enough."

Kal frowned, and leaned forward. "That is not fair, Eric. We were in northern California, in a battle, when it happened."

"You're right, Kal. What about Eric and Erica?"

"Neither of them are Alter-Egos, but there is something going on with Erica."

"What?"

"There is something special about your daughter. I can't figure out what it is, but I've felt it for years."

Eric remembered what it was, and smiled. His daughter was a 'sanctioned' mate. That was one thing Kal couldn't know. At least not yet. He smiled wider. "Of course my baby girl is special."

Kal stood up. "Let's work out, man. I need to get you up to par."

"I'm not ready to go back to that drab place."

"Me either," Kal replied. He leaned down and kissed Nanette. "Let's go to our battlefield. The guys are waiting."

Eric stood up. "Let's do it."

They vanished.

"I LOVE YOU," Nanette shouted out loud.

"I love you too," Eric replied, and cracked up.

"Shut up! I ain't talking to you!"

"Sorry, Net," Kal replied. *"I LOVE YOU, BABY!"*

She laughed. Her husband was too excited about Eric being in his natural state. *"That's okay, I understand. Make sure Eric knows he is welcome to stay with us."*

"I will."

...

CHAPTER 32

Erica was tossing, and turning. As exhausted as she was, she could *not* fall asleep. It was strange that she hadn't remembered Ariel, for eighteen years. Now that she did, she couldn't bear the separation. She missed his invisibly furry embrace.

She understood why he couldn't stay in her room, but it didn't make her feel any better. She wanted to lay in his arms, like she'd done under the tree.

She turned on her side, and embraced her bed pillow. She tried to pretend it was Ariel. It wasn't working though. It didn't smell like Ariel. It didn't feel like her Lion. It was cold, and too soft.

After about ten minutes, she slung it across the room and sighed. She threw the covers off of her, and punched the mattress with her fists. It didn't feel right either.

Nothing she was accustomed to felt right. Because none of it was Ariel. She groaned. This was going to be another long…long night.

•••

"Why are you groaning, Ms. Erica George?"

"Ariel!" she shouted, and sat up. "Where are you?"

"Talk with your mind, girl; otherwise your mother will come running."

She couldn't believe the peace that swept over her, just hearing his voice. Every fiber of her being was excited, and rejuvenated. *"Where are you?"*

"Stretched out, all comfy, on the roof."

She laughed. *"On the roof!"*

"Michael forbade me from coming in your room. He did not forbid me from being over it," he replied, and cracked up.

"I can't sleep, because I miss you, Ariel."

"Would you care to join me?"

"Yes! Yes!" she exclaimed, out loud.

"Be quiet, girl! Are you trying to get me in trouble, as payback?"

"Sorry." She couldn't help herself, though. She was too excited. Plus, technically she wouldn't be breaking any rules.

There was a stairway down the hall that led to the attic. The attic had a glass door that led to a flat part of the roof. She assumed that's where he was.

There was patio furniture up there, and plexiglass railings. The plexiglass was so that no one would accidently tumble off the roof. Mainly her. Her brothers never came near it.

They all had private patios in their upstairs bedrooms. Her patio was on the first floor, and could be communal.

She often laid on the hammock on the rooftop, and glanced up at the stars; with her father. Many nights she'd fell asleep in that spot, reading by flashlight.

Sometimes she went up there to get away from her smurf brothers. Especially if some of their friends were over.

Her parents hadn't cared, because she was still at home.

Now, she'd have to open her bedroom door gently. She didn't know if her mother was asleep, or tossing and turning too. If she were, she'd want to join her.

Plus, she'll have to turn the alarm system off. That

was going to be a little trickier, because the darn thing talked. It warned everybody that a door, or window, was open. It would actually shout which one.

It warned everybody with the blaring announcement, 'Alarm set! Alarm off!' It was worth the gamble though. She needed Ariel.

She headed for the stairs that led to her loft. *"On my way."* It was barely a whisper even though she was talking with her mind.

Ariel laughed. *"You don't have to whisper to my mind. You can scream and no one but me will hear it,"* he said and laughed again.

"OOOOO....KAAAAY!" she screamed in his head.

He cracked up laughing. *"Stay where you are. I will teleport you to me."*

Then he teleported her to the hammock. To his waiting arms.

...

"Ariel," she whispered. She snuggled up close to him, and sighed. Once again, she didn't feel the hardness of his frame, but soft downy fur. He felt like an all over bed pillow. It amazed her that even though she didn't see fur, she felt it. *"I can't believe you found a way."*

"I told you I was here to stay, didn't I?"

"You did, but I thought Michael made you leave."

"Nope. He just made me leave your bedroom." He wrapped his arm around her waist. She had goosebumps on the surface of her skin. *"Are you cold?"*

She placed her hand over his heart. *"Not at all."*

It was a little cool out, but it didn't matter. Just being in his arms, warmed her body. She snuggled closer, and threw one leg across his.

Just being with him, wrapped in his arms, eradicated

her insomnia. He didn't know it, but this had just become their bedroom. *"I couldn't sleep without you,"* she whispered, and yawned.

She closed her eyes, and sighed again. It was a satisfied sigh this time.

...

It was his turn to groan. She was dressed in skimpy sleepwear. Really – really - skimpy! It didn't help that she wasn't wearing a bra. But, by the position of her breasts, it appeared she didn't need one. They were standing tall, and firm.

Those thin straps, and the V-neck of her top exposed the cleft of *full* youthful breasts. Even if she wasn't cold, her breasts were. The coolness of the air caused her nipples to perk.

The skimpy bottoms of her pajamas was *wow*. It left little to the imagination. The thing exposed more leg than he even imagined. Long, sleek, sexy legs. Legs that evoked a desire, and a provocative vision, he never once had in Heaven.

He loved her in Heaven. He'd longed for her, for eighteen years. He'd been drawn to her, when he first saw her at the country club. He'd even felt weak in the knees. But this was unbelievably worse.

He was grateful he hadn't been standing, when he teleported her to this roof. He surely would have lost his footing, and fell at her beautifully painted toes.

He was even more grateful that she hadn't had to walk to him. If she had, Michael would have most definitely yanked his chain, again. He would have welcomed that this time.

Although, in all honesty, her leg slung across his was just as dangerous. He stroked his hand up and down her thigh. He had more than an urge to pull her all the way on top of him. Man, he could see it in his mind. That was not a vision to be having. At least not now. He couched that thought, and fast.

He wrapped his arm around her, and pulled her even closer. *"Is this better?"* It surely wasn't for him. In fact, it was worse.

He'd blocked his view of her form, but he could still feel her. Her softness! Her warmth! Her warm breath! Her heart beating, next to his! Her breasts nestled up against his! Her hand over his heart! Her knee provocatively laying against his groin! He moaned again. *"LORD, you gotta help a brotha!"*

When she didn't answer, he looked down. She was sound asleep. *"Thank you, LORD!"* That was the answer he needed. He'd never attempt anything, or be tempted, while she was sleep.

He kissed her temple, and stroked her hip. *"Sleep tight, Ms. Erica George."*

She purred, and tried to snuggle closer.

···

He gazed up at the Heavens, and smiled. The constellation smiled back. It was the perfect picture of Jehovah-Sabbaoth's best handiwork. Next to Ms. Erica George, that is.

They still needed to discuss Jacques, but that could wait until tomorrow. That boy may have been clothed, but he certainly wasn't in his right mind.

Michael said that Jacques had been handled. He trusted Michael explicitly, but he needed to see for himself.

He propped his free arm behind his head, and cast his glance toward him. He frowned. Jacques was asleep.

Heavily doped, in fact.
But *his* brothers were there. Why?

...

CHAPTER 33

The Archangels were about to start on the last room. Dorothy had already instructed them on what color to use for every room. She liked soft earth tones. Beiges, tans and browns. The lady had all around exquisite taste.

They could tell that by the furnishings in each room. Men didn't select this type of furniture. They bragged about it, like it was their idea; but it never was.

Raphael had already come and healed all three of them. Jacques was still asleep, but was no longer in turmoil. Beaux had asked them to yank the carpet up, because it too had chemicals in it. He wanted a fresh, chemical free start for his family.

Chamuel immediately vanquished the carpet throughout the house. Beaux and Dorothy were amazed at the amount of dirt left behind on the beautiful wood floors. Lead filled dust.

They both attempted to sweep it up, but Chamuel stopped them. "That will only stir it up more. Plus, if you do it, the dust will still be in the cracks. Allow us to handle it all."

Beaux was overwhelmed. The angel that had scared the crap out of him, eighteen years ago, was as nice as they came. "Thank you."

"Why don't you guys sit with your son, and let us handle everything. You have to be tired."

They both nodded. They were tired, but grateful too. Their house smelled like roses, through and through. Dorothy assumed it was the angel's doing. Beaux knew it was Varachiel's doing. If there was one thing he knew, it was his angels and demons. He'd been afraid of them both, but he knew them. "Thank you," he said again. Then he and Dorothy went back upstairs.

...

The minute they left, Ariel asked, *"What are all of you guys doing in that fool's house?"*

"Be careful, Ariel. Remember that you should not call your brother a fool," Chamuel reminded him. *"You might be in danger of Hell's fire, brother."*

"Oh please. First of all, that 'fool' is no more my brother, than Lucifer is. Secondly, it is perfectly okay to call a fool, a fool. It is only wrong when you call someone a fool, that isn't."

"He is not a fool. He is sick, Lion," Varachiel informed him. *"This house has caused damage to his right mind."*

"See. If you aren't in your right mind, you're a fool. A sick fool," Ariel replied, and cracked up.

"You ain't right, Ariel," Chamuel admonished. *"Where is your compassion?"*

"When have you ever known Recompense to have compassion, Sap?"

"Now look here, fool!" Chamuel replied. *"I'm tired of you calling me Sap!"*

"Did you just call me fool?" Ariel asked, and cracked up laughing.

The other Archangels roared. All of the Heavenly host was watching and laughing. The friction between those two was always a moment away from conflagrant.

Neither of them realized that they complimented each other. One was overly gentle. The other overly gruff. Chamuel could be extremely sensitive, and compassionate. Ariel was extremely combative, and overly ruthless. Both had been designed that way, by the call of the Master.

Chamuel blushed. Ariel was right. He'd just called his brother a fool. Then again, Ariel always could work his nerves. *"Why do you continue to agitate me?"*

"It's the nature of the beast. I'm the Lion. Hear me roar," Ariel replied, and chuckled. *"Why are you guys there?"*

"The walls are covered in lead paint," Varachiel responded.

"Fried his brain?"

"His parents' brains too."

"That's too bad," Ariel commiserated. Humans were always trying new things, and then learning years later that they're harmful.

Like everything God created, lead had its purpose. It just wasn't in paint, or pencils. It was poisonous when confined indoors. Or used as a passageway, for liquids.

He knew at first glance that, unlike Erica's home, Jacques' house was not a modern structure. It was well kept, but old. *"Be sure to check the water pipes. They're probably corroding by now, too. That waterline is the same one that waters their herbs, in the greenhouse."*

"That's a good idea," Gabriel replied. He couldn't believe that Ariel was being helpful.

"Let's just change them out, to be on the safe side," Varachiel suggested.

"Is that all you have to say, Ariel?" Chamuel asked. He thought Ariel should at least feel bad for the way he'd treated Jacques. He himself felt awful about the way he'd treated Winston, and his cousins.

"Oh yeah, my bad. Just make sure that fool stays

away from my mate. Otherwise, your changing the pipes will be for naught."

Chamuel couldn't do anything but laugh. Ariel was as stubborn as Araciel. When God called them, He commanded, *"Love and Recompense come forth."* They appeared at the same time. Deep affection and deeper reward.

"You know that Jacques, and his father, think you're one of Lucifer's minions."

"Two peas in the same fool's pod."

"Considering the way you acted, in the greenhouse; who did you expect them to think you were?"

"Considering his father remembered how you acted in New Orleans, I'd have to say you. Cupid!"

His brothers roared. Ariel always was quick with a comeback. But then again, Chamuel was too. They looked at Chamuel, and waited.

"Why are you bothering me? And why are you not with your mate?" Chamuel asked. Then he chuckled. *"Oh that's right, Michael escorted you out of her bedroom, didn't he, Lion? He forbade you from ever crossing the threshold, am I correct? In a minute I'll be snuggled up to my mate. Where will you be, Lion? Leaning over the balcony, peeking in?"*

His brothers cracked up. That was a low blow.

Ariel smirked. Evidently none of them had looked to see where he was. He immediately materialized a blanket and threw it across both he, and Erica. He didn't want them to see her, in all her sexiness.

Then he replied, *"See that's your problem. You listen with your sappy heart. While I, on the other hand, listen with my ears. I stalk the silence, and prey on what has not been said. You should try it sometime, Sap."*

Just as he suspected, they took a look see. He kissed Erica's temple. *"Any more questions?"*

Chamuel roared. Michael told Ariel he couldn't sleep in Erica's room. He never said he couldn't sleep somewhere else with her. His brother, the untamable Lion, was a trip.

"Hey, why don't you and Erica come by the Haven tomorrow? Kay can't wait to see her, and for some reason you, too."

That was actually a good idea. He needed to get Erica out of the house. Take her on a date, without chance of her adversary showing up.

He mimicked Chamuel, *"Why that's a splendid idea, Old Chap."*

"Just don't call me Sap or Cupid, in front of our mates, Ariel," Chamuel stipulated.

Ariel chuckled. *"You know I'd never do that, man."*

Chamuel was a formidable warrior, just like all Archangels are. Whenever he did battle it was always in the name of agápē. The highest form of God's *unconditional* love, for His people.

He liked ribbing Chamuel, when it was just him and his brothers. Chamuel also ribbed him too, whenever he saw an opening. He just hadn't found one, recently.

Neither of them would ever do that to each other in public, though. That would be insulting to all Archangels, and to their Father. Just like it offended Him when humans acted uncomely, while claiming to be His followers.

He often got mad when humans referred to his brother as Cupid. Especially the ones Chamuel had brought together. They fashioned a holiday around 'cupid'. They sang songs about cupid drawing back his bow, and letting his arrow flow through their lovers' hearts. Please! They'd better hope Chamuel didn't hit them with an arrow!

They didn't recognize that it was God, through Chamuel, that had blessed them. They preferred to give the glory to a fictitious character. A character that wore a diaper, at that.

...

Chamuel was listening to Ariel's thoughts. Ariel was right. He was formidable, they both were. He smiled. They were the antithesis of each other, but they were the closest in Michael's inner circle. *"We need to finish cleansing this house. See you later, Ariel."*

"Good night," Ariel replied, and closed the link. Then he kissed the top of Erica's head. He'd have to teleport her to her bedroom soon. The sun would peak over the horizon in a little while. She needed to be in her room, before it came up; just in case her mother checked. But for now, he embraced the moment of holding his mate.

He wondered how Eric was doing. He knew he was in Kal's yard. He cast his gaze toward Kal's backyard. They weren't in the yard, but they were going at it.

"How do you like the aerial view?"

...

CHAPTER 34

Eric had told his children years ago that angels walked on the air. He had no idea how he knew that, but it just stood to reason. He never imagined that he – himself - would one day be able to do so.

But, here he was walking in the skies, over California. Over his house. And just like he hadn't been able to see the angels, no one could see him. That is except that angel laying on his patio, with his daughter Erica.

The way he was holding her, touched him to his core. Even if he couldn't be there, Ariel could. And the way he held her, said he would. The LORD knows that he could not have asked for a better mate for his daughter.

He stopped fighting and said, "I need a break from this scrimmage. I want to walk around the Heavens alone, for a while. If you guys don't mind."

"Sure, man, take your time," Kal said.

He could not see Ariel, or Erica; so he didn't know the motives behind Eric's request. It didn't matter though, because he didn't feel the need to monitor Eric's behavior.

He knew Eric would not break the rules and attempt to go home. Even if Eric were to try, Michael would stop him.

"The sun will be coming up shortly anyway, and we have to go," he replied.

Watchers couldn't be outside when the sun came up; let alone levitating in the skies. "Plus, I need to check on Nanette anyway. She said to tell you that you will be staying with us."

"That's perfect. I'll be there in a few."

"See you then," Kal replied. Then he, and his Watcher friends, vanished.

As soon as they left, Eric responded to Ariel, *"I love the Ariel view."*

Ariel laughed. Even though they sounded the same, he knew what Eric meant. *"I'm talking about your view from the sky, not your view of me."*

"Man, I have never felt so light."

"What I wouldn't have given to be a part of that scrimmage, man."

It was unfortunate, but he couldn't. Not as long as those Watchers were a part of it. Nevertheless, being a spectator was good. It reminded him of the many battles he, and his brothers, fought. They often fought demons in the sky, right over humanity's heads.

Eric knew why Ariel couldn't join him. Kal and his friends weren't allowed to know about the Archangels' relationships to their 'sanctioned' mates. *"Maybe one day you and I can do it together."*

"We will. You can count on it. I want you in shape, and at my side, when I go after your daughter's attacker."

"You can set your heartbeat by that shit!" Eric promised. *"Oh wait, can I still curse?"*

Ariel laughed out loud. It was so robust, it caused Erica to stir. He squeezed her, and kissed her head. She sighed, and settled back down.

"Man, you're going to get me in trouble with your wife."

Eric laughed. *"You didn't answer my question."*

"I'm not sure, but God doesn't change who you are. Your awareness, and your basic nature, remains the same.

The only difference is you are not weighted down by Sin, Iniquity, or the clay," he replied. Then he laughed. *"If it were up to me I'd say express yourself. Besides, I know how you feel about your family. I feel what you feel about those who are after my mate."*

"My daughter has never done anything to anybody. She has always been my sweet child. I was so grateful when I learned of her existence. I took one look at that sweet little girl, and I was convinced. She... was... mine! I didn't know how she came to be, but I didn't care! I fell in love with my baby girl, at first sight. I have loved her ever since."

Ariel's heart lurched. He not only felt the emotions behind Eric's words, he identified with them. *"I feel ya, man. I did, too."*

"It angers me that she has so many enemies. It angers me that Jacques wanted to kill her, even if he was sick."

"Exactly! Being sick is no excuse. At least not in my book. It's even worse that you didn't know how her doctor felt."

Eric hadn't seen the fight while it was going on because Michael had blocked his view. Now that he was hovering over his family's house, he could see past, and present. He took a look.

It upset him so bad, he appeared on the patio; next to the hammock. *"You have got to be kidding! Grayson?"*

Ariel nodded.

"That sorry ass, low down, bastard! The only damn reason he was as successful as he was, was because I referred my clients to him. I am tempted to go down in the bowels and kick his back stabbing ass."

Ariel laughed out loud again. *"Yeah, that would be*

fun. I might go with you."

"It's not funny, man," Eric countered. He reached down, and stroked Erica's hair. *"I put her, and my wife, in harm's way.   That bastard planned to kill my entire family!"*

"Be easy, Eric. His plan was not my plan. He'll never get near them, or anyone else, again."

"Thank you for looking out for them, when I couldn't."

"I will always look out for them."

"Did you retrieve my daughter's blood from Grayson's freezer?"

Ariel had actually forgotten about that. Those vials needed to be destroyed, immediately. He reached out, and grabbed them.

Dr. Grayson had made sure no one else would touch them. He'd labeled them all 'hazardous'. He hadn't lied, though. In the end, they were hazardous to *his* health.

He held them up for Eric to see. Then he crushed them. *"Done!"*

"What about all of the tests he ran? He has to have a file somewhere of his findings. Paper, and computer files. My daughter's charts too."

"I wouldn't know what to look for. You grab them, man."

Eric smiled. He liked his new abilities. *"I can do that now, can't I?"*

"Yep."

He reached out, and found the files. Erica's personal file was in the file room. That one was for all of the staff's viewing, but there was another one. It was secured, in a locked drawer in Grayson's desk.

That one had the findings of all the private tests he'd

ran. That one told the nature, Grayson presumed, of Erica's blood. That bastard called his daughter 'the humanoid alien'. He destroyed both of them.

He burned all the floppy disks, and the hard drives on the computers. Then he destroyed the server. That wasn't enough, though. The more he thought about it, the angrier he got.

He looked to make sure no one was in, or around, the building. He saw the janitor was getting in his car, and waited. The minute the janitor drove away, he disarmed the smoke and fire alarms. Then he opened the file room door.

Next, he waited for the janitor to get far enough away, so that he could not see anything in his rearview mirror. When the janitor turned the corner, he jumped into action. He set the whole damn building on fire. Starting with the file room; and Grayson's desk.

"Hey, man! That's a good idea. Hold up, I'm going to dump Grayson's worthless body in those flames!"

"That's the shit I'm talking about! Smoke his ass!" Eric replied. *"Too bad he's already dead!"*

Ariel laughed. *"Did you not hear me say you don't lose your awareness? You didn't lose yours did you?"*

"Let's have a barbeque then," Eric replied. *"Roast that swine, whole."*

Ariel reached for Dr. Grayson's body, and spirit. Just as he grabbed it they heard Michael.

"Do not go overboard, Eric. You may place Grayson's body in the fire, but leave his spirit be. Would you please not encourage this type of beastly behavior, Ariel. You are not in the wild, Lion."

"You tell Verenda yet?" Ariel retorted.

Michael did not respond.

Ariel and Eric cracked up. Nevertheless, they left Grayson's spirit where it was.

"Listen. My wife gets up really early, to let the maid in. You need to put Erica back in her bed now."

Ariel squeezed her, and groaned. He didn't want to. He was enjoying her soft breath, against his chest. He was enjoying her soft flesh, up against his.

He didn't know if he could be civil enough for her. After all, he was the untamed Lion. However, there were a few things he did know, without a doubt.

He was never going to let her go. He was going to do his best to make her happy. He was always going to protect her. He was going to stay under Michael's skin, like a tick; until he handled his business.

He looked up at Eric, and asked, *"What is an appropriate time for me to knock on the door?"*

Eric knew how Ariel was feeling. He hadn't wanted to leave Libby, when they first met. He hadn't wanted to leave her, the day he died.

He'd loved that woman from day one. No one else could've ever measured up. No one else would have accepted his daughter. What he wouldn't give to be with her this moment.

He loved his daughter, but he was so grateful his family knew how she came to be. He was grateful his wife knew he hadn't strayed, after all. He was grateful to learn himself, that he hadn't.

In the past he'd always appreciated a glass of fine wine. From the time he found out about Erica, he never had another drink. That was because he'd just assumed that someone had put something in his drink.

He'd totally forgotten that he was a sperm donor. He wondered how many more of his children were out there. He needed to find out, for his son's sake. He didn't want Eric to unknowingly fall in love with his sister.

He didn't want one donated sperm to fall in love with another, either. That would be cruel, and messed up. He'd check later.

Ariel was listening to Eric's thoughts. That dude was spot on. In ancient days Abraham had actually married his sister, Sarah. They shared the same father, but not the same mother. Others had done the same. But, it was frowned upon now. And it would be cruel if they didn't know in advance, that they were siblings.

"I'll help you seek out your other seeds later. But right now, let's deal with the matter at hand. What time is acceptable for me to come calling?"

Eric also heard Ariel's thoughts. It made him nervous, as hell. *"Good LORD, I was a prolific donor, man. Every week for years on end! I could have as many children as Abraham!"*

Ariel roared. That would be too funny! *"What time, man?"*

"You can knock around 8:00. My daughter likes to eat breakfast at the country club."

Ariel nodded. Then he kissed Erica's cheek, and vanquished her to her bed.

He stood up, and stretched him muscles. "You going to Kal's?"

"Yeah. Check you later."

They both vanished, just as Libby's alarm went off.

...

CHAPTER 35

Libby had showered, dressed, and made her way downstairs. She'd called the maid, and told her not to come. She couldn't deal with the noise today. She couldn't deal with outsiders today.

She wondered what her days would be like, without Eric. One thing she knew for sure. They'd be long. The nights even longer.

She jumped when she felt a kiss planted on her cheek. "Eric!" she whispered.

"I'm sorry, Momma. It's just me," Erica said, and wrapped her arms around Libby's neck.

Libby smiled. "Hey, baby. How did you sleep?"

"Good," she replied and smiled. Her mother couldn't see her smile, for which she was grateful. The woman always could read her face. She couldn't let her know where she'd slept.

She walked around and sat next to Libby. "How about you?"

"I don't know if it was the totality of all the information given to us last night, but I crashed."

Erica smiled. "Really?"

"I didn't wake up once, until this morning. Even when Eric was alive I always woke up a few times during the night. If for nothing else, to go to the bathroom."

Erica cracked up. "He used to complain that you'd blow up the bathroom, and then leave the door open," she said, and squealed.

Libby laughed too. "He'd wake up complaining."

Then she mimicked him, *"'Damn Libby! Can't you let a brotha rest! Either you learn to close the door, or we gon' change sides of the bed!'"*

"Daddy would come downstairs the next morning, tired and complaining. He kept telling us that something died inside you, and escaped during the night."

They both burst out laughing.

"That's when he started buying all that fiber crap," Eric said from the doorway.

Libby and Erica looked around.

All four of the boys were standing in the doorjamb. They were cracking up laughing.

Ian squeaked out, "Dad warned us about just walking in you guys' bedroom."

"He said, 'If your momma's in the bathroom-'" Remington started.

"Hold your nose-" Eric added.

"And run for your lives!" Carson finished.

Erica hit the table. "Daddy said, 'Normal people had morning constitutionals. Not your momma! That woman has, wake the dead, *midnight* explosions!'"

They all roared. Then they started telling one story after another about their father. The man was funny as hell. "He never got used to other people's bodily functions," Eric said.

"Remember when he put Ian out the car, because he kept passing gas?" Carson asked, and howled.

They all burst out laughing.

They'd gone to a Mexican Restaurant for dinner. Ian had overeaten, and the food gave him gas. He kept releasing stink bombs, one after another.

Eric looked in the rearview mirror. *"What the hell's wrong with you, boy! Hold that shit in, until we get out the car!"*

Ian let one rip again, and said, *"I can't, Daddy!"*

As soon as they hit the driveway their father slammed on his breaks. *"Get out!"* He made Ian walk to the house.

Libby was laughing so hard, she was crying. But they were joyful tears. It felt so good to remember Eric, and his antics, with laughter.

She wiped her eyes, and said, "Eric would scream from the other side of the bathroom door, 'You being named Liberty does not give you the liberty to assault my sense of smell. Flush as you go, woman!'"

They all roared. They were laughing and having such a good time, they didn't hear the doorbell. It wasn't until Perry walked in the kitchen, with Ariel in tow that they remembered Perry even lived there.

"Good morning, everyone," Ariel greeted.

Erica stood up. "Ariel!" she yelled, and hugged him.

"Hey, Ms. Erica George," he said and stroked her back. "Do you want to go out to breakfast?"

"Y'all eat?" Remington asked. He never wondered if angels ate before, but it was a good question.

"We don't require sustenance, but we can."

"Do y'all go to the bathroom, and fart?" Ian asked.

The entire room roared.

Perry playfully popped Ian on the back of his head. Then he took a seat next to him. It did his heart good that Eric's family was sitting around the table. They were laughing, and having fun; at Eric's expense.

The man would be dearly missed, and not because he was the provider. He would be missed because he was the life pulse of this family.

He nudged Ian, and said, "Nobody does it like you." Then he looked at his sister. "And your momma!"

"See!" Ian exclaimed, and put his arm around Libby. He kissed her cheek. "I AM my momma's son!"

Everybody roared.

Ariel was cracking up too. He sensed Erica didn't want to leave, because she was having too much fun. She wanted to take this trip down memory lane, with her family. He was good with that.

He held the chair for her to retake her seat, then he sat down next to her. "You can't handle the truth, Ian," he said and laughed.

"Yes I can!"

Ariel laughed. This was the strangest conversation he'd ever heard. Nevertheless, he felt how joyous their spirits were. That amazed him. Something as simple as a memory of Eric's rants, made them feel like he was close.

"I've never had much interaction with humanity. Being the Lion, and all. I am beastly, and combative, by nature. From time to time I've hung out with Chamuel, and his mate, Kay. But, you guys blow me away," he voiced.

He looked around the table at everyone's faces. Chamuel had extended family that he adored. He'd met them all, and liked them all; but they were Chamuel's family.

He'd also met Jeremiel's extended family too. He really liked Melvin Foster. That man, and his brothers-in-law, were a hoot. So was Ms. Ima. But, again, they were Jeremiel's family.

These people sitting around this table, was his extended family. A gift from the Master. "I'm learning that the human spirit is resilient. In spite of what's happened, you've resigned yourselves that you can go on without Eric. You know what he is, and you've accepted that. It amazes me that memories, as silly as these, have eased your spirits; and made you smile. No wonder God loves you guys so much."

"Who are Chamuel and Kay?" Eric asked.

"Chamuel is my brother, and Kay is his mate," Ariel added.

"Where are Kay *and* Anita?" Erica asked.

"Kay is in New Orleans, with Chamuel. Anita is in Galveston, Texas, with Jeremiel."

"Chamuel and Jeremiel are Archangels, too?" Carson asked.

Ariel nodded.

"God gave all of his Archangel sons a wife," Perry told them.

They all looked at him. "You never preached that, Uncle Perry," Remington replied.

Perry laughed. "I didn't know that! Not until they all came by, yesterday afternoon."

"They were all here?" Libby asked. "Where were we?"

Ariel laughed. "Trapped in the closet."

"What?" Perry asked.

Libby and her children burst out laughing.

"Eric's clothes fell on me, when I tried to get them ready for charity."

"It was like Dad was saying leave my clothes alone," Carson added. "If he's not really dead, he may want them."

They all gasped. Was that what it was all about? Was Eric saying that, for real? They all looked at Ariel.

"Tell us," Erica insisted. "Have you seen our

father?"

Ariel nodded.

Erica's heart leaped, and her eyes teared. "He's here, isn't he? He doesn't want Momma to get rid of his clothes, does he?"

Ariel shook his head. "He's not in this room, but he is close. And I'm sure he will want his clothes, eventually."

"Where is he?" Libby asked.

"He can't be distracted by family ties, right now. He is vigorously training."

"For what?" Ian asked.

"Your father is an Alter-Ego, now. His job is to help Watchers fight demons."

"Real demons exist?" Ian asked. "That's worse than Vampires."

Eric and Erica rolled their eyes.

Ariel cracked up laughing. He was going to enjoy this family. When he wasn't fighting he was laughing. There was no middle ground, for him. These boys were going to keep him roaring, and not like a lion.

"Boy! How many times do I have to tell you that vampires are not real! You watch too much television."

Ian laughed. At first he wasn't sure he'd like Ariel, but he was cool. He might just like having an Archangel as a brother-in-law. "Yeah well, them Watchers sure act like vampires."

...

Ariel reached out. *"May I tell them now, Michael?"*

"NO!"

...

"Have you ever thought that Hollywood got the idea from demons?" Ariel asked.

"What?"

Ariel nodded. "His human name is Vlad III, Prince of Wallachia," he explained. Then he went on to tell his history, and his madness. The human version.

"You mean the Impaler?" Erica asked. She'd read about him in school. He was into cannibalism. He also cut his victim's heads off, and spiked them in the ground. He was a scary, scary man. She was grateful he was dead, and gone.

"Yes. The Impaler," Ariel replied.

"You said his name *is*, not his name *was*!" Ian voiced.

Ariel laughed. "I did, didn't I?"

They all slowly nodded.

"Oops!" he answered, and cracked up.

...

CHAPTER 36

Erica wanted to get off this foolish subject. Her brothers could talk about vampires, werewolves, and other creatures of the night; all night.

They got that from their father telling them stories, while camping out with them. Even after she came along, he'd have boys' night out once in a while.

She could hear them screaming and laughing, outside her patio. She'd never liked ghost stories, or anything spooky. She still didn't. Now she knew why. She knew demons personally.

"Tell me about Kay, and Anita," she asked.

"Kay has invited us to come visit today. She can't wait to see you again."

"How do you know Kay, Erica?" Eric asked.

"She was a friend of mine, before we left Heaven."

"That's what I don't understand. How in the world were you in Heaven, before being born?" Ian asked.

"It's because you were a test tube baby, right?" Carson asked.

"Oh, that makes perfect sense!" Remington added.

"No it doesn't," Perry countered.

"We all were in Heaven before we received our bodies," Erica added.

"What?" Carson asked.

"Erica is correct. You just don't remember. Like she didn't," Ariel informed them. "Everybody comes from the breath of God."

"Even you?" Ian asked.

"No," Ariel denied, and arrogantly leaned back in his seat. "While humanity was formed by God's holy hands, angels were *called* into existence."

They all knew that God spoke everything into existence, but humanity. They knew that God breathed life into Adam.

"The Bible never said he breathed into Eve, though. Nor did it say how angels came to be," Ian stated.

"That's true. However, unlike Adam, Eve was not formed from the dust of the ground. She was formed from the rib of Adam. From his flesh and bone. There was already life in the cells of that flesh, and bone. Spirit, but not soul. He still had to breathe her soul into that living flesh."

"Really?" Libby asked.

Ariel nodded.

"So Archangels were never children, either?" Carson asked.

Ariel shook his head. "What you see, is what I've always been."

"Like Adam and Eve," Eric added.

"Yes. Except they were formed with God's hands. We were formed with His thoughts."

"We have always believed that angels are deities. Now I'm not so sure," Ian stated.

"We are not deities. We are fellow servants, of the same God. My brothers and I just live with Him, in the glass darkly."

"What is Heaven like?" Perry asked.

Ariel looked around the room, and smiled. It did his heart good to see that his mate had grown up in this type of environment. Her brothers had not liked her. Nevertheless, their disdain did not sway, or overshadow, her parents' love for her. Even the mother who hadn't birthed her, adored her.

Kay had grown up in a hotel, but it lacked parental love. Anita had grown up with parental love, but in the hood. His mate had grown up with an abundance of material, and emotional wealth.

His gaze fell on all of them. "By man's standard this is a mansion. The architectural design is amazing. I've never seen anything like it."

He looked out the window, and back at Perry. "That well-kept sprawling yard is absolutely stunning. Not a weed in sight."

His gaze perused the trees, and beyond. "This house was designed, with an excess of windows. That was done so that you guys can sit in any room in this house, and see the beauty of Mother Nature. You can witness the sun going down over the water, every night. You can see the trees standing erect, with their boughs pointing towards the Heavens. You experience, and benefit, from the shade they provide from the scorching California sun."

They all nodded.

"You guys have lived a privileged life. Yet, I feel it in your hearts that you don't take any of it for granted. And you don't worship the structure, or the terrain."

They all shook their heads.

He looked back at all of them. "You give credit to Eric, for what he has provided. You credit him for raising his family, on this street; in this neighborhood."

They all smiled, and nodded.

"If your earthly father could provide this type of dwelling, how much more can your Heavenly Father provide?"

They didn't answer. Not even Perry.

"Your eyes have not seen, nor have your ears heard, the things that my Father has prepared for *you*. You can't even imagine it in your hearts," Ariel continued.

Perry was feeling something, but he remained quiet.

"But, every now and then, Holy reveals Heaven's greatness to your spirits. He reveals that Heaven is better than what you have. You know in your hearts that there is no kind of burden, trials, trouble, or tribulations. Not in the Home of the soul."

He glanced at Perry, and said "That's why every now and again some of you get, just a little, homesick. That's why you sing songs like 'I'm going to lay down my burden', 'Sweet Home', and 'Walk around Heaven...all day'. You know there's no night! You know that there is one more river to cross."

Perry sat up straight. He felt movement in his spirit. A praise coming on!

Ariel looked around the kitchen. The cabinets were carved from Sycamore wood. They were natural in color, with a shiny clear stain on them. The grains within each section of the cabinet were different, yet uniform.

The ceiling had two layers of symmetrical Sycamore beams. The top layer was shorter than the bottom one. It sat in the groves that separated each beam. They extended from the four walls, and came together around the light fixture in the center of the room. Even the table where they were sitting, was Sycamore wood. It was classic, and pristine.

He rubbed the tabletop, and said, "You know in your soul, that Heaven is better than *this*. On some level, your *souls* remember. That's why you long for it."

. . .

"LORD, yes," Perry replied. He thought about the

second verse to his song. He shouted, "I haven't been to Heaven, but I'm on my way!"

...

Ariel smiled. Then he tilted his upper body, sideways. "There is a river, in Heaven. It flows, like a bridal train; from each side of the Master's throne. Mingled in the water is a perpetual iridescent rainbow. The water is filled with His glory, and is crystal clear. It flows outward, on each side of the golden street."

He looked out the window again, and back at them. "There are also trees in Heaven. Only three. One in the middle of that golden street. One planted on each side of the rivers of water. Although more beautiful than any beach, there is no sand. There is no need for it. Not in *Heaven,*" he said, and shook his head.

"The trees are unmovable, and are fed by the rivers of *holy* water. They cast no variation of a shadow, or shade; because there is no darkness, or night. Not in *my* Home.

"They are called the 'trees of life'. The same as the one planted in the Garden of Eden. Like that tree, each one bears twelve different types of fruit. Like that tree, they yield fruit all year around. Like that tree, the fruit is for sustenance, and the leaves are for healing."

...

They were all mesmerized by his words. His description was so vivid they could see it, with their minds' eyes.

...

"Unlike earth, there is no division. Not by ethnicity, and not by class. There are no neighborhoods, subdivisions, states, or countries. There is a city, though. Just one! Most of its residents are blood bought, forgiven sinners. It is the Holy city. Saints of old are clothed with garments of salvation. Wrapped in long white robes of righteousness. The twenty-four elders sit on their own thrones. Waiting for that Great Day of Judgment. The Son sits on the right hand of our Father. The Seraphim, and Cherubim, sing songs of His holiness, all day long."

...

The telephone rang, but no one moved to answer it. They couldn't, they were lost in Ariel's words. He stopped talking, and frowned. Not only did the telephone distract him, but he found *himself* homesick. He glanced around at everyone gazing at him, through glazed eyes.

He smiled, and said, "That's what *my* Home is like."

...

CHAPTER 37

Ariel stood up and reached for Erica's hand. "Shall we go visit Chamuel and Kay?"

Erica had forgotten all about going to see her friend Kay. She wanted to hear this story, more than she wanted to breathe. "I *know* you ain't gon' stop there, Ariel," she complained.

"Yeah!" her brothers all chimed in.

"How big is Heaven?" Remington asked.

"What's Jesus like?"

Ariel cracked up laughing. "I'll finish the story later. Chamuel and Kay are waiting on us, Ms. Erica George."

Erica sighed. She was double minded. She really couldn't wait to see her friends, especially Kay. But she wanted to hear this story too! Not to mention, she didn't want to leave her mother, by herself. But she really wanted to go.

"Do you mind if I go, Momma?"

"No, baby, go ahead. Y'all have a good time."

Ian really wanted to ask Ariel a lot more questions. One was personal. "Can I ask you something before you go?"

Ariel sucked his bottom lip, because he knew what Ian was going to ask. "Go ahead."

He looked Ariel's chest. The first three buttons on his shirt was open, like it was yesterday. "Why don't you have any chest hair, man?" he asked.

"IAN!" Perry shouted.

Ariel chuckled, and sucked his bottom lip again. "You *really* don't want to see me with hair on my chest, Ian," he warned. Then he gave Ian a visual of his hairy chest.

"OH!" Ian shouted and reared back. Ariel's chest was covered in black fiery hair. "I get! The lion!"

Ariel laughed. "See you guys later."

"Can we go?" Carson asked.

"No," Libby replied. "Let your sister enjoy herself."

Ariel laughed again. He knew what Libby was going to do, once he left. He didn't know how Michael was going to like it, but it was cool with him. He wrapped his arms around Erica, and said, "See you guys later."

They vanished.

...

The minute they disappeared, Libby reached for the wall telephone. She had to talk to her oldest friend. Just as she went to lift it, it rang.

"Hello," she greeted.

"Hey, Libby."

"Hey, Nanette. I was just getting ready to call you."

"Are you busy?" Nanette asked.

"No, I'm not busy. Just sitting in the kitchen."

"Can I come by? I just want to make sure you're okay."

"Yes, I'm more than okay," Libby replied. Then she winked at her sons, and brother. "But come on over."

"Okay, see you in a few minutes."

"See ya," she replied, and hung up the telephone.

"You're going to ask her about Dad," Eric asked.

"You damn straight."

Perry raised his eyebrows. "You are getting mighty comfortable with cursing, Liberty."

"I earned the right," she defended.

They all laughed.

...

The minute Nanette walked through the door, Libby asked, "How is my husband?"

Nanette frowned. "What?"

"You heard me, Nanette. How is my husband? I know he's at your house."

Nanette looked past her at the boys, and Perry, sitting at the table. They were all looking at her side eyed, and smiling.

Her eyes bulged. "Oh my God! Y'all know, don't you?"

They all slowly nodded.

She wrapped her arms around Libby's neck, and started crying. "I'm so sorry I had to keep it from you, all of these years!"

Libby was crying too. "I knew he wasn't dead."

Nanette pulled away from her. "How did you find out?"

"He was here all day yesterday! My Eric is still alive!"

"Did you see him?"

Libby shook her head. "I felt him. He kept hugging me."

Nanette thought she'd just stepped in it. Feeling your dead loved one's spirit, didn't mean they were alive. "Then how can you be sure it wasn't just your imagination?"

"Michael told us," Libby replied.

"Michael!"

"He was here yesterday too!"

"What did he tell you?"

"Come on and sit down," Libby directed, and led her to the table.

...

Once they were seated, Libby started telling her everything that had happened the night before. Nanette jumped and said, "Dr. Grayson was trying to kill Erica?"

Everyone at the table nodded.

"Son of a bitch!" she shouted. She also heard Kal growl in her ear.

...

"I didn't realize that by giving my blood to Eric, it would pass to his children, Nanette."

"I know you didn't. Thank God Michael destroyed Grayson."

...

"That's not all," Libby continued. "The accident that killed Eric, wasn't an accident."

"What?"

"Whoever it was, was trying to kill Erica."

"What?"

They all nodded.

"What in the world is going on?" she asked, out loud. But she was speaking to Kal.

...

"I don't know, but I damn sure plan on finding out," he responded. *"This is crazy!"*

"You need to hurry up, and get Eric up to par, Kal. His entire family is in danger!"

...

"That's not all, Ms. Nanette," Libby added.

"What else!"

"Michael told us that Kal is a Watcher. I know that Eric is Kal's Alter-Ego."

Nanette smiled. "Thank God the façade is over!"

"Your husband looks good for his age, woman!" Perry added.

They all laughed.

"What else did he tell y'all, Libby?"

...

Libby knew she couldn't tell her about Ariel. It kind of felt good that she'd be able to keep a secret from her. Sort of like payback. "That's about it. What else is there?"

Nanette's eyes glowed. "You told me once that you fell for Eric's mind, way before you fell for his face."

Libby nodded. "That's true. It was mind, body and finally face. In that order."

"That's a good thing, because he doesn't have the same face, girl."

"What?"

Nanette shook her head. "That face belongs to the clay body. That body is dead and buried."

Libby grabbed her chest. She loved her husband's face. That actually made sense, though. Eric was Kal's Alter-Ego. For all intents and purposes, his son. She looked at Eric, Jr. He looked just like his father. It stood to reason that Eric would look like his. "Does that mean he looks like, Kal now?"

Nanette roared. She didn't know who was laughing the loudest. She, or Kal. She wiped her eyes and looked across the table. They were all looking at her like something was wrong with her.

Her voice was high pitched when she squeaked out, "He looks like the male version of..." She beat her chest and squealed, "ME!"

"WHAT!" they all shouted.

Nanette was laughing too hard to answer them. The expression on their faces was priceless. She tried to stop laughing, but she couldn't. She could hear Kal laughing up a storm in her head. That was making her laugh that much more.

They were all trying to envision Nanette, as a man. It was not working. Nanette was a knockout! They just couldn't see her face on a man. Especially Eric!

"That can't be," Eric voiced. "I'm the spitting image of Dad!"

Nanette wiped her eyes, and howled. "You used to be!" she replied and screamed.

...

CHAPTER 38

Eric was training with Raphael, but he was listening to their conversation. Neither Kal nor Nanette realized that he was listening.

He wasn't laughing, though. He couldn't. He saw the shocked look on Libby's face. He feared that she wouldn't be able to handle it. He feared that she'd reject him.

"I need to see my family, Raphael. May I go?"

•••

Michael appeared in front of them. He had not kept a direct eye on Eric, while he was in human form. That was because Leizalak fell under Raphael's leadership. He did however, know the man; because of Erica. He'd been a disciplined human, with exceptional character. That discipline, and character, bled over into his change.

It pleased him that Leizalak was doing as well as he was, staying away from his family. It also pleased him that Leizalak was up to speed on his fighting skills. The man was as accomplished, if not more so, as the original Alter-Ego. That was thanks to Kalaziel.

Kalaziel was the only Watcher, to date, that had kept an eye on his Alter-Ego. It was something they all should do. Especially, those who chose to be rebirthed, in human bodies.

All of the other Watchers were more interested in the 'spirit' mates, they'd finally found. They gave no thought to the spirit that had been with them from day one.

Adabiel had kept up with his Alter-Ego, but Leibada

chose to remain a spirit. Leibada had, in fact, never left Adabiel's side. Even so, Adabiel hadn't taken the time to teach Leibada the art of war. Raphael had.

Kalaziel, on the other hand, had been forward looking; and leaning. He had prepared Leizalak for the day when he would give up the clay.

It was fortunate that Kalaziel was one of the original twenty Watchers. Leizalak was just as powerful as Kalaziel.

...

"Good morning, gentlemen."

"Good morning," Eric replied.

"Hey, Michael," Raphael spoke. He knew his brother. Michael never came to this place, unless he came to deliver a message. "What's up?"

"Kalaziel has just declared he is going to look out for Leizalak's family."

"He promised me he would, last night," Eric responded.

"He cannot. Not yet."

"Why?" they both asked.

"Ariel is untamed. No one can reign him in. He might refuse to hide his identity from Kalaziel."

Eric laughed. "My future son-in-law is out there, but I like that about him."

"It is not an endearing quality to be untamed one hundred percent, Leizalak. Especially when recompense is not on the agenda."

"Are you saying he lacks a learning curve?"

Michael's eyes twirled. "Without equivocation."

"Well, you're wrong. I witnessed his gentleness, last night. There was nothing untamed about the way he held my daughter."

"You witnessed his gentleness toward his mate," Michael countered. "Even while he was holding her, he was agitating our brother."

Eric laughed. That was the truth, but he really liked Ariel's personality.

"If we do not do something, Ariel is going to turn Leizalak into an untamed beast, Raphael. We need to give this Alter-Ego *balance.*"

Raphael nodded. He'd witnessed Ariel and Leizalak's attempt to retrieve Grayson's spirit. He would have stopped them, but Michael beat him to it.

"This is an opportune time for Leizalak to go home, because Ariel is not there. He and Erica have left for New Orleans. They will be gone for most of the day."

Raphael nodded, again. All angels yielded to Michael's authority, even if they didn't agree. This time he agreed wholeheartedly. "You are right, Michael."

Eric didn't like their reasoning, but he liked the end result. "I can go home?"

"Yes, you may," Michael answered for Raphael. "However, do not tell Nanette, or Kalaziel, about Ariel. Or mention the fact that Perry, Libby, and your three sons are Alter-Egos."

Eric frowned. "I didn't realize that Perry was an Alter-Ego, too."

Michael and Raphael nodded. "Kalaziel wasn't aware, because Perry's Watcher is another Ultimate Watcher. That Ultimate Watcher used to have this territory. I moved him shortly after he found his mate, and replaced him with Kalaziel."

"Why?"

"This is where Nanette *and* Liberty lived," Michael responded.

"Oh, that's right," Eric replied.

He didn't remember everything at once. He remembered as the information became necessary. Kal needed to be here, so that his and Nanette's paths would cross. That also made way for him to meet Liberty, his Alter-Ego better half.

"Everyone in my family is Alter-Egos."

"With the exception of the two children you fathered, yes."

"Why aren't they?"

"Firstly, because Erica is Ariel's 'sanctioned' mate. She could not be both a 'sanctioned' mate and an Alter-Ego."

Eric nodded. It totally made sense to him. Alter-Egos had to be separated from their human bodies, through death. 'Sanctioned' mates will never die. "One negates the other."

"Erica is the first of her kind. Two Alter-Ego parents, and a 'sanctioned' mate," Raphael added. He was in noticeable awe. "Extraordinary!"

"Indeed," Michael replied. "Secondly, you and Liberty are Alter-Egos. You could not birth anything less than a healthy baby."

Eric felt privileged. Even though Jr was not an Alter-Ego, he was special. He almost regretted his and Libby's decision not to have more children. Four boys had been a handful, especially with their special needs. Then Erica came along, and five children was more than enough.

"Thank you for allowing me to go home," he voiced.

However, he was concerned about their opinion of Ariel. He appreciated their concerns, but Ariel was his boy. His personality, although aggressive, was engaging. He did what he did without remorse.

He smiled and vanished. They both heard him say to their minds, *"By the way, have you told Verenda yet?"*

Raphael roared.

Michael grunted, and said, "I might be too late, Raphael.

Raphael nodded, and kept laughing.

•••

Eric appeared in his kitchen, and smiled. It was good to be home. To be back with his family.

"Hello, Liberty. Hello, sons. Hey, Perry. I'm back."

•••

CHAPTER 39

Ariel and Erica appeared inside the Haven. The lobby was empty, except for Kay and Chamuel. Kay turned beet red. She didn't realize how much she'd missed her best friend, until she saw her.

Just like Anita, Erica was darker than her, but absolutely gorgeous. Erica was also younger than her, but she had an air of sophistication about her. Like she came from a classy background. That didn't matter, because she was still her long lost friend.

"Erica," she whispered.

Erica smiled. She'd missed Kay so much; she just didn't know it. Kay had left eighteen years before her, and the others. She didn't look as old as she was, and she was stunningly beautiful.

She's seen Kay's life, from the balcony of Heaven. Kay's father didn't want her. Had never laid eyes on her, in fact. Kay's mother was more evil than Jezebel. An unrepentant witch. She had abused Kay, all of her life. That made her sad, for her friend.

Her own father had sought her out, at the risk of his reputation. And his marriage! She'd had two mothers who adored her.

She hadn't talked to God since He took her father. Now she was ashamed of herself, because she was immensely blessed.

Standing here with Kay, she realized that was why she didn't have any friends. On some level she must have remembered seeing how Kay's classmates treated her.

Or else, she knew that no friend could ever measure up to those she had in Heaven. Those who got in trouble on the balcony with her.

That didn't matter now, though. There were seven of them on that balcony that dreadful day. Verenda left first. Then Kay left.

The last five of them left Heaven on the same day. She had no doubt they would all eventually be reunited. She also knew time wouldn't change how they felt about each other. She was feeling it now, just being in the same space with Kay.

"Kay," she greeted. Then she walked over and hugged her friend.

They hugged, and rocked each other back and forth. No words needed to be – or even could be – spoken. Their embrace said it all.

The memory of their mishap on the balcony accosted both of their minds. Erica pulled away. "We can't have children. Can we?"

Kay shook her head. "It was the only way we could keep our mates, Erica. Remember?"

Erica looked behind her at Ariel, and smiled. She remembered him, from their days in Heaven. She remembered all of her friends, in Heaven. She even remembered her mothers, and her father, in Heaven.

She also remembered a private conversation they'd all had, with God. One that their mates didn't know about. It wasn't until this moment that she remembered the child she gave up, for Ariel. A son! It broke her heart, but Ariel was definitely worth the swap. Nevertheless, her eyes glazed.

She turned back toward Kay. "It was a good trade."

"And, we'll always have each other, Erica," Kay

promised, and hugged her again.

She knew what Erica had just remembered. She'd remembered her own, years ago. Life was about choices. Her eyes watered, too. They both sobbed.

...

Ariel and Chamuel stood back, and let their mates have their emotional reunion. Chamuel thought it was touching, the way they clung to each other.

"I guess you think that's sappy too, Ariel," Chamuel voiced. *"Or should I call you Lion?"*

Ariel didn't hear him, at first. He was focused on Erica's emotions. They were twofold. She was grateful for him, but sad over the child she'd never know. At least on this side of Heaven.

He knew who the child was, and where he was. He was tempted to tell her, but that would not be good. Or fair!

"Did you hear me, Lion?" Chamuel asked.

Ariel snapped out of his daze, and glared at Chamuel. Then he had total recall. *"See that's the difference in you and me, Cupid. I have no problem being called Lion. It gets an understanding right out the gate."*

Chamuel grunted. *"Listen, I got a lot of humans living in the Haven. Behave yourself."*

"So long as I'm not given a reason to do otherwise."

Chamuel stared at him. He almost felt sorry for his brother. This was a new era in his life. He couldn't continue to be combative at every turn. Not with a 'sanctioned' mate.

"Listen, you do know that you and Erica are only together, as long as she wants to be, right?"

"Of course."

"You are going to have to learn how to mellow out, Ariel. Otherwise you will lose her."

Ariel scoffed at that. *"I am not combative with Erica! Nor will I ever be. She remembers who I was. She knows who I am."*

"That may be true, but your behavior will cost her, dearly. It already has."

"Cost her how?"

"Take a look in her kitchen."

Ariel did, and frowned.

"Michael allowed Eric to come home," Chamuel added. Then he frowned, and carefully said, *"Because you were not there."*

"Why would he do that to her?"

"Because Watchers can't know about 'sanctioned' mates. Neither can 'spirit' mates. You have proven that you will not hide your true nature from Kal."

"I know they can't know about us. I would never upset the order of things, Chamuel. Michael should know that!"

"How would he? You are fighting him at every turn, about Verenda."

"You think I'm wrong? You didn't think I was wrong, in the beginning."

"True. I agree with you on every level, except one."

"Which one?"

"My reason for wanting him to get a move on is selfish. So is yours. As much as we want him to hurry up, Michael knows his mate. He knows what she can, and cannot handle. We weren't there when he found her, man. We didn't see her condition."

"Please. I understand what she went through, but it's been years, man. How long does it take to move on?

He needs to step up and coax her towards him, instead of sitting on the sideline."

"You haven't been around humans very much. I have. Sap or not, I know how their emotions work. Especially when they have been hurt as badly as Verenda has. Their safety is in building a wall, around their hearts. Shielding it from even more pain. The more they want to be loved, the more they shut themselves off."

"Yet she married another man!"

"Now that I don't understand," Chamuel admitted.

"Nobody understands that! Michael knows she's his mate, even if she doesn't. It's asinine, and out of order."

"He says he wants her to learn how to live. He felt like her husband could've helped her get over her past."

"That makes no sense, and you know it. Michael could have had Uriel minister to her, years ago. After all he is the Archangel of Peace. Not only that, but Michael can command Peace to embody her."

"If Michael did that he'd have to overrule Free Will."

Ariel laughed. Michael did not like that spirit. Plus, that was the one spirit that Michael couldn't control. *"Yet, Uriel overrode that 'fool's' will."*

Chamuel rolled his eyes. *"Jacques is not a fool, Ariel. Plus, he was begging for help. Verenda has yet to ask Father to ease her troubled mind."*

"That makes no sense. Why would she want to wallow in it?"

"Sure it does. She understands that with love comes hurt, and pain. That's why their wedding vows say for better, or worse. Her peace has to be birthed, over time."

"Kay had her own heart breaks. It doesn't get any

worse than not being loved by your parents. Her mother tormented her every day of her life, Chamuel. Yet she accepted you the minute she met you."

"Of course she did. I am the Archangel of 'love', after all," he replied and laughed.

"I hear you, Sap," Ariel replied, and laughed. *"Listen, you told that 'fool' to stay away from my mate, didn't you?"*

"I told his parents the importance of it."

"Did you tell them that I was an angel, and not a demon?"

Chamuel laughed. *"Nope! Beaux finally got over being afraid of us. I wasn't about to send him back there."*

Ariel cracked up. That was okay. As long as Jacques stayed away from Erica, he would never see him again. Not in any form. *"We're two of a kind, aren't we?"*

"I'd have it no other way," Chamuel responded. That was the truth. If he had to be called into existence with someone, he was glad it was Ariel.

Ariel was right. He could sometimes be too sappy. Ariel, on the other hand, could sometimes be filled with too much reward. Together, they balanced each other out.

Ariel heard Chamuel's thoughts, and smiled. He was spot on. That was why God called them together. Their Father believed in balance. *"Where are we taking the ladies?"* he asked.

"Antoine's, of course."

"Can we do it another day? I don't want Erica to miss her father's first day at home."

"Sure. However, do not teleport into the house, Ariel. They have company."

"I appreciate your concern, but trust me. I know

what I have to do, Chamuel."

Chamuel nodded.

Ariel spoke to Erica's mind, *"Eric is with the family now."*

"I want to be there, Ariel."

"That's what I figured."

Then they walked over to Erica and Kay, and broke up the reunion. They didn't tell Kay why, because she didn't know about Alter-Egos; yet.

Instead Erica came up with a plausible excuse. She told her that her mother was having a meltdown, and she needed to get to her.

"We'll be back in a day or so," Ariel promised.

"Maybe Anita can come, when we come back," Erica added.

"Yes!" Kay agreed. It would be fun for the three of them to get together. She hugged Erica. "Just let us know when you guys are coming, so Chamuel can arrange it."

"We will," Ariel agreed. Then he and Erica vanished.

•••

None of them knew Michael had been listening to them. He nodded. They were indeed a pair. He appreciated Chamuel explaining things to Ariel.

Michael eased into Chamuel's mind. *"Thank you, Chamuel."*

"You are welcome, Michael. However, I believe he will continue to rib you, like he does me."

Michael chuckled. *"I'm sure he will. It is the nature of the beast."*

•••

CHAPTER 40

Jacques opened his eyes, and stared at the ceiling. Man, where had his mind taken him now. He closed his eyes, because he didn't want to know. They popped back open. Something didn't feel right. Not wrong, though. Different! He was too calm! Easy! Stress-less!

Even the memory of what happened last night, wasn't bothering him. His mind was clear, for the first time in his life. Even his brain didn't hurt.

"Am I dead?" he asked himself. That had to be it. If he was, he was okay with it; because he felt *great*. He didn't even care if Erica hadn't died with him. He didn't care about anything.

...

"Good morning, son," Beaux greeted from his seat next to the bed.

Dorothy slept in Jacques' bedroom, too. At the sound of her husband's voice, she woke up. She really didn't want to, though. It had been the most peaceful sleep she'd had in years.

At first she didn't know where she was, either. Then it all came crashing back. The angels, the paint, the carpet. Dr. Grayson. Her son's real life fright night. Beaux hanging in there with them. The last memory made her smile.

She stood up and walked over to her son's bed. She leaned down and kissed his forehead. "Good morning, baby. How do you feel this morning?"

"What's going on? What happened? Why are these

walls a different color?" he asked. He remembered the creature, but he wasn't stressed about it. "Did that creature come back? Are we all dead?"

"No, son," Dorothy replied. "How are you feeling?"

He sat up in his bed. "I feel fine. What happened, Momma? Why are you guys in my bedroom?"

Beaux sat up in his chair. He couldn't believe how good Jacques looked. He'd never noticed that his son's face had been etched with an eternal scowl. That is until now. Thank God it was gone.

Even Dorothy looked better. The burden she carried, for years, over their son's condition no longer showed on her face. He imagined his facial expression had changed too. He knew his heart was lighter.

"You don't remember what happened last night, son?" he asked.

Jacques thoughtfully squinted, as it all came rushing back. "Now I do. I remember everything."

Then he smiled. "Even while I was asleep I was aware of what was going on. There were a lot of angels in this house, man."

Beaux frowned. He'd been referring to his son's maniac behavior last night. He looked at Dorothy, and back at Jacques. "You saw that? While you were sleep?"

Jacques ran his fingers through his hair. That had been the most amazing experience he'd ever had. "Yes. That angel that scared you guys in New Orleans' name is Chamuel, right?"

They both nodded.

"He appeared to me, in my sleep. He apologized for what he'd done to you guys. Then he tried to leave. I wouldn't let him. I fought with him, Dad."

Beaux leaned forward. "You did what?"

Jacques laughed. "I wrestled with him. I wouldn't let him go. Not until he helped me."

Dorothy couldn't believe her ears. Her mind slipped backwards. She remembered what Chamuel had done to those demons in New Orleans. "He could have killed you, son!"

"And that would've suited me just fine. I'd wanted to die anyway."

"Oh God!" Beaux exclaimed. His hand actually trembled. He couldn't imagine fighting that angel.

"I told him I couldn't keep going on the way I was. I said I didn't want to live the rest of my life on drugs. I told him that I didn't mind dying. I told him that he had to either take me with him, or heal my mental illness. He said it wasn't my time to die. I told him he'd better heal me, then."

He laughed when he saw the shocked looks on his parents' faces. They'd both run from Chamuel, years ago. The difference was, they were trying to live. He was trying to die.

Plus, Chamuel didn't frighten him, especially since he'd seen what that creature had done to Grayson. But then again, that wasn't a creature either. That was another Archangel!

"Chamuel finally agreed to heal me."

"He did?"

"He said it was provided I stay away from Erica."

"I told him that I loved her. He said that she wasn't my mate, and I'd have to move on."

"What?" Beaux asked.

Jacques nodded. "The next thing I knew, another angel placed his hand on my head."

"You saw that?"

Jacques nodded again. "I stopped wrestling after that. It was two against one," he said and laughed. "Then the second angel beat the walls, and the paint started chipping away."

"Oh my God! That's exactly what happened," Beaux replied.

"Then they replaced all the sheetrock, and starting painting this room."

"I'm sorry, son. I had no idea that it was the lead paint doing that to you," Beaux apologized. "I didn't know it was killing you slowly."

"That's alright, Dad. It's not your fault. I know that you didn't deliberately try to hurt me, and Mom. Mom knows that too."

"So are you okay with staying away from Erica?" Dorothy asked.

"Yeah. Strangely enough I am. If she doesn't want me, it's no sweat off my back. It's her loss. There are plenty of girls out there who will appreciate, and love me. It's time I start testing the waters."

WOW! Even he couldn't believe how calmly he'd said that. But he meant it. Life was too short to be chasing after the unreachable.

"I want a woman like you, Mom. One that will weather the storm, at my side."

Beaux looked at Dorothy and smiled. "For better or worse."

"That's what I'm talking about, Dad. Tristen's mother ran off and left him, and his father. Even though she was abused, she still left him behind. I understand she was scared to take him, but c'mon. Mom never would have left me, if you were abusive."

"I would have killed him," Dorothy replied.

"I know you would've. You stayed with us, through our craziness. You tried everything you could think of, to make your family emotionally whole. Even though we were driving you off the mental cliff too," he said and laughed.

"In sickness, and in health, son," she promised.

"Yeah well, we were some kind of sick, weren't we, Dad? Mom really got screwed, didn't she?"

Beaux laughed. His son had never had a sense of humor. He did now, and he was funny. He himself used to be funny, too. That's how he snagged Dorothy, in the first place. They hadn't had anything to laugh about in years.

He looked at her and cracked up. "Yeah, I guess she did, son."

Dorothy laughed too. She and Beaux had definitely run the gambit of the wedding vows. Even though she hadn't been to church in years, she knew what she'd promised. Through sickness, poorer, and worse.

In the end, those vows were not the cohesiveness that held her there. It was her love for both her husband, and son.

"Now that everybody is in their right mind, there are going to be some changes around here," she declared.

"What changes, Mom?"

"First of all, I want to go to New Orleans."

"What for?" Jacques asked.

"Your father and I need to go back to where we first lost it." Then she looked at Beaux. "And I want to visit my parents' graves."

Beaux nodded. Neither of them had ever gone back to New Orleans, after they left. Not even for their parents', or any family member's funerals. "We can visit both of our parents' graves. Maybe place some flowers on them."

Dorothy nodded, and smiled. "Then when we get back, I want to find a church home."

"That's a good idea," Beaux replied. They needed to get back to where they first fell in love. They'd gone to the same schools, but they'd met in church.

He looked at his son and said, "Your mother and I got married, the first time, when we were only seven years old."

Jacques frowned. He looked from his father to his mother. "What?"

Dorothy laughed. "We were the bride and groom, in the church's Tom Thumb Wedding."

Beaux cracked up. Back then he thought they were married for real. He kept crying because he couldn't take her home with him. "Your mother looked beautiful in her wedding gown."

"You were quite handsome in your tux," she complimented. "I guess fate knew back then that we were destined to be together."

"Not fate. God," Jacques corrected. "Chamuel told me that Erica is not my mate. He said God has predestined her to be someone else's soul mate. He said God predestined everybody. He also said that he, himself, was the Archangel of love. And that he had tied the binds that bound you two together."

"Really?" Dorothy asked.

Jacques nodded. He did not tell them who Erica's mate was. That knowledge would send his father back over the cliff. "He also said we are all predestined."

Beaux nodded.

"One more thing," Dorothy said.

"What?" they both asked.

"If I catch either of you smoking weed again, I will kill you both."

They both laughed, until they realized she wasn't. They nervously coughed.

She stood up, and walked out the room.

They looked at each other, and nervously smiled.

"It's a good thing weed ain't addictive," Jacques said.

They both laughed.

...

CHAPTER 41

Libby jumped. She almost couldn't believe it. This man was fine, but didn't look a thing like her Eric. She looked back at Nanette, and then back at him. He really did look like the male version of Nanette. They could, in fact, be twins.

She stood up. "Eric?"

He took a few steps toward her, and then stopped. He was concerned. She didn't look accepting of his change. He knew it would be a shock to his family, but he'd been hopeful.

He looked from her to his sons. They all had a shocked look on their faces. It may be harder than he thought, to pick up where they left off.

"It's me, Liberty Belle."

Libby slowly smiled. It may not be her husband's face, but it was his voice. It was his eyes. She anxiously moved toward him. "Eric!"

"I'm home, Liberty." He moved toward her, at the same time. This kitchen was too big! He felt like he couldn't get to her fast enough.

They met up half-way. He lifted her in the air, and turned his back on everyone else. Then he passionately kissed her. He pulled away, and spoke to her mind, *"I'm home, baby! I'm never again going to complain about your midnight bathroom habits."*

Liberty wrapped her arms around Eric's neck, and laughed. Yeah, this was her Eric. His kiss was the same. You can't fake that. She didn't know how this would work, and she didn't care. She had her husband back. She squeezed his neck, started crying. "I missed you, Eric."

"Can you love an immortal?" he asked.

"Not just any immortal," she replied honestly. "But I still love you, Eric."

"Even though I look like that fast tail Nanette?" he asked.

Nanette screamed from behind them. She hadn't told Libby that Eric had seen her naked. "Shut up, boy!" Then she frowned, and mumbled, "Oh my God."

Eric didn't notice that her facial expression had changed. He was looking at Libby. He chuckled, and kissed her again. He hadn't thought about it, but he couldn't continue to be called Eric. Everyone thought he was dead. The old Eric was. For humanity's sake he needed a new name.

He sat her back down on the floor, and looked at his four sons. They'd all gathered around him and Libby. He reached out and pulled all of them into his embrace.

"Dad," they all said.

This felt so right to Eric. Him and his boys. He pulled back, and looked at his three youngest. "It never mattered to me that I didn't seed you boys. I loved you from day one. I love you just as much, if not more, now. You three boys are mine. Just like Eric, and Erica. Understand?"

They nodded, and hugged him again.

Eric took a step back. He was seeing something that he never would have known, in human form. He looked at them sideways. He looked at Nanette, and then back at his three sons.

"Dammit Nanette!" he shouted.

She knew he was seeing what she'd just seen a

moment ago. "I didn't know, Eric. I swear I didn't. Kal doesn't either."

"Didn't know what?" Libby asked. Eric had a different face, but the same scowl.

"What is it, Dad?" Eric asked.

"Kal knew that I'd adopted my sons, Nanette. How could he not know?"

Nanette stood up and walked over. She could see that Eric was sincerely upset. She touched his arm. "Kal didn't know. He still doesn't."

"I know now," Kal said from his house. He couldn't join them because it was daylight. Eric's house had too many damn windows. *"It wasn't my place to know sooner, Eric."*

Eric didn't know if he should tell his sons, but he'd spoken out loud. He looked at them. "You boys are mine, no matter what."

"What's the *what*, Dad," Remington asked.

Libby looked at her three youngest sons, and her eyes bulged. She looked at Eric, and back at her sons. She'd never noticed that before. She did now. She looked at Nanette. "My sons look like Eric does *now*. Like *you*. All three of them."

Nanette nodded. "I never saw that before, Libby. I swear."

"Who is their father, Nanette?"

"I don't know. I don't have any siblings. I did have a couple of male cousins, who I wasn't close to. It has to be one of them. Or their sons."

"It was one of their sons," Eric replied. How ironic that his adopted sons looked like him now, instead of the son he fathered.

Either way, they were all borrowed bodies. His

family just didn't know that. "He was a drug addict too. He was the one that kept Annette strung out. She couldn't get right, because she loved him."

"We all had the same birthfather?" Carson asked.

Eric nodded. "With emphasis on *birth!*"

"Where is he?" Remington asked.

"Dead. A drug overdose, shortly after Annette died. He evidently loved her too."

"They loved each other, but not us," Remington replied.

"It doesn't matter," Ian stated. Then he hugged Eric again. He finally got it. It's not about who planted the seed. It's about who nourished it. "This is the man that loved me back to health. This is the man that planted my childhood memories. This is *my* father."

Eric kissed his son's cheek. "I always will be, son."

His eyes teared. This was a better reunion than he'd hoped for. He reached out and hugged all four of his sons again. He was still a blessed man.

He looked over his sons' heads and saw Perry standing in the crowd. He was feeling a bonanza of gratitude toward his brother-in-law.

He released his sons, and embraced Perry. "You kept your word. You've been looking out for my family since the accident, man."

Perry squeezed him, and patted him on his back. "If I hadn't already believed in God, this would be a game changer. It is so good to have you home, man."

"I never left," Eric countered, and laughed.

"You *were* in that closet, weren't you?" Carson asked.

Eric laughed. "I couldn't let Liberty get rid of my clothes."

They all laughed.

"Plus, I needed to make you boys remember how much I loved you. I never saw you as anything but my sons. I'm sorry if you thought otherwise, once Erica arrived."

He looked around the kitchen. "Where is Erica? Where is my daughter?" He knew where she was, but he had to ask. For Nanette's sake.

"She went out to breakfast," Libby answered. She didn't say with who. Nanette couldn't know that Ariel was an Archangel.

Everyone nodded. They all knew.

"With who?" Eric asked. "Not Jacques, I hope."

"No. Her new boyfriend," Ian replied. "While we were grieving, she was trolling," he added, and laughed.

Eric Jr. hit him on the back of his head. "Stop! Erica was just as devastated as we all were, and you know that."

Ian rubbed his head. "I was just playing."

...

Erica was alone, when she walked in the kitchen. Ariel was there, but he was invisible. As far as Nanette was concerned, humans couldn't know about their supernatural world. That meant that he could not witness the reunion.

If he'd been allowed to witness it, he'd know that Eric had somehow transformed. That would raise Nanette's suspicions, about *him.*

...

"That was a very wise call, Ariel," Michael stated.

"You have always underestimated me, Michael."

"It may have something to do with your behavior."

"That is not true, and you know it. You want me to

wear a hat that doesn't fit my head, man. I was called by the Master with the temperament that I have."

"That is indeed a fact. Nonetheless, Father did not plan for you to constantly be the Lion. If that were so, He would not have given you a 'sanctioned' mate. You must embrace the new dawning in your life, Ariel. You must learn how to tame the beast within, brother. Erica deserves a little sentimentality. Or as you call it sappiness."

"The same can be said for you, big brother. Have you – sentimentally - talked with Verenda yet?"

Michael laughed. Chamuel and Eric did too. He had just broadsided Ariel with a truth he could not deny. His only response was to mention Verenda.

"No, I have not, Lion. She is not ready to hear it. Trust me, when she is, I will let her know. Does that satisfy you?"

"Not really, but at least you gave us a reason. It'll have to do, for now."

"Would you force Erica to accept something she was not ready to deal with?"

Ariel didn't even hesitate. *"No."*

"I did not think so. When Verenda is ready, I assure you I will be as sentimental as I need to be."

"Fair enough."

...

"Hey," Erica spoke. "What's going on?"

They all fanned out.

Her eyes genuinely teared, and she pouted her lips. "You were on the hill with me. You were in my dreams. You're my father, aren't you?"

Eric's heart thumped. He loved all of his children, but Erica gave love an entirely different meaning. There was something about daughters that overwhelmed their fathers' hearts.

Libby's father had felt the same way about her, and Annette. That's why he grieved himself to death over Annette's death. In spite of how unruly she was, she was still his baby girl.

He understood that feeling, the minute he found out about Erica. She'd reached through that first picture he saw of her, and captured his heart. From that point on, all bets were off. He'd missed her first nine years, but he was not willing to miss any more time with her.

He hadn't even paused, other than to ask for forgiveness. Then he immediately went to Libby, and told her about his daughter. The daughter he wanted to bring home. They flew out the same day to bring his baby *home*.

He opened his arms. "Erica, baby."

Erica ran into his arms. "Daddy!"

He kissed her cheek. "I told you to never let anyone tell you that you weren't mine. You are flesh of my flesh. Bone of my bone," he said and squeezed her. "You will always be my own. I love you so much, baby."

She was genuinely crying. To dream about him was one thing. To have him here, was another. She didn't care what his face looked like. This was the man that rescued her, when she was all alone. This was the man that proudly declared he was her father.

His face may be different, but the way he held her was the same. She squeezed him tighter. "Daddy!"

Eric cried for the first time. His face was drenched. She had so many enemies, to be so young. There was still one out there. The one that had hit him with that car, trying to kill her.

"We'll get him," Ariel spoke to his mind. *"You and*

me."

"You damn straight!" Eric replied.

He stretched out his arms, and his entire family walked into his embrace. He was definitely a blessed man. "No one is ever going to hurt any of you, again," he promised.

Ariel nodded.

Nanette felt like this was a family affair. At the moment, it did not include her. Kal couldn't come get her, because it was daylight. He sent a shout out to Michael to teleport her home.

She vanished.

•••

CHAPTER 42

The minute Nanette vanished Ariel blocked her, and Kal's view. Then he materialized. "Hey, man. You look pretty good, for a stiff."

Eric laughed, and released his family. He gave Ariel a one-armed hug, and said, "I feel pretty good for a stiff."

"Y'all already know each other?" Libby asked.

Eric wrapped his arm around her. "This is my partner in crime."

Ariel laughed. "Michael is concerned that I am going to corrupt Eric. He thought he could sneak Eric back to the family, while I was away."

Eric cracked up laughing. "He damn sho did! He said hurry up, go. Ariel is out of town."

He and Ariel were the only ones laughing. The others were confused, even Erica. She asked, "Why would he want to do that, Ariel?"

"Michael is concerned that Eric will become untamed, like me."

"That doesn't make any sense. Being the Lion, untamed is your forte. You were called in that manner."

Ariel nodded, and wrapped his arm around her. He knew his mate remembered who he was. Her statement pleased him. "Eric, on the other hand, has another assignment altogether. His calling has a different task."

"Plus, if I trespassed into Ariel's territory God will instruct Raphael to destroy my silver bowl."

"What's the silver bowl?" Carson asked.

"Let's have a seat," Ariel suggested.

...

Once everyone was seated, Ariel and Eric explained how Eric was able to exist. The family was in awe, and amazed. Perry thought about what Michael said about the mysteries of this universe. Humanity didn't know the half.

Scientists used to say that humans only use ten percent of their brains. That theory had been debunked, through research studies of the brain.

He wasn't so sure the original thought wasn't the correct one. At least to some degree. He now believed that it didn't have anything to do with humans setting limits. It was limitations that were set in place by God.

"It's the premise of the 'glass darkly'," he stated. "In 1 Corinthians 13, the book of love, Paul declared *'We know in part'*."

Eric and Ariel nodded.

"If humanity knew all, like we do, there would be no need for faith, or hope. There would be no need to strive to please my Father," Ariel replied.

"In human form we cannot handle it all, Perry. We can't even imagine it," Eric added. "The knowledge that has been imparted on me since I gave up the clay, is unimaginable, man."

"What have you seen, Dad?" Ian asked.

"It is more awareness, son. For instance, not only do I know when the test will take place; I know the outcome."

"Test?"

"Life struggles in every human's life."

"Even ours?"

He nodded.

"So you know when we all will die?" Remington asked.

He scowled. Then smiled. "And how."

"Tell us!" Carson demanded.

"Would it make a difference, if you knew?"

"Yeah! I'd be really...really good days before," Carson replied.

They all cracked up.

"That's my point, son. You should live every day as if it were your last. What would've happened if you'd died while mistreating your sister? What would have happened if you'd died while challenging your mother, over my will?"

The memory of that scene agitated him. His sons had done to his wife, what they wouldn't have done, if he'd been there.

"Which, by the way, upset me immensely. Your mother and I never once skimped on our commitment to you boys. We gave you guys all the love we had to give. For the three of you to turn on my wife the minute I was gone, hurt her and *me*. Your behavior made your mother resent me for leaving her with a mess. We were not trying to keep a secret from you guys. We never told y'all, because it never mattered to us."

He looked at Perry. "You should have beat their asses, man! I left you in charge. How could you not? In one day you let my boys get out of hand!"

Perry knew Eric was serious. Eric had always been a disciplinarian. He wasn't too quick on using the rod. He didn't have to be. His mouth made his children feel like they'd been whipped. He didn't answer.

"You guys' behavior at my repast was reprehensible! Your mother and I taught you better than that. When did you guys develop a love for money? I know we never taught you that."

Carson swallowed hard. His brothers did too. They never thought, for a minute, that their father could see them. They never imagined he was witnessing their unruliness. They looked down, and remained quiet.

"Cursing at your mother, and your uncle! Calling her a liar! To her face! In what universe did you boys think that shit was acceptable?" he asked.

They didn't respond.

"The only reason I didn't reach out, and tighten up your asses, was because Ariel wouldn't let me."

Ariel nodded. It took all the strength he had to keep Eric from materializing. That dude had been warm.

"I'm back, but I can't stay. Nevertheless, the ground rules have not changed."

"What?" Libby asked.

Eric held a finger up to her, and continued his reprimand. "No matter where I am, I will be watching. I expect you boys to behave yourselves. I expect you to remember the things your mother and I taught you. I expect you to respect you mother, and her authority, in my absence. Perry too. Am I clear?"

They nodded, but didn't look up.

"Because let me let you in on another secret," he said. "Look at me!"

They looked up. Everybody in the room did. They all jumped, even Erica. She not only jumped, she jumped in Ariel's lap. There was a dozen, or more, Erics in the kitchen.

Ariel cracked up laughing. He really liked this dude. Little did Michael know, *he* didn't have to corrupt Eric. The man was already twisted! "Multiplicity! You wrong, man!"

Eric didn't laugh. While still seated, he placed a

hand on all of his children's shoulders. "No matter where I am, I can reach out and touch you. Get out of line with your mother one more time, and I will not hesitate," he warned, and squeezed all of their shoulders.

They got the message.

"We're sorry, Dad," Remington responded.

"Did you apologize to your mother?"

They shook their heads.

"Well, what are you waiting on?"

They looked at their mother. "We're sorry, Mom."

Libby smiled. If she doubted before, she didn't anymore. This was her Eric! The love of her life was immortal. He was never ever going to leave her, again. Oh wait!

"What do you mean you can't stay?"

"My commission is to fight alongside Kal, and other Watchers, Liberty."

"Fight who?"

"Demons, and demon possessed humans."

"What?"

"Demons roam the earth, just like Watchers do. Just like my kind does." Then he looked at Ariel. "Just like angels do."

Ariel nodded. "There is a constant war going on, in this world. A hidden war. We war for humanity against beings they are too weak to defeat."

"Is it a demon that is still after my daughter?" Libby asked.

"Demon possessed human," Ariel responded.

"Why is he after her?"

"He is filled with the spirit of Jealousy," Ariel replied. Then he looked at her brothers. "Just like you guys were."

"We never tried to kill our sister," Ian argued. "Never!"

"Why is he jealous of me?" Erica asked.

Ariel stroked her side, and laughed. "You have something he wants, Ms. Erica George."

"What does she have?" Libby asked. "And when did she get it? Where did she get it?"

"It's not tangible, is all I am at liberty to say."

Erica and her family assumed it was her blood. They wondered who else had gotten a look at her blood samples. It was scary to have an enemy, and not know who he or she was.

Libby looked under eyed at Eric. "You won't let them hurt our daughter, will you?"

He shook his head. "I took the blows of a moving car in her stead, didn't I? I was human when I did that, Liberty. I'm immortal now. How much more do you imagine I will be able to do?"

"Not to mention me," Ariel injected. "I promise nothing will happen to my mate. Or any of you."

• • •

CHAPTER 43

Eric heard Raphael calling him. He stood up. "I have to go now." He leaned down and kissed Libby. "I'll be back, before nightfall."

Libby stroked his cheek. "Okay."

He spoke to her mind. *"I can't wait to make love to you, without the clay. It'll be like the first time."*

She thought about all those hands, and blushed.

"I heard that, Ms. Liberty Belle! I felt your womb clinch, woman."

She blushed again. Then she felt his hand stroke her. This was unbelievable. He really was her Greek god. She shifted in her seat. She'd never been more turned on. *"Hurry home."*

He looked at his sons. "When I get back, I'm going to start training you guys how to use the weapons of my warfare. You too, Perry."

"The 'Samburu' spear?" Eric Jr asked.

Eric nodded.

"Cool!"

Perry had never been one to physically fight, but this might be fun. For once he'd be in on the boys' night out. He hoped that would bring him even closer to his nephews. "I'm game."

Ariel smiled, and spoke to Eric's mind. *"That's a good cover, man."*

He knew why Eric was doing this. He wanted his sons and brother-in-law to be trained beforehand. Just like he'd been. Not only would they be up and running, but it would make the transition easier. *"But what about Liberty?"*

Eric looked over at Ariel. *"I'm never going to let my wife die, man. Never!"*

Ariel slightly nodded. *"I understand."*

Eric really needed to leave, but he looked at Erica, and frowned. She was sitting on Ariel's lap.

He was old school to the bone. Mortal or immortal, that had not changed. He needed to get something straight with his daughter, and Ariel.

•••

"Give me a minute, Raphael."

Raphael laughed. He knew what Eric was going to do, and say. *"Take your time. I'd love to see you handle the Lion."*

"Me too," Michael injected. *"Chamuel! Jeremiel! You boys might want to listen."* He would have called the other three, but their hands were full with their newly found mates. *"Listen up, Varachiel, for future reference."*

They all bent their ears toward Eric's kitchen.

•••

Eric sat back down, and stared at his daughter. A week ago his stare would've spoken volumes. Not anymore, evidently. She was quite comfortable. Maybe it was due to him having a different face.

He never took his eyes off of her, when he said, "Different face, same rules."

Erica looked confused. "What?"

"Is something wrong with your behind?"

"No, sir," she replied, and blushed.

"Get off of Ariel's lap, and sit your butt in your own chair!" he demanded. His children knew he didn't allow that. It was disrespectful to him, and their mother.

"Chill out, man," Ariel replied. "You're the one who scared her onto my lap, with your parlor trick."

"She's not scared now, is she?" Eric came back. "I don't care how you guys act when it is just the two of you. But do not disrespect my wife, Ariel. Or me. Not in my house, man. Angel or not, I won't put up with that crap."

Erica eased off Ariel's lap, and sat in the chair next to him. "Sorry, Daddy."

Libby looked side eyed at Erica. She knew better than that.

"And another thing," Eric continued. "What made you think you could disrespect my wife, by staying in my daughter's room. Have you lost your damn mind!"

"Uh-oh!" Ian said, and laughed. This was the hard disciplinarian he remembered. "Dad's home, y'all!"

"Dad don't play," Carson added, and laughed.

"I don't care if my daughter is eighteen. She still lives in her mother's and my home. She will still abide by the rules. And so will you, Ariel. I said my children could not entertain company in their bedrooms. My body may have changed, but there is no waffling in my mind. I meant that when I had the clay body. I mean that shit now. Stay...out...of...Erica's...bedroom! Don't even peek in there. Understand?"

...

"What you gon' say to that, Lion?" Chamuel asked.

"Shut up and get yourself some business, Cupid!"

"Don't forget they were on the balcony, Eric!" Chamuel reminded him.

"I have no problem with them being on the balcony, Chamuel. And why are you in a conversation that doesn't concern you?" Eric asked. *"Especially since we have not even met yet. Now do you mind?"*

"My bad! Keep going."

Ariel chuckled.

...

"When you guys go out on a date, have my daughter home at a decent hour. You understand?"

"Lighten up. I will not do anything to disrespect your daughter," Ariel replied. *"You sound like Melvin Foster, man."*

"Did I hear my father-in-law's name mentioned?" Jeremiel asked.

"Yeah! Eric is trippin' like Melvin!"

"Man, I hope not!" Jeremiel replied and laughed. *"What is he calling you?"*

"Nothing yet, but I'm sure he'll come up with something."

Eric paused, and checked to see who Melvin was. He smiled. He couldn't wait to meet that dude. There was something about fathers, and their daughters.

He also checked on Chamuel. Unfortunately, Chamuel's mate didn't have a father figure. Although he didn't understand why Rufus did not step up. *"That father got that shit right! The same rules apply, Ariel. If you have to, go ahead and run your butt home with your boys! Keep in mind, unlike Melvin, I can see you! I will know if you peek in my daughter's bedroom, or shower. I'm telling you in advance...don't!"*

Jeremiel and Chamuel cracked up laughing. *"Dang! I never thought about the shower,"* Jeremiel said.

"Me either," Chamuel admitted. *"I might have to try that."*

"Don't!" Eric replied. *"It's disrespectful."*

"You know that all of our women will remain chaste, until Michael handles his business," Chamuel

replied.

"I'm not talking about chaste, Chamuel. I'm talking about 'virtue'. In case you didn't realize it, they are two different things. My daughter needs to carry herself in a manner that says she's my daughter. A George! I'm sure Melvin feels the same way."

"Did you gentlemen hear that?" Michael injected, and laughed. *"Very well stated, Eric. You might be the only one who can tame the Lion!"*

"Have you talked to Verenda, Michael?" Eric asked. It was one thing for him to get on his future son-in-law. It was another for Michael, Jeremiel and Chamuel to add their two cents.

There was one thing he'd been good at. Laying down the law in his house. Nothing has changed since he now had an immortal body. He was still the man of his house. He still expected his children to behave like they were *his*.

Michael howled. These two together were going to be interesting. *"I am out!"*

Ariel roared. *"Bye!"*

•••

Eric stood up again. "Now I really do have to go. Please remember whose children you are. You all are your mother's, and my *treasures*," he stated. "Carry yourselves accordingly. All of you."

He gazed over at his son, Eric. He hadn't given him any instructions. His oldest didn't need it. He'd always been responsible, and compliant. A real chip off the old block.

He spoke to his mind. *"Thank you, son. For just being you. You have always made me proud."*

Eric Jr smiled, and slightly nodded. He knew none

of his father's speeches had been for him. He always followed the rules. Not because he was a goody two-shoes, but because he was the oldest. The responsibility was always on the oldest, to set the tone for his siblings. *"I love you too, man. Glad you're back."*

He leaned down and kissed Libby's head. "Until tonight," he said, and vanished.

CHAPTER 44

Libby and Erica were lounging in the backyard when their pool man arrived. He had a hose draped over his shoulders, a pole in one hand, and a skimmer in the other.

"Good morning," he politely spoke.

"Good morning, Zander," they both replied.

He hadn't been there since Eric's death. At first Libby wasn't emotionally capable of dealing with outsiders. Then Eric came home, and she hadn't wanted to be disturbed by outsiders.

Her family needed to get used to having Eric back. They needed to get used to his new, albeit handsome, face. He'd been back over a week now. His return had stimulated the family's appreciation for each other.

Like when he had a human body, he was gone quite a bit. Only this time he returned at a moment's notice, instead of waiting on the next flight.

He'd pop in their bed, late at night. Just long enough to make mad desperate love. Her man still had the touch, only heightened. As soon as she dozed off, he'd pop back out. But, he was there every morning when she woke up.

According to him, he was the first Alter-Ego that had returned home to his family. He just couldn't stay away. Others had been afraid to do so, or either didn't know they could.

They griped to Raphael for not telling them that they could have. Raphael informed them that Eric was a test case. He said all of the Heavenly host was watching. Scrutinizing to see how well it worked.

He, their four sons, and Perry, scrimmaged with the spears every evening. Kal and three of his Watchers friends came every night, too.

Libby had never seen Eric wield that spear. The man looked like he was born to be a warrior. She guessed he was. It was sexy as all get out.

Her sons seemed to be catching on with ease. Her three youngest, and Perry, were more proficient with it than Eric Jr. But he was getting there.

...

The family was finally back on track, in most instances. The one area that had changed was they couldn't call Eric 'Daddy', or even 'Eric' in public. Eric didn't like that. So he stopped going out during the day with them.

Their maid had been devastated, when she saw Eric lounging in their bedroom. She couldn't believe that Libby had fallen for another man so soon.

She accused Libby of being coldhearted. She even insinuated that Libby had a man on the side, all along. Libby fired her on the spot.

That was fine with Eric, because he could clean the house with just a thought. He didn't though. It was time his children learned to be self-sufficient. Especially his three youngest sons. Those boys gave an entirely new meaning to the word 'lazy'. That was his and Libby's fault. They'd never required their children clean up behind themselves.

All in all, life was good.

...

She looked over at Erica, and smiled. "Where are

you and Ariel going today?"

"We're finally going back to New Orleans," Erica advised. Her father didn't have a regular schedule. She never knew when he'd appear, or how long he'd stay. She hadn't wanted to miss a moment of time with him.

"That's good. New Orleans is a beautiful city. We used to go to Mardi Gras every year, before you kids came along."

"Really?"

Libby nodded, and smiled. "We used to do a lot of traveling, when it was just the two of us."

"We cramped you guys' style?"

"Not at all. Eric Jr wasn't an accident. We decided to start a family, when we were ready."

"You guys didn't count on your youngest four, though. If you'd only had Eric, you could've still travelled."

Libby reached for her hand, and squeezed it. "If we hadn't adopted your three brothers, we would've had more children, Erica. We always wanted a large family. As far as you are concerned, you were a breath of fresh air. Can you even imagine me stuck with all those men, and no other woman in this house?"

Erica laughed. "We're still outnumbered, Momma."

"The point is, your father and I have no regrets. Not about any of our children, baby. You are, and have always been, my favorite daughter."

They both laughed. She really didn't have a favorite child. They were all hers.

Erica squeezed her hand, and sat up. "I'm going to get some more tea. You want some more?"

"Yes, please."

Erica stood up, and looked around the yard then at

the house. The large pillars stretched from the ground to the second story.

The tops and bottoms of the pillars were Corinthian, with grooved leaves. She'd never noticed that they were just like the ones in Greece. They supported her and Ariel's half-moon shaped private patio.

She gazed across the yard. It was more stunning than she realized. In the past, she'd taken everything she had for granted.

Her parents gave her anything she wanted. Their bedroom. Her decorated ceiling. Jewelry! A new deep purple Corvette! The car was her graduation present.

She had yet to drive it, though. She hadn't even thought about it until now. After her father died, she hadn't thought about anything, except her loss.

She wasn't emotional, by nature; but she was now. She'd stopped talking to God for a week, because she was mad. She wasn't mad now. Not anymore. She started mentally counting her blessings, one by one.

She was unbelievably grateful her father was home, and he was never leave again. She was equally grateful that she had her Ariel. He wouldn't ever leave either. She was so grateful that she and her brothers were getting along. She was even more grateful that her mother had accepted her. She loved this mother, as much as the one she'd lost.

She leaned over and kissed Libby's cheek. "I'll be right back."

...

The minute Erica walked through the patio doors, Zander walked over to Libby. He squatted down next to her, and grabbed her hand. He started to massage it. "I was sorry to hear about Eric. He was a good man, Libby."

"Thank you," she replied, and tried to pull her hand away. For some reason he was giving her the creeps. He'd never been presumptuous enough to stroke her hand, in the past.

He squeezed her hand tighter, and continued to stroke it. "You know I lost my wife four months ago, to cancer."

She nodded. She and Eric had gone to the woman's funeral. "Would you *please* let go of my hand."

He ignored her request. "I am part of a support group for widows and widowers. We know that we will never love anyone like we did our beloved spouses. None of us will ever marry again."

Libby understood that sentiment. If Eric hadn't come back an immortal, she knew she'd be single for the rest of her days. She relaxed for a moment.

"You are a lovely woman, Libby. Maybe you and I can comfort each other."

That statement caught her off guard. "Let go of my hand. I don't need your comfort. I certainly have none to offer you!" She tried to pull her hand away again.

He gripped it tighter. "My friends and I are swingers. There's a whole community of us. We get together once a month. We want to swing with you. Men and women can satisfy you, Libby."

"How dare you! You creep!" She slapped him with her other hand. "Let me go, you damn pervert!"

"Let go of my mother!" Erica screamed from the doorway. She'd heard everything he said. This yard was big, but he hadn't even tried to whisper. The next door neighbors could've heard him. She was disgusted.

She ran towards them. "Get away from her!" When she got close enough, she threw her glass of iced tea at him. It hit him in the head, but he still didn't release Libby's hand. She tried to push Zander away from Libby.

Zander shoved Erica back, with his free hand. She tripped over a stone, and screamed.

Libby sat up, and screamed, "Erica!" Then she punched Zander in his face. "You son a bitch!"

He grabbed her other wrist. "Give us a chance. We're all widowers and widows. I told everybody about you, the minute Eric died."

Erica jumped up and kicked him in his back. Then she grabbed a handful of his hair, and tried to pull him away. "Get off my mother!"

Libby's sons and Perry heard their shouts. They came running out the door. "Get away from her, you bastard!" Perry shouted.

"Let her go!" Eric Jr and his brothers, shouted. They tackled him, but he still didn't release Libby's hand. The awkward position of her arm made her scream.

Perry was trying to pull his nephews off the man, so he could get to him. It wasn't working. His nephews were pissed! That was understandable though. Libby was their mother.

He tried to get her arm untangled, but couldn't. He realized that Zander had a nervous death grip on Libby's hand. He couldn't release it, even if he wanted to.

Erica screamed, "Ariel! Daddy!"

Libby screamed at the same time, "ERIC!"

...

CHAPTER 45

Eric and Ariel were scrimmaging in the place of invisibility. They heard both of their women scream, and felt the men's rage at the same time. They vanished, and appeared on the scene.

Ariel was as old as Time. He lived and fought by Biblical law. Old Testament Recompense. At least where it applied to offensive body parts.

This offensive human evidently didn't know those scriptures. He went to pounce on him, but Eric snatched him back. *"No! He's mine!"*

Ariel growled. He hated being yanked. He hated chains! He wasn't used to taking a back seat. *"He attacked my mate, too!"*

"He's mine, Ariel!" Eric replied, and moved past him. *"He offended my entire family, man!"*

Ariel nodded, but he wasn't just going to do nothing. He wasn't designed to stand on the sideline. He decided to introduce this creep to Old Testament law. He reached out, and clawed Zander's offensive hands - plum off! Then he vanquished them.

Zander's scream was loud, and agonizing to their eardrums. All except Ariel's. The sound pacified the Lion.

Zander tried to get away from Libby's sons, but couldn't. Those boys meant to make him pay.

They all had angry tears in their eyes. The thought that their mother had been attacked, in their own backyard. They all were thinking what the hell is going on.

···

Eric could not believe Zander had done this thing. He'd been their pool man for over five years. Never once in all of that time had he gotten out of line.

Being that he was immortal now, he could hear Zander's thoughts. The ones overshadowed by the thoughts of pain. He'd always been a pervert. Even before he joined that group of swingers.

He actually saw all of the women Zander had had an affair with. Married women. Those whose pools he cleaned, while their husbands were at work. Even now, with all of this pain, the bastard still had an erection.

He teleported his family to the patio. Out of *his* way! Then he reached down. His hand was upside down, when he wrapped it around Zander's throat.

"Get your immoral perverted ass off my property!" he shouted, and yanked him backward.

···

Zander went airborne. He kept going higher, and higher, as he flew across the yard. His body scraped the tree tops, but he kept going higher.

Libby and her children's eyes grew. Eric had thrown that man damn near three thousand feet in the air. They could see that he was still airborne, even though he was no longer on their property. As far out as he was, they knew that he was over the water.

"Oh my God!" Erica whispered.

Ariel wrapped his arms around her. She was still trembling. He eased her spirit. Then he called forth a few of his water friends. They were untamable, like him.

···

Zander was still screaming when his body started to descend over the ocean. People along the beachfront looked up. Eric immediately gave the onlookers a vision of a small airplane overhead. They all assumed he fell out of the plane. Or jumped!

Zander couldn't remember the what, when, where, or even how. All he remembered was falling from the sky. He was afraid of heights. So, what in the world was he doing up there? How did he get up there?

He could hear the muffled sound of people along the beach screaming, and shouting. They were waving their arms, and shouting for him to get out of the water. He was too far out for anyone to help him, especially seeing that he was surrounded by a frenzy of sharks. Angel sharks!

He was trying to escape, but there was no way out. They were gnawing on his arms, and legs. One even went for his groin. He tried as hard as he could to fight them off - especially that one.

Two bit his wrists. He struggled to get free. When the sharks released him, he realized his hands were gone. He flapped his stubs, and screamed.

He assumed they bit them off. Thank God his adrenaline, and the shock factor, prohibited him from feeling the pain. He kept screaming, anyway.

His blood was pooling, and drawing the attention of other, more dangerous, sea creatures. He screamed, "Help! Help!"

He heard the crowd on the beach shouting, "Look behind you!"

He turned around. Someone was in a speed boat, speeding towards him. He tried to swim toward it. That was a bad decision, because he was stirring his own blood.

He felt something grab his legs, and pull him under. He kept going further, and further down. He tried to bend and untangle his legs from whatever was holding him under.

He screamed, and kept screaming, when he saw a white haired man. Bubbles were coming from his own mouth, and nose. He knew he was swallowing too much water.

The sharks knew who this man was. They hurriedly swam away, out of his reach. He knew who he was, too. This was it! The end of the road for him. His gigolo days were over. He stopped fighting.

Sammael snatched his spirit, but allowed his body to float back to the top. He stayed below, to be sure the speed boat grabbed it. Or what was left of it.

The minute they had Zander's corpse onboard, he vanished with his spirit.

...

Eric reached for Libby's hands. Both of her wrists were bruised from Zander's grip. He stroked them with his thumbs, and removed the bruises. That wasn't good enough though. "I hate this!" he voiced. "That bastard never would have tried this, if he knew I was still alive."

"I know. I want to tell the whole world that you're back, Eric."

"I don't care how it looks, Liberty. Introduce me by whatever the hell name you want. But introduce me!"

She smiled. She never cared what people thought about her. Her college roommates thought she was crazy for being attracted to Eric.

They laughed at her for being desperate for a man. They even accused her of being scared to date the good looking guys that were after her. They didn't understand how a young woman, as fine as she was, could settle for magnified eyes.

That is until he took his glasses off, and stopped

acting nerdy. Then they all wanted him. They even tried to take him from her.

Eric was very polite toward them. He didn't tell them that he was a one-woman man. One woman would've implied any of them could have been *that* one woman. If they'd given him a chance *first!*

He wanted to make sure that there was no confusion, or misunderstanding. He told them that he was Liberty Belle's man. And he damn sure was. Still was.

"I don't care what anyone thinks. You know that. I would call you by your Alter-Ego name; but I can't pronounce it," she replied. "I'm going to call you Eric."

He loved how he could hear her thoughts. All of her sorority sisters had hit on him. They promised him a night that would blow his mind. They hadn't realized that his mind had already been blown.

He wrapped his arms around her, and kissed her. "That's my Liberty Belle."

...

Their sons, and her brother, were still fuming. They wondered how Zander was able to get inside their yard.

"Michael promised us that we were all safe," Eric commented.

His brothers nodded. "He said that nothing evil could breach our yard. This attack was evil, and as demonic as it got!" Remington added.

"How was Zander able to get in, Ariel? You promised us too," Perry asked.

Ariel stared at them, staring at him. He was just as confused as they were. They were right, to some degree. No one evil should've been able to breach the parameters. Then he realized that Zander wasn't so much evil, as depraved. Still, he should not have been able to get in.

Not with that vulgar thought on his mind.

He remembered that Depravity and Vulgarity were spirits! He remembered who the chief of those spirits was. He reached out to see if he could sense that demon. He growled. Just as he suspected, this was that perverted demon's doing.

He shouted, "SAMJAZA!"

"Who?" they all asked.

"I never would have touched the woman," Samjaza responded, from the bowels of Hell.

Everyone in the yard heard him. Their eyes bucked. Erica and Libby trembled.

"But you did! You bastard!" Eric replied.

"Ariel pretended to be me, when he chased Tristen and Beaux in the greenhouse. Now we have an unspoken agreement. He can pretend to be me, and I can entice the women in his life. His mate looks as sexy as her mother. I think I'll try her next. Maybe while she sleeps, wrapped in his arms. I will make it so she assumes it is you," he replied, and laughed. *"I may even do to her what I did to Mary Magdalene. Now that would be fun."* Human's thought that Mary Magdalene was possessed by seven demons, but she wasn't. He'd split himself seven times and possessed her. He had that woman doing all kind of sexual things, that is until Jesus called him out. Jesus wouldn't stop him this time. *"I can't wait!"*

Erica trembled again. That demon wanted to possess her! What would he make her do? The Bible didn't call Mary a prostitute, but some ministered alluded to it. Her uncle never did, but still. She also knew that demon could appear in her dreams, because that's how she saw her father. She was more than a little frightened. "Ariel!"

"We'll see about that, you bastard!" Ariel argued. Samjaza was just talking noise about possessing her. He couldn't do it as long as *he* was around, and he'd always be around. He could also appear in Erica's dreams, and contend with Samjaza, but he wouldn't. That would turn her dreams into nightmares.

Plus, he knew Samjaza was twisted. That bastard would start out with Erica, but he wouldn't stop there. Or even with just the females. He'd go after God's man – Perry – with a vengeance. No way was he going to let that happen. He reached out...

"Just watch-" Samjaza started then stopped. He felt a sharp pain in his head, and lost his concentration.

•••

Ariel went to teleport, but Eric stopped him. "I'm going with you."

"No, you are not. I gave Zander to you, because it was the right thing to do. Samjaza is mine, without negotiation! Understand! You stay here with your mate, and mine. There ain't no telling who else Samjaza will try and send."

"Who is Samjaza?" Erica asked.

"A Fallen angel," Ariel replied.

Eric saw the fear on his family's faces. Even Perry looked concerned. This was a whole new way of life for them. His state of being, and Ariel's too, had opened his family up to all kinds of evil spirits.

Ariel was right. He needed to stay with them. He nodded. "Alright, but you make sure to fix this shit!"

Ariel kissed Erica. "I'll be back in a minute," he promised. Then he vanished.

•••

CHAPTER 46

Word in the underworld was that no one could defeat Samjaza. Maybe Azazel could, but they were on the same evil team. Whereas good fights good all the time, evil never fights evil.

Even during the Great War, none of the other Archangels attempted to contend with Samjaza. They all left that battle up to Michael. For eons it had been widely speculated that Samjaza was still more powerful than most of the Archangels.

Supposedly he gave his oldest son, Seraphiel aka Brock, all that he was. Therefore, Seraphiel was powerful enough to take down his father, provided he caught his father off guard. Both theories had yet to be proven, or disproven.

All of the Heavenly host proclaimed that Seraphiel was more powerful than any Archangel, except Michael, Gabriel and Raphael. Ariel was okay with that conclusion, and had no need to challenge it.

He was, however, up to pitting his powers against Samjaza's. In fact, he'd thirsted for that opportunity for eons. There was one thing his brothers, and the Heavenly host, seemed to forget.

Samjaza was a perverted *demon*, with a one track lascivious mind. He, and all other demons, lost the light of God's glory, when they rebelled.

From that point on they became adversaries of God, and His faithful sons. Therefore, none of them were more powerful than any angels. Especially an Arch imbued with the Creator's recompense.

In truth, demons were not as powerful as God's 'so' loved humans, either. Humans just feared the supernatural. They didn't realize the power they held in their tongues.

They were so busy teaching, and believing, the hype about God being a hard taskmaster. And He was. Still, He'd given them all an angel. A witness, in the clouds.

He'd reached out, before he left Erica's side, and attacked that cretin. He pierced that demon's brain, with all ten of his animalistic digits. He dug so deep, his claws on his left hand overlapped the ones on his right hand.

That was just the beginning of what he had in store for Samjaza. He meant to wipe his mate's name out of this demon's memory bank.

...

Samjaza had been trapped in his dungeon by Michael, eons ago. His fellow Fallen brothers, and other demons, could visit him; but he couldn't breach the threshold. It was the ultimate punishment for his leadership role in the births of the Nephilim.

However, he was still able to play mind games on humanity, at will. He enjoyed attacking humans, while they slept. He enjoyed stimulating their sinful and iniquitous nature. He enjoyed making the Creator sit on His throne, and watch.

Now somebody was playing a mind game on him. An excruciatingly painful one. His head felt like someone had all but scrambled his brain. He couldn't remember who, or why. He only had four brothers that were more powerful than he was.

Azazel, Gabriel, Raphael, and Michael. Azazel wouldn't attack him, because they were on one accord. He couldn't imagine Michael, Gabriel, or Raphael would be attacking him, either. If they were, why after all this time?

He tried to resist the attack, but couldn't. Something was terribly wrong. His temporal lobe was under attack. All of a sudden, he couldn't remember who, or what he was. He couldn't even remember where he was.

He forgot that he was a prisoner in this small confinement. He walked towards the entryway. The minute he got to the threshold something slammed him backward. He palmed his head and screamed, *"Who's doing this?"*

• • •

His scream echoed throughout the underworld. A few of the Fallen realized it was him, and came running. They were followed by lower level demons, and imps. They all hesitated at the entrance of the dungeon.

He was leaning over a stone bench, holding his head and mumbling. It appeared he was being tortured, but they didn't see anyone. They couldn't even sense anyone's presence.

"What's happening to him?" Pain asked.

"He looks like he's being attacked, by *you*," Apathy replied. Then he looked at Pain. "Are you doing this? If so, why?"

"Of course not." Pain was insulted by the notion. "Why would I hurt my brother?"

"Then who's doing it?" Lucifer asked from behind them. He couldn't see or sense a presence, either.

"THE LION!" Ariel shouted.

• • •

He appeared in front of them, at the entrance. His eyes were all ablaze, when he asked, "Do y'all want a piece of me, too? I have both the will and the authority to deal with you, and this Hellhole you call home."

They all moved away from the doorway. He was their untamed, and unchained brother. The one that the Creator uses to destroy worlds that He created. Hell may not be as nice as Heaven, but for the moment it was home.

Lucifer wasn't afraid. He knew why Ariel was attacking Samjaza. He knew all about Erica George. He'd sent Jealousy to kill her weeks ago. The damn demon had killed her father, instead.

That was not good, because her father's death released the Alter-Ego, Leizalak. He hadn't known that her father was an Alter-Ego! That was okay, because Ariel's mate was still human. She was still destroyable.

He stepped over the threshold. "I am not afra-"

Today was not the day to mess with Ariel. He was not a novice when it came to shutting his adversary's mouth. Before Lucifer could finish his statement, he clawed the hell out of his jaw. His claws went straight through the bone.

Lucifer screamed, and tried to get loose, but he couldn't. He extended his claws and reached for Ariel's face.

Ariel pushed his arms to the side. Then pierced his eyes with the claws of his other hand. This was right up his alley. It'd been a minute since he'd expressed himself.

Lucifer screamed, and grabbed his eyes.

Ariel didn't release Lucifer. He gripped his jawbone tighter, and glared at the others. "Anybody else want a piece of me?"

They all backed up even further.

"Why are you attacking Samjaza?" Apathy asked.

"I answer to neither angel, nor demon. Even if I

were compelled to explain, why would I? Especially to you, Apathy," Ariel retorted. "The bigger question is, why are you in my affairs? Why do you, of all demons, care?"

"I don't! I was just curious," Apathy replied. That was the truth. He cared for no one, and nothing.

"Humans have a saying," Ariel commented.

"What?"

Ariel's eyes perused the crowd. Then he glanced at Lucifer, and back to Apathy. He smirked, and said, "Curiosity *killed* the cat. Seeing that I am the lion, and you all are nothing more than pussies – cats that is – I suggest you all get out of my business!"

Apathy turned and walked away. He'd fought with Ariel during the Great War. He knew what Ariel could, and would, do to him.

Ariel retracted his claws, and pushed Lucifer through the doorway. "Take my advice and leave."

Lucifer was holding his jaw when he stumbled away. Ariel was their enemy, no doubt. But this was *not* their fight. He would get him back though. He just needed to rally his best warriors, first.

•••

Ariel chuckled, and turned his attention back to Samjaza. He grabbed a handful of his hair, and slung him backwards, up against the stone wall. "You worthless demon! You seriously thought you could get away with threatening my mate?" he asked. "I won't be as gentle with you as Jesus was."

Samjaza wanted to fight, but the pain was too great. Plus, his motor skills were paralyzed. He couldn't even stand up straight. His legs buckled, and he started to slide down the wall.

Ariel replaced his invisible claws, with his physical

ones. He pierced Samjaza's skull, just above his earlobes. Then he lifted him up to his eye level. He held him there, with his own mind.

He glared into the bastard's eyes, while he twirled his claws forward, and backward. Slicing his cerebrum to shreds as he went.

Samjaza tried to reach out with his mind, but that skill was gone too. All he could mumble was, "Who are you?"

Ariel laughed. It had been a minute since he'd dealt with one of his Fallen brothers. "It won't matter, if I told you. By the time I'm finished, you're going to be nothing more than a mindless vegetable," he promised.

Then he pulled back and twisted Samjaza's brain sideways. His frontal lobe was now where the temporal lobe was supposed to be. That pushed his motor speech right behind his ear.

Samjaza tried to grab Ariel's arms, but his own were leaded. He screamed, and then went totally silent. The sound of his scream was going inward, and vibrating against his insides. "What's happening to me?" he mumbled. His words were slurred. That didn't matter, because no one heard that, but him.

Ariel kept on lobotomizing Samjaza. He shifted his temporal lobe to where the cerebellum once was. That placed his sensory speech area at the back of his head, where the occipital was once located. That shift moved the occipital, and parietal lobes, out of joint.

Once he'd adjusted this fool's brain, he pulled his hands back, just a little. Then he viciously clapped! Just savagely smacked the crap out of that deviant's bleeding lobes.

The veins in Samjaza's head started to snap, from

being twisted and tangled up. Orange and black blood started seeping from his eyes, nose, and mouth. "Why are you doing this to me?" he moaned, but only he could hear it.

...

Araciel was sitting in his dungeon. He was more than a little amused. Who else would have thought to attack Samjaza's brain? As seamless as Michael was, he wouldn't have thought of this. Gabriel and Raphael either. But they all had limitations.

Ariel's ruthlessness knew, and had, no bounds. It was the axiom of his existence. He was called to handle that which God had turned his back on. Be it demon, human, or world.

When God turned *His* back, He no longer cared about what happened to you. He cared not about the manner you were removed from His sight. When God turned *His* back, Grace and Mercy did, too. When God turned *His* back, Ariel stood at it. With his eyes set on you.

He crossed his arms over his chest, and threw up a cone of silence. No one could hear him, but Ariel. *"That's enough, Lion. I think you have made your point."*

Ariel looked into Araciel's dungeon, and smiled. Just the sight of Araciel lightened his heart. He hadn't seen his brother in eons, and he missed him. All of the Heavenly host did.

From time to time God sent Michael with a message for Araciel to come home. A few times He'd even sent Gabriel and Raphael with the same message. They all came back home, without Araciel.

"I'll stop, if you allow me in your dungeon." He wasn't going to try to persuade Araciel to come home, that

wasn't his job. He just wanted to see his brother.

"You really need to see about your mate first. She is quite concerned about you, Lion," Araciel advised. *"You are welcome to visit me another time."*

Ariel took a look. Erica was stressed over what happened to her mother. She wanted him to be with her now.

"Fair enough, Araciel. I will leave as soon as I make sure Samjaza can't reach out and mess with Erica."

"I will handle that for you from here," Araciel promised. He knew what Samjaza had been doing to humans for years. He never got involved, because his involvement might make these demons aware that he was not a demon.

He appeared in front of Ariel. *"Go. He will not be able to touch her, or anyone else."*

"Thank you, brother," Ariel replied. He knew that Araciel could be just as vicious as he was. He also knew Araciel was a man of his convictions, that's why he was still in Hell. He gave him a one-armed hug. *"I'll be back to see you soon."*

They both vanished.

...

Once in his own dungeon, Araciel restored Samjaza's brain. He left the memory of what had happened to him, but not who had done it. Or why.

If Samjaza was allowed to remember who attacked him, he would remember why he was attacked. He would also remember his plans for Erica, and her family. It was to his benefit not to remember.

He bound Samjaza's spirit in the dungeon, for his own sake. Ariel lacked tolerance for his Fallen brothers. The next time Samjaza tried to attack, Ariel would finish

Samjaza off.

•••

Samjaza knew he had been attacked, but he didn't recall by whom. All he knew was that he'd felt that kind of pain only once before. That was when his son, Seraphiel, and all of his vicious personas had attacked him, eons ago.

He'd known all along that he'd given his son too much of himself. He had no idea how much too much was. That is until their confrontation.

That boy couldn't have been any more than seven years old, but he was fierce. To this day it amazed him that he was as old as time, but lost that battle. And not just lost! That boy had annihilated him. It still angered him that he'd gotten beaten senseless, by his *seven-year-old* son.

Only a few of his brothers knew that he'd been bested by his progeny. That boy's dark side had kicked their asses too. He was too ashamed to ask them if he'd been attacked by Seraphiel again.

He wiped his bloody nose. "I'll find a way to repay you. You ungrateful lil bastard!"

•••

Araciel and Ariel both laughed.

•••

CHAPTER 47

The family had moved back inside the house. They were all in the game room, waiting on Ariel's return. Erica was still visibly upset about what had happened to her family. Neither she nor anyone in the family knew about demons' ability to possess humans. "How was that demon able to embody Zander, Daddy?"

"I'd like to know that too," Remington added. They'd all seen the movie "The Exorcist", but thought it was just a movie.

"It's a scary thought that something can take over our minds," Ian stated.

"I know that Catholics practice exorcisms, but I never bought into demon possession," Perry stated. He was just as thrown off as his niece and nephews.

He was a son of the greatest spiritual leader of their time. Pastor Thomas Maulsby. Never once did Maulsby teach them about the validity of demon possession. He'd have to talk with him about that.

Eric, on the other hand, believed wholeheartedly in the possibility. Even when he was human, he believed there were powerful evil forces.

Unlike Perry, he'd studied every religion known to man. He even read the writings that the Canon rejected for the King James Version of the Bible.

Those writings were replete with witchcraft, and other supernatural practices. The Maccabees were the worst, or at least the more detailed.

He now knew that his knowledge had been peeking

from his subconscious, and spiked his interest. He remembered the Maccabees from his days of being hosted by his Watcher. He just didn't know that that was the root of his belief. In truth, it wasn't even belief. It was knowing, without a doubt, that evil existed beyond the movie screen.

"You have preached on the man in the graveyard, Perry. Remember what he said?"

"We are legion, because we are many."

"What else did they say?"

"Cast us into the swine."

"And Jesus did just that," Eric replied. "Swine was known to be the filthiest of animals. The Bible does not record it, but Jesus said, 'Okay. Filth get in that filth.'"

"He did?" Perry asked.

Eric laughed. "No, I added that last part."

They all laughed.

•••

Ariel appeared in the game room, next to Erica. It pleased him that she wasn't concerned about his wellbeing. Over the last week she'd remembered how powerful he was. She also remembered how untamed he was.

He hugged her, and promised, "Samjaza will not be bothering this family again."

Eric was just staring at Ariel. He had witnessed everything that Ariel had done. Not only that, but he was able to see inside Samjaza's skull. Ariel's hands had virtually turned to furry paws. His fingernail claws. He had never seen anything like that in his life.

He was a doctor, or at least he used to be. He'd been in on many brain surgeries, over the years. Never in his wildest dream could he have imagined that a brain could be twisted around. Why would he?

Two things he knew for sure. If Samjaza had been human, he'd be dead. If Ariel had been a doctor, he'd be sued.

He frowned. "You are warped, and fiendish as hell, man."

Ariel hunched his shoulders. "I thought you knew." That was what he was called to be. "You will learn soon enough that spiritual warfare is vicious, Eric. If you are going to fight demons, you have to fight them on their level."

"How do we do that?" Eric Jr. asked.

"We don't. If we are *tempted* by Lucifer, we can resist him with the power of our words; and he will leave us alone," Perry answered. "However, when we pray God dispatches His angels to fight demonic forces in our stead, Eric."

"His angels, and Alter-Egos," Eric added.

Ariel nodded. "That degenerate bastard I just contended with, is twisted. I thought I'd let him see what twisted really felt like."

"You did do that," Eric replied, and roared.

He also saw what Araciel had done. He wondered why an Archangel was living in Hell. That made no sense. Unless he was God's Watchman, in the bowels of Hell. He'd ask Ariel about it later.

"What did you do?" Erica asked.

Ariel didn't respond, at first. He didn't want Erica to know how twisted he was. He didn't want her to see, in his eyes, how much he'd enjoyed it.

He slowly shook his head, when Eric went to tell her. "I eliminated the threat," he told her.

Eric understood why Ariel was being so vague. He appreciated that. His son-in-law was borderline crazy. It made perfect sense that Erica was his mate. His daughter was sweet enough to tame the beast.

He changed the subject. "Hey, Libby said you guys are going back to New Orleans."

"Yeah. Erica wants to see her friends."

"Do you mind if we tag along. Libby and I haven't been there in years."

"Not at all," Ariel replied. "I'm sure Chamuel won't mind."

"Can we go too?" Ian asked.

"We've never been," Remington added.

Carson was nodding. In truth, none of them wanted their father to leave them behind. They'd almost lost him just a few weeks ago. They'd been clingy ever since.

"It could be my graduation trip," Eric suggested.

Eric and Libby frowned, and then slowly smiled. They both had forgotten all about the two-month trip they'd planned to take with their children. It was supposed to be Eric and Erica's graduation gifts.

"Do you mind if everyone comes?" Libby asked. "We'll do our own thing."

Erica wanted time with her friends, but she also wanted her family trip. She looked at Ariel. It was really up to him. "Is that okay with you?"

Ariel nodded. He actually liked the idea of hanging out with the family. He'd observed Chamuel and Jeremiel interact with their human families, for years. Periodically he'd visited both families, but they weren't his. He'd secretly envied them that relationship.

Not only that, but Michael was right. Erica was still very young. She'd eventually be diving into her college education. This time was what humans called vacation. Whatever she wanted to do was alright with him.

...

"Did I hear you just admit that I was right, Lion?" Michael asked. *"Did you gentlemen hear that?"*

"I heard it," Chamuel responded.

"I did too," Jeremiel added.

"Get out of my business, Michael!"

Michael roared. He was actually enjoying his banter with the Lion.

"Hey, Chamuel, you don't mind the entire family coming, do you?"

"Not at all. Plus, I am looking forward to meeting Eric, face to face."

Eric could hear the conversation going on. *"I am looking forward to it as well. Jeremiel, bring your father-in-law."* He looked at Ariel and laughed. *"I can't wait to meet Melvin Foster."*

Ariel chuckled.

"We'll be there, but keep in mind my family does not know about Alter-Egos yet," Jeremiel advised. *"There are a few in my area, but the family doesn't know about them."*

"They don't?"

"The Watchers can't know about the 'sanctioned' mates, so there is no way the two can meet yet."

"Okay. I understand." It was the same as his host couldn't know about Ariel. Everything hinged on Michael's relationship.

"I have a few Alter-Egos, in the region, that want to meet you, though. I'll advise them of the gathering."

"Really?"

"Absolutely."

"We'll make a party week of it," Chamuel added.

"May I come?" Michael asked.

"Are you bringing Verenda?" Ariel asked.

"We have an agreement, Ariel. Remember? When my mate is ready you will be the first one I advise."

"Yeah. It's cool."

"See you guys later today," Chamuel said.

•••

Ariel rubbed Erica's waist. This celebration would be a good distraction to keep him from crossing the line. "I have no problem with that at all, Ms. Erica George."

"How about we go to New Orleans for a week, and then on to Rome and Africa?" Libby asked.

"Yes!" her sons shouted.

Rome was Eric's choice, Africa was Erica's. She smiled, and nodded. "I need to repack."

"We all do," Libby replied.

"When are we leaving?" Eric asked.

"As soon as you guys get packed," his father responded.

"I'll help you pack," Ariel said, and kissed Erica's cheek.

"You most certainly will not. Her bedroom is still off limits, Ariel!" Eric reinforced. "You will wait in the game room with me while they pack."

The Archangels cracked up laughing in Ariel's and Eric's ears.

"You thought you'd catch him off guard, didn't you?" Jeremiel asked.

"It was worth a try," Ariel replied, and laughed.

"Trust me. Daddies don't play when it comes to their daughters. I think Eric and Melvin Foster together are going to make this gathering interesting."

"I think they will, too," Chamuel agreed.

•••

CHAPTER 48

Eric led Ariel to the game room. Once inside, he closed the door. He didn't even wait for Ariel to take a seat, or offer him one. He needed to get an understanding with this Archangel.

"Listen, man," he started. "I respect the hell out of you. I couldn't have asked for a better husband for my daughter. I know that as long as she has you, she'll be safe."

Ariel grinned, and said, "But?"

"I didn't change, once I dropped the clay. I am still a protective father. I still have rules that all my children have to abide by."

"As long as they are in your house."

"Location has nothing to do with it. True, I have rules for my house, but that is not what I'm talking about. At least not at this moment. But, since you bring it up we can go there."

He pointed to a chair for Ariel to sit. Once they were both seated, he continued. "I have five children, man. Two of them younger than Erica, two older. The older three are legally grown, but they still eat at *my* table. The roof over their heads, belongs to me. They say 'their' bedrooms, but trust me, I own all five of them. Their clothes, shoes, cars, gas allowance; all paid for out of my pocket."

"You guys listening to this?" Michael asked.

"Yep!" they all answered, and cracked up.

Ariel heard Michael calling out to all of their

brothers. They were all laughing. He chuckled himself. *"I never realized how nosey Archangels were. You boys ain't got nothing else to do? Like mind your own business!"*

"Nope!" Chamuel replied.

They all cracked up.

•••

Eric crossed his legs, and stared at Ariel. He knew the Archangels were listening. Good! He kept talking. "All of them are still single, but dating. Just because Erica is mated to you doesn't mean the rules are going to be lax. I meant it when I said it. I mean it now. My children cannot have company, in their bedrooms."

Ariel laughed. "Man, I was just kidding about helping Erica pack for the trip. Trust me, I will not disrespect you, Libby, or Erica. Not only can I not cross the threshold, thanks to Michael, I wouldn't anyway."

"I really don't care what Michael said, one way or the other. This is between you and me. Just so long as you and I understand each other. That's all that matters. Did y'all hear that? Michael!" he prodded.

Ariel, and all the Archangels, cracked up laughing. Even Michael. They all liked Eric. He was just as untamed as Ariel. Or maybe it was that he was the man of his house.

"I heard that," Michael replied out loud.

•••

"So if that is not what you planned to talk about, what was on your mind?" Ariel asked.

"The trip."

"Listen. Let me stop you right there," Ariel stated. "I'll give you your props, in *your* house. However, do not think for a minute I am going to take orders from you, while in New Orleans."

Eric went to interrupt him, but couldn't.

"Erica is my mate. I plan to wine, and dine her, without a chaperone."

"I have no problem with you wining and dining my daughter. It is when the night is over that I'm concerned about."

"Why? You and Libby did a lot of 'when the night is over', before you married."

Eric had to laugh, himself. They damn sure did. They stayed in the dorms at college then eventually moved into a co-ed apartment building.

The girls' rooms were on the second floor, and the boys on the first. They had a den mother, and father. Those two people were digging each other, and didn't really pay attention to their wards.

His dorm room mate was into Libby's roommate. He snuck up those stairs, every single night. Libby's roommate snuck down to his room.

They didn't consummate their union, until they got married. By that time, he knew everything he needed to know about Liberty Belle.

He kept laughing. "If her father had known what was going on, *Eric* would have died over twenty-five years ago."

They both laughed.

"All I'm saying is Erica is still *my* daughter. As long as she carries the surname George, she represents her upbringing."

"Your point?"

"Do not go to these people's house and cause my daughter to embarrass me. Or my name. There are children in that hotel. My sons will be there."

"Again, your point."

"Get your own bedroom, Ariel. Do not shack up with my daughter in her mother's, and my face. I will not tolerate that blatant disrespect, under anybody's roof."

Ariel heard his brothers laughing, and making fun. They always underestimated him. While they were listening to what Eric was saying, he was listening to what wasn't said.

"That's cool, man. I'll give you your props. I won't cross the threshold of her bedroom in New Orleans either."

Eric knew his future son-in-law. He saw it in his eyes. That Archangel was scheming. "And she will not cross the threshold of yours," he added.

"That never even crossed my mind," Ariel replied. Then he cracked up laughing.

His brothers, and now Eric, were always trying to tame him. Didn't they know it was virtually impossible to completely tame a lion? That's why those captured by zoo keepers were kept imprisoned, behind caged bars. That's why he himself hardly ever left the balcony.

He'd come out to help Chamuel in New Orleans. Then again, to help Jeremiel in Houston. He'd even visited their homes, now and again. But for the most part, he stayed in Heaven. Waiting for his next assignment.

However, he had to admit that there was one person who would hold the reins. The addictive Ms. Erica George.

...

He'd had enough of this conversation. He looked around, and took stock of the room. He hadn't been in this room before, but he liked it. It wasn't as pristine as the other rooms. It looked like a place where one could just relax, and hang out.

There were several table games, a large television, and exercise equipment in the room. It had one overstuffed sofa, loveseat, and windows galore. The ambiance was warm, cozy, and lived in.

The walls were covered with clearly varnished sycamore wood paneling. Even the floors were sycamore. To the ordinary observer it would appear that Eric was obsessed with the sycamore tree, and he was. He understood Eric's love for that tree, more than Eric himself did. It went far deeper than an obsession.

Eric was listening to his thoughts. "How so?"

Ariel looked at him and smirked. "You might not want to make a habit of reading my mind. You might get a glimpse of something you don't want to see, hear, *or* know."

Eric laughed. Ariel was probably right. "Just answer my question, man."

"The sycamore is similar to you, in several senses. It exemplifies what happens to all Alter-Egos. The bark of the sycamore is not pliable; therefore, it cannot stretch with the growth of the tree. Your clay body couldn't be stretched beyond its own limitation, either. The sycamore sloughs off its old skin. You gave up the clay."

Eric took a seat across from Ariel. "That makes sense." His clay body was not able to do the things his glorified body could. Neither could it take the hectic fighting. During their scrimmages, Ariel, and Raphael took no mercy on him. Neither did Kal.

"Just as you can now split yourself, the base of the sycamore splits itself into several different trunks," Ariel added.

Eric nodded. Those splits had helped him climb to the top when he was a kid. They'd saved him from the bullies.

"Somewhere in your mind, you knew you were different. Your refusal to look in a mirror attested to that. Because the face that kept looking back at you was not Eric, but *Leizalak*. The girly boy had been trying to send you a message."

"Oh man! It really was this face I'd see, every time I looked in the mirror. I couldn't figure out why this mug kept reflecting back at me."

"I know," Ariel replied. "I don't think that has ever happened to any other Alter-Ego. You are, by far, the most powerful Alter-Ego I have ever encountered."

"I doubt that," Eric disagreed. He didn't imagine that to be in the least bit true. He had been scrimmaging with Leibada for weeks now. That Alter-Ego was a force. She drove him and drove him.

Every time he wanted to rest she told him it was all in his mind. She said, "Only the clay body had limitations."

And she was right. But still, he knew she was more powerful than he was.

"It's a fact, Eric. All of the heavenly host bears witness to that truth."

Eric grunted.

...

CHAPTER 49

"May I join you gentlemen?" Raphael asked.
Eric smiled. *"Certainly."*
Raphael appeared in the room.

...

"Ariel is right. You are the most powerful Alter-Ego."

"How is that possible?"

"It just is," Raphael advised.

He took a seat in the armchair next to Ariel. He stared at Leizalak for a moment. He'd seen how this Alter-Ego had tossed Zander in the ocean. The tossing had been no big deal. It was the distance in which he'd tossed Zander that was unheard of. No other Alter-Ego had this one's reach. "We need to discuss your leadership role, Leizalak."

"Leadership? What? I'm new in the game, man," Eric replied. That didn't seem quite fair. He knew there were thousands already out there. They'd been warring hard for the cause, while he was still in the clay.

"That has no bearing. You will be in charge of all Alter-Egos."

"What? What about Leibada?" Eric asked.

"Leibada is over the northern region."

"Region?"

"The Alter-Egos are sectioned off, all over the world. Leibada is over the northern part of the US. She has a team that works under her."

Ariel laughed. "Leibada is neither male, nor

female."

"What?" Eric asked. "Neither male nor female?"

"Leibada has no physical body."

"Oh. That's right." He remembered that he was the only one that chose to stay with his family. The ones he'd met were quite upset about that. None of them had realized they had that choice.

Raphael replied to his thoughts. "They didn't."

"Why?"

"It was not the will of God."

"Am I going against His will?"

Raphael shook his head. "You are doing exactly what God has permitted you to do."

"How is that possible?"

"You are able to remember beyond the clay, Eric. Examine your past, you will be able to recall the decision."

...

Eric did just that, and was astonished. There were thousands of souls at the meeting. They were all standing at the foot of the Throne.

He heard God ask the question, *"Whom shall I send, and who will go for us?"*

God asked the question, but He didn't tell the mission. It didn't matter, because if the LORD wanted somebody, he was willing. He heard himself reply, *"Here am I, LORD. Send me. I'll go."* His soul was immediately bathed in the light of God's glory.

One after another soul started to respond just as he had, but the light did not encompass them. In the end, they'd all agreed to stand up and be counted.

God nodded, and said, "You shall all be Raphael's army. He shall lead you."

The next scene showed all those souls seated in a

meeting. He was able to see the faces of all of his team members. Including his sons', Perry's, and Liberty's.

Raphael was standing at the head of the table. He was marshalling orders to his newly formed brigade. The first order of business was that he – Leizalak – would be the Ultimate Alter-Ego. He would report to Raphael, and all the other Alter-Egos would report to him.

"Why me?" he asked.

"You did not hesitate to accept the charge. For that blind willingness, God has given you a greater measure of strength," Raphael replied.

"Why are we needed?" he asked.

Raphael informed them of the reason for their creation. Who their enemies would be, when they would be born, and who their host Watcher would be.

It shocked him so much, he jumped out of his memories. He looked at Ariel, then Raphael. "God knew about the fall, before the fall?"

Raphael laughed. "Be specific. Which fall are you talking about?"

Eric squinted. "There was more than *one?*"

"Look again," Ariel advised.

He went backward in his memories again. Only this time the Alter-Egos weren't sitting at the table. They were witnessing Lucifer, and his followers, huddled together. They were scheming about overthrowing the Kingdom. Lucifer wanted to take Michael down first, and then his *ancient* Father. God!

He mumbled out loud, "Lord, have mercy Jesus."

The next thing he saw was Lucifer, and his followers, caught up in the angry whirlwinds of God. They flew across the sky, like lightning. He could even hear the crackling. He could hear their shouts of rage. He could see the defiance on their faces.

He saw the light of God's glory being ripped from them. It looked like they were being destroyed - from the inside out. He knew it was their souls being freed. The sacred breath of God could not dwell in those powerful unclean temples.

He closed his eyes, but it didn't help. Eyes open or closed had no bearing on an Alter-Ego's ability to see. At least it didn't without their host Watcher. He was seeing this through the lens of Leizalak's memory, not Eric's.

Then he saw the faithful Archangels battling against them in the sky. That army was led by Michael. Raphael had one of his Fallen brothers, the Seer, by the throat. He planned to kill that traitor.

He heard Michael shout for Raphael not to go too far. Raphael immediately stopped his attack. He grasped that even though Raphael was the Alter-Ego's leader, he answered to Michael. That also meant the Alter-Ego's answered to Michael as well.

Ariel was fighting like a wild beast, as he tackled one Fallen, after another. He was just as untamed, in that battle, as he is now. If not more so. His claws had invaded Apathy's chest. It looked like he was syphoning out what residual light was left. Michael was not trying to control Ariel. He wondered why.

He noticed that some of the Fallen were trying to find a way back into Heaven. The Alter-Egos were standing in front of the twelve gates. They were shielding their view from those deviants. It was their first battle, although non-combative.

He jumped out of his memories, again. He'd meant the fall in the garden, but wow. He could not believe that he'd been there for the original fall.

He looked at Ariel, and then Raphael. "Both."

Raphael nodded. "First of all, Michael is the General in God's army, and all angels answer to him. Secondly, Father knows our thoughts, before we do. He knows which ones we will resist, and the ones we will embrace."

"Why didn't He forewarn the Fallen what would happen?"

"He also allowed His called into existence sons free will, Eric. They had the right to choose to defy Him, just as Adam and Eve did," Ariel injected.

Eric nodded. "I understand free will. I practiced it with my children. I told them that it was within their right to disobey me, and their mother. But, I always stipulated that there would be consequences to their disobedience. Mainly, me practicing my free will to beat their asses!"

Raphael and Ariel howled. It amazed them that as professional as Eric had been in life, he had a foul mouth. His tongue didn't concern itself with the company he kept. Be it in the company of the president of the free world, doctors, lawyers or his family; he always expressed himself.

Eric laughed too. He'd learned how to cuss from his earthly father. His ole man said people understood expressive language. "I still don't understand why He chose *me*."

"Search your memories again, Eric," Ariel suggested.

•••

Eric went back in. As soon as that light encompassed him, he and God had a one-on-one conversation.

God showed him what the future held for him.

When he saw Liberty and his sons he smiled. He also saw his other children, but they were not conceived through Liberty's womb. When he saw Erica, he was disturbed. Not about her birth, but her foes. She had many!

He'd asked, *"May I stay with my family, Father? They will need me."*

God replied, *"If they will have you, so be it."*

He jumped out of the vision. He didn't mention what he'd seen. He was sure that Raphael and Ariel already knew.

However, he surmised that Libby had the option to reject him. His children too. He was grateful that they loved him beyond the clay. He certainly loved them beyond it.

He looked back at Raphael, and asked, "Who is over the southern region?"

"I will introduce you to all of the leaders later," Raphael promised.

"Okay." Then he frowned. "It still doesn't seem fair, man. Leibada is the first Alter-Ego."

"What does birth order have to do with anything? David was Jesse's youngest son, was he not?" Raphael asked.

Eric nodded.

"Yet, he was chosen to be the king," Raphael continued.

Eric nodded again. Humanity had overlooked David, because he was so young. He mumbled, "God's ways are not man's ways."

Raphael nodded. "You saw for yourself that the foundation was laid, in the ages. God decided, at that time, that you would head up the Alter-Egos."

"Your teams, all over the world, have been waiting

on your arrival," Ariel added.

"They knew about me?"

"Yes. Didn't you see them sitting at the table?" Ariel replied.

Eric nodded.

"We will discuss your role in greater detail later," Raphael informed him.

"Alright," Eric replied. He still had concerns, though. It was human nature to resent the new guy. They often balked about the new person coming in, and taking over. In some instances, they acted up; and ended up losing their jobs.

Growing up, he saw how his own father struggled with that. The man had been overlooked time and time again, even though he was more qualified. His father said it was because of his ethnicity.

He himself hadn't given two shits about America trying to hold the black man down. He was never going to be *anybody's* ox. He'd had no intentions of being an employee, but rather the employer.

He staked his claim, and charted his course at a young age. That's why he studied so hard, on multiple degrees. Medical, legal and finance.

If one career failed he had a plan B, and C. He hadn't set out to be ordinary in either of those fields. He'd aspired to be the best in all of them, and he was. Evidently he was the best at being an Alter-Ego too.

He quietly wondered if any of the Alter-Egos would object to him coming in at the head. It wouldn't matter, in the long run. He'd run from bullies when he was a child, true enough. Once he grew up, he put that mindset in check. The bullies too, for that matter.

He hadn't backed down from anybody in years, not

even when he pretended to be a nerd. He certainly wouldn't back down now.

"Stop thinking like you are still human, Eric. Neither you, nor any of the other Alter-Egos are human. Not anymore. You have worked hard on your physical change. You need to work on renewing your mind, man," Ariel reprimanded.

"Your former self has passed away. You are a new creation," Raphael added. "There will be no conflict. Trust me."

Eric nodded.

...

CHAPTER 50

Ariel and Erica finally made it back to New Orleans. When they arrived at The Haven, Anita Foster and Jeremiel were there. The reunion was just as emotional as it had been with her and Kay.

"You're beautiful," Erica told Anita.

"So are you," Anita responded.

"I can't believe we are all back together," Kay injected.

"Me either," Erica said. She hugged Kay again. "I'm glad we are. I missed you guys so much. I just didn't know I did."

They all laughed.

"I remember the day we left Heaven. We were so scared, and crying," Anita reminded Erica.

"Hey, wait a minute," Erica cut in. "We have the same birthday, don't we?"

Anita nodded, and giggled. "Happy late birthday, girl!"

"Happy late birthday to you too," Erica replied.

"There were five of us that left that day, remember?" Anita reminded her.

Erica nodded her head. She also remembered Michael's mate. Ariel had advised her not to mention Veranda, today. Jeremiel had advised Anita of the same thing.

Kay remembered everybody but *her.* They didn't know how she didn't remember Verenda, because she was the first. They were sure Michael had blocked her view of their seventh cohort. They just didn't know *why*.

What was even more confusing was why Verenda didn't remember them, or Michael.

"Brandi, Wanda and Charlotte, right?"

Anita nodded. "I can't wait to see them again, too."

Kay knew about the other three. Their mates were with them, this very minute. Like all three of them, they'd had to be rescued. Chamuel had been with them a few days ago.

She didn't understand why Michael let everything get down to the wire. Just like it had with Anita and Erica. Chamuel told her that Michael couldn't do anything, until God gave him permission. She accepted that, but she didn't understand.

If Chamuel had been a day late, that demon would have gotten her. But, she'd learned over the years that, no matter how hard you tried, you can't hurry God.

"How long are you guys staying?"

"A week."

"We'll have to have a late birthday party for you guys. Let's go into the lounge and discuss it," Kay suggested.

They did a three-way hug, and all of their eyes teared again. Then the three of them walked away, arm in arm. They'd totally forgotten that their families were standing around.

...

They spent more than an hour in the lounge. For the first time in their lives, they were with others who understood. Erica was quizzing Kay and Anita.

"What has it been like being with Chamuel and Jeremiel?"

"I was ostracized by the entire Parish, because of my

mother," Kay told them. "Then on my eighteenth birthday a demon showed up to claim me as his property."

"What!" Erica and Anita asked.

Kay nodded. "Chamuel showed up just in the nick of time. He did battle with that demon and his followers, in St Louis Cemetery. It was the night of my mother's funeral."

"I didn't know that, Kay," Anita stated. She'd gotten reacquainted with Kay weeks ago, but they hadn't talked about their experiences.

Kay nodded. "He had to fight that demon twice, because the demon wouldn't give up. Jeremiel and Ariel were there for the second battle."

"Really?"

Kay nodded again. "He made sure that demon was no longer a threat to me. He saved me, and he has been here with me ever since."

"Why was the demon after you?" Erica asked. She had people after her, but not demons. She wasn't sure she could handle that.

"My mother unwittingly sold me to him."

"Oh my God!" Erica replied.

Kay actually laughed. "She was a witch herself. So it wasn't really out of character."

Erica just kept shaking her head. Then she looked at Anita. "Did you have demons after you too?"

"No. My great aunt, and my schoolmates."

"What happened?"

"My great aunt, and my schoolmates, didn't like me because I'm black."

Erica frowned. She'd never experienced woes of racism. That was because of her family's wealth. She, and her brothers, had gone to the best private schools.

They hung out at the country club. Shopped at the best stores.

There wasn't anywhere, in California, that her family wasn't welcomed. They'd never once had to make a reservation. Fine restaurant owners kept their family's table on reserve. Just in case Eric George, or his family, decided to grace them with their presence.

White people, all over America, loved her father; because of his vast array of knowledge. Even so...

"Black? Your aunt's not black?"

Anita laughed. "I am too dark skinned."

"What?" Erica asked.

"My aunt is half white, but she looks all white. She couldn't stand me, or my father."

"And your schoolmates?"

"They picked on me all of the time, even the dark ones. Then Jeremiel showed up as a fourteen-year-old boy."

"Fourteen?" Erica asked.

Anita laughed. "He was so cute as a kid. We didn't know he was an angel, though. He told us his name was Jeremy. Sammael pretended to be his father."

"Death!"

Anita nodded. "Jeremiel even started going to school with me. He gave one of my classmate's the devil, for picking on me."

She told them how Jeremiel had bounced Leslie on his legs. They were all laughing at that. She stopped laughing, and said, "Leslie tried to do a drive-by on me, and my family."

Erica had heard of a drive by, but she'd never experienced it personally. Only in the movies. "A real life drive by?"

Anita nodded. It didn't surprise her that Erica seemed appalled. Erica looked, and dressed, like she had no idea what went on in the hood. Thankfully, she didn't act snooty. "That's when we all found out that Jeremiel's name wasn't Jeremy, and he wasn't human. He, Ariel, Chamuel, and all the others showed up, including Michael."

"Wow. Did your aunt still treat you bad?"

"Jeremy got her straight too. Now we are as close as ever. She lives with me and my parents, in Galveston. You gotta come visit."

"I will. So you're happy being with Jeremiel?"

"It has been wonderful being with him," Anita replied. Then she burst out laughing. "Not so much for my father though."

Erica laughed. "Girl, my father is tripping out. Setting all kinds of rules. My momma too! Even Michael put his two cents in. They've all barred Ariel from coming in my room. Thank goodness Ariel thinks outside the box."

They all cracked up.

"We saw Ariel thinking outside the box, when he went after your old boyfriend," Kay voiced, and laughed.

Erica stopped laughing. "What?"

"Uh-oh," Anita said and laughed. "We thought you knew."

"Knew what?"

"Ariel went to Jacques' house. That Lion wasn't nothing nice. He had them running and screaming for their lives," Kay told her. Then she cracked up. "It didn't help that Jacques' father was a schoolmate of mine. He left New Orleans, on foot, the night Chamuel fought with those demons."

"Mr. Beaux?"

Kay was laughing so hard, she was choking. "Chamuel scared the crap out of Beaux," Kay said between her howls. "Beaux ran off and left his pregnant girlfriend, Dorothy. Wait a minute!" Something had just dawned on her. "She was pregnant with *Jacques!*"

Erica had stopped laughing. She didn't like Jacques anymore, but she didn't want him hurt. She remembered that Ariel had kept asking her about Jacques, but she forgot that Samjaza had mentioned the incident. "Did Ariel kill Jacques?"

Kay stopped laughing. Chamuel had told her the sordid story. She actually felt sorry for Jacques, and his parents. "No. In fact, Chamuel went to visit him and his parents. Jacques was sick, Erica. That's why he wanted to die."

"I knew something had happened. He changed too quickly. I thought he was the one who killed my father, but Ariel assured me it wasn't him."

Anita frowned. "Wasn't that your father, that came with you?"

Kay frowned too. "Chamuel told me that your parents, and brothers, were coming. Your father died? Who brought him back?"

"Daddy died saving me and Momma, from a hit and run," Erica replied. Then she smiled. "That's when we found out that my father wasn't human, after all."

"What was he?"

"They call themselves Alter-Egos."

"What is that?" Anita asked.

"You guys know about Watchers, right?"

"Yes. My three cousins are 'spirit' mates. They met their Watchers a few weeks ago."

"Well you know that the Watchers live with demons in them, until they meet their 'spirit' mates, right?"

Anita and Kay nodded.

"Well some of the Watchers don't have demons. They have what is called an Alter-Ego. They are good guys."

"Get out!" Anita replied.

"Shut up!" Kay added. "I'm going to kill Chamuel! I've been with him eighteen years. He has never told me about them."

"Jeremiel never told me either," Anita added.

Erica laughed. "Well, that's what my father is. He's one of the good guys!"

"I can't wait to meet him," Anita stated.

"Oh Lord. We were so rude. We were so glad to see each other, I didn't introduce you to my family," Erica said.

"Or mine," Anita added.

"Let's go back out there. We'll talk more when we go out."

They all headed toward the door. "Oh wait," Erica stopped them.

They paused.

"Watchers can't know about my father."

"They can't know about our Archangels either," Kay reminded them.

"Your cousins don't know, Anita?"

She shook her head. "My cousins do, but their mates don't. Jeremiel shields his essence from them. They just think he is a big human."

They all cracked up, and walked out the room.

...

CHAPTER 51

Ariel, Jeremiel and Chamuel had stood off to the side, and let their mates have their moment. They'd assumed once they settled down they'd introduce their families. Now it was obvious that was not going to happen. Those women just walked away.

"While the ladies are getting reacquainted, let me introduce Erica's family," Ariel proposed. "These are her parents, Eric and Libby George. Her brothers, Eric Jr, Remington, Ian and Carson. Her uncle, Pastor Perry Busby."

"How rude of us. Good to meet you all," Chamuel replied. Then he extended his hand to Eric. "I'm Chamuel, Kay's mate."

"Good to meet you, face to face," Eric replied. Then he laughed. *"With your nosey butt."*

Chamuel laughed in his head. *"I couldn't help myself. I love witnessing Ariel being challenged."*

Jeremiel followed suit. "I'm Jeremiel, Anita's mate. These are her parents, Melvin and Sandra Foster."

They all greeted each other, and shook hands. Eric slapped Melvin five. "You and me," he said, and laughed. "We gon' talk."

"Daddy business?"

"What the hell else?"

"I feel ya, man," Melvin replied. "You get an understanding yet?"

Eric grunted. "Right out the damned gate. How about you?"

"Jeremiel and I understand each other." Then he looked under eyed at Jeremiel and said, "Don't we, Billy Boy?"

Jeremiel smirked.

Eric roared, and slapped Melvin five again. He was digging this brother. No doubt they were going to be friends. Then they took turns volleying their tangents.

"This dude thought he was going to just move in my daughter's room with her," Eric vented.

Melvin scowled. "In your house, man?"

"Right across the hall from my bedroom."

"I know you nipped that shit!"

"First Libby, and Perry, did. Then when I got back home, I squashed that crap."

Melvin looked at Jeremiel, and smirked. "This dude talkin' bout my baby his 'sanctioned' mate. I told him not yet she ain't!"

Sandra looked at Libby, and laughed. "I'm really glad to meet you. We can be each other's support group."

"Between our husbands, these Archangels, and daughters, we're going to need it," Libby agreed. "Is your daughter eighteen?"

"She is now. But when Jeremiel first arrived Anita was only fourteen."

Libby and Eric were shocked. Their children weren't even allowed to date at that age. "Fourteen?" Eric asked. "I'd be damned if that shit would've happened."

Melvin slapped him five. "I put my foot down on that dude's *'she's my mate'* notion!"

Sandra laughed. "Melvin almost gave *himself* brain damage."

Melvin rubbed his head. "That ain't no lie. I almost became a stay at home father, too."

Everybody in the lobby roared.

"Melvin went straight off on Jeremiel, and the other Archangels. He put his foot down, in the middle of the street, girl. I was so embarrassed," Sandra said.

"Eric didn't pull any punches, himself. My husband has a very colorful way of expressing himself."

Everybody laughed again, even Ariel. Eric reminded the Archangels of Peter. That boy could cuss, too. Even so, Peter was the Son's sidekick. Jesus loved that foul mouthed disciple.

He kept telling Peter that what came from his mouth came from his heart. A few times He'd had to tell Peter to mind his own business.

Peter still kept right on cussing. Nevertheless, even though his mouth was colorful, he loved himself some Jesus, too.

...

Ariel dropped the bomb. "The difference in Melvin and Eric is, Melvin's eyes are limited. So, Jeremiel can get away from his nosey view. Eric, on the other hand, has all seeing eyes. I have to be creative. It's a good thing that I think *outside* the box."

His brothers cracked up laughing. Eric did too. Then he said, "I got all of my eyes on you, boy!"

Melvin looked at all of the Archangels. They were all smiling. He looked at Eric. That dude was cheesing, from ear-to-ear. "What does that mean, man?"

He felt someone tap him on his right shoulder, and turned. He jumped, and whipped his head back around! "What the hell!"

Sandra almost screamed. She was seeing two of Eric. She shouted, "What!"

Eric kept cheesing, as half a dozen more of him

joined the crowd. One standing next to his wife, Perry, and each of his sons.

Libby hit him. "Stop it."

His sons cracked up.

Ariel chuckled. "He's just showing out, now."

"What are you, man?" Melvin asked.

"Up until a few weeks ago I was human."

"What the hell happened?"

"One of my daughter's enemies killed me."

"What?"

Eric explained, to Melvin and Sandra, what had happened to him. "He was trying to run my baby down with his car, as she and Libby crossed the street. I pushed them to safety, but I got trapped on the bumper. I died on impact. He dragged my body for a block."

"You didn't really die from the impact, Eric," Ariel told him.

All of the Archangels shook their heads. "Your spirit was so enraged it jumped out of the clay, on its own," Chamuel added.

"I didn't realize that," Eric replied. "No *wonder* I didn't feel the impact."

"That's why Michael was there. If he had not been there you would have created a scene, in the middle of the street," Jeremiel informed him.

"You would have been fighting, with the strength you have now. All the while your body would've been laying on the ground," Ariel said, and cracked up. "You would've scared not only Erica's attacker, but your family too."

"I know it messed with my head, when I saw his spirit and Michael standing there," Perry injected.

"You saw his spirit?" Chamuel asked, then squinted.

He looked at Ariel. *"Both of them are Alter-Egos."*

Ariel slightly nodded. *"The entire family is, except Erica, and Eric Jr."*

...

Melvin had a flashback. Leslie was in a fast moving car too. He was fortunate that he had good aim, because he'd had no plan to duck, or dodge. "Maaan. But how did you end up still here?"

Eric smiled. There was no reason for them not to know the entire story. Before he started, he made it clear that the Watchers could not know about his kind.

"You're a ghost?" Sandra asked.

Eric shook his head.

"An angel?" she asked. "I didn't know that humans become angels when they die."

"They don't," Eric replied. "I am, what is unknown to humanity and Watchers, as an Alter-Ego."

"What the hell is that?" Melvin asked.

Eric allowed Melvin, Sandra, *and* his family to see how he came about. Not the intimate part of it, but just his being released from Kal's body. He allowed them to see his spirit enter the deceased baby Eric's body.

Perry's heart enthusiastically quickened. His three nephews' hearts did too. They couldn't put their fingers on it, but there was something familiar about that scene. They shrugged it off. "Oh man!" Perry voiced.

Libby looked under eyed at Eric. He'd allowed her to see what the others didn't. She whispered to his mind, *"We all died, at birth?"*

"Yes, Liberty."

"How could my parents have two stillborn babies, back to back? What happened?" She and Perry were only a year apart. Three hundred-sixty-five days, to be exact.

"They lived in the backwoods country. You were delivered by a midwife, instead of in a hospital. The cord was wrapped around yours and Perry's necks."

"What about Annette?"

"By the time she came along, your parents had moved to the city. They were able to get hospital care."

She sighed. She'd quietly bemoaned the day of her death. The day that she would be in Paradise, and Eric would still be roaming the earth.

She was more than relieved to see, through his eyes, that her children would still be around too. Even though Eric Jr was not an Alter-Ego, neither he nor Erica would age, or die.

She wanted to blurt it out, but her sons were too young to know their fate. Like a moth to the flame, Perry would run towards his demise to be like Eric. She played it off by hugging him. "You are mine, for all times."

He laughed in her ear. *"At least until the Son returns. But, I'm never going to let you die, Liberty, or age. I couldn't handle it."*

She was fine with that. *"Okay."*

•••

Everyone was watching them. The Archangels knew Eric had shown Liberty hers, and the family's fate. With him being over all the Alter-Egos it was okay. His judgment call was good. That was evident by his not revealing the information to Perry, or the boys. He knew his family better than anyone. He knew who could, and couldn't handle the truth. They all nodded.

Sandra and Melvin were feeling some kind of way. After all of these years, they wished there had been an Alter-Ego available for the baby they lost.

Melvin was the first to speak. "That was awesome.

Look here. Can you keep an eye on Billy Boy, and Anita?"

Eric shook his head. "I'll have my hands full with keeping up with the Lion."

"Don't waste your time, man," Ariel warned.

Everybody cracked up.

...

CHAPTER 52

Viola walked out in the lobby. She and the other women had been in the kitchen preparing a brunch for Kay's guests. It did her heart good that Kay finally had female friends, besides the ones that lived at the Haven. She couldn't wait for Verenda to be added in that number.

"Hello," she greeted.

Everyone turned around. "Hey, Viola," Ariel spoke. Then he introduced her to the family.

Jeremiel did the same.

"Brunch is ready, if you all are ready to eat," she informed them. Then she looked around. "Where is Kay?"

"Right here," Kay replied from behind her.

When they reached her, Kay introduced Anita and Erica to her.

"You ladies are beautiful," Viola said, and hugged them.

Before Erica and Anita could reply they noticed some of the young residents coming down the stairs. Erica's chin dropped, and she looked at Eric.

Chamuel smiled at the young ladies. "Where are you young ladies going?"

"To the game room," one of the girls replied. But she wasn't looking at Chamuel. She was all eyes, and smiles, for Eric Jr.

Eric Jr frowned. She used to go to the same college he did. They'd even started dating. Then one day she went missing, without a trace. He'd always thought she was *cute,* and wondered what had happened to her.

There was no shame to his game. His voice was deep, and questioning when he spoke. "You live here, Jean?"

"Hi, Eric." She'd had a crush on him, for two years. Just as they started dating, her father went crazy. He'd dead bolted the doors, and then set the house on fire. She and her mother were trapped inside. He was outside screaming, *"Burn, baby, burn!"*

The Archangel Michael appeared in the burning house. He whisked them away, and they landed here. Across the country.

Not seeing Eric anymore, was the worst part of her leaving school. She'd really liked him, and had never stopped thinking about what could have been.

She boldly walked over and hugged him. "My mother and I moved here last year, after my father tried to kill us. I missed you, though."

Eric was somewhat angry when he hugged her. Not at her, but at her father. "Why was your father trying to kill you?"

She pulled back from him and gazed in his eyes. She'd already been told that she'd mother 'spirit' mates. Now she knew who her babies' daddy was. "It's a long story," she replied, and took his hand. "Let's talk." They walked away from the crowd.

The other girls invited Remington, Ian and Carson to go with them to the game room. They readily agreed. The adults watched as they all walked away.

"I'll be damned," Eric stated. Not only was that Eric Jr's mate, but those three ladies were Alter-Egos.

Ariel cracked up. *"All those eyes, and you couldn't see that?"*

"Give me a break. Thanks to your antics, my eyes have all been on you!" Eric replied.

"Peek a boo!" Ariel taunted, and burst out laughing.

The Archangels cracked up laughing.

...

"Brunch was wonderful, Kay," Liberty complimented. "It's been years since Eric and I have had real Cajun food."

"Viola is the best cook ever," Kay praised.

"So what's the deal with Jean? How did she end up living here?" Erica asked.

"We shelter women, and children, that are future mates," Kay replied.

Erica did not know that. "Really?"

"We do too," Anita injected. "There are a lot of future mates that are in danger, from their parents."

"You're kidding, right?" Libby asked.

"No, she's not," Melvin answered. "The day we opened our shelter they came running, by droves. Their fathers, dead on their asses."

"How did you stop them?" Erica asked.

"They can't cross the threshold, because our shelters are hallowed," Chamuel answered.

"How do you keep them safe, when they leave the property?" Liberty asked.

"During the day Alter-Egos watch out for them. At night Watchers look out for them. The Watchers don't know why they are looking out for them, because they can't know about 'spirit' mates."

"I can't believe Michael hasn't talked to you guys yet," Jeremiel stated.

"About what?" Erica asked.

"All 'sanctioned' mates are charged with keeping

the young mates, or parents of the mates safe."

"'Sanctioned' and 'spirit' mates," Chamuel added. He was concerned about the same thing. Why hadn't Michael prepared this couple, and this family?

"Michael has not mentioned it to them, because their charge is different," Ariel explained.

"How so?" Eric asked.

Before he could answer, Michael and Raphael appeared in the dining room.

...

"Good afternoon, everyone," Raphael spoke.

"Good afternoon," Michael echoed.

"Hello," everyone greeted.

Viola immediately came into the room, with a large mug of coffee, and a regular cup of coffee. She handed the mug to Michael. "You eating?"

"Not today. Thank you. I will only be here for a few minutes."

"How about you, Raphael?"

"I wish that I could, Viola. But, I have another engagement. I'll take that cup of coffee, though."

"I'm sure you will." She handed him the cup and exited.

Michael and Raphael took a seat at the end of the table. Michael enjoyed his coffee, while Raphael did the explaining.

"By now, everyone knows that Eric is an Alter-Ego," he stated, and took a sip of his coffee. Man he loved this stuff, especially if it was piping hot. If he weren't careful, he could become addicted to it.

Everyone nodded.

He put his cup down. Then thought about it and took another quick sip. His eyes actually rolled back in his head, as he savored the flavor.

Michael laughed at him. "Raphael, you can keep the coffee as hot as you want it. Get on with it."

Everyone laughed.

Raphael chuckled. "What you all do not know is that Eric is the Ultimate Alter-Ego."

"What?" Libby asked. "Ultimate?"

Raphael and Michael nodded.

"What does that mean?" she asked.

"Eric is the Michael of Alter-Egos," Raphael continued. "There will never be one more powerful than him."

Melvin looked at Eric. He was cheesing again. He looked back at Raphael. "Get...out!"

"With that knowledge it is obvious that Ariel and Erica will not be housing 'mates'," Michael informed them.

"Why not?" Chamuel asked.

"Are there no 'sanctioned', and 'spirit' mates that need protecting, in California?" Jeremiel asked.

"Of course there are," Michael replied. "Just as I protected Jean from her father, I will continue to protect them. I will usher them to the shelters where they need to be, to meet their mates."

"So what will Ariel and I do?" Erica asked. She didn't want to be the odd man out, and not participate. She was only eighteen, but she had a lot to bring to the table.

Michael smiled at her. "You, your mate, and your parents will be responsible for housing future Alter-Egos."

"Say what?" Eric asked.

"It will be up to you, Leizalak, to train all future Egos," Raphael stated. "They are in as much danger as 'sanctioned' and 'spirit' mates. Kalaziel, and Ariel will work with you, but at different times. Kalaziel cannot know that Ariel is an Archangel."

"It does not have to be at different times," Michael injected. "Ariel has the ability to shield who he is. He can pretend that he is training also. I am commanding that he does so, when in Kalaziel's presence."

Erica frowned. She didn't like the way Michael said that. This was the second time he asserted his authority over Ariel. It was one thing to command he stay out of her bedroom. This was different. Michael was acting as if Ariel was an out of control child. Good grief, the man was as old as Time.

Sure Ariel was the untamed Lion, but he knew where to draw the line. She didn't appreciate Michael's choice of words, in the least bit. She raised her eyebrows, and belligerently asked, "Command?"

"No command is necessary, Michael. I have no intentions of revealing myself to Kal, or any other Watcher," Ariel promised. He hated the way they always acted like he was out of control. Evidently Erica did not like it, either.

He squeezed Erica's hand, and eased her spirit. This was between him and Michael, not her. "I am well aware of the rules, and what is at stake. I have not revealed myself to Kal, to date. Why would I do it later?"

"You are correct, Lion. Forgive me," Michael offered. He realized that he had not only offended Ariel, but his mate as well. It was those pesky spirits. "Forgive me, Erica. I have to work on getting past the fact that Ariel is untamed."

"I know that he is untamed. That's what I love about him, Michael. But, untamed is not unreasonable, now is it?" she replied.

Michael smiled. "No, it is not the same thing."

"I didn't think so. Listen, my mate doesn't need to be handled. You and my parents need to back up off of him. You guys worry about your mates, and leave my mate to *me.* I promise you, I will let *my* mate know when he has gone too far. Deal?"

Michael chuckled. No one but Ariel had ever told him to back off before. He and Erica were a perfect match. "Deal."

Ariel smiled. Ms. Erica George had her man's back. She was so right. If anybody could tame the beast within, she could.

He leaned over and kissed her cheek. Then he looked side eyed at Eric, Michael and his brothers. They all looked shocked that she'd gone in, like she had. He wasn't though. After spending years under attack by her brothers, Ms. Erica George knew how to speak up. "Y'all heard that, didn't you!"

Eric grunted. "Alright, baby girl. Just make sure *you* don't go too far. Understand?"

Erica sheepishly nodded.

Kay and Anita stood up, reached across the table, and slapped her a high five. Anita looked at Melvin. "Did you hear that, Daddy? We know how to handle our men."

"Sit your fast tail down!" Melvin demanded.

"Yes, sir," she replied, and plopped down in her seat.

Melvin slapped Eric five over the tops of their wives' heads. "That's how I handle my house!" he bragged.

"Archangel or not, rules are rules," Eric replied.

Anita rolled her eyes. Erica smirked. Everybody else cracked up. These two couples and their fathers were going to be entertaining.

•••

"What will I be doing, while Ariel and Daddy are training the Alter-Egos," Erica asked.

"Dr. Grayson was right. Your blood has healing powers. It will come in handy for all of the shelters. Some of the children are plagued with diseases brought on by Lucifer, to kill them. 'Sanctioned' and 'spirit' mates, as well as Alter-Egos," Michael replied.

"Really?" she asked.

"The mates cannot be allowed to die, before their mates find them. The Alter-Egos cannot be allowed to die, until they are ready for battle," Raphael replied. "Eric Jr's blood will be useful as well."

Libby nodded. Erica and Eric had their father's blood. Or at least the blood he had, when he had the clay.

Michael stood up. "If there are no more questions, I will take my leave."

Raphael also stood up. "I must leave as well. However, Eric, I am not sure a two-month vacation will be feasible."

"Why?"

"Children in need will be coming to you in a few weeks."

Eric nodded. "Alright."

•••

CHAPTER 53

Kay and Chamuel showed everyone to their bedrooms. Erica's and Anita's fathers wanted them to stay in their suites. The women rejected that notion, especially Kay.

"They are not children. They know how you guys feel. There is no reason to embarrass them like this," she voiced.

For the first time in forever, she was glad she didn't have parents. She gazed at her friends, and then at their fathers. "That is unless you are questioning your own parenting skills."

"She is absolutely right," Sandra agreed. Melvin needed to get off of his high morals. He didn't feel that way about sleeping with her, when she was eighteen. In fact, he bragged about putting his mark on her. "That's enough, Melvin. You are being hypocritical. Anita can stay in her own room. And you will mind your own business."

Melvin grunted, but didn't say anything.

Jeremiel laughed.

"I agree with Sandra, Eric. Plus, this is not our house," Libby voiced. She wasn't a hypocrite. She knew about raging hormones, at the age of eighteen.

She and Eric had their moments at that age, too. The beds in their dorm rooms were an open invitation for them. And they took full advantage. They knew how far to go, and so did Erica and Ariel.

"Erica knows how we feel, and what we expect.

Besides, what about your son, Eric? You aren't demanding he stay in our room, are you? By the way, where *is* your son?"

Eric looked around. Dammit, if that wasn't the truth. They hadn't seen Eric Jr all day, or their other three sons. Even Perry had been whisked off, by Jean's mother. They hadn't given any of them a second thought. For all they knew Eric could be in Jean's room, right now. He reached out to see, and jumped.

Ariel was watching Eric, and listening to his thoughts. He'd known all along where Eric Jr was, but who cared. The man was twenty-two years old. Jean was twenty-one. Plus, they'd been bequeathed to each other by God, Himself.

He spoke to Eric's mind, *"They aren't doing anything you and Libby didn't do, except they are older. Besides, you have all seeing eyes. If you take your eyes off of me and my mate, you'll see that Jean is Eric's wife."*

Eric looked under eyed at Ariel. *"I still don't like it, man."*

"Only in Heaven does a tree produce different types of fruit. On earth, a tree is known by the fruit it bears. In both cases the fruit doesn't fall far from the tree. No matter how untamed I am, I am my Father's son."

Eric chuckled. Ariel had just told him that Eric was his father's son, too. He couldn't deny that. *"I heard that."*

"I told you that I would not disrespect Erica, or you and Liberty. Erica will not disrespect you, either. You need to apologize to my woman, for being an ass."

"Did you just cuss?"

"The ass that I speak of is the stubborn four footed beasts. The one that is just as unreasonable, as you are."

"Um Hm," Eric replied. Then he looked at Erica. She looked embarrassed. Just as she'd been the day Libby tried to force her to marry Ariel.

He needed to do better by her, because above all else she was his sweet child. She'd never been quick to spread her legs. She kept telling him that she wasn't sexually active. Without the clay he now knew she wasn't lying. She hadn't felt that way about anybody. In fact, he now knew that she still had all of those condoms. His baby was a good girl. She never even allowed Jacques to grope her.

His boys were a whole other story. All four of their mannish butts! They not only used up their entire box of condoms, they'd used many more boxes. He guessed he should be grateful, because at least they'd used protection.

Erica had waited until she was legally grown. Until she was in love. He leaned down and kissed her cheek. "I'm sorry, baby."

"Thank you, Daddy."

She thought her mother had persuaded her father. She hugged her, whispered in her ear, "Thank you, Momma."

Libby thought she'd persuaded Eric too. She hugged Erica. "That's okay, baby. I love you. Just remember who you are, and carry yourself accordingly. Okay?"

"I will," she replied, and kissed her mother's cheek. In times like these, she felt less guilty about how she felt about her. Her birthmother was gone. She had been for nine years. It was time she let her rest in peace, and appreciate this one. "I love you, too, Momma."

"After everyone gets unpacked, and settled, let's meet with my team," Eric suggested. There were about a dozen in New Orleans.

"There are a few in my area too," Jeremiel injected. "They can't wait to meet with you."

Eric nodded. He already knew who they were. "I'm aware of them. I'd like to meet with them on their turf, though."

Jeremiel smiled. "So after your visit here, you guys are coming to Galveston?"

Eric nodded. This just put a kink in his family's vacation plans, but it needed to be done. They were charged to protect humanity. That took precedence over everything else. "We'll meet with this group, your group, and then Ariel and I will meet with California's group. Does that work for you, Lion?"

"Of course it does. This is your party," Ariel replied. He picked up Erica's luggage. "Give me about an hour to help Ms. Erica George get settled." Then he escorted Erica into her suite.

Eric frowned. "An hour! It won't take no damn-"

With the backwards swipe of his foot, Ariel slammed the door in Eric's face, before he could finish.

Chamuel howled. "I'm glad he has you to pick on this week."

Libby hugged Eric. "Ariel reminds me so much of you, Eric."

Eric smirked. "Don't insult me, Liberty Belle."

She laughing and released him.

Jeremiel reached for Anita's luggage. Her room was across the hall from Erica's. Kay's room sat at the end of the hall, between theirs. He was politer, when he escorted Anita into her room, and left the door open. He was smiling when he gazed beyond the threshold. "I bet you're glad I'm Anita's mate, instead of Ariel. Aren't you, Melvin?"

"All things considered, I'd have to say yeah," Melvin replied, and cracked up. Eric had his hands full, with that Archangel.

They were all laughing, as they followed Kay towards their own rooms. Kay was mindful to put both sets of parents at the far end of the hall, closer to the stairs. She'd assign their sons, and Perry their rooms later.

···

Ariel was still laughing when he placed Erica's luggage on the bed. "I just love messing with Eric," he bragged, and stretched out on the bed.

Erica started unpacking. "What did he mean about meeting with *his* team?"

"Eric is the General over all of the Alter-Ego army."

"What?"

He nodded. "That's why I like messing with him," he replied and laughed.

She looked up, from her unpacking. "Yeah well, you'd better get up, before he sees you laying there, Ariel."

He slid off the bed and walked up behind her. He wrapped his arms around her waist, and pulled her back up against his chest.

Then he nibbled her ear. *"Your father has a lot of eyes,"* he said, and kissed her ear. *"But, he can only see what I allow him to see, Ms. Erica George."*

She loved the feel of him holding her. Sometimes he was soft as down. Other times, like now, he was rock solid. The softness gave her comfort, like a warm blanket. The hardness gave her security, like armor.

She turned in his arms. His eyes were playfully dancing. He loved messing with her father. It was written all over his face.

She remembered more about him, with each passing

day. When he was in Heaven he was laughing. When he leaped over the balcony he was going to fight. There was no middle ground with her mate.

Strangely enough that was her persona too. She was either fighting her three brothers, or laughing with her parents, and Eric. Laughing with Jacques, or fighting against him.

She snuggled closer to him. *"Even so, you can't stay in here with me, Ariel."*

He kissed her nose. "I have no intentions of staying in this room," he replied out loud. That was for Eric's benefit. He knew the man was listening.

He released her, and reached inside her open suitcase. The cloth that he lifted was unfamiliar to him, but he had an idea. It was soft, and skimpy. It was made mostly of pure silk. He held it up and asked, *"What have we here, Ms. Erica George?"*

Erica blushed, and snatched it from his hands. *"Get out of my suitcase, Ariel!"*

He read her mind, and heard what she hadn't said out loud. He burst out laughing. He picked up another one. Just like the first one, it was black, lacey and frilly! *"What is a G-string?"*

"Give me those, Ariel!" she shouted, and tried to snatch it. She was so embarrassed.

He laughed, and raised his arm over her head. Then he wrapped his other arm around her waist, and growled. *"Do you have on a pair now, Ms. Erica George?"*

"I'm not telling you!"

"You'd better, or I'll peek," he replied.

He moved his hand from her waist to her butt, and squeezed. She was soft, tempting, and perfectly endowed. And she definitely was wearing another pair. He moaned,

"Ummm."

Erica melted, and her hormones stirred. No one had ever caressed her backside. It felt like the palm of his hand had reached inside of her clothes.

She scraped her nails down his massive biceps. What she wouldn't give to make love with him this moment. That wasn't going to happen though. Not this moment, and not the next.

They were on Michael and Verenda's timeframe. More so Michael's than Verenda's. She didn't know all of the details, but she knew Michael was at fault. For whatever reason he'd elected not to tell Verenda everything.

She gazed in Ariel's eyes. His seductive gaze was tempting, and torturous. She sighed and asked, *"May I please have my G-string?"*

Ariel slowly brought his arm down. He seductively stroked the flimsy fabric with his thumb, before he handed them to her.

Then he cupped her cheek, and passionately kissed her. *"Remember how I held, and stroked them, while you sleep tonight. I promise you will have sweet dreams of me, Ms. Erica George."*

Her womb didn't just spasm, and tingle. It straight up gushed. She swore she felt his hand stroke her. She'd never felt anything like that in her life. She knew he felt it too, because his tool jumped to attention, up against *her* thigh.

"Okay," she breathlessly replied.

Ariel moaned. He was in serious trouble. He needed a distraction, like five minutes ago. Something to force him out of this room. He didn't have the will power, or the desire, to leave on his own.

For the first time in his existence, he needed his chain yanked. *"Lead me not into temptation, Father!"*

...

"We're ready to go, Ariel," Eric shouted at him.

"Alright. I'm on my way," he replied, and chuckled. Then he added, *"Once again, my Father has used a donkey to talk."* Although, at this point, any distraction would do. *"Thank you, Father."*

Eric howled. *"C'mon man!"*

Ariel kissed Erica again, and begrudgingly released her. "I have to go, Ms. Erica George. *See you later.*"

He vanished.

...

CHAPTER 54

Before the men left, Chamuel introduced everyone to Winston, Spencer, Sherman, and Rufus. Then he introduced them to their spouses: Paulette, Vergie and Johnnie Ruth. Next he introduced their parents: Clara, Cynthia, and Diane.

Finally, he shared with his people what Eric was.

Winston was blown away. "Just when you think you've seen it all, here comes another group of unknown warriors."

The Archangels and Eric laughed.

Chamuel explained the role they'd all played over the last eighteen years. "These men have been fighting demons, most effectively. The women have helped with the children. These men should be allowed to meet the Alter-Egos, as well, Eric."

"For real," Sherman agreed.

Eric smiled. "This is your territory, Chamuel. If you think it will be beneficial, I am okay with that."

"What about us?" Perry asked. Speaking of him, and his nephews. Melvin too.

Eric nodded. This was actually good. Perry, and his sons would get a chance to see how their network worked. "Absolutely."

They all vanished.

...

While the men were at their meeting, Sandra and Libby decided they wanted to go sightseeing. They knew their daughters wanted time together, without them. Viola,

Diane, Cynthia and Clara offered to be their guides.

They walked out the front door chatting, like they'd known each other forever.

...

Erica spent the evening rekindling her relationship with Kay and Anita. They shared their remorse about never being able to have children. At the same time, they all agreed the tradeoff was more than worth it.

"I can't wait for you guys to come visit me," Anita told them.

"Me either," Erica replied.

"My cousins Sha, Quay and Cola wanted to come. Their parents did too. Daddy told them to wait, because he was sure you guys would be visiting us too."

"I'm actually a little jealous of both of you," Kay injected. And she was.

"Why?"

"Your parents and family love you guys. All I have is Viola."

Erica smacked her lips. "Family doesn't necessarily mean blood relatives. Family is those you can count on, in and out of season. Liberty is not related to me by blood, but she's still my mother."

"She's not your birthmother?" Anita asked.

Erica shook her head. "She's only Eric's biological mother." Then she went on to tell their history.

"You were a test tube baby?" Kay asked.

Erica laughed, and nodded. "But my mother loves me, like I came from her womb. From what I can see you have a lot more family than we do, Kay. It's not about blood, it's about devotion."

Anita nodded.

...

Erica was exhausted by the time she went back to her room. Ariel had not returned from their meeting. Even if he had, she doubted he would come to her room. She showered, and dressed for bed.

She laid in the spot Ariel had lain on. She swore she felt his body heat. Then she turned on her side, and hugged the pillow his head had rested on. It smelled like him. She sighed, and dozed off, hoping for the sweet dreams he'd promised.

•••

The meeting with the men was going well, but into overtime. Eric was going to be a great leader. He laid down his expectations, and took suggestions. All of the Alter-Egos were excited to finally meet the man.

They were surprised that he elected to stay with his family. Most of them had had horrible lives, as humans. They hated being confined to gender identification. They hated, even more, being limited by the clay. Some claimed to be placed in ugly babies, who grew into ugly men, and women.

One raised his hand and declared, "I was a damn pygmy, in Central Africa! Why would my host put me in that body?"

"You didn't see the baby, before being placed?" Eric asked

"Yeah, but how was I supposed to know it wasn't gon' grow any taller than it was at birth? Know I didn't appreciate that shit! When I see that damn Watcher again, I'm going to kick his ass!"

They all cracked up laughing. You couldn't tell it looking at him now. There wasn't one Alter-Ego, in that room, under six feet four.

They started going on and on about the advantage of

being genderless, and bodiless. Eric looked at his three youngest sons. All three of them were five eight. In comparison, they were short too. Not pygmy short, but short. He laughed. Man his boys were in for an awakening.

"I'll tell you what. You guys do it your way, and I'll do it mine. I happen to be very fondly attached to my gender parts."

They all laughed.

Ariel decided this was a great time for him to make his exit. He wasn't needed here. Eric had his group's undivided attention, and they had his.

He unapologetically stood and said, "I'm out!"

He vanished before anyone could comment.

...

He pulled the covers back, and eased in the bed next to Ms. Erica George. He propped his back up against the headboard and just stared down at her.

She'd done as he requested, and wore that sexy little G-string. He hadn't asked, but she'd put on the matching bra. A man would have to be made of *stone* to resist this woman.

He imagined that was Jacques' problem. Jacques had had sexual thoughts about her, for years. He wanted to see this Ms. Erica George. She'd never once let him touch her. It was never going to happen, now.

Her hair was in disarray, and wildly splayed over her pillow, and her face. She was softly purring, with elicit thoughts of him.

He put up a cone of silence around the room. Next a blinding shield to block Eric's, Michael's, and everyone's prying eyes. He leaned over and stroked her hair out of her face. Then he cradled her cheek, and said, *"I love you,*

Ms. Erica George."

Erica opened her eyes, and smiled. She sat up, reached for him, and whispered, *"You're here."*

He nodded, leaned down, and passionately kissed her. Her lips were more inviting, and desperately more demanding. He lifted her up with one arm, but didn't relinquish her lips. *"I couldn't stay away."*

The way he'd effortlessly lifted her sent shivers down Erica's spine. Or maybe it was his fingers, holding her waist that did the trick. She straddled him, and caressed his cheeks.

She broke the kiss, and gazed in his eyes. They were sensually heavy with desire, and defiant. Like hers! The *purplish* was now full blown purple, with hints of lilac. She embraced his cheeks, and tilted his head slightly backward. That spot of hair just below his bottom lip was too grown, and too sexy. She licked his bottom lip, and whispered, *"I love you, Ariel."*

He nipped her tongue, swirled his own around it, and released it. Then gazed in her eyes. He saw in them, what he already knew. Yearning, passion and desire had just overruled caution.

He caressed her quivering thighs, and slid his hands toward her cheeks. He decadently squeezed and lifted them. Then he spread his legs, and planted her womb right up against his manhood. They both moaned.

Right or wrong, there was no turning back. They'd already crossed that prohibited line. Her womb knew it; his manhood did too.

It was too much to expect them to abstain. It was unfair that they had to wait on another couple's mating, before they could enjoy their own.

Both of their bodies were in virgin territory, sizzling

with reckless anticipation. Both of their minds willing to forsake it all, for this unsanctioned moment. If they ended up in Hell for this, at least they'd be there together.

She kissed him, again. Her tongue desperately sought out his. His met hers, half way. As if rehearsed, or perhaps remembered from days of old, their tongues danced. From the first contact, the twirl, swirl and warmth heightened their need.

She loved the way his felt, against her own. Her buds were salivating with each swirl. He cherished the way hers felt against his. His heart raced with every twirl.

He marveled that she was as reckless as him. He pulled her closer, moaned, and stroked his hand up and down her form. The feel of her breasts meshed against his chest caused him to want more. *"This silky fabric feels good, but it is in my way, Ms. Erica George."*

She reared back, and unhooked her bra. She gazed in his eyes, as he eased the bra straps off of her shoulders, and down her arms. The tips of his fingers slightly grazed her skin. She tremored.

His breath hitched, at the sight of her exposed beautiful full breasts. He cupped them, and smiled. The cold air in the room caused her nipples to rise. Or maybe his touch was the enticer.

The feel of her breasts heightened his desire to see, and feel more. That G-string was tiny, but not tiny enough. He gazed in her eyes, as he seductively trailed his fingertips down her sides. She shivered, and he did too. He looped his fingers in the strings, around her hips, and snapped them.

Erica leaned in, kissed him deeper, and moaned. She lifted her hips, to give him more access. Her womb was ripe for Ariel's touch. She whispered to his mind,

"Don't stop."

He growled, as he removed the G-string. That never crossed his untamed mind. He tore the string off and tossed it, and the bra, across the room.

She shivered when his manhood bounced against her exposed womb. Odd as it were, she'd never seen, or felt, a grown man's manhood. Not even in Sex-Ed, at school. She'd seen her little friend's weeny, when she was six years old. What was throbbing against her womb was anything but little, or weeny!

She ran her hand between them, because she had to feel it with her own fingers. At first contact, they both jumped. Her womb was weeping for her mate, and had drenched his manhood. She moaned as she stroked up and down the shaft. The feel of the sleekness made her womb clap. It jealously wanted what her fingers held.

Ariel moaned at the unbelievable tender fingers that greeted his manhood. His hips literally bounced off the bed. He wrapped one hand around the nape of her neck, the other around her waist. He suckled her breast, and very *slowly* turned.

Erica hadn't even felt him turning them. She was now laying on her side, with one leg still splayed across his body. Their hands crossed between the two, as she continued to stroke him, and he reached for her. Her head wobbled backwards, in total ecstasy, when his hands made contact with her quivering, and anxious womb.

Ariel was entranced by the feel of his mate's womb. He had not been prepared for its warm, sleek and animated contact. With every stroke, her womb was gripping, and driving him to satisfy her. At the same time, her hand was well on the way to doing the same for him.

He was the lion but, in this instance, he was nothing

like the beast of the wild. And neither was his mate. Not where mating was concerned. Lions, and lionesses, physically mated for procreation purposes only.

He wasn't trying to procreate. He couldn't even if he were. Sanctioned or not, he was simply trying to get to know his mate. Devour her, in fact, in the biblical sense.

He slowly turned again. He smiled when her leg didn't fall away. Instead, she'd looped it around his lower back. That was sexy!

He leaned down and kissed her. Then he gazed in her eyes, and said, *"I love you, Ms. Erica George,"* as he eased into her spastic womb.

Erica felt no pain, but was overwhelmed. All she felt was the fullness of her mate. Her womb on instinct clapped, and clapped. And clapped some more. Between each clap she felt every stroke.

She had no idea that making love could be this intense. She thought she'd be shy, when they finally made love. She wasn't! In fact, her actions were driving his.

Her body was doing things she hadn't imagined. So were her hands. Her screams, and moans, were drowned out by his.

With their gazes locked on each other, her womb clapped one last time. Deeply seated in her womb, his manhood gave her a standing ovation!

•••

Erica was laying in the cuff of Ariel's arms. She was soaked, and as weak as she'd ever been. Her womb was still throbbing, and quaking.

She stroked her fingers across his drenched pecs. "That was amazing, but I cannot believe you, Ariel."

Ariel was grateful that he wasn't an ordinary Archangel. He was untamed, and *always* thought outside the box. Like he said, he always listened for what was *not* said.

He kissed her temple. "Where there's a will, I'll find a way."

...

CHAPTER 55

Erica was all smiles, when she stepped out of the shower. That had been the best dream she'd ever had. It was erotic, and felt unimaginably real. Her body was *still* tingling. She still felt his hands caressing her. Her womb still felt his strokes. She didn't know how Ariel did that, but she was looking forward to tonight's dream. Or fantasy!

She started singing, *"Dream lover, where are you?"*

Ariel chuckled. *"I am on your balcony, with your father. We've been scrimmaging most of the night."*

She smiled. *"You are such a sneak."*

He could see her smile, and her eyes. She was glowing. *"Keep a straight face, Ms. Erica George. I can block your father out of your mind, but not your face. Don't bust me out, girl. You're going to get me in trouble."*

She laughed. *"Can Michael read your mind?"*

"Not if I don't allow him to."

"How is that possible?"

"I am the Lion. Father sends me on many missions that the others are not privy to."

"Can God read your mind?"

"He can, but I didn't step over the line."

"Are you sure?"

He laughed. *"Yes, I'm sure. It was your dream, not mine."*

"My dream that you planted."

He laughed. *"All Angels have the ability to deliver*

messages to humans, in their dreams. That's what happened to Nebuchadnezzar, isn't it? That's also what happened to Pontius Pilate's wife. Samjaza was called into existence to be the messenger, through dreams. Of course, that was before he rebelled against Father."

"You didn't exactly deliver a message, Ariel," she admonished, and blushed.

He cracked up laughing. *"I most certainly did. I was there with you, and all of your sexiness. I delivered the audible, and demonstrative message that I love you, Ms. Erica George."*

Her heart lurched. He'd certainly done that. *"I love you too, Ariel. Untamed and all."*

"You are the only one that can tame, and chain, the Lion. Look at your finger."

She looked down. On her left ring finger was a ring shaped like a chain. The band was gold, and studded with purple diamonds. In the center was a large, perfectly round, diamond, with a lion's head etched inside. She'd never seen a ring like that. She hadn't even felt it being placed on her finger. When had he put it there?

She hugged her hand against her chest. *"You were really there, Ariel!"*

He reached across space and kissed her. *"Yes, ma'am."*

"It's beautiful, Ariel. Everyone will wonder when you gave it to me."

"No one can see it, but you and me."

"Sneaky!"

He laughed again. *"We'll be there in a moment. Remember to keep a straight face."*

"Okay. I love you."

"I love you more!"

•••

By time she made it downstairs, her family was already there. So were Melvin and Sandra. They were all talking, and eating from the breakfast bar.

"Good morning," she greeted.

"Good morning, baby," Libby replied. Her daughter was glowing. "You slept late."

Erica's womb jumped, and started to weep. She heard Ariel growl in her ear. Then she felt him reach out and caress her womb. She blushed. *"Stop it, Ariel!"*

He laughed. *"I'll stop, but only until tonight!"*

Her womb clamped down with such force, she almost climaxed on the spot. Goodness! She needed to get herself together. He did too.

Thank God Kay and Anita walked down the stairs at that moment. She knew that Anita and Jeremiel had left for their island, after they separated. Kay didn't have to put on a façade. Everyone knew she and Chamuel slept in the same bed. Every single night. She wished!

"I stayed up late talking with Kay and Anita," she replied to her mother's question. "How was your sightseeing? I didn't hear you guys come back."

"We had a ball. I forgot how much there was to see in New Orleans. We're going out again today. Are you going to join us?"

She nodded, and poured herself a cup of coffee. Her hand was as steady as ever. That is until Ariel and her father appeared in the room. Then it slightly trembled; so did her womb. No one noticed it but Ariel.

•••

Eric leaned down and kissed his wife. "Good morning, Liberty."

"Good morning. Where have you guys been?"

"We've been scrimmaging most of the night." Then he looked at Melvin, and laughed. "That's how I run my house. Keep him *busy!*"

Melvin slapped him five. "Next time take Billy Boy with you."

Ariel chuckled. Then he kissed Erica's cheek. "Good morning, Ms. Erica George."

"Ariel," she answered. She couldn't say anything else, or she'd give them away.

"What are your plans for today?"

"Momma said she wanted to go sightseeing. Do you want to do something else?"

"No, that's good," he replied. Then he took her coffee cup from her, and drank from it. "Black? No cream or sugar?" He'd never seen anybody drink it like that, but Michael.

She smiled at a long forgotten memory. It was when she first moved to California. She'd gotten up before everyone else in the house. She was still nervous about her new surroundings, and was roaming around the house. She'd never seen a house that big, or with so many windows.

When she got to the kitchen her father was already in there, sitting at the table. He'd smiled and told her to come sit with him. When she eased into her seat, he squeezed her hand, and said, *"I'm so sorry I didn't get there in time for your mother's funeral. The letter came too late."*

She'd just nodded, but her eyes watered. His did too. She'd wiped her eyes, but they kept running. She was so brokenhearted, she couldn't speak.

He'd reached over and pulled her into his arms. He hugged her, and kissed her cheek. *"I'm sorry I didn't know about you, before now."*

She started to straight up bawl. He rocked her trembling body back and forth and said, *"I can't bring your mother back, but I love you, Erica. I'm going to do everything in my power to make you happy, baby."*

They cried together that morning. Her over her loss, him over her tears. When they settled down, he handed her a cup of coffee. It was her first. She didn't like it, but she wanted to be a big girl. She wanted to be like her daddy. After that, they had coffee every morning together when he was in town. Over the years, she learned to like it.

Her eyes were glazed when she looked across the room at her father. "I learned how to drink it that way from Daddy."

Eric knew where her mind had gone. His eyes watered too, but for a different reason. His eyes watered, because if he'd known about his, and Erica's blood, they both could have healed her birthmother.

He wouldn't have had a problem with joint custody, or visitation. Libby wouldn't have either. They would've loved Erica, no matter what.

His eyes also watered, because if he'd known about her, and her mother; he could've saved the woman's life. Erica did not know, nor would she ever know, that they'd misdiagnosed her birthmother.

He'd looked at all of her medical records, blood work, and X-rays. They'd gotten her entire file mixed with another patient's. She hadn't died from cancer. She died from her insides being fried, by a cancer treatment she hadn't needed.

He smiled at Erica. "It was our morning ritual. Just the two of us."

Erica smiled.

Ariel was touched by the way Erica and Eric smiled at each other. You didn't have to be an angel to feel the emotional fabric of their bond. It was tightly woven. "You can continue your ritual, can't you?"

They both smiled, and nodded.

He took another sip of her coffee. This was the last time he'd share a cup with her. "It's good," he said, and gave the cup back to her.

...

"So what sights do you guys want to see," Kay asked.

"We want to go down by the cemetery," Ian replied. "Some of the guys here said it's haunted, and really spooky."

Remington looked at his father. He'd acted a butt when Eric died, but it was a macho defense mechanism. He was never more glad that he was wrong, when he declared *'he's not coming back.'* Although he'd resented Erica in the past, he'd never once resented his father.

He shook his head. "It may be spooky, but I've seen enough of graveyards for a while."

"Aw man. C'mon. Don't be a wuss," Carson shot back. "I wanna see where Chamuel took those demons down."

"How do you know about that?" Chamuel asked.

"The guys told us about it last night. They said you walked all over their graves!"

Chamuel chuckled.

"Hey, can I see your wings?" Ian asked.

Chamuel cracked up. "Not now. Maybe later."

Erica smirked. She didn't understand her brothers' affinity to scary things. As long as she could remember they were obsessed with monsters, dead people, and ghosts. "I do not want to go to a cemetery, either. I want to visit Louis Armstrong Park, and Bourbon Street."

"Of course you don't want to go," Ian teased. "You're a chicken."

"Maybe that's because I know monsters up close and personal. After all, I live with Lucifer's sons," Erica taunted and laughed.

"That ain't even right," Carson replied.

"What are you saying?" Ian asked. Then he smirked and said, "Oh, I get it. She just called *you* the devil, Dad!"

Eric cracked up. This was definitely a different family he'd come home to. A united one. "How about this. Everybody do your own thing, today?"

"I'm game," Eric, Jr. replied. He liked that idea. He didn't want to sightsee in a group. He wanted to rekindle his relationship with Jean privately.

He hadn't realized until she was gone, that he was in love with her. That last thing he wanted was his youngest brothers making fun.

• • •

CHAPTER 56

Jacques and his parents had been in New Orleans for a week. On the first day, they went to visit relatives that were still alive. Even though his parents had never come back, they kept in contact with their families.

Both of their families remained close, over the years. In fact, one of his father's cousins had married his mother's cousin. He also met cousins that were close in age to him. He'd been enjoying getting to know them all week.

The family had been elated to see them, and meet him. They kept going on and on, in their deep accent, about how much he looked like his grandfather.

On the first day, they threw a spontaneous crawfish boil. He'd never seen anything like that, in his life. Mounds of crawfish, potatoes, and corn, piled on a table; clad with a checkerboard table cloth. Everyone just dug in, and grabbed what they wanted.

On the second day, they had a catfish and shrimp fry. It was the same thing. Food galore! Kegs of beer! Music, dancing, and laughter abound. His New Orleans family loved to celebrate each breath they took. He was experiencing something he'd never experienced. Life!

On the third day, the entire family went to the infamous St. Louis Cemetery. They visited every grave that belonged to their loved ones.

Even that turned into a celebration, as musical family members brought their horns, and drums. They marched onto that hallowed ground to the beat of 'When the saints go marching in'. Even though surrounded by the dead, he had never felt so alive.

However, his parents were feeling some kind of way, being back. A sense of homecoming, but at the same time no longer belonging. He understood that. While their families talked about events of the past, his parents were getting the info secondhand. In most instances, years after the fact.

Even still, they were enjoying themselves. More importantly, they were enjoying seeing him interacting with his cousins. His mother was more than a little relieved that Tristen was not with them. He'd had no idea she did not care for his friend.

...

He and his cousins, Miles and Chase, were hanging out in Louis Armstrong Park. They'd introduced him to many of their friends. Every one of them were friendly, and seemed happy to meet him.

He'd never once experienced being happy, for happy sake. He'd never once experienced being happy! It was like a drug, and it drew him in. "Man, I could get used to this."

"Why don't you move here," Miles suggested. He really liked his cousin. Plus, after talking with Dorothy, he didn't care much for Tristen, either. Unfortunately, Dorothy didn't know how the world worked, so she misunderstood what was going on. "I can get you on at the docks."

"I can work at the docks in Cali, man."

"Yeah, but as long as you are on the west coast, Tristen will never stop stalking you."

Jacques' jaw dropped. "What are you talking about?"

Miles grunted. "Man, you are slow as hell. I've never even met the dude and I know he's stalking you."

"Ain't that the truth," Chase cosigned.

Jacques was still confused. "What are you talking about? You don't even know Tristen."

"I know the dude has the hots for you. Is that plain enough?" Miles asked.

Jacques cracked up laughing. "Y'all trippin'. Tristen is not gay!"

"Have you ever seen him with a woman?"

Jacques stopped laughing. "No, but that doesn't mean he's gay."

"We're not wrong, Jacques. Dorothy thinks that he's in love with your ex-girlfriend, Erica, but she's way off. That dude only has eyes for you, cuzzo."

"You haven't even met him. How can you judge him like that?" he asked defensively.

"We know the type. We've experienced it first hand," Chase replied. "They aren't attracted to other gay men. They get their rocks off by turning out a newbie."

"You being the newbie," Miles added.

"I'm telling you that man wants to get in your ass, literally!" Chase added, and cracked up laughing.

Jacques frowned. That didn't sound cool, at all. Could they be right? His mind was much clearer than it had ever been, thanks to those angels. He started thinking back, to when he first met Tristen. It hadn't been at school. It had been at a beach party. From that day on, Tristen had been around. Every single day!

He thought about them in the showers, after gym class. A few times he'd caught Tristen staring at him. The dude had even slapped him on his naked ass, with a rolled up towel. He hadn't realized until now that it was inappropriate. Who thinks another dude is looking at him the way a woman would? Not a straight man, that's for damn sure.

He thought about all the dates he'd gone on, with Erica. Tristen always tagged along. Even if he wasn't invited, he somehow managed to show up.

Tristen practically lived at their house. All of this time he thought it was because he had a bad home life. When they got high, in the greenhouse, Tristen always wanted to do the mouth-to-mouth 'shotgun'. Although their lips never touched, it was evidently close enough for Tristen.

Last week, Tristen had been upset that he couldn't come to New Orleans with them. Irate was more like it. He'd even accused him of trying to get rid of him. He'd blatantly declared, *"That is never going to happen, because you are min- my family, Jacques!"*

He hadn't given in another thought, but Tristen had almost said *mine!* All of a sudden, a sinister thought crossed his mind. It was accompanied by a wave of nausea, as bile rose to his throat. That creature had chased Tristen, not him or his father. Just before it left, it roared at *him*. Not because of anything he'd done, but because he was a fool. It was because he couldn't see what was right before his eyes. He could see it now, and it was as plain as day. He was sick, but Tristen was crazy. Tristen was a psychopath!

He needed to get to a pay phone, and warn Erica. He jumped up, and shouted, "She's in danger!"

He was already on the move before his cousins could respond. He was practically running, across the park.

"Who?" Miles asked, and ran behind him.

"Erica! Erica's in danger!"

"What?" Chase asked, as he caught up to him. He grabbed his arm. "Stop!"

Jacques stopped, but he was jumpy. "Someone killed Erica's father."

"What?"

"They ran him down with their car."

"What does that have to do with her?" Miles asked.

"Her father pushed her out of the way, man! He wasn't the one they were trying to kill!" he shouted. "They were trying to kill her!"

"And you think it was Tristen?" Chase asked.

"YES! He was trying to kill her, because of me, man!"

"Shit! That dude *is* crazy!"

Jacques took off again. "I gotta call and warn her!"

"There's a pay phone by that café'. Let's go there!" Chase suggested.

They all took off, in an all-out run, across the park. He was in his right mind now, and he was scared. Before he romantically loved Erica, he platonically liked her. She was his best friend, in fact.

He liked her because she didn't have that rich valley girl mentality. He liked her because she didn't think she was better than anybody, especially him. He liked her because she didn't care that he lived in the hood. He liked her because she was the sweetest person he'd ever met. He liked her because she helped him overcome his dyslexia. He liked her because she made him feel normal, even though both knew he wasn't.

He didn't want her, or anyone else in her family, hurt. Not because of some screwed up punk's misguided affection. Not for any reason!

They were across the street from the café, when he came to an abrupt stop. He leaned down and breathed deeply. "That's her sitting outside the café."

His cousins looked across the street, and then down at him. "That's her?" Miles asked.

He nodded. He was so relieved, he actually wanted to cry. He'd been concerned that Tristen had already gotten to her. She wouldn't have known to be careful, because like him, she had no idea. None! "She's in New Orleans, too. Thank God she's out of harm's way."

"Why is she here?"

"I don't know, but thank God she is."

"Damn. She fine as hell, man," Chase voiced.

"Inside and out," Jacques replied.

"Who's that dude with her?" Miles asked.

"I don't know. Probably her new boyfriend. I still need to warn her, though. She'll eventually go home. Her father is dead, but she has an uncle, and four brothers. They'll protect her, and her mother."

"You need to call the police, before you guys leave. They can arrest that crazy ass punk," Chase suggested.

"That's a good idea," Miles agreed. "You are probably in danger too, Jacques."

"I think I'll take some vacation time, and go back to California with you for a while," Chase informed him.

"Me too," Miles agreed. "If he can't have you, he won't let anyone else have you."

Jacques cringed. That's the way he'd felt about Erica. He'd wanted them to die together, but it wasn't to keep anyone else from her. He was obsessed, because he was sick. Tristen, on the other hand, is crazy. Maybe that's why his mother left him. She knew he was beyond help. Or maybe she knew his father was the only one that could keep him in line. Either way it didn't matter, not anymore. All he cared about was making sure Erica was safe, and out of harm's way.

"Okay, but let me warn her first."

Just as he went to step off the curb, his heart sped up! Not again! He shouted, "WATCH OUT!" and took off running again.

•••

Like most humans, they didn't know that angels keep a watch over them. All night...all day! Ariel was definitely watching. It pleased him that Jacques understood what he'd been doing in that greenhouse. Even if Michael hadn't. It also pleased him that Jacques had a genuine concern for his mate's safety. That alone took him off the 'fool' list. It also earned him protection, as opposed to recompense, from the lion. That was a first!

He sent a shout out, *"Jeremiel!"*

"I'm on it!"

"Thanks, man!"

•••

Neither Jacques nor his cousins saw Jeremiel standing in front of them. They did however feel a force so strong it pushed them backwards. With eighty miles an hour winds at their faces they stumbled three feet backward, and then to the ground. They tried to get up, but kept stumbling and rolling backward. The force was holding them down.

Jacques screamed, "I can't move! What is that?"

His cousins shouted, "I don't know!"

They all heard Jeremiel's voice. *"You will all die if you attempt to cross the street."* Then he materialized, nodded and said, "Be easy. Erica has a host of angels encamped all around her."

They didn't try to get up, but they sat up, and just stared at him. Strangely enough they were not afraid. Especially since this dude sported dreads. Not only that, but Miles and Chase has seen him in the Quarter before. They just had no idea he was not human.

"You're an angel?" Chase asked.

He nodded. "I am Jeremiel, the Archangel of hope."

"You are always in the Quarter, man," Miles stated.

Jeremiel smiled. "I have close friends who reside in New Orleans."

"Other Archangels?"

Jeremiel nodded.

"Y'all know about Tristen?" Jacques asked.

Jeremiel nodded. Then he sat down on the ground with them, and drew his knees up. "We always keep a watchful eye on God's 'so' loved. Tristen will not be able to get near Erica, or you Jacques. It is about to get ugly on the street. I just need you guys to stay out of the way."

They nodded.

"And Jacques, you are going to see something that will make you want to run," he warned. He heard Ariel laugh in his ear. He chuckled and said, "Don't! Trust me, it will be better for you to stay put."

"Alright," Jacques replied.

...

CHAPTER 57

Erica was enjoying her time alone with Ariel. They walked hand-in-hand through the Quarter, and took in all of the sights. Ariel told her the Mexican, and French history behind New Orleans. He also told her about the last time he'd been here. "We helped Chamuel, when the demon Mammon was after Kay."

"I can't believe a real demon wanted her," she replied.

Ariel grunted. "What do you think Samjaza is?"

"Yeah, I know, but that was just his spirit."

He nodded. "That's true, but look what he made the pool man do to Libby. His attack on you would've been the same, if not worse. He would've relentlessly assaulted you, while you slept."

She tremored. That thought scared her. To be raped in your sleep was nothing she wanted to think about. "Are you sure he can't still do it, Ariel?"

He felt her concern. He released her hand, and wrapped his arm around her neck. "The only person you have to worry about, in your dreams, is me."

She wrapped her arm around his waist, and immediately relaxed. "I like it here, but I can't wait to get back to our patio, Ariel."

He laughed. He knew what she was thinking, but it was not going to happen. No way! No how! "Listen. On the nights that we are on the patio, I will *not* be visiting your dreams."

"What? Why not?"

"I can't do both, Ms. Erotica George." Then he nibbled her ear, and confessed, "I don't have that kind of will power."

"I don't understand?"

"I can't hold your physical body, while making love to your mind. The two would get crossed up, for sure. Then my Father would spank me, or demand Michael do it. Either way would be very painful," he explained. Then he whispered to her mind, *"I've never been spanked, Ms. Erica George. I'm much too old to get spanked now."*

She laughed. She thought about all the whippings her and her brothers had gotten over the years. Her mother never once hit them. Her father wasn't quick to hit them either, but when he did he didn't hold back. Ariel was right, whippings were very painful!

"I'll spank you in my dreams, tonight."

He squeezed her neck, and growled. "Don't make promises you can't keep."

She cracked up laughing. "Let's stop and eat, before we go to the park."

"Okay."

•••

They stopped at a small outdoor café, just outside the park. The bistro tables were extremely small, but that didn't bother Ariel. This was a perfect spot, because the street dead ended at the café. He pulled out a chair for her, and then sat with his back to the street.

When the waitress arrived he ordered shrimp po boys for both of them, coleslaw, and two grape sodas. They continued to talk, while waiting for their meal.

"So which do you like better, New Orleans or Cali?" Erica asked.

He hunched his shoulders. "They both have their

own appeal. One has sprawling mountains, the other's below sea level. They both are a part of Mother Earth, that the deep made way for."

"I'm talking about the people, Ariel!"

He laughed. He knew what she meant. He was trying to keep her distracted. There were things going on that she couldn't see yet. "I've spent more time in New Orleans, than anywhere else on earth. I'm just learning California. So, I haven't made up my mind yet."

"You never roamed, like Michael?"

He shook his head. "Not really. In the past I've only left home on a mission. Either to help my brothers, or to handle my father's affairs."

"So how do you know so much about New Orleans?"

"I know about the entire earth. I was there when Father flooded the earth, the first time. I was there to witness the ruin, when He parted the waters, afterward."

She nodded. "The earth was void."

"And without form," he finished.

Something crossed her mind. "That means that you can not only walk on the air, but under water too."

He nodded. "Yes, ma'am. Chemical formulas have no effect on Archangels. Unlike humanity no part of us is water based. No part of us is terrain."

"Does fire hurt you?"

He shook his head. "Nope."

"The sun?"

"I can sleep on it if I chose to."

She thought about those bullets. "Nothing manmade can hurt you either, can it?"

"Nope." Then he shook his head. "Nothing manmade can hurt you anymore either, Ms. Erica George."

"How is that possible?"

"I won't let it." Then he took her hand. "I really need you to trust me on this. I know that Zander hurt you. That was my fault, because I didn't consider Samjaza's reach. I am never going to let anyone else get close enough to hurt you."

"We don't even know who else is after me, Ariel."

"You don't, but I do."

She jumped. "You do?"

He squeezed her hand, and nodded.

"Who?"

"His name is Triste-"

"TRISTEN! WHY?"

"He is obsessed with Jacques. He thinks you are in his way."

"Jacques? What? Jacques is a lot of things, but gay is not one of them, Ariel."

"I know that. Tristen seems to think if you were out of the picture he can persuade Jacques."

"That is just stupid! Either you are gay or you are not!"

Ariel laughed at the expression on her face. She looked appalled. But then he got serious. "Listen. No matter what you see, I need you to sit still. Don't move. Don't make a sound. Don't even blink, okay."

"Okay." But she was all of a sudden nervous. Why would he tell her to be still? She wanted to ask him what was going on, but was too afraid to know.

She looked over his shoulder and saw Jacques and two other guys, running toward them. What in the world was he doing in New Orleans? He was shouting, "Watch out!"

Then she saw them being hurled backward. Her

hand trembled, when they stumbled and fell. The wind was high on that side of the street. It was pushing them further back, away from her. Something was about to go down. Was Jacques still after her? Her voice trembled when she whispered, *"Ariel!"*

He pulled her hand to his lips, and kissed it. *"I see them. Be still."*

Then he sent another shout out, *"You in the area?"*

"Just around the corner."

"We've got a lot of company coming."

"I'm aware of that. I keep my eyes on my baby girl, man."

Ariel laughed. *"Your reward or mine?"*

"Mine."

Ariel was okay with that. Under any other circumstances recompense would've been all his, but not today. He was content to sit and enjoy the spectacle. That and keeping Ms. Erica George calm. Her peace of mind was much more important than his pleasure of reward. Yeah, she was taming the lion alright. He chuckled. *"That's fine."*

"You don't want in?"

"Nah. I know how much you want him."

"I want to drag his sorry ass, by his own car!"

"What's your plan?"

"Just sit tight and learn a thing or two."

Ariel laughed. *"Don't get too cocky, boy!"*

...

Ariel knew that Chamuel was entertaining the remainder of Erica's family. He sent a shout out to him. *"Keep them away from the Park, Cham."*

"What's going on?"

"Erica's last threat has arrived."

"Oh man."

"Jacques is also in the park, but Jeremiel is handling him, and his cousins. Plus, Beaux and Dorothy are on their way to the park." Then he added, *"Feet don't fail me now,"* and cracked up laughing.

Chamuel laughed out loud. Poor Beaux was about to witness another attack of an Archangel. That man was going to take off running, again. He decided he couldn't let that happen. *"I'm going to teleport the family back to the house, and then see if I can distract Beaux."*

"See that's why I call you Sap. You don't know how to have fun!"

Chamuel laughed, again. Then he teleported Erica's brothers, and Perry back to the Haven. He didn't tell them what was going on, because they'd want to be there. From what he could already see, the less people on the streets the better.

He saw that Libby was already back inside. She looked extremely nervous, and anxious. No doubt Eric had brought her back, and told her what was about to go down. She was worried about her daughter, but there was no need. "Everything will be fine, Liberty. Stay here until I return," he instructed, and vanished.

Unfortunately, he got to Beaux, and Dorothy, too late. They were cattycorner from Jacques, and Erica; and only a block and a half away. Both of them were anxiously running down the middle of the street, toward their son.

He read their minds. They could tell that Jacques was making his way toward Erica. They thought he was going to make a scene, because she was with another man. Both of them were wondering what the hell she was doing in New Orleans.

He flapped his wings, and created a gust of wind. In doing so, he reversed their momentum. They both staggered sideways, out of the center of the street. The force was so strong; they were headed for a plate glass store front.

...

Beaux was nervous, and concerned for his son; but he didn't run. He grabbed Dorothy with one arm, and a light pole with the other. He wrapped his arms her waist, and mashed them both to the light pole. He held on tight enough to steady them against the wind.

Dorothy's eyes watered. Not because of the wind, or fear. It was because Beaux hadn't abandoned her. She'd waited eighteen years for him to show some sign of valor. For him to show that his love for her was more powerful than his fear.

He not only stayed there, but he positioned her in the safest place! His shoulders, and torso, were pressed hard against her back. The gale force wind was at his back, but he was at hers! She sobbed.

Beaux squeezed her waist. "Ssh. Don't cry. I got cha, Dorothy. That's Chamuel."

Neither of them saw Chamuel, but they knew that that unexpected wind was supernatural. It was too strong not to be. It brought back the memory of Chamuel, in the cemetery, when he'd angrily flapped his wings. One snap had pushed the entire crowd in the cemetery backwards.

She nodded. After everything those angels had done for them, she knew Chamuel wouldn't hurt them, or their son. But what was going on? What had upset him this time?

...

Their rationale pleased Chamuel, more than he

could've imagined. The wind died down, and he appeared in front of them. "Be at ease. I still mean you no harm," he assured them. "Jacques is trying to warn Erica, not hurt her."

Beaux released the pole, but kept one arm around Dorothy. "Warn her. About what?"

A car sped past them at that moment. Dorothy gasped. If Chamuel hadn't pushed them to the side, that car would've come up behind them. It would have plowed them down, in the middle of the street.

Beaux had the same thought Dorothy had. Chamuel had just saved their lives. "That was close, man. Thank you."

Chamuel nodded, and smiled. Then he looked toward the back of the car. He frowned. "Tristen is behind the wheel of that car."

"Tristen! What is he doing here?" Dorothy asked.

"He followed you guys."

"Why?" Beaux asked.

"To keep an eye on Jacques."

"Oh my God," Dorothy stated. It all made sense now. It was a love triangle alright, but she naturally got the dynamics wrong. "He's not in love with Erica! He wants my *son!*"

"What?" Beaux asked. Then he recalled Tristen's distaste in Jacques' feelings for Erica. He remembered how Tristen had left the night Jacques had his breakdown. He remembered Tristen telling him that he'd been in love. He hadn't questioned it until now, but he'd never seen Tristen with a young lady.

He also remembered something else, and the thought sickened him. They hadn't heard about Erica's father's death from the news. They heard about it less than thirty minutes after it happened, from Tristen.

He'd very matter of fact stated, *'Erica's father was rundown by a speeding car, a few minutes ago.'* Then he'd bluntly said, *'The bigger they are, the harder they fall.'*

It was only later that they'd learned that Erica and her mother were almost hit. That in fact, Eric had died pushing them out of the way. He wasn't the intended target, Erica was! Now come to think of it, they hadn't seen Tristen's car since that night. "Erica is in his way. He tried to kill that girl, that night. Not her father!"

Chamuel nodded. "He killed her father, trying to kill her. He's on his way now, to finish what he started that night."

"We didn't even know Erica was in New Orleans. How did he know?" Dorothy asked.

"He didn't. Not until he spotted her in the Quarter, earlier today," Chamuel explained.

"I'm concerned, Chamuel," Beaux admitted. "My son is not gay. Even if Tristen were to succeed in killing Erica, Jacques still wouldn't want him. Will he go after my son, next?"

"Jacques is also under Archangel protection. I assure you, no harm will come to him."

Dorothy breathed a sigh of relief. She'd been thinking the same thing. "Thank you."

"Battling evil is what we Archangels do. Most times in the darkly. Other times, like now, out in the open. There are mysteries in this world that humanity has yet to discover. I must warn you guys that you are about to witness another supernatural phenomenon. One that will undoubtedly leave you confused, afraid even. Be of good courage, and keep your feet planted where they are."

They both nodded. Neither of them were afraid. Not anymore. They both knew that when this was over, like that demon in the cemetery, Tristen would be out of their lives forever. That pleased Dorothy beyond her wildest imagination.

They also knew that Archangels were exact in their disbursement of justice. There would be no friendly fire, or unintended casualties of war. No innocent human, like Eric George, would be hurt. Not them. Not their son. Not Erica.

...

CHAPTER 58

Tristen was seething. In fact, he was so irate he could chew on steel, and spit out glass. Jacques had refused to let him come to New Orleans with him, and now he knew why. His pathetic ass was still chasing after Erica.

Why couldn't he get it through his head that that bitch did not want him? Why couldn't he get it through his head that no woman was worth it?

He'd learned that at an early age. His trampy mother was the biggest bitch of them all. His father, like Jacques, was a wimp. Chasing after a woman that didn't want him. Forgiving her over and over, even though he knew she'd cheat again.

He wasn't that forgiving. He hated her from the first time he saw her with another man. When he got old enough he killed her cheating ass.

"It wasn't enough to kill me, and your mother," a voice spoke in his mind.

The car swerved just a bit. He recognized the voice. "Hell nah, it wasn't enough!" he shouted out loud. "I'm going to kill that deceitful bitch, or die trying!"

"Do you think I'm going to let you kill my daughter?"

"You can't stop me! You're dead!"

Eric appeared in the passenger seat. So there was no misunderstanding, by Tristen or the onlookers, he appeared with Eric's face. Not Leizalak's. He hadn't even known he could do that, but was glad that he chanced it. "Am I?"

Tristen screamed. Then he shouted, "YES!" He'd been getting high since he saw Erica in the Quarter, with another man. The only weed he could score was Bohemian. That shit was strong. He had to be hallucinating. He had to be. "I KILLED YOU!"

"I came back."

"You're not real," he replied, and laughed. "Just a figment!"

"Then who is that standing between this car and my daughter?"

Tristen looked ahead, and screamed. A dozen Eric Georges were standing in a half moon shape, just up ahead. They were all holding an ancient scepter, poised to strike. One by one, they threw them at the car. He jerked the wheel sideways, in an effort to dodge them. It didn't work!

The precision was spectacular! The Erics hadn't aimed for the windows, the doors, or any part of the car's body. Instead, five of the scepters went through both front tires. Five went through both back tires. The tires blew out, slowing the car's momentum; but the scepters were still sticking out the sidewalls. The ends started to scrape the ground.

The remaining two scepters pierced the gas tank, from the left, and right sides. Gas began to spew, like a clogged fountain. The smell permeated the air, inside and outside the vehicle.

...

Erica jumped, and tried to stand, when she saw her father. It wasn't his new face, but her daddy's face. The one she looked like. The one she loved. Her eyes teared. She wanted to run to him. She wanted this Eric to hold her, one more time! "Daddy!"

Ariel squeezed her hand, and held her in place. He knew this was a shock for her, but at the same time a precious gift. One that her family would never witness.

He knew Eric was going to do this, that's why he'd told her not to move. He also knew why Eric did what he'd done. He wanted his daughter to know that it was really *him*, that was fighting for her. He wanted to dispel any lingering doubt that he loved her, and he always had.

That mindset was amazing to him. He himself never once had split emotions, when exacting recompense. Yet, as enraged as Eric was he had the wherewithal to comfort his daughter. To assure her. He could learn a thing or two from the man.

He moved to her side of the table, and wrapped his arm around her. *"That's how strong his love for you is, Ms. Erica George,"* he whispered to her mind.

Erica remembered what her father told her. *"You are my daughter! Don't ever let anyone tell you that you're not."* She laid her head on his chest, and smiled.

...

Beaux was glad Chamuel had warned them, but that warning wasn't clear enough. What the hell! Twelve Eric Georges just appeared out of nowhere. Twelve of one dead man standing right in front of him, in a half moon. "Oh my God," he shouted.

If he would've run, Dorothy would have understood. She certainly wanted to. What the hell was Eric George? No wonder he was able to get into their home, without setting off the alarm. The man could not have been human, when they thought he was alive.

There he stood, all twelve of him, in whitewashed jeans, and a white tee shirt. Muscles in his legs and arms protruding, like jagged rocks. He was no angel, that's for sure. With the exception of his clothing, he looked like a Greek god. "What is he? How is he here?" she nervously asked.

"He is one of the mysteries beyond the darkly," Chamuel replied. He knew the warning Eric had given this family. He knew Beaux and Dorothy were remembering it too.

Their hearts were racing. They were wondering if Eric's revenge would be retroactive. Would he punish everyone who had ever hurt his daughter? Was their son next? Did he know that Jacques acted the way he did because he was sick? Did he know that Jacques wasn't sick anymore?

"Be easy. He is not a threat to you, or yours," he assured them.

...

Jacques slapped his hands over his eyes. Then he peeked through his fingers. Mr. George was still in his view. A bunch of Mr. Georges! Was he losing his mind again? He didn't want to be sick anymore. "It can't be!" he shouted.

"Who is that?" Miles asked.

"What is that?" Chase asked.

"That's Erica's father!" Jacques shouted.

"WHAT!"

Miles' heart thudded. "I thought you said he was dead? You said Tristen killed him!"

"HE DID!" Jacques shouted.

Neither Chase nor Miles believed in ghosts. Even being raised in New Orleans, they didn't believe in the 'doos' either. Not hoodoo! Not voodoo! None of it! But God help them. There were twelve of the same man standing in the cobblestone circle of the street. All of them protecting Erica!

They all tried to get up, at the same time. Miles and Chase thought to run to the church. Jacques thought to follow in his father's footsteps, and run back to California.

They all paused when they noticed the shadow of an angel's wings, all around them. They'd forgotten that Jeremiel was on the ground beside them. They all gazed at him. They didn't see any wings on his body. They looked back at the ground. Sure enough they were sitting in the shadow of wings.

Jeremiel was showing all of his pearly whites. Even though he felt their fear, he was amused. "How y'all gon' just run away from the protection of my wings?" he asked.

"Man, this is some scary shit!" Jacques replied, and eased closer to him. "I thought I was losing my mind again."

Jeremiel laughed out loud. "Nah. This is how we do it, man. Normally humanity is not allowed to see our warfare, but this is a special dispensation."

"Why? Why us?"

"So you young men will know that God has an all seeing eye. So you young men will know that angels are always watching. All night, and all day. So you young men will know no matter the trial, if you ask God, He will send me, and my brothers."

"So Erica's father is an angel?"

He shook his head. "No." Then looked across the street. Their eyes followed his. Erica was still sitting at a table, with her new boyfriend. "Erica's mate is an Archangel, like me. The only reason that he is not contending with Tristen is because her father needed this. Tristen killed the man, trying to kill her. Her father is one of God's special beings."

"I should say so," Chase replied. He could not believe how human these angels looked.

···

Eric stretched his arm across the seat and relaxed. He was grateful he was who he was. If he had been totally human, he wouldn't be here. And Tristen would've never stopped coming after his family.

Of course Ariel would spend the remainder of time protecting his baby girl, but that wasn't good enough for him. He wouldn't have wanted to just witness the battle from Paradise. He was grateful that the answer to his lifelong question, *'will a man live again'*, was yes!

Something occurred to him. Nobody really dies. Everyone goes from one type of existence to another. As a rule, your faith determines your final destination. He'd witnessed that on his visit to Paradise, and Hell. He saw the Georges in Paradise. He saw his sister-in-law Annette, the atheist, in Hell.

He glanced over at Tristen. With his new eyes, he could see beyond the terrain. His heart was black, and so was his spirit. Like Annette, he didn't believe in a benevolent God. He didn't believe in the devil either.

No one had taught the boy that there were only two choices. It wouldn't have mattered if he believed in God, but not the devil. That mindset might have been enough to please God.

It did however matter that he didn't believe in God. That made him the devil's own, whether he believed in him or not. He'd believe in both, in just a minute or two.

Tristen could not see them, but two demons were also in the car. They'd taken up residence in his heart, years ago. Now they were trying to get out, but couldn't. Forget days, their *minutes* were numbered.

•••

"It won't be long now," he warned.

"SHUT UP! You're dead!" Tristen shouted, and made a sharp turn.

"You will be too, in a second," Eric replied. "But don't worry, I am in no ways finished with you! Do believe, death will not save your no good ass, from my wrath."

"SHUT! UP!" Tristen screamed, as he struggled to control the car.

The rims, and the scepters, kissing the concrete kindled dangerous sparks, but the car was still in motion. It bounced over the curb, where Jacques and his cousins had been standing. The sparks from the back wheels hit a pool of gas; and set off combustible blue flames.

A stream of fire ran along the trail, following the sparks, and the gas coming from the tank. The minute the fire caught up with the car, the undertow exploded. The car moaned and bounced. Then it caught fire.

Smoke bellowed toward Jacques and his cousins. They jumped. Then they watched in amazement as the smoke literally did a backstroke. Just turned around mid-air, and seeped through the hood of the car.

"DAMN!" Chase shouted.

Jacques was holding his mouth. It wasn't until then that he saw yet another Mr. George sitting in the car. The man was sitting there like the damn car wasn't burning all around him. He noticed Tristen screaming, and trying to get out the car, but he couldn't. He knew Mr. George *could* get him out, but he wouldn't. He didn't want to see this, but like the average rubbernecker, he couldn't look away.

•••

Erica closed her eyes, and hid her face in Ariel's chest. He shook his head. "You have to witness this, Ms. Erica George. Your father is doing this, for the love of *you!*"

...

Dorothy hid her face in Beaux's chest. She couldn't witness this. She'd have more nightmares, if she did. Beaux wrapped his arms around her, but never diverted his eyes. One of them needed to witness the removal of their family's threat. It was his job, because he was the man of the house. He didn't smell the smoke, but he did smell the burning flesh. It made his stomach churn, but he held his position.

...

Tristen tried to open the door, but it was jammed. He started stomping the fire coming up through the floorboard. His shoes and pants caught fire. He started beating his pants, and screaming, "LET ME OUT, YOU BASTARD! LET ME OUT!"

Eric's arm was still relaxed across the back of the seat. Fire was swirling in the backseat, but didn't cross his arm. He turned sideways and said, "That's not going to happen. You forced my daughter to watch you drag my body under your car. You forced my daughter to watch me die a horrible death - at your hands."

Tristen kept beating the fire and shouting, "HELP!"

"You forced me to hear her screams, and cries, as she watched her father's tragic death. I can still hear her screams. I can still see her kneeling by my deceased body, begging me not to leave her. She fell across my casket, begging her daddy not leave her, but you knew that didn't you. You stood your murderous ass there and watched my baby crying for her father."

Tristen saw Jacques sitting on the ground. He started beating on the car window. "HELP ME, JACQUES! HELP ME!"

Jacques couldn't move or respond, and he didn't want to. Jeremiel had allowed him to hear the conversation going on in the car. Tristen killed his own mother. Who would be next? His friend was a psychopath. That was different than a chemical imbalance. If he were allowed to live he wouldn't stop killing. One more kill would classify him as a serial killer. The world would be safer without him in it. Erica would be safer without him in the world. He shook his head.

···

"He can't help you. No one can," Eric informed him. "It is only fair that my daughter sees you die, a gruesome death, at my hands. It is only fair that I hear your sorry assed screams, begs, and cries. That is the only sound that will drown out my daughter's cries."

"IF YOU DON'T GET ME OUT YOU'LL DIE TOO!"

"I'm already dead. You killed me. Remember?"

"I DIDN'T MEAN TO KILL YOU!"

"You meant to kill my daughter. Do you imagine that shit makes me feel better or worse? Do you think that will get you a reprieve, or an acquittal? It doesn't, and it won't! Your judgement is merciless death, by excruciating pain. That is the only way my daughter will be safe from a piece of shit, like you." Then he removed his arm. "Burn, you no good son of a bitch!"

Tristen screamed as the fire jumped up from the back seat, and engulfed his head. He was bouncing around in the car, screaming in agony. Never in his life had he felt this level of pain. It felt like his brain was on fire.

The demons were also screaming. They jumped out of Tristen, into the backseat. They kept trying to vanish, but couldn't. They noticed that Eric was not burning, and tried to jump in his body. They couldn't!

Eric did not say another word. He sat in the flames, until Tristen's charred body stopped moving; and his voice silenced. At the same time, the demons turned to ash.

He nodded when he saw Sammael holding Tristen's spirit. His baby was safe now.

He opened his car door, and stepped out.

•••

CHAPTER 59

Eric momentarily glanced at Jacques. He was no longer a threat to Erica, but a warning glance was in order. Jacques jumped. His cousins did too. They couldn't believe the man stepped out of the car spotless! No burns! No singed hair! No smoke! No soot on his white clothes! Nothing!

"Gon' man," Jeremiel said, and laughed.

Eric chuckled, and turned around. His glance fell across the way, on Beaux. Beaux stared back at him, and then nodded once. Dead man or not, he was not afraid of Eric George. Not now. In fact, he was grateful to the man. What this man had done, had just saved his son, too. Possibly saved his family.

Chamuel had let him, and Dorothy, hear the conversation in the car. He could not believe Tristen had killed his own mother. For some reason he believed that Tristen's father knew. He helped his son get rid of the body. That's why he became a drunk. He loved his son too much to turn him in.

He understood that, because he wouldn't turn Jacques in either. He rubbed Dorothy's back. He was so grateful that she was a better woman than Tristen's mother had been. He was so grateful she'd been faithful to both of them, in spite of their flaws. He kissed the top of her head, as he gazed at Eric George. Then he mouthed, "Thank you."

Eric nodded back. That one glance, was a meeting of the mind. He knew Beaux understood that his original threat was still in play. Even more so now. Nevertheless, just to clarify he spoke to the man's mind. *"As long as Jacques stays away from Erica, none of you will ever see me again."*

...

He turned and arrogantly swaggered across the street. When he made eye contact with Erica he smiled. Then he stopped, and opened his arms.

Erica was crying, when she jumped up. She ran to the middle of the street. To her father's open arms. "Daddy!"

Eric swooped her up in his arms. He squeezed her much too tightly, and kissed her cheek. "Erica!"

In this moment, she wasn't an eighteen-year-old young woman. She wasn't the daughter he'd given his life for. She wasn't the 'sanctioned' mate, to the Lion of God! Not to him, and not to her.

In this moment, she was that nine-year-old that he'd rescued nine years ago. She was that scared little girl, that he comforted in the kitchen. She was that scared little girl who wore thick glasses, because she'd inherited his eyesight. She was that little girl who laid in his arms, on the patio, and glanced at the stars. She was that little girl that he promised he'd always protect.

She was that little girl, who came to be years after he'd frozen his seed! She was his unexpected blessing! His unexpected treasure! His baby girl! He squeezed her tighter, and kissed her cheek. "Don't let anybody tell you that you are not mine."

"I won't," she sobbed. She was an emotional mess. Not because of what her father had just done. She was an emotional mess, because he'd done it for her. She was so grateful her birthmother sent for him. She was so grateful that he hadn't hesitated, or denied her. He came with open arms, and one purpose in mind. To claim the daughter he didn't know he had; but desperately wanted. "I love you, Daddy."

"Daddy loves you too, baby," he replied, and kissed her cheek. "I always have; from the moment I knew you existed."

•••

Jacques and his cousins wiped their eyes. This was the most amazingly surreal thing they'd ever witnessed. Mr. George loved his daughter enough to die in her stead. He loved her enough to come back from the dead. Not to avenge his own death, but to save her from a similar fate.

Just like the story of the angel battling with the demons in the cemetery, this story would live on. They couldn't wait to give their eye witness account. They knew some would believe, others wouldn't. That didn't bother them, though. There are still those who don't believe that Jesus is the Son of God. It didn't matter who believed, and who didn't. In the end, truth was truth. And this truth would impact *their* lives, forever.

•••

Jeremiel was deeply affected by Eric's actions. His mate's father loved her, too. He'd been willing to go up against a street gang, to protect her. He'd been willing to kill his own cousin's son, for her. He'd even ran and grabbed Anita out of *his* arms, after she'd been trapped under that house.

Even so, Eric's display of love for Erica was different. It was revering love for the daughter he hadn't originally known about, but was grateful to have.

He wiped his eyes.

•••

This was one of the most endearing scenes Chamuel had ever seen. One that his mate would never experience. One that he was grateful his mate was not witnessing. It would make her sad, because of what was lacking in her own life. What had always been lacking. Her father's unconditional love. A love that rose up from the grave, stronger and everlasting. One that was abiding!

He was the Archangel of *abiding* love, so of course he was affected. He wiped his eyes. He knew his brother would tease him about being a sap. So what if he was. This was a touching moment. He looked across the way at Ariel. *"Well I'll be. What is that liquid in your eyes, Lion?"*

...

Ariel sniffed, and wiped his eyes. He'd never spent much time with humanity. Of course he'd watched them from the balcony, but he'd never examined their affections. That was the Sap's job.

He was recompense. Emotions had never meant anything to him. He destroyed fathers, mothers, and children; at the Master's will. Never once had he stayed around to see the effects.

He had no idea humans could love one another this *hard.* Eric's and Erica's emotions, and words, put the *'so'* in their love for each other.

He heard Chamuel mocking him. He wiped his eyes again and said the only thing he could. *"Shut up!"*

Then he stood up, and walked toward his mate, and her father.

...

Eric put Erica back down on the ground, and extended his hand to Ariel. They gave each other a one-armed hug, and patted each other's back.

"I think you are just as fiendish as I am, man," Ariel voiced.

Eric chuckled. "If I am not mistaken, that is my commission."

"In the darkly, man. In the darkly!"

Eric cracked up laughing. Ariel was evidently off his game. He was so busy watching, he failed to see what had really happened.

He looked around at all of the people going on about their business, in the park and on the streets. Then he looked back at Ariel. "Only those who needed to see…saw."

Ariel looked around too, and his eyes grew. The park was crowded. So were the streets. Yet, no one had, or was running toward the burning car.

In fact, people were walking through the burning car as they traversed. None of them the wiser. None of them aware of the battle that had taken place.

He was the Lion of God. He watched all night, and all day. How was it possible that he didn't know that they were not visible? How was it possible that he didn't know that he, himself, was operating in the darkly?

He wondered if Jeremiel and Chamuel were aware. They both appeared next to him. They had the strangest look on their faces.

They both shook their heads and said, "No!"

"Not a clue," Jeremiel added. He was just as confused as Ariel was.

So was Chamuel. Normally operating in the darkly felt differently; than out in the open. He had felt no such difference. He'd always known about the Alter-Egos. However, this was his first time seeing one in action. "Is this how you guys operate?" he asked.

The sound of their response said they were in as much awe as Ariel was. Chamuel had asked a good question. He added, "Is it?"

Eric chuckled, and nodded. "We are Alter-Egos. That just means we are the alternative to the Arcs. Where you guys handle warfare in the present, we can handle it in any timeframe."

"What?" Erica asked.

"If I wanted to I could go back in time and stop the accident from happening. But why would I do that? My family has accepted my new face. My life hasn't changed in the least bit. That is with the exception of my multiplicity of bodies," he replied. Then he stroked Erica's cheek. "This form of existence is better for me. I have more eyes to watch over you, baby."

Ariel scowled at Eric, and said, "Damn!"

Eric cracked up. "Can angel's curse, boy?"

Ariel laughed too. That was the first time he had. Michael was concerned about him rubbing off on Eric. It was evidently going to be the other way around.

He pulled Erica into his embrace. "Ms. Erica George, you have two untamed men, who love you greatly."

Erica wrapped her arms around him. "And I love you both."

Eric changed his face back to Leizalak's. Then he vanquished the burning car, and removed the veil. "Let's go back to the Haven."

...

CHAPTER 60

The minute they walked through the door, Libby grabbed Erica. She hugged her, and rocked her back and forth. "Are all the threats to my baby finally gone?" she asked her husband.

Eric and Ariel nodded.

"Thank God," she replied, and hugged Erica again.

"Who was it?" Remington asked.

Erica's family freaked when they found out who her last foe was. They were even more freaked out as to why she'd been his target.

"I didn't like Jacques, but even I knew he wasn't gay," Ian voiced.

"Tristen was so ugly, he knew he couldn't get a woman," Carson added.

Eric Jr laughed. "That may be true, but I've never seen an ugly gay man. Some of those dudes are fine as hell."

Everyone looked under eyed, at him.

He laughed again. "Man, I've seen some queens that look more she than he. The only way I could tell they weren't women was because of their mannerisms."

"What was the difference?" Remington asked.

"They overly exaggerate *everything*. Their walk. Their voice. The way they use their hands. The way they sit, and cross their legs. Everything is done with conscious graceful precision."

"You were very observant," Eric voiced.

"Man, they are all over the college campus. They

are all over New Orleans."

"What?" Libby asked. "That doesn't bother you?"

"Shoot nah. Times are not like when you were growing up, Mom. My generation is lot more open minded. We don't care about other people's lifestyles. To each his own."

"Eric and I even went to a drag queen contest, with a friend of ours," Jean added.

Everybody looked at her.

"What?"

She and Eric laughed. "Those drag queens made me feel inadequate," she informed them. "Even their hair and makeup was perfect. And you know something else?"

"What?" everybody asked.

"They are the kindest people I have ever met. One night there was a snow storm. I asked Eric if he would go get me a pack of cigarettes."

Eric laughed. "I told her she'd better turn her light off, turn her butt over, and go to sleep. Besides, she didn't need to be smoking anyway."

Jean smirked. "I called my gay friend, Buster. In less than an hour, he was knocking on my door. Not just with a pack, but a carton. He said just in case the storm lasted longer than expected. He wouldn't even let me pay him for them."

Eric Jr rolled his eyes, and smirked. "Whatever!"

Chamuel was remembering Sodom and its original meaning. "That was indeed hospitable. That's all the Master wants is for humanity to be kind, one to the other."

"That may be true, but I wasn't about to get out in that snow storm," Eric replied. "I didn't grow up around snow. I don't like snow. And I wasn't going out in it to get her any cigarettes."

Everybody cracked up laughing.

•••

"What about Jacques, Dad? Is he going to leave Erica alone?" Ian asked.

Eric and Ariel laughed. "He got the message, trust me," Ariel replied.

Chamuel spoke up for Jacques. "He'd had a change of heart, before he witnessed Tristen's death."

Jeremiel nodded. "I actually had to stop him from trying to warn Erica."

"He was trying to warn her?" Libby asked.

"He realized it was Tristen who'd killed Eric. He was afraid that Tristen would still come after Erica. He was about to run right in front of Tristen's oncoming car, to warn her."

"Ump," Libby replied.

•••

Eric Jr decided to change this subject. He had a more pressing matter. "Anyway," he said. Then he looked at his parents. "I'm not going back to California."

"What?" Libby asked.

He put his arm around Jean. "California is not safe for Jean. Her father is still a threat to her and her mother. I can't lose her, again."

Eric felt his wife's heart breaking. New Orleans was too far away. She wanted her son to come home. He did too.

"Here's the deal. You are a grown man, and can certainly make your own decisions. Just keep in mind that I, along with Ariel, Kal too for that matter, can keep her safe. Jean, and her mother, are welcome to stay with us."

"They are?" Eric asked. He'd much rather go home with his family. New Orleans had too many floods. He'd take a ten second earthquake over that any day of the week. But not without Jean. For her, he'd weather the elements.

"Yes. However, the rules still apply. You will not disrespect my house, understand? She cannot sneak in your bedroom, under any circumstance. Unlike your den mother, and father, I will always be watching. Grown or not, I will beat your naked – mannish – disrespectful – ass, boy!"

Melvin slapped Eric a high five. "That's what I'm talking about!"

Sandra jabbed him in the side. "You didn't think that when you were sneaking in my window, Melvin. Right under Aunt Ima's nose."

"You evil, San!" Melvin replied. "Why can't you let that go?"

Sandra laughed. "The truth will make you free. Especially of self-righteousness."

He smirked.

"What?" Eric asked. "I know you didn't disrespect that woman's house like that, man."

Jeremiel cracked up laughing. He loved his future mother-in-law. "Yes, he did. Every single night. Poor Ms. Ima didn't have a clue."

"Shut up, Billy Boy!" Melvin demanded.

Libby burst out laughing. Sandra and Melvin were hilarious. Every time Melvin opened his mouth, Sandra shut it for him. She really liked them. She looked forward to spending many years as friends. She couldn't wait for them to meet Nanette, and Kal. She couldn't wait to meet Sandra's two cousins, and their husbands.

However, her husband was as serious as his death had been. In most cases he was easy going, but he had rules. Rules that there wasn't even a sliver of room to negotiate. One being nobody had sex in their house, but them. She loved her Greek god, no matter what his face looked like.

She also knew her son. He was as over the top for Jean, as Eric had been for her. As Eric still was for her. The desire to make love with Jean would out way the chance of getting caught.

Her husband would beat Eric's butt, in front of Jean. How embarrassing would that be for her son, and for Jean? She couldn't let that happen. "If you love her, why don't you marry her, son?"

Eric Jr was laughing up a storm. He was glad his father was back, but the man was a stone. He said what he meant, and meant what he said. His parents didn't have to worry though. He'd never done anything to disrespect them; he wouldn't start now.

He also had no intentions of disrespecting Chamuel's house. Too many impressionable children lived in the Haven. He'd snuck in her room, last night, but his training stepped in this morning. He knew better, and he told Jean as much. He was not going to do that again.

Suggesting he and Jean get married, was different from *demanding* Ariel marry Erica. Plus, his mother's suggestion was too late.

He lifted Jean's hand, and stroked her finger. "I planned on doing that, Mom. We went ring shopping today."

Libby screamed! Not only was she getting a daughter-in-law, but she knew grands would soon follow. She hugged Jean. "Welcome, daughter."

Erica screamed too! She loved the thought that she was going to have a sister-in-law. She hadn't spent a minute with Jean, but that was about to change. Especially if they came back to California. She hoped they would, because that would mean another female in the house.

Kay and Anita both had women that lived with them, that were their closest friends. She wanted the same thing. "I can't wait, Jean," she said, and hugged her.

Eric palmed the side of his son's head, and pulled him into an embrace. "Alright, son. I'm proud of you."

He released him and hugged Jean. "Welcome to the family."

Ariel reached for Erica's hand. He wanted to show off her ring too. He made her ring visible. "Erica and I did the same thing."

They all looked at Erica's finger. That ring was stunning. It had a message that only the Archangels understood. Chamuel explained it out loud. "She hold the chain, and the rein, right?"

Ariel kissed Erica's cheek, and replied, "Ms. Erica George is the only one who *could* tame the beast within."

Erica smiled and said, "I love the untamed Lion, Ariel. Don't go changing, for me. I love you, just the way you are."

Sandra and Libby sighed. "Awwww."

Eric pulled Eric and Erica into an embrace. He kissed the sides of both their heads. He was as proud as he'd ever been, of both of them.

They would keep his original face alive, because they both looked like he used to look. They were the proof, that Eric George had even existed. Their flesh, their blood, and their bones, was a living testimony.

Then he hugged his youngest three sons. The ones that look like him *now*. They would keep his current face alive, for years to come.

He released them and hugged Liberty. The mother of all of his children. The woman he'd chosen, in Heaven. The woman he couldn't bear to leave. The woman who couldn't bear to let him go, no matter what his face looked like.

He kissed her cheek. He'd heard her thought. "You can't wait for the pitter-patter of grandbabies' feet, can you?"

She laughed. "Nope!"

He kissed her cheek again. "Neither can I."

He still believed things had to be done decently and in order, though. It may be old fashioned, but marriage before babies. He knew Erica couldn't get married yet. Even if she could there would be no children. Eric could, though. He needed to marry first.

"Would you consider having your wedding in our backyard, Jean?" he asked. "It will give my family a better memory than the last time they were there."

"What happened?" she asked.

"Our pool man thought that Dad was dead. He attacked Mom, in the backyard," Eric Jr replied.

"What?" Sandra asked. Libby hadn't told her that.

Libby nodded.

Melvin looked at Libby, and scowled. Then he looked at his own wife. He shook his head. He couldn't even conceive that scenario happening to her. "I know damn well you handled that shit, man."

Eric smirked. That comment was ridiculously insulting. It didn't even warrant a verbal response. He planted the scene in Melvin's head.

Melvin was mesmerized by what he was seeing. He tilted his head backward, and turned it, as his mind followed Zander's body flying across the air. "Damn."

"So are you willing, Jean?" Eric asked again.

She'd seen the vision too. She smiled, because Mr. George was as powerful as Chamuel. She and her mother would definitely be safe from her father. "Yes!"

Liberty was elated. "Let's forget about taking a two-month vacation. Let's go home and plan a wedding."

...

CHAPTER 61

They'd been home for a week. The hustle and bustle of planning for the wedding made for merriment throughout the house. Everyone was involved, including Kal, Nanette, and their three children: Amber, Aniesha, and Prince Kaiden.

Kal's son and daughters were glad the cat was finally out of the bag. Prince Kaiden, and his wife, owned a flower shop. Like his sisters, he'd always thought of Eric's children as his family. As a wedding gift, he and his wife were providing all of the flowers.

As it turned out there were two weddings going to take place. Eric and Jean's. Perry, and Jean's mother, Nancy. No one saw that one coming, not even Ariel.

Libby was excited for her brother, but concerned. "Aren't you still legally married, Nancy?" She thought Nancy was still married to the man who tried to kill her, and Jean. He thought they died in the house, but they hadn't.

Michael answered for Nancy, "I can assure you he signed the divorce papers. He just does not remember that he did."

Libby relaxed. She was so happy for her big brother. He'd finally moved on, and found happiness, again. He was marrying a healthy woman this time around. One that would not die.

She hugged him, and cried like a baby.

Perry hugged Nancy. He never thought he'd love again. He blew his family's mind when he said, "It wouldn't have mattered if she was still legally bound to another. Nancy is my destiny. I'd gladly live in sin with her."

Nancy smiled. She felt the same way he did. She hadn't wanted anything to do with any man. Not until he walked in the Haven. She'd literally felt the clouds roll away, taking her fears with it. He was her haven now. Her port in the storm. "Thank God we don't have to, Perry."

●●●

Kay, Chamuel, and almost all of the Haven had been in and out, all week. Chamuel was going to give Nancy and Jean away.

Anita, Jeremiel, and their entire family came to help, also. The minute Perry saw Chris Miller he laughed, and hugged him. "This world is smaller than we know, man."

"Ain't that the truth," Chris agreed.

"Y'all know each other?" Libby asked.

"We have for years," Perry said. Then he explained, "We are brothers in the ministry. Both of us are sons of Pastor Thomas Maulsby."

Chris nodded. "Indeed. You know he married me and Tammy, man."

Perry nodded. "I've already contacted him. He's going to perform ours too."

"Just keep in mind Pastor Maulsby cannot know about Watchers, Alters, or Archangels," Michael told them.

He, and his brothers had known Pastor Maulsby, since he was a young man. Even though he was the grandson of an Ultimate, it was not his season to know about them.

●●●

Ariel was in and out. At night he knocked on the door, because Kal, Nanette, and their children were always there. As well as Kal's sons-in-law, and the Watchers from Galveston.

Eric introduced Ariel to Kal, and Nanette, as Ari. Kal thought he was a twenty-year-old street punk, especially with all of those earrings, and the nose ring. He assumed Eric had told Ari about their world. Still, he added his own two cents worth of warning. He told him how they'd gotten into Jacques' house, while the family slept.

He assured him that walls, and locked doors, were not a problem for them. He warned that no place was too far out of his, or Eric's, reach.

Then he said, "Treat Erica with anything but respect, and her father will be the least of your worries. Understand, young man?"

Ariel heard Eric, Michael, and all of his brothers cracking up in his head. *"You heard that, did you not, young man,"* Michael voiced.

Ariel sucked his bottom lip, and inwardly grunted. He was tempted to jack with Kalaziel, just to show him who was boss. Kalaziel would not be the wiser, as to where the attack came from.

He could see himself appearing in Kalaziel's house. Maybe he'd rearrange the furniture while he slept. Possibly move the bed outside. Maybe even leave claw marks on his bedroom door; or the headboard.

Then shrink his manhood, to the size of a thumb. He could make him sexually impotent, too. Or maybe invert his manhood. Turn his pee-wee, into a she-wee. Leave him that way, until Michael told Verenda about their relationship.

Perhaps he'd put up a blockade, so that Kalaziel couldn't teleport back inside his own house. He might just make the entire house disappear. Make that Ultimate Watcher wet his pants, just as the sun was about to come up.

He just might restore Samjaza's mind. Make that sexually perverted demon stalk Kalaziel in his dreams. He'd make that Egyptian Moor wish he could crawl his butt back inside the safety of his mommy's womb.

Better yet, make that Negro pine for the days he was nothing but sperm! Beg for the opportunity to dodge his mommy's fertile egg, at all cost.

...

His brothers, and Eric, were listening to his spiteful, and deviant thoughts. All of Ariel's life the weapons of his warfare had no bounds. No chains, or rein! He had a vivid imagination, that's for sure. Like most beasts of the wild, he thrived on the smell of fear; while stalking his prey. Like most wildlife, he antagonistically played with his food.

Of course, they knew he'd never do any of those things. At least they hoped he wouldn't. Kalaziel wasn't exactly one of God's 'so' loved. He was, in fact, an abomination in the sight of God.

Even though this was serious, they couldn't help themselves. They laughed, out loud.

Michael did not laugh. He did not put anything past Ariel. Ariel believed in recompense for any offense, at any level. Kalaziel has just offended the Lion with his admonishment.

He was not about to spend all of his time cleaning up Ariel's spiteful behavior. *"You had better not, Lion!"* he commanded. *"You are dealing with creatures born in sin, shaped in iniquity. For once in your life, stop being so litigious."*

"I'll be cool, man."

"Good!"

"For now!" he added. *"But the minute you connect with Verenda, it's on! I'm going to revisit this conversation with Kalaziel. No matter how long it takes. I'm going to introduce him to the Lion of God,"* he threatened.

Erica wrapped her arm around Ariel's waist. She was laughing too. *"Behave, Ariel."*

He chuckled, in her head, and wrapped his arm around her waist. *"I will,"* he promised.

"Kal is my uncle, Ariel."

"I said I'll behave, Ms. Erica George. Didn't I?"

Then he outwardly replied to Kal, "Yes, sir, *Mr. Kelley.* I understand." He sounded nervous, respectful, and truly sincere. *"Just you wait, though."*

Erica elbowed him.

His brothers and Eric roared! Even Michael laughed.

...

CHAPTER 62

Because so many Watchers were in attendance, the wedding could not be held during the day. It turned out to be a beautiful night ceremony.

Prince Kaiden and his wife decorated the yard. It was filled with a rainbow of flowers, from birds of paradise, to daisies, to lilies. All in various colors.

Colorful garden lights were staked in the ground along the tree lines, but aimed toward the center of the yard. They crossed each other, mid-air, and formed a rainbow canopy.

There were trellises, wrapped in clear holiday lights, lined on both sides of a white carpeted path. They were filled with white roses, and baby's breath.

•••

Jean wore a white lace filled wedding dress, and veil. Eric Jr wore a white silk tux. Nancy wore an eggshell white linen suit, and pillbox hat. Perry wore a white double breasted linen suit. They walked their own brides down the aisle.

•••

Pastor Thomas Maulsby stood under the brightly lit floral dais. In a deep, resounding voice he stated, "Dearly beloved. Before 'in the beginning' was penned, 'amen' was already done. Each and every one of us was already predestined, justified, sanctified and glorified, by our Creator. We are merely gathered here today to formally bind on earth, what God has already bound in Heaven..."

The tenor of his voice had everyone mesmerized,

even the Heavenly host. He performed one of the best worded wedding vows, any of them had ever heard.

All the married couples wished they could renew their vows, under the sound of his authoritative voice.

...

"By the power bestowed upon me, I verbally announce God's decree. In the sight of man, God, and the Heavenly host…" He stopped, took his glasses off, wiped his eyes, and put them back on.

Then he smiled and said, "I pronounce you husbands, and balls and chains."

At first everyone was caught off guard. How could Pastor Maulsby end this sacred ceremony like that? He chuckled at the expressions on everyone's faces. He looked at the grooms. "Trust me, over time you will find those words to be an accurate assessment."

Ariel was holding Erica's hand. He rubbed his thumb across her ring, and laughed. She looked at her ring, and back at him. That's exactly what her ring was. The purple stone was a ball. The band a chain. She cracked up laughing.

Melvin looked at Sandra. She was as evil, as can be. She yanked his chain about being self-righteous, every opportunity she got. He nodded. "Yep. Ball and chain is accurate, alright."

She laughed, and elbowed him.

The men in the crowd looked at their wives, and began to slowly laugh, too. Pretty soon the women were laughing too.

...

The reception was just as nice. All of the couples were slow dancing to Kenny Rogers' song "Lady". Ariel and Erica were gazing in each other's eyes, when he crooned, "Lady, for so many years I thought I'd never find you. You have come into my life and made me whole."

The Watchers didn't think that was a big deal. So what, the brother could sing. The Archangels didn't either. All of them were called into existence with perfection, in all things.

Erica, her brothers, mother and Perry were tripping out. They all started speaking at once, in his head.

"Man, you told us you couldn't sing!" Remington accused.

"I didn't know Archangels were permitted to tell an out-and-out bald-face lie," Ian added.

Ariel chuckled, but kept on crooning to his mate. There had never been a better song written. It exemplified his, and all Archangels' plight. They'd all waited to find their mates. Some were still waiting. He crooned, "You're the love of my life, you're my lady."

Ariel's deep baritone voice was erotically smooth. It was sweeping through Erica, and giving her a thrill. *"You have a beautiful voice, Ariel. Why would you say you couldn't sing?"*

When the song ended, he squeezed her and kissed her ear. Then he replied, *"Hang around me long enough, and you will learn to listen for the words not said."*

"What words?" Carson asked.

"What did I say to you guys?" Ariel countered.

Eric Jr reminded him, word for word. *"You said, 'I am an angel, but I'm not a Seraphim, or Cherubim. I have never sung in anybody's choir. In fact, I can't hold a monotone note. I was not fashioned to do so.'"*

Ariel nodded. *"Where in those words did I say I could not sing?"*

"You said you couldn't hold a monotone note,

Ariel!" Libby added.

"I can't!" he replied.

Eric Senior burst out laughing. His family thought Ariel was double talking, but he wasn't. They hadn't figured out that Ariel spoke what was obvious. He listened in that same fashion.

Michael had told him that he couldn't lay with Erica in her bedroom. Ariel heard he *could* lay with her *everywhere else*.

He, himself, had said the same thing to Eric Jr. His son just didn't hear what he had not said. He'd said, *"She can't sneak in your room."* He hadn't said, *"Y'all can go somewhere else, and make love."*

By the time his son-in-law finished he was going to have his family thinking outside the box. He liked that, because he never much cared for 'the box'.

The box said he was a black man. Therefore, great success was not in his future. The box said African Americans were second class citizens. He'd burst out of that box years ago.

He laughed and said, *"His voice was anything but monotone, Liberty."*

It took a minute for his family to get it. His sons, and Perry, cracked up laughing. Libby smacked her lips. *"I'm not about to play with you, Ariel!"*

Ariel cracked up laughing.

Perry and Nancy were laughing up a storm. Ariel was messing with all of their minds. *"We'll just have to read between the lines, from now on."*

"That's your best bet, Perry," Ariel advised, and kept laughing.

•••

Erica wrapped her arms around Ariel's neck.

"You'll have to sing me to sleep tonight."

"Your room, or ours?" he asked.

Her room meant she'd lay in her bed alone, and make love to her *dream lover*. All night long. Their room meant he'd hold her in his arms, on the patio, while she peacefully slept.

Those were their only two choices, until Michael talked with Verenda. She was more than okay with Michael taking his time in informing Verenda. He *should* do it at Verenda's pace, not his brother's. Verenda had spent her life having no control over what people did to her body. Slow and easy was what the woman needed.

She knew, like Michael knew, you can't *make* someone love you. The heart can't be forced to bend to someone else's will. It responds to affection in its own way, and in its own time. Tristen found that out, the hard way.

She understood Verenda, because she'd held on to her birthmother, for nine years. Even though Libby always treated her like her daughter, she couldn't let go. It took her nine years to completely embrace her mother.

Thanks to her untamed mate always thinking outside the box, they could be intimate; if only in her dreams.

Tonight the newlyweds were going to light up the house, with their moans and groans. She didn't want to be anywhere near them. Tonight, she wanted to feel his physical arms around her, caressing her. She wanted him to hold her, while serenading her under the light of the moon.

"Our room," she replied.

Ariel kissed her, and they vanished…

•••

EPILOGUE

Ariel took a seat, and crossed his legs. At first, he didn't say a word. He just took in his surroundings. The only light in the room radiated off of him, and his brother.

"Why are you so stubborn, man?"

"Look who's talking."

"You know you cannot stay here forever, Araciel."

"Says who?"

"Father."

Araciel's heart quickened. He missed his Father. He missed his brothers. He missed his home. But, not enough to face the music. "Are you here to visit, or here to speak on His behalf?"

"Michael, Gabriel and Raphael are Father's messengers, not me. I just thought maybe I could reason with you, on my own. How can you choose to live amongst our Fallen brothers? You could be living in Father's glorious light. It'll heal you, and ease your troubled mind."

Araciel shook his head. "This is where I belong."

Ariel shook his head, but didn't respond. Araciel knew he didn't belong down here. Nothing he might say could add anything to that fact.

Araciel also knew he had a 'sanctioned' mate. If that didn't compel him to come home, nothing would. He said the only thing that merited saying, "Thanks for helping me with Samjaza."

Araciel nodded. "You didn't need my help, but it was my pleasure." What he'd really like to do is throw all of these Fallen, demons and imps into the abyss. End their tirade on humanity, once and for all. He wouldn't because it wasn't his Father's will.

Ariel smacked his lips. "Since when do you care about Father's will? His will is for you to come home, but you won't! His will is for you to claim your mate. You won't do that either. Even though you know Lucifer knows who she is! How could you do that to-"

Araciel muted him. He didn't want to know her name. Whoever she was, she was better off without him.

Ariel smirked. "I have never met a more stubborn, and frustrating man!"

Araciel laughed. "You haven't? Let me introduce you. Ariel meet the Lion."

Ariel slapped his leg, and roared. He guessed he was stubborn. He stood up. "I have to go. It was good to see you again. May I come back, from time to time?"

Araciel stood up too. "By all means. By the way congratulations on your mating."

Ariel shook his head. Araciel was hiding from his own mate. His guilt over his sons' mothers was greater than his desire to claim his mate. That was just sad.

He hugged his brother. "I wish I could destroy that useless spirit, Guilt! I wish you could see how much Heaven misses you. I wish you'd listen to what is being said about you, in Heaven. All of the good things, Araciel. All of the prayers being said, on your behalf. The lamenting Father does, for His lost son. Just like it repented Him for creating His 'so' loved; it repents Him for banishing you, brother."

Araciel moaned, and squeezed him tighter. He couldn't believe what Ariel had just said. His Father was sovereign. He didn't have to feel sorry for, or have regret over, *anything* He did.

Something stirred in his heart, because he knew Ariel was telling the truth. Just hearing those words alone was tempting.

He didn't want to keep hurting his Father. He wanted to run home. Kneel at his Father's feet, and apologize for disappointing Him. But he couldn't, because he was too ashamed.

He pulled away from Ariel. "Take care, Lion."

Ariel nodded, and vanished.

...

Michael was standing on the Throne, on the left side of God. They, along with all of Heaven, were listening to Ariel and Araciel's conversation. He sighed. He wished the Lion would have pushed just a little bit more. "He almost persuaded Araciel, Father."

God nodded. "All things in their season, son."

...

BOOKS BY THE AUTHOR

Brock's Redemption
Ramiel's Symphony
Denel's Lillian
Chaziel's Hope
Batariel's Robyn
Bezaliel's Destiny
Arakiel's Faith
Weddings & Births
Baraqiel's Dawn
Henry's Pia
The Brothas & The Greatest Gift
Separate Vacations
Yomiel
Adam
The Promise
The Wrath of Seraphiel
The Walker Brothers
The Archangel, Michael
The Archangel, Araciel
The Kingpin's Vitriol
Much Ado
The Archangel, Chamuel
Rogue's Rage
TEKEL, The Weight of Mercy
The Archangel, Jeremiel
The Archangel, Ariel
In The Corridors of My Mind
Brock's First Noel

SOME OF MY FAVORITE AUTHORS

Dr. Jay Winter
"The Book Of Enoch"

Melinda Michelle
"Color Me Blind"
"Chronicles of War Series"

Aja
"I Am Yours"

Perri Forrest
"Rapture"

Trisha Sroka
"The Reclaimed Smile"

Heather Rae
"Two Worlds"

AD Davis
"Discovery"

Amber Nichole
"Masquerade"

Made in the USA
Middletown, DE
01 September 2023

37762224R00265